Gatsby's Girl

BOOKS BY CAROLINE PRESTON

Jackie by Josie

Lucy Crocker 2.0

Gatsby's Girl

Gatsby's Girl

Caroline Preston

HOUGHTON MIFFLIN COMPANY
Boston New York 2006

For information about permission to reproduce selections
from this book, write to Permissions, Houghton Mifflin Company,
215 Park Avenue South, New York, New York 10003.

Visit our Web site: www.houghtonmifflinbooks.com.

Library of Congress Cataloging-in-Publication Data
    Preston, Caroline.
    Gatsby's girl / Caroline Preston.
        p. cm.
    ISBN-13: 978-0-618-53725-9
    ISBN-10: 0-618-53725-2
    1. King, Ginevra, 1898–1980—Fiction. 2. Fitzgerald, F. Scott
(Francis Scott), 1896–1940—Fiction. 3. Rejection (Psychology)—
Fiction. 4. Authors—Fiction. I. Title.
    PS3566.R397G38 2006
    813'.54—dc22
    2005026166

Book design by Lisa Diercks
The text of this book is set in Perpetua.

Printed in the United States of America

QUM 10 9 8 7 6 5 4 3 2 1

For my mother,

    Sylvia Peter Preston

He talked a lot about the past and I gathered that he wanted to recover something, some idea of himself perhaps, that had gone into loving Daisy. His life had been confused and disordered since then, but if he could once return to a certain starting place and go over it all slowly, he could find out what that thing was. . . .

F. SCOTT FITZGERALD, THE GREAT GATSBY

Prologue

Scott Fitzgerald's daughter called long distance, out of the blue. Her voice sounded apologetic, as if she was afraid I wouldn't remember who he was. She explained that she had had no idea how to get in touch with me. She decided to give the number in his old telephone book a try, even though Scott had been dead for ten years. "I can't believe you're still in the same place, Mrs. Granger."

That made me sit down, hard, on the hall bench. Scott had bounced around from St. Paul to New York to Paris to Baltimore to Hollywood, and here I was, still in the same house where he'd come for a visit, back in 1916. "I'm not Mrs. Granger anymore," I said. "Now I'm Mrs. John Pullman." At least that part had changed.

She told me her name had changed too, to Scottie Lanahan, and she lived on a farm in Chevy Chase. Judging from all the racket in the background, she had a couple of small children and a dog. "My father always used to talk about you. He said you were the first girl he ever loved."

"I'm afraid I wasn't very nice to him," I said lightly, as if I hadn't had years of regrets about the way I treated Scott.

"He said you threw him over without a second thought." She let out a merry little laugh, as if she didn't take any of her father's heartbreaks too seriously. "Anyway, that's why I'm calling. I'm sorting through Daddy's papers to give to the library at Princeton, and I found something I know he would want you to have."

"What?" I asked, thinking maybe it was one of my letters, even though he was supposed have destroyed them all.

"Let's just say it's something unusual. You'll have to see for yourself," she said in a teasing way. It reminded me of the game Scott used on girls at parties. "I'm thinking of two words that describe you," he'd say, "can you guess?" "I'm going to be in Chicago next week and I was hoping I could give it to you in person. I've always wanted to meet you."

I tried to think of someplace cheerful and uncomplicated to meet, in case Scottie was prone to cocktails and mournful moods like her father. "How about the Walnut Room at Marshall Field's? You'll be my guest, of course. The Welsh rarebit is famous."

"My favorite." There was a huge clatter in the background, like a stack of pots and pans falling off a top shelf.

"Uh-oh," said a small voice.

"Better go," Scottie said. "See you next week. At the Walnut Room. I want to hear all about you and Daddy. Your version."

I hung up the phone and studied the front hallway, trying to remember what it had looked like that summer Scott visited. The house was brand new then and still had all the fripperies my father had insisted Mr. Shaw include. The iron balusters had been gold-leafed, the black-and-white marble tiles were hard-waxed and buffed once a week by Mrs. Coates, the privet by the front door was clipped into poodle balls. Daddy had bought a second-rate salon portrait at auction to hang in the stairwell—three sons of some unknown Austrian aristocrat, dressed in ostrich feathers and satin pantaloons, with oddly enlarged heads.

My image of Scott when he'd stepped through the front door came in disconnected fragments. His white linen suit was rumpled across the back, and his collar had a ring of grime from the long train ride. His hair was bright blond, like a Dutch boy's. The chin and nose were strong, but hadn't firmed up into the famous profile yet. He dropped his battered suitcase on the marble floor with a bang and surveyed the hallway as if it were a cathedral—first staring up at the ceiling and then rotating slowly to take it all in. Then his girlish mouth pulled back into a tight grin, as if he was trying not to laugh. Even though Scott's family lived in a rented flat in St. Paul, he could see that an Italianate villa smack-dab in the middle of the prairie was pretentious. Later, after he'd had a couple of my father's gin and tonics, he announced that Lake Forest consisted of nothing more than the palaces of meatpackers.

I could remember Scott's letters more clearly than his face, which wasn't surprising. I saw Scott only a few times, but there had been dozens and dozens of letters. Each sheet stamped with the Princeton seal, the letters so thick that the envelopes bloated like a puffer fish and needed extra stamps. For a while, I found one every day in my wooden mail cubby at Westover. The letters seemed clever at first, filled with the flattery and clippings of his latest in the *Tiger Lit.*—he was the only boy I'd ever met who fancied himself a "writer." But then he came for a visit to Lake Forest, and under Daddy's judgmental gaze, Scott and his avalanche of love letters began to seem foolish, tiresome. And I'd met someone more dashing, at least in my sixteen-year-old opinion—Billy Granger.

The subject of Scott's letters was bound to come up when I had lunch with Scottie, and I'd have to admit the truth. That a week after Scott's visit in August 1916, I'd gathered his letters into a heavy, wobbly stack, carried them down the back stairs, and dumped them in the trash can outside the kitchen door. I could still see the cream envelopes with the black-and-orange crest landing on a mound of coffee grounds and eggshells. My excuses would sound lame. He asked me to destroy his letters, said he was afraid I'd use them as "incriminating evidence," which was such nonsense. How could I have ever guessed that the Princeton boy who wrote silly songs and poems would turn into a famous author?

Scottie had probably read the description of our meeting in *This Side of Paradise: She paused at the top of the staircase, like a diver on a springboard or a leading lady on opening night*—something like that. So typical of Scott, to take a punch party at a shabby country club and fill it with flickering lamplight and romantic interludes. To take a stuck-up pre-debutante and turn her into a noble creature capable of deep feelings.

I wondered what memento of our romance Scottie had found in her father's papers—a clipping about the party at the Town and Country Club in the St. Paul paper, a ticket stub for *Nobody Home,* the sash from the Hawaiian costume I'd worn the night I broke it off with him? I had my own secret collection of mementos about Scott, hidden away on the back shelf of a cedar closet behind a pile of unused evening bags. But I wouldn't share those with anyone—not his daughter, and certainly not the Princeton library.

I would tell Scottie my version of F. Scott Fitzgerald, without the moonlight.

The story began in the dormitory of Westover School, second floor, last door on the left. I could see myself then, a girl strolling jauntily down a long, dim hallway, her high heels clacking on the bare wood floor, a pale blue moiré jacket slung over one shoulder like a college boy. I was two months shy of my sixteenth birthday and stood a pinch below five foot four. I had been told I was pretty far too often for my own good, but my only unusual features were a thick coil of dark hair and large, doe-brown eyes that could turn wistful. Dramatic coloring was my claim to fame back in the days when girls weren't allowed to wear rouge or lipstick.

I was still bristling from the injustice of my father's words as he put me on the train. He'd said that Westover was my final chance to prove my character and warned me not to dilly-dally at Grand Central or I'd miss my connection to Middlebury.

I do have a good character, I fumed. I am good on the inside, and I never say things I know aren't true. Sometimes I'm too emotional and don't think things through, but why is that such a character flaw? But I had dawdled for a few minutes, to have some cinnamon toast in a real English teashop with organdy curtains and to window shop, and missed my connection. I caught the next one, but I was three hours late.

Part One

1

St. Paul Girl

I found my roommate hanging her uniforms in the left-hand side of the closet. She had gotten there first, and had already spread her satin comforter on the bed by the window and appropriated the top two bureau drawers. The second bed was pushed against a bare white wall, two battered desks stood side by side against the other.

She whirled around and gave me an open-mouth, friendly-girl grin. "I'm Marie Hart. From St. Paul." She had a pretty, round face with light brown hair springing loose from a sagging pompadour. She was the kind of sensible girl Daddy had probably requested for my roommate— someone who played on the field hockey team and sang in the glee club, and would exert a good influence on me.

"In Minnesota?" I asked. Even though I was from the Midwest, I was a little hazy about anywhere west of Chicago.

"What other St. Paul is there?"

"St. Paul's."

"What's that?" Her freckled brow furrowed.

Better not get off on the wrong foot with my roommate, have her think I was stuck-up. "It's a school in New Hampshire. That's a pretty blouse," I added. It was just a candy-stripe middy, but she looked pleased.

She sat on her bed and watched as I unpacked my school uniforms—the four khaki skirts to wear to classes, and four white dresses for dinner. Then I pulled out two evening dresses in case I got invited to a prom, a green wool suit for shopping trips to New York, a beaver coat for Yale football games. Unfortunately, they took up so much of the closet that Marie's dresses got shoved into a corner. Then I arranged my silver dresser set, jar of hairpins, and a jewelry box across the dresser top.

"There," I said.

Marie sat on the foot of her bed, swinging her heels. "Ginevra. That's a funny name. Is it after a relative?"

I stood on tiptoe so I could see myself in the tiny mirror above the bureau, pulled out my combs and hairpins, and started brushing out the tangles. "My father named me after a woman in a painting by Leonardo da Vinci he saw in some old book. He seemed to think she was pretty." I shrugged. Frankly, in the smudged illustration I'd seen of Ginevra de Benci, I thought she looked a little horsey.

"I wish my parents had named me after a painting. I'm named after my Great-Aunt Marie, who tried to close all the saloons in St. Paul."

The bedroom door banged open and in stepped a large gray woman—iron-gray hair raked into a tight twist, sallow skin, a gray worsted dress with a high starched collar.

Marie leaped to her feet, clasped her hands in front, and dropped a small curtsey. "Good afternoon, Miss Hillard."

The woman snapped open the watch hanging off her belt. "Late afternoon. Five-fifteen to be exact. You must be Miss Perry," she said, her pale squint zeroing in on me. "My letter to your father said no later than two o'clock."

I dropped my hairbrush and spun around to face her. I considered making an excuse—the connection to Middlebury was late, the trunk was misplaced. But I could already tell that Miss Hillard was the type who wanted you to try an excuse so that she could bat you down with the back of her witchy hand.

"I'm sorry," I said in a meek voice, dropping my chin.

Her fierce glare swept from the closet to the bureau, and then landed on my earlobe. "Are you wearing earrings, Miss Perry?"

Only pearl drops—my tiniest pair. "Yes."

"Yes, *Miss Hillard.*"

"Yes, Miss Hillard."

"Westover girls are not allowed to wear jewelry. I am sure you know that already, Miss Perry, from your close reading of the Student Rule Book." Her voice was heavy with sarcasm. "Items like silver brushes and makeup of any kind are not allowed. I can't imagine what you think you might need a fancy dress or a fur coat for. New girls are on bounds. Please pack all that nonsense back in your trunk and carry it down to the basement storeroom. And be quick about it. The dinner bell is in twenty-two minutes, and you will get a half a conduct mark for every minute you are late." With that, Miss Hillard replaced the watch under her belt and marched out of the room.

"She sure has it in for you." Marie's voice was trembling.

"My parents sent me here because I got in trouble back in Chicago. Hillard finally agreed to accept me on probation. Twenty conduct marks and I'm fired." I grabbed an armful of clothes and slung them back into the trunk.

"Let me help. You can't get a conduct mark your first night. You get dressed while I pack your trunk."

"Thanks," I said, surprised and grateful. Most girls didn't like doing me favors.

I changed into my uniform while she carefully folded my dresses, and then I wrapped the jars and brushes in tissue paper. Together we dragged the trunk down three flights to a dank basement store-room, and stumbled into the dining hall just as the bell was ringing, our dresses wrinkled and faces flushed, choking back giggles during grace.

The senior proctor, a weak-chinned girl who carried a watch on her belt like Miss Hillard's, checked to make sure we were in bed at the ungodly hour of eight-thirty. "Half a conduct mark if you are caught talking after lights out," she warned, snapping off the light.

I lay in the darkness and listened to her footsteps retreat as she made her rounds down the hall, the stern voice and slamming doors growing fainter and fainter. I made out the ghostly shape of my desk chair in the slit of light seeping under the door, and listened to Marie's raspy breathing.

Mother had warned me that I would be homesick. "I'm sure you'll cry yourself to sleep the first night," she said. You'll be sorry you misbehaved, her tone implied. You'll miss your bedroom with its rose-sprigged bedspread and the balcony with potted gerani-ums. You'll miss being able to scatter your clothes all over the floor for Edith to pick up. You'll miss having Mrs. Coates serve coddled eggs and toast on a breakfast tray at whatever hour you feel like waking up. You'll miss your father caving in to your every whim—the dressing gown you saw at Field's, the beaded handbag just like Weezie Ryerson's, the weekend trip to Lake Geneva for a house party you could not miss. Mother was right, I was feeling blue but I pinched the palm of my hand so I wouldn't cry.

Marie cleared her throat. "Ginevra? Are you still awake?" she breathed in a tiny whisper.

"Yes."

"What did you do? To get sent here?" Her voice was timid, as if she wasn't sure she should hear the answer.

"My parents found out I was secretly engaged."

"At sixteen?" she squealed.

"No." I paused for dramatic effect. "Actually I'm only fifteen."

"Was the boy fifteen?" Marie sounded relieved. Fifteen-year-olds pretending to be engaged—that probably happened in St. Paul too.

"Nope. He was twenty. A junior at Harvard. His parents made him leave school for a year and he's working on an uncle's ranch in Montana. We're forbidden to write."

"Do you miss him?"

"Of course." I made pudgy, asthmatic Aldus Hutchinson sound much more romantic than he was. How was I to know that no girl had ever paid him any attention before, and that he'd go over the edge after a little mild flirting at the Winter Club Christmas Dance? He wrote me lots of boring letters, then withdrew two thousand dollars from his trust fund and presented me with a four-carat sapphire ring over Fourth of July weekend. He seemed desperate and the ring was pretty, so I said yes, we could be engaged, but made him promise to keep it a secret. But then his trust officer informed his father, and all hell broke loose.

Even though Aldus was five years older and should have been the one to know better, my parents seemed to think I was partly to blame. You must have led on him somehow, my father said. All I did was show him how to do the Castle walk, I insisted, and act interested when he said he'd seen Jupiter through the new telescope at the Harvard Observatory. I was just being polite.

Ever since I turned thirteen and boys started paying attention to me, I'd been accused of being false. No one believed that I was always truthful about my emotions—I would never tell a boy I liked him or allow him to steer me into the butler's pantry if I didn't care. Sometimes I changed my mind later, but I never knowingly told a boy a lie.

"Golly. That's so sad," Marie sighed. I twisted my comforter tight around my shoulders and closed my eyes. Marie was going to be a true friend, I could just tell, who wouldn't misjudge me like the rest.

It was the first time I'd ever been in New England in the fall. The snap in the air and the desperately bold colors of the leaves as they swooned onto the brick paths filled me with a new resolve. I'd become a model "Westover girl"—I'd show Daddy and Miss Hillard that they'd underestimated me.

Every Sunday and Wednesday we had services in the mock-medieval chapel, with new girls banished to the back pews with no cushions. Miss Hillard, decked out in a velvet robe with a fake ermine collar that she'd gotten from some English women's college about fifty years ago, delivered the homily from the pulpit. Hillard's talks usually started with stories about unfortunate people. Once it was about poor Armenian children who had been chased by Turkish Cossacks into the desert without any food or water. Another time it was about the mothers in France who were willing to let their sons get gassed in muddy ditches because they loved their country. Sometimes the stories were about long-suffering people in the Bible, like the Israelites who were held as slaves in Egypt. Then the talk would work its way around to how lucky Westover girls were by comparison, and how many of us didn't appreciate the advantages we'd been handed by our parents and teachers.

I'd heard this kind of lecture before, but now that I was trying to become a proper Westover girl, I hung my head and tried to open my heart. Even if I did get cross at Daddy, I realized he'd showered me with everything a girl could possibly want and I should count my blessings. I signed up to donate fifty cents of my allowance every week to the starving Armenians, and when Adele Craw, the head proctor, came around with a box for used clothing to send to the poor Frenchwomen, I tossed in a navy wool skirt and two shirt-waists. Mother would probably have a fit, since she'd just bought them from Marshall Field's, but it wasn't my fault that I didn't have any old clothes.

Adele Craw decided that as the official wayward girl of the junior class, I was in need of a role model, and offered her services. At her suggestion, I joined the French Club and helped with their fall play, *Jeanne d'Arc*. My French accent wasn't considered good enough for me to have any lines, so I played an awestruck peasant who fell to his knees and a soldier in a cardboard breast shield painted silver.

Adele also urged me to go out for intramurals, the Wests and the Overs, and I was glad to oblige. I'd always been keen on sports. Racing around on a tennis court till my heart pounded seemed like a much more productive way to spend time than plodding through some useless book in study hall. Marie and I played doubles tennis for the Wests, and we made it to the semifinals. We would have won if Marie knew how to serve overhand. I tried to be a good sport. After we lost, I stayed on the bench and bellowed our fight song.

> Watch out, Overs!
> We'll run you over.
> Here come the Wests.
> And we're the best!

My reputation as a woman with a past proved hard to leave behind. Even though I had sworn her to secrecy, Marie eventually broke down and told the other new girls on our hall about my tragic engagement. After that I was considered an expert on the wild side of love, and girls would gather in our room after evening study hall for details.

"Did he write you poetry?"

"Was the sapphire round or square cut?"

"Did you kiss?"

"Of course. All engaged couples kiss," I said in a wise tone, even though I'd only kissed Aldus three times, all fairly unpleasant because he perspired so much.

The girls, with their bony knees poking up under their baggy uniforms, looked shocked. "My older sister's kissed two boys. But she's a senior at Miss Porter's," said a girl with chapped cheeks.

"Girls in Chicago get kissed early," I explained.

Once we glanced up to find Adele Craw standing in the doorway, arms crossed over her erect chest, eavesdropping. When her clear no-nonsense gaze met mine, it seemed to film over with disappointment. "I'm sure you girls can think of better things to do than bother Ginevra," she said mildly, and the cowards jumped to their feet and scattered.

After that, Marie's and my conversations about boys took place after lights out. Since Marie was now my official best friend at Westover, I was careful to be just as interested in her life and love prospects as she was in mine. She told me that she lived on something called Summit Avenue in St. Paul, which she implied was a fancy address. Their house had over twenty rooms, and three bathrooms that had just been modernized. Her father was a lumber exporter, which she said was "a pretty big business, since Minnesota's got a lot of trees. That's where Paul Bunyan's from, you know."

"Tell me about the boys in St. Paul," I said.

"There's Reuben Warner and Tubby Washington. They both go to the U."

I guessed that "the U." must mean University of Minnesota, if such a place existed. "Do any of them go east for college?"

"One does. Scott. He's a sophomore at Princeton."

"Everyone in Chicago says that Princeton men are clever. I'd love to meet him."

"Maybe you could visit after Christmas. Scott will probably be back in St. Paul. And my friends are all dying to meet you."

It gave me a little thrill that Marie had written nice things about me to her friends back home. The more I thought about it, the more I warmed to the idea of a trip to St. Paul after Christmas. Maybe Marie's friends in St. Paul didn't gossip or make snap judgments like Lake Forest girls.

In truth, the misunderstanding with Aldus Hutchinson hadn't blown over yet. Sally Swift admitted in a letter that her mother had called me "nothing but a showoff," and had suggested that Sally "branch out into new friendships" now that I was away. Weezie Ryerson didn't answer my letters at all. The only Lake Forest friend who wrote me on a regular basis was Millie Jordan, but that was only so she could give me a hole-by-hole description of her latest golf game. "Was shooting a 49 on the front nine until the last hole. Then a turribel wind carried my ball right into the ditch. Rats!"

Two weeks later, Marie's mother sent a proper invitation to my mother, who accepted eagerly. "Your father and I are very relieved that you are choosing to spend time with a serious young woman your own age," she wrote. "I think a quiet visit to St. Paul after Christmas will be more constructive than the tiresome round of holiday parties at home."

I wrote back: "Marie says that St. Paul winters are so bad that the police find two or three frozen corpses on the sidewalk every day! I think a fur hat with a matching muff might be wise. Since the Harts live on Summit Avenue (the Astor Street of St. Paul), I might need a new formal dress as well. As the Boy Scouts say, Semper paratus! You will be glad to know that I am being more conscientious in Latin this year."

2

Bob Party

On New Year's Day, I boarded a mustard yellow car with CHICAGO, MILWAUKEE & ST. PAUL lettered on its side. As the train pulled across snow-covered fields, frigid air seeped in along the edges of the frosted windowpane. Every few miles, a farmhouse perched mournfully under a stand of naked cottonwoods, half-buried in trackless drifts, the windows black. I wondered if there was a poor soul huddled inside, waiting for spring. I shivered and wrapped my fox scarf tight over the shoulders of the dove-gray traveling suit with the jet buttons.

I opened my handbag and pulled out a pocket diary with a soft leather cover and a tiny mechanical pencil that Mother had tucked into the toe of my Christmas stocking. I folded open the first page and slipped the pencil out of its slot in the spine.

> January 1, 1916
> Mother told me to use this diary to copy inspirational lines from Hillard's sermons, but I have other ideas.

I am on a train bound for St. Paul to see my roommate and new best friend, Marie Hart. I was dying to
get out of Lake Forest. Mother checked all my mail to
make sure I didn't get forbidden letters from Aldus, as if
I wanted to hear from him again after all the trouble he's
caused me. Weezie and Sally are thick as thieves now
that I've been sent to Westover. All Millie can talk about
is going to Santa Barbara next month to play golf.

The conductor came lurching down the aisle, clicking his metal
punch as he walked. He had a tan, rugged face that looked like it
would be more at home under a cowboy hat than a gold-braided
conductor's cap.

"Ticket, please?" he said, showing a lot of square, even teeth that
I guessed he was proud of.

I handed him the same ticket I'd shown him four stops ago. He
gave it three officious punches. "Whatcha writing in that book?"

"Secrets," I said, with a saucy smile.

"What kind of secrets?" He propped a bold foot up on the arm
of my seat and leaned over far enough to blot out my reading light.

When I boarded the train, Daddy had warned me about getting
overly familiar with strange men. "Secrets about our Lord Christ,"
I said. I remembered a hobo propped in a doorway on Wabash
yelling this at passersby. "Would you like me to read a few?"

His foot dropped to the ground and he straightened his cap. "Not
right now, thank you. We're coming into La Crosse."

I arrived in St. Paul four hours later. Marie and her father, a jolly
man with a humpty-dumpty shape and a handlebar mustache, met
me at the station in their Buick touring car with chains around the
tires. It sputtered along the icy pavement, wheels spinning, while
Marie and I huddled under two horse blankets on the frozen leather

back seat. "I've planned a party so everyone can meet you," she chatted, her breath a damp plume against my cheek. "Reuben and Tubby. Scott's going back to Princeton two days late so he can meet you." The car drifted around a corner.

"Here's Summit," Mr. Hart yelled from the front seat.

I peeked over the scratchy folds of wool and made out a wide boulevard lined on either side by wedding-cake houses, their cupolas and iron fences frosted with swags of snow.

The car skidded to a squeaky halt in front of a hulking mansion made of jagged stones like a fortress. As we shuffled up a slippery path, a rounded oak door with an iron latch clanked open. A matronly version of Marie trotted across the porch, wiping flour-dusted hands on an apron. "So this must be the famous Ginevra from Chicago. Excuse my appearance. I've been helping the cook roll out an apple cobbler. Marie asked that I make her favorite." Mrs. Hart grasped my gloved hands, leaving thumbprints of dough, which made me feel oddly welcome—Mother never set foot inside the kitchen, much less made my favorite dish. "Marie's letters have been nothing but Ginevra this and Ginevra that."

"Mama, please," said Marie, kicking off her galoshes.

The blast from the hissing radiators made me so woozy I wriggled out of my overcoat and scarf. The faces of Marie's two little brothers pressed against balusters, mouths agape with wonder.

Mrs. Hart stepped back and scrutinized my traveling suit, then her eyebrows creased together. "Marie said you'd have very smart clothes, and she was right. I'm afraid you'll find all of us very unsophisticated."

"I'm sure I won't!" I said, giving Marie an apologetic shrug. Dressed in a red plaid jumper with her hair hanging down her back in a braid, she looked even more like a schoolgirl than she had in her Westover uniform.

After supper, Mrs. Hart ushered us into the living room for cups of hot cocoa in front of a walnut mantel carved with wheat sheaves.

Marie and Mrs. Hart demurely blew on their hot chocolate while Mr. Hart took charge of the conversation. "What is your father's line of work, Ginevra?"

"He's in investments," I said vaguely. My father, like the fathers of my friends, never talked about business. I knew that he was a partner in Perry and Hamill Investments, which had its offices in one of the new "skyscrapers" in the Loop. I knew that he went off to work every morning dressed in a gray flannel overcoat and felt hat, that the desk in his study was covered with bond certificates printed in curlicue type, ledgers, and adding machine tape. But Daddy mostly talked about his hobbies and clubs—the weekly lesson with the golf pro to improve his swing, the duck-hunting shotgun he was having repaired at Abercrombie's, the lunches with his fellow members of the Chicago Community Fund, the upcoming weekend at his fishing club in northern Wisconsin.

My mother said that discussing how a person earned his money was uncouth, something the older generation did because they didn't know better. Grandpa Perry often told the story over Sunday dinner about how he'd made his fortune after the Chicago Fire. "An ember landed on my parents' roof, and twenty minutes later there was nothing left but the chimney," he'd say. Even though the Chicago Fire had happened barely forty years ago, it sounded as distant and primitive to me as Marquette paddling down the Mississippi. "They had fire insurance. Only problem was the policy got burnt up with the house. So I decided right then and there, even though I was only nineteen years old, that I would invent a fire-proof vault that would be small enough and cheap enough for the average house. And five years later," he would say, pausing to set down his fork so he could thump his chest with his thumb, "I had my first patent for the C. L. Perry Fireproof Vault."

Once he caught my parents exchanging eye rolls and bridled. "My son thinks he's too high bred to dirty his hands with fireproof vaults," my grandfather complained. "But where do you think I got the money to send him to Yale? Where do you think he got the money to pay for all this fancy stuff?" he said with a wave toward the crystal chandelier hanging low over the dining room table and the sideboard weighted down with silver candlesticks and cake baskets.

Daddy crossed his legs and lit a cigarette, which he exhaled with a flourish. He was a handsome man, with a full head of wavy dark hair that he was vain about and wetted down each morning with imported French cologne. "Nonsense, Father." He pronounced it *fah*-ther—four years at Yale had cleansed the prairie vowels from his accent. "We all have great admiration for the Perry Patent Fireproof Company. I just think there might be more educational topics to discuss with the children."

My grandfather shifted his indignation from Daddy to my little sister. "What could be more educational than a lesson on how to earn a living? Right, Evvie?" he asked.

My little sister, who had been intent on making an indentation in her mashed potatoes and filling it with gravy, glanced up and nodded. Grandpa considered Evvie the only one with a sensible head on her shoulders. Every Saturday, I took my allowance to Dayton Five and Ten and spent it on whatever caught my fancy in the wooden bins—Japanese fans, Mexican jumping beans, wax lips. Evvie marched her allowance down to the Lake Forest Bank and already had a savings account balance of $22.75.

Mrs. Hart, seeing my attention drift off, decided to try a domestic topic. "Does your mother keep many servants?"

My mother would also have considered it vulgar to brag about the number of servants. "A few."

"We feel lucky that we can always find Swedish girls." I had already met Irma, the cook, a flush-faced woman with braids wrapped around her head who'd served up a whitish heap of stewed chicken and dumplings. "I don't suppose there are so many Swedish girls in Chicago."

"We have Irish girls. And a few coloreds for ironing and heavy cleaning. But they don't sleep in."

"Of course not," Mrs. Hart said with a smile, pleased that the servant situation in St. Paul was obviously more reliable.

"This is such a comfortable house," I said, which sounded like a social lie but was the truth. The green plush parlor set had crocheted doilies on the backs so men did not leave grease spots from their hair pomade. Small, spindle-legged tables were covered with fringed shawls and watercolors of flowers set on easels. It reminded me of Grandpa Perry's parlor on Prairie Avenue, where you could sit by a fire and read a book. Ever since Mother had gotten our living room redecorated, Evvie and I weren't allowed in unless it was Christmas or Thanksgiving. "I'm so glad you asked me to come."

"We will make sure you have a perfect visit, Ginevra," Mr. Hart announced, as sonorous as Moses.

The next morning, Marie flipped to the society section of the *St. Paul Dispatch* and pointed out the lead article. "I didn't tell you about this yesterday," she said. "I wanted to surprise you."

WILL GIVE BOB PARTY AND SUPPER TONIGHT FOR GUEST
In honor of Miss Ginevra Perry of Chicago, who is a
houseguest of Miss Marie Hart, 475 Summit Avenue,
a bob party at the Town and Country Club. Among the
guests will be Misses . . ."

I skipped over the list of girls to the boys.

> Messrs. Vernon Rinehart, Frank Hurley, Reuben
> Warner, Gustave Schurmeier, . . . and Scott Fitzgerald.

I set the paper down, my cheeks growing hot with pleasure. My name had appeared three times in the *Chicago Tribune* society pages as a guest at this or that dance, but I had never been the subject of an entire article, one on the front page no less. St. Paul wasn't such a backwater after all. I leaned back with the hum of impending destiny in my ears. Something momentous would happen tonight that would change the course of my life forever—I knew it. "What's a bob party?" I asked.

"You'll see," Marie said with a secretive smile.

We spent the afternoon sprawled across Marie's puffy eiderdown comforter, rolling each other's hair into pin curls, trying on various outfits and standing on a chair so we could see our reflections in the rippled mirror hanging above a high chest of drawers. I produced a lipstick and a compact of rouge powder that I'd secretly bought at a drugstore near Union Station, and Marie dabbed them on, then furiously wiped them off with the back of her hand. "Mama would keel over if she thought I was wearing makeup," she whispered, her face flushing scarlet with her daring.

I pumped Marie for details about each male guest—who was the richest, the best-looking, who had a reputation as dangerous and tarnished as my own. "Well, Reuben's the richest, I'd say. His papa is head of the Lumberman's Trust. You can see his house catty-corner from ours." She led me over to an icicle-covered window, and I peered down the snowy street at a vast ramble of porches and ells.

"And there's Gustave, who used to be kind of chubby, but now he's a tackle on the freshman team at the U. Vernon is probably the smartest, and is going to finish up engineering at Macalester in three years."

I picked up a nail file and pushed down my reddened cuticles. All the snow and blasting steam heat in the Harts' house had made my skin crack. "Who's the most handsome?"

She considered while rerolling one of her pin curls. "I guess that would be Scott, the one I told you about who's at Princeton. He's very blond and he's got a profile a little like Richard Barthelmess." Marie had been swooney over Richard Barthelmess ever since he'd rescued Lillian Gish from Yankee marauders. She kept a scrapbook about him at school.

I put down the nail file—Scott sounded much more promising than Reuben, Vernon, or Gustave. "Tell me more."

"Everyone thinks he's talented, and he writes songs for the Triangle Club."

I'd seen a Triangle Club show last Christmas when it came to Chicago—a lot of screeching boys dressed up in ball dresses and crooked wigs who weren't nearly as funny as they thought they were. But still, Scott Fitzgerald from Princeton was the best St. Paul had to offer. I stretched my arms and patted my pin curls, which were now as bone dry as my cheeks. "Do you think he'll like me?"

"Of course he will," Marie said, squeezing my arm, glad that I'd shown interest in one of her friends. "I made you sound fascinating."

By six o'clock, I was dressed in the new bottle-green velvet evening dress that I'd bought for the occasion. My cheeks and lips were rosy from a layer of artfully applied makeup. The effect was somewhat spoiled by the raccoon coat and galoshes Mr. Hart made me wear, saying, "It's going to be ten below tonight, and I don't want you losing the end of your nose in that bobsled."

After a half hour of skidding turns, we pulled up at the Town and Country Club, a ramshackle shingle building perched on a bluff above the dark void of the Mississippi. Male heads bobbed restlessly in the blazing first-floor windows. Someone was doodling "Good Night Ladies" on an out-of-tune piano.

Marie grabbed one of my fur sleeves and dragged me over a snowbank toward a side door. "Quick. We don't want them to see us until we're ready." We scooted up a back staircase, down a dim hallway, and through a door marked LADIES DRESSING ROOM. We tossed our coats on top of the mound of furs stacked on a wicker couch and kicked our galoshes into another pile in the corner. Suddenly we were surrounded by a dozen girls, all pale-haired like Marie, with pastel, frilly gowns that looked as if they'd been sewn by the same dressmaker.

"We've been waiting for you. The boys are all going crazy," one whispered.

Another poked her hand out and gave me a brisk shake. "Gin-er-va. That's a funny name."

"It's Ginevra, and she's named after a painting by Leonardo da Vinci," said Marie, my defender.

I stood in front of a dressing table and smoothed down my hair with an ivory-handled brush.

"That's a lovely dress," a girl said, running a curious finger down my silk sleeve.

I looked down with a vague expression as if I never gave my clothing a thought, even though I'd had the seamstress redo the neckline twice. "Why, thank you."

A high male voice whooped up from below. "Ladies . . . are you coming?"

The girls giggled and marched out two by two. I trailed a few steps behind, moving in small, deliberate steps, taking my time. I tilted my chin up, pressed my lips together in a slight frown, as if my heart was overflowing with some secret sorrow. I paused on the landing until the herd of girls had thundered down the broad, curved staircase, feeling almost giddy, like an actress waiting in the side wings for her cue. All I could see from that angle were several pairs of men's evening pumps, and I wondered which pair was attached to Scott Fitzgerald.

I ambled down the stairs with a distracted air, studying my hand inching along the honey-oak rail, as if I were trying to remember where I had dropped a glove. On the bottom step, I stopped and raised my eyes to the waiting circle of boys, slowly let the serious look melt into a surprised half-smile, let my eyes dart to life. It was an effect I'd practiced and practiced in front of the mirror.

Marie linked her arm through mine and rattled off the names. "This is Reuben and Vernon and Scott and Gustave . . ." The faces kaleidoscoped together—all shiny-cheeked, sandy-haired, and voice boxes jutting out over starched collars. I tried to pick out which was the special one, Scott.

One of the boys insinuated himself next to me and squeezed my hand in a possessive way. "You're the famous Ginevra Perry," he whispered, as if he were sharing a confidence that no one else should hear. The face turned sideways showed a graceful nose and a sharp chin—this must be the romantic profile of Scott Fitzgerald, I thought, and felt my spirits droop. I had been expecting a more looming, impressive male, not this boy with buttercup-yellow hair and Cupid's-bow lips who was barely an inch taller than me. But still, I would force myself to fall in love—otherwise, I'd have spent my Christmas vacation in St. Paul and missed Franny Bard's New Year's dance for no good reason.

"And you must be Scott Fitzgerald," I whispered back, as if I were reading his name off a billboard.

"Would you like some hot chocolate?" He slipped a casual arm around my waist and steered me through the crowd to a bench in the chilly corner behind the silver urn of hot chocolate. He held my hand while I sat, then wedged himself so close that the edge of his jacket fell across my lap and his arm had no place to rest except on top of my knee. A smooth, bold move—I liked being laid claim to.

"We've been coached for each other," he said.

"I want to hear everything that Marie told you."

"Hmm, let me think." Scott dropped his head as if in deep thought, and managed to nudge even closer in the process. "She said you were considered very beautiful." He paused, as if he was considering whether to say more.

I played with his pocket flap. "Go on. Don't spare me."

"That some poor boy had to leave Harvard and go brand cattle out in Montana because of you. That's why your parents packed you off to Westover."

I burst out laughing. "Marie was supposed to keep that a secret. I hope you aren't shocked."

"I like girls who are shocking," he said in a world-weary voice. He pulled a brass case from his pocket, lit a cigarette, exhaled with a practiced flourish. "Now, tell me everything that Marie said about me, even the bad things."

"That you were considered to be good-looking." I edged away a bit so I could make a show of assessing his face. The clear green eyes were a plus, I decided. So was the thick fringe of dark lashes. Now that we were sitting side by side, I wasn't so aware that he was slight and slope-shouldered. His cuffs jutted a trim two inches from his sleeve, the cuff links were silver ovals set with jet—tasteful but not showy. He was wearing a kind of soft corduroy vest that I'd seen on a few fashionable Chicago boys lately. "That you wrote all the songs for the Triangle show, but that your grades are so bad you're not allowed to be in it."

His elfin smile faded with a sigh. "I failed algebra and hygiene. I even went to tutoring school, but spent the night before the exams carousing, so I flunked a second time. I'm sure I'll do better this term." He sounded unconvinced.

I glanced over at the guests we had deserted, who now stood in awkward clusters, wearing pained expressions as if they'd gotten stuck with the person they least wanted to talk to. "That heavyset boy with the crooked nose keeps glaring at you," I whispered through a pasted-on smile. "I don't think you're supposed to be monopolizing the out-of-town guest."

"Marie said to take care of you, and I am. By saving you from Reuben Warner."

"What's so bad about Reuben Warner?" Besides his red wool vest.

"Nothing, if you want to talk all evening about the Stutz he got for his birthday. He'll tell you about how the cylinders are nickel-plated with a patented process, and that he can get it up to forty-five miles an hour on the Fort Road. Then he'll show you a picture of it in his watchcase, and offer to take you outside and let you look under the hood."

"What about the muscular one with the spiky black hair? He's not so bad-looking."

"That's Gus, who finally made the freshman football squad at U. after two years. He only got to play for three games, and I know he'd love a chance to describe every tackle. We've all heard about them ten times already. Vernon's the one who's squinting down the front of Margaret Bigelow's dress. His mother told him he looked more distinguished without his glasses, so he doesn't wear them to dances and stumbles around, blind as a mole. And finally, there's Rufus, who's very proud of his baritone and will find a chance to break into 'K-K-K-Katy.'"

"Do you always sit along the wall and size people up?" I waved over at Marie, who was being cornered by Reuben.

He didn't answer, and his mouth pinched in a mournful way. "What?" I squeezed his hand. Sad men were attractive.

"I'm an outsider, I guess. I feel like the little boy with his face pressed to the window, looking in at the party he wasn't invited to."

"Don't act pathetic. Marie says you live right on Summit Avenue with the rest of them."

He shook his noble head hard. "I live on the unfashionable end of Summit in a shabby row house with weeds growing over the windows. I'm sure Marie was too polite to mention that my mother wears eccentric feathered hats and passes out religious tracts."

"Everyone has embarrassing relatives," I said. "My great-grandfather was a station agent back in Massachusetts, but Mother thinks I shouldn't tell people that."

"Being an outsider's not so bad. It helps me see the truth in people. That's why I'm going to become a writer."

"What kind of writer?" I asked, hoping that wasn't a foolish question.

"I'm going to write a novel someday, and everyone will know my name." He spoke with such quiet confidence that I decided he wasn't just boasting.

"What's the truth you see in me?"

Another pensive pause as he clicked open the brass case and pulled out another cigarette. "I'm not sure I should say. Most people don't like hearing the truth about themselves."

"Tell me. I promise I won't be upset."

"People misjudge you just because you're beautiful. The girls think you must be conceited, and the boys decide you must be a hardhearted flirt who's toying with them. But I think you're just shy and lonely."

My scalp tingled at this new notion of myself. It was true that a lot of girls back in Chicago and at Westover thought I was full of myself, no matter how hard I tried to be just like them and fit in. My only true friends were Marie and Millie.

"That's why I came to St. Paul." I pressed his hand against my waistband. "I was looking for someone who'd understand me, someone I could really talk to. Not just the meaningless chitchat I have in Chicago. 'Did you hear that Gifford Chandler broke off his engagement with Eliza Blair? Who could blame him—she's gotten so heavy, she looks like a heifer!'" My voice turned shrill, as if I were imitating some harpie. Scott didn't need to know that I'd repeated the gossip myself to Weezie and Sally. I needed someone like Scott to bring out my sterling qualities. "I'm glad I found you," I whispered.

A thunder of footsteps made me glance up with a start—the crowd had moved over to the front door and was bundling up into overcoats and galoshes. Marie stood in front of us, hands on hips. "I hate to break up your tryst," she said, glancing first at Scott and then at me, pleased that her matchmaking plan seemed to have worked. "But the bobsled's waiting. The driver says the horses will get frostbitten hooves if we make them stand much longer."

I jumped to my feet, smoothed my skirt, readjusted my hairpins. "Come on, Scott. We don't want some poor horses to get gangrene because of us," I said, hooking my arm through Marie's and skating toward my borrowed raccoon coat, which was being held up like a furled sail by a pair of husky arms.

"Good man," said Scott officiously, as Gus the quarterback wrapped the coat around my shoulders and twined the foxes around my neck. "I'll take over from here."

Grasping my hand as if I were a small child, Scott led me down a snowy path, the crust crackling under our boots, toward an ancient barge-shaped sleigh hitched to a pair of woolly horses, exhaling white plumes into the inky air. He pushed me up a wobbly iron step toward the one free seat, a bench along the back that was scarcely big enough for one person. "I guess we'll have to fit in here." We crammed in side by side, and he pulled a musty buffalo robe over both of us, right up to our noses. The sleigh lurched forward with a jingle of bells and a creak of harness leather.

"Where are we going?" I whispered into his ear, close enough to feel the prickle of beard and a whiff of lavender shaving soap.

"Nowhere special—just across the golf course, down to the river and back. The point is to stay out long enough so everybody gets frozen through and has to snuggle up." A snowy blast rolled up from the river, jamming ice shards into my cheeks.

Scott pulled off his glove, and wiped the frozen drops off my eyelids with still-warm fingers. His arm snaked around my waist and pulled me tight; my face nuzzled into his scratchy lapel. "I'll protect you," he said, a hot breath on my forehead.

"From what?"

"From frostbite. From stupid people who don't understand interesting girls. From everything."

The scrape of runners through crusty snow and the rocking of the sleigh lulled us like a cradle. Scott's bare hand slipped under my coat, stroked the velvet nap along the back of my dress. My fingers crept up his pant leg, along the bumpy surface of his corduroy vest. His body stiffened with a sudden shudder.

"Cold?"

He exhaled a laugh, like a swimmer popping up for air. "Hardly." His hand slowly moved up my spine, over my shoulder blade, up along my neck. All the places a boy's hand roamed when we were dancing, but now his touch felt molten.

After what seemed like an hour of groping under buffalo fur and wool, Scott detached himself. "Ginevra," he murmured, as if calling out to an apparition. "I'm glad I found you."

"Me too," I whispered back. As the sleigh crested the next green, the lights of the clubhouse twinkled ahead.

"We're almost back." Scott sounded urgent.

I knew what was coming next, and my body had its usual reactions to an approaching first kiss—the heartbeat sputtering, the lungs squeezing for breath, the eyelids clamping shut, the tongue wetting the lips, parting them. I waited, listened to his raspy sighs, to the rustle and murmurs from the other couples. A finger ran along my jaw line, tipped my chin upward; another pause. I could tell without opening my eyes that Scott's face hovered above mine. I imagined the knife-edge of his fine nose against the starry night, the loose tendrils of my hair blowing across his cheek. Then his lips dropped down against mine, first a faint brush, then a firm, smooth pressure. I gave him a quick hard kiss back.

The sleigh lurched to a halt. We pushed apart and I snapped my eyes open. Scott's face looked chafed and somehow more manly. "You seem so sad," I said.

"My train for New York leaves in two hours. My suitcase is already at the station."

"What can we do?"

"I'll write you a letter on the train."

I had an image of Scott hunched over in an empty dining car, covering a sheet of paper with an emphatic scrawl. A rosy dawn seeped in under a half-drawn shade, catching in the blond stubble of his day-old beard. An ancient colored waiter in a starched white uniform refilled the thick porcelain coffee cup for the fifth time.

"What will it say?" I wondered how a real writer would describe what had just happened.

"Be patient," he teased. "It'll be waiting for you when you get back to school."

Scott yanked his arm from under my coat and pulled his gloves on. I straightened my hat, which had slipped sideways. He sprung down with a surprisingly athletic leap, then grasped me under the elbows and spun me around and down. "Oopsie daisy."

The winter constellations, which I couldn't name, whirled over-head and my boots landed weightless on the snowy ground. Scott turned to me, his face grave, as if he was tamping down every emotion, while the others gathered around us in a watchful circle. He bowed stiffly at the waist and grasped my hand with one of his, which I shook, just as I had done to every other hand stretched out to me that evening. Some boys let out disappointed groans, as if they'd been expecting what our maid Edith called a "moving-picture clinch." They didn't know that the slight squeeze between our gloved fingertips was more ardent than any kiss.

Later that night, back at the Harts', Marie seemed oddly grim and silent. As we peeled off our fancy dresses, unpinned our hair, and climbed between the icy sheets, she refused to meet my eyes.

In the darkness, I hoped we could fall into one of our old chats, as if we were back at Westover. "I think I'm falling for Scott," I tried, but her only answer was to thump the pillow and turn her back to me. "I thought you wanted me to like Scott."

"I did," she said, her voice muffled and distant.

"Then what is it?"

With a sigh, she flipped back over. "I never suggested you should fall in love. Scott's different than you, Ginevra."

"What's that supposed to mean?"

"The Fitzgeralds are poor. Papa says that Mr. Fitzgerald is a dipso who lost his salesman job, so now they live on handouts from Scott's grandfather McQuillan. His mother is very queer, with witchy hair and mismatched shoes. People make fun of her. Every September they move to another apartment."

"Do you think I'm such a snob?"

Another painful silence. "Well, not a snob exactly, but it seems like all your friends in Lake Forest are pretty well off."

"Maybe they are, but that doesn't mean I'd look down on Scott's family. And neither would my parents. They're always nice to everyone."

"I don't want to see him get his feelings hurt."

I let out a small laugh. Marie was being so silly, it was hard to take her seriously. "He's the sophisticated Princeton man, and I'm the little boarding school girl. You should be worried that I'm the one who's going to end up with a broken heart."

3

Letters

It was waiting for me, propped sideways in my wooden mail cubby—a cream envelope embossed with an orange-and-black Princeton seal. The mailroom was thronged with girls, clucking over a letter from this or that boy flirted with at a Christmas dance. I slipped out the letter—bulging and so heavy it required three extra stamps —jammed it between the pages of my French grammar, and headed with a nonchalant stroll toward the door.

"No letters today?" asked Cassandra Reid, a polo player's daughter from Oyster Bay. She sat cross-legged in the middle of the mailroom floor, shuffling through a thick stack addressed in various sloppy scrawls—boys seemed to find her large bosom and plump knot of honey hair irresistible.

"I guess not," I said in a soft, sad voice.

I wandered across the quadrangle, searching for a place where I could savor every word in privacy. The study hall and library would be swarmed, dorm rooms were off-bounds until after five o'clock. I decided on the stone chapel, which sat forlornly down a steep slope, surrounded by high drifts from the last snowstorm. I trudged up the unshoveled front steps, tugged at the iron ring until the oak door broke open with a crackle of ice. I slipped into a frigid pew under a murky stained-glass window of Saint Francis feeding a flock of starlings, took a deep whiff of the moldy air, and tore Scott's letter open. Eleven numbered sheets of Princeton stationery, covered back and front with script pitched forward at an eager tilt.

> January 3, 1916
> 4:32 A.M.
> half an hour past Oconomowoc, Wis.
> Dear Ginevra . . .

My eyes swept across the pages, absorbing his words in disconnected chunks. This was unlike any letter I'd gotten from other college boys, which were usually nothing but tedious descriptions of physics exams and baseball games. Scott wrote like I did in my diary —a gush of emotion and sensation, unchecked, unafraid.

> It's hard to write to you what I really feel because I feel so much . . .

> Our evening together seems as far away as a dream . . .

> I think over what you said last night and wonder how much you meant. I'd heard about how popular you were. It's hard to believe that you like me best . . .

> Sorry my handwriting is shaky. Maybe it's love, or maybe it's from the three Bronxes I had. I hope you don't mind that I like cocktails.

He described his first glimpse of my face as I walked down the staircase at the Town and Country Club—the mouth downturned, the eyes bright with a sympathy that swept him and every other boy right in. The hem of my dress moved like "a damask curtain in a summer gust," my voice was "an addictive melody I can't get out of my head." He re-created the sound of metal runners cutting through crusted snow, and the heat of our hands under the buffalo robe. He named the mysterious constellations that had spun above us—the Big Dipper, Perseus, Orion's Belt.

Scott described the bob party so it seemed more vibrant and romantic than I remembered it. Tiny details that had seemed insignificant to me at the time, like the snap of the horse's leather harness or the ice on the plank sleigh seat, took on a symbolic meaning. This is what a true writer does, I decided. Makes real life better than it is.

I reread the letter, whispering the words out loud. I sank back in the pew and enjoyed the cryptlike gloom. The poinsettias left over from the Christmas service were shriveled black with frost, the altar candles had guttered into ghostly puddles, the drops of water seeping from the stone walls had turned to icicles.

That evening, while Marie was off at glee club practice, I sat at the splintery kneehole desk.

> January 4, 1916,
> Westover School, Middlebury, Connecticut
>> Dear Scott,
>> Your letter was marvelous. Marie was right—you certainly have a flair for words!

I paused, cleaned off the nib on the blotter, nibbled on the cap of the pen. If this had been a letter to one of the stolid boys with a good pitching arm, I might have dashed off any stupid thing—how

I'd scribbled out his name ten times over on the back flyleaf of my composition notebook, that I'd gotten jealous when Lydia Cudahy had said that his eyes crinkled shut when he grinned. But now I imagined Scott holding my letter up to a slant of light streaming in through a leaded-pane window, sizing up the measure and heft of every phrase with his writer's eye.

I'm not used to writing long letters, so please try to be patient. I thought about you all the way back to Westover. I even wrote silly stuff about you in my diary, like "I'm just over the moon about Scott." I was afraid you might have forgotten your promise to write me, and was beside myself when I saw that thick envelope with extra stamps.

You are the first boy to realize that I am a serious and emotional person. Sometimes I'm too emotional, I admit, which has gotten me into trouble in the past. But I meant every word I said to you in St. Paul, and my kiss, although I wouldn't admit that to anyone.

Now, since I promised you a long letter, and I don't want to write pages and pages of mush, let me tell you what's been going on here.

It was very cold last night with a full moon, and Miss Hillard announced at dinner that there was a special surprise. Instead of going to study hall, we would be allowed to go for a late night skate on the big pond in the woods behind the schoolhouse. Marie and I wrapped ourselves up in plaid mufflers and polo coats and had a fine time playing crack-the-whip and pom-pom-pull-away. The snow sat on the tree branches like fleecy clouds. I think all that moonlight on my head made me go a little crazy. I'm surprised I didn't start to howl.

You said that you were afraid I was fickle and that you didn't think I liked you best. Well that's just not true. You are head and shoulders above all the other boys I know.

I'm dreaming of the time when I can see you next. Wouldn't it be wonderful if we could spend one perfect hour together, in front of a roaring fire or in a moonlit garden?

But don't get your hopes up. Miss Hillard runs this place like the state penitentiary, and the convicts don't get sprung until June!

I had better finish up, because Marie will be back from glee club practice any second now. I have not mentioned your letter, because I'm afraid she'd ask what you said and maybe even want to read it. For the time being, I want you all to myself.

Of course I don't mind if you like cocktails. All men like cocktails, including my darling dad.

There, I've written the kind of letter you wanted. Write back as soon as you get this!

Yours in haste,
Ginevra

Two days later, another, even thicker letter landed in my box.

Dear Ginevra,

Your letter came and it was wonderful! I read it over about six times until I had learned it word for word by heart.

Do you think about our bobsled ride constantly like I do? Tell me everything you remember.

He closed with another string of questions. *What were you like as a little girl? What's your favorite book? What do you dream about?* He needed to ask people personal questions for his writing, he explained. He hoped I didn't mind.

Dear Scott,

I'm afraid I'm not poetic like you are. I just remember queer things like the mothball smell of Mr. Hart's raccoon coat, the metal clank of galoshes' buckles, the hot chocolate burn on my tongue, the soft ridges of your corduroy vest. I admit that the exact features of your face have gotten a little blurry, so please send me a photograph if you have one.

I don't mind you asking me personal questions at all. It's probably because I'm so self-conscious, as Miss Hillard says.

My mother will tell you that I was a very unpleasant child. Whenever I thought I was going to get punished, I held my breath until I got blue in the face.

When I was about twelve, I wouldn't have anything more to do with dolls or tea sets. I only wanted to play model trains and baseball with the boys. That's probably when I first got my reputation for being boy crazy.

The last book I finished was *The Last Days of Pompeii,* which sounds romantic but was really quite boring. My favorite writer of all is Tennyson. Don't you agree?

As for dreams, I dream about spending one perfect hour with you.

Winter exams are next week, and I really should be studying instead of writing you a long letter. I am such a bonehead, and I get down in the dumps when I think of all the 30's and 40's I am going to get.

You should probably do a little "greasy grinding" yourself, so you can get yourself off probation.

Your Ginevra

When I slit open his next letter, a newspaper clipping fluttered to the floor. It was a rotogravure of a saucy girl with the neckline of her frilly dress daringly pushed down to reveal bare shoulders. The caption underneath said "Scott Fitzgerald is considered the most beautiful 'show girl' in the Princeton Triangle Club's new musical play, 'The Evil Eye,' coming to the Waldorf next Tuesday." Scott made an alarmingly pretty girl.

Dearest G.,

When this ran in the New York Times, men sent me mash notes. You said to send a photograph!

Please send me one back and I will put it in my watchcase. I am writing this with all the lights off except my desk lamp. It's easier to picture your face in the dark.

Dear Scott,

I would prefer a photograph of yourself dressed as a male! I went to a grubby little studio in Waterbury and had this mug shot made. I think it makes me look swarthy and foreign, so please don't show it to anyone.

Two girls in our dormitory came down with scarlet fever and were quarantined in the infirmary, which we call Pink Eye Hall. One was our proctor, Adele Craw, who disapproves of me, and we had to pray for her in morning chapel. Now they say she's recovering nicely and will be back after Easter holiday. Tant pis! I was hoping she would have to be out for the rest of the year.

Hillard ordered that all our uniform dresses and toiletries be boiled in bleach. My uniform shrunk so much it wouldn't fit a ten-year-old, and the bristles fell out of my Mason & Pearson hairbrush.

I probably should have spent more time studying for my exams and less time writing letters. I got 45 in French, and a 57 in math. So now I'm on academic warning and have to be in monitored study hall.

How'd you do on your exams?

Dear Genevra,

Managed to pass all my midyears except chemistry. Might have passed that one as well if I hadn't spent so much time writing to my Westover siren. But at least I'm off probation and can run for club elections. I've already taken the maximum number of cuts for the whole year and it's only February.

Here's the first stanza of a poem I'm writing about Robert Frost for the Tiger.

> A rugged young rhymer named Frost,
> Once tried to be strong at all cost
> The mote in his eye
> May be barley or rye,
> But his right in that beauty is lost.

Of course, I could never be a poet like Frost, because I don't catch subtle things in nature. There are only a few obvious things that I notice as beautiful: women, spring evenings, music at night.

Let me know what you think.

He closed with two more questions. When did I realize that I was beautiful, and what kind of man would I like to marry?

Dear Scott,

I think your poem is very clever, but I'm not sure who Robert Frost is. Should I have heard of him?

I wish I were a poet like you, but this is the best I can come up with:

> Shake!
> Spear!
> A kick in the rear!
> A box on the ear,
> And a Happy New Year!

Well, I'm not beautiful at all. I think you're trying to trick me into saying something conceited and making an ass of myself. In fact, last summer when we were in Maine, a very famous artist named James Montgomery Flagg was in the cabin next door. Mother actually suggested that he use me as a model, and he told her straight out he thought I was full of myself and babyish.

As for the man I plan to marry, I change my mind all the time. Sometimes I think I'll be an old maid who tats doilies and has a little pug dog (aren't they revolting?). Sometimes I think I'll marry a careless fellow with dangerous habits so I can reform him.

I'm afraid you must be getting tired of me and losing interest. I wish you could visit some Sunday, but I can't have visitors now that I'm on academic warning. It's probably just as well. You'd keel over at the sight of me in my white uniform.

He wrote back:

I'm sorry I won't get a chance to see you in your uniform.

I wrote my fourteen-year-old sister a letter on how she could make herself more attractive to boys.

Annabel has no self-confidence and is not a good conversationalist. She slouches, can't dance, and has no control over her facial expressions. So I advised her to become more like Ginevra Perry.

I told her that she should never try to convince a boy that she is popular. You tell boys that you are unpopular and don't have any beaus.

I told her that every girl should develop a pathetic appealing look, and that you are a specialist at this when you are delivering your "I'm so unpopular" speech. You open your eyes wide and droop the mouth a little. You hang your head and then look upwards directly into the eyes of the boy you're talking to.

I instructed her to practise this look every day in front of the mirror.

I replied:

I feel sorry for your poor sister. If she follows my example, she'll probably end up an old maid. I'm sure if I ever meet her, she'll spit in my eye.

It makes me feel queer that you see right through me. Am I that obvious?

Really, Scott, you are a punk speller! The word is beaux, not beaus. And practice has a "c," not an "s." I'm not a bluestocking, but I am a good speller because Mother is such a stickler. She writes cross notes to the maids when they misspell things. She would probably wonder how they ever let you into Princeton.

Miss Hillard gave us a talk in chapel today about the battle in Verdun. She explained that the French and English soldiers who have sacrificed their lives aren't much older than we are. It made me realize that I have not given enough thought to the serious suffering that is happening in the rest of the world.

By March, Scott seemed to lose interest in my inner thoughts about love and marriage. His letters concerned mostly himself and the upcoming club elections.

Got elected secretary of Triangle, which should help with my bids. All the clubs have different characters. Ivy is the aristocrats. Cottage is the most fashionable. Cap and Gown is for teetotalers. Tiger Inn is for the football and baseball players. Quadrangle is for the Nassau Lit. crowd.

I am leaning toward Cottage, but maybe it's too snobbish for a boy from Summit Ave.

Being in the right club is like having the top girl.

A week later he wrote:

Got bids from Cap, Cannon, Quadrangle and Cottage.

Sap and I are going with Cottage. When we heard, we went out on Nassau Street and romped in the snow.

I'm afraid you'll forget me when you go home for Easter. Even now you may be having a rendezvous with some mysterious Chicagoan with midnight hair and a glistening smile.

I wrote back:

Dear Scott,

You must be thrilled to pieces about Cottage. I wonder what club I'd get a bid from if I were a boy.

It feels very boring being back home. Weezie and Sally are off at Hot Springs. They would probably ignore me even if they were here. The only boy here who fits your description is old John Pullman, who sat next to me in third grade at the Bell School. He has sandy hair, but he is dark in a way. He has dark circles under his eyes! He does have a nice white smile, though. I read him that part of your letter.

When you act jealous about other boys, I wonder if you are just fed up with me and trying to start a fight.

When I got back to Westover, the forsythia was in bloom and tender shoots of grass had sprouted up in the playing field. The promise of spring seemed to put Scott back in a romantic mood.

Dear Ginevra,

Somebody is playing "Love Moon" on a mandolin far across the campus, and the music seems to bring you through my window. Now he's playing "Goodnight,

Boys, I'm Through," and how well that suits me. I meet
new girls all the time at club dances, but I know I'll
never fall in love again. I couldn't—you've been too
much a part of my days and nights to let me think of another girl . . .

The spring nights make me feel so sad. I'm afraid that
they will never come again, and I'm not getting all I
could out of them. I wish my girl was close by, to share
them with me.

Please promise me you will come to the Prom. I will
reserve some rooms for you and your mother at the
Nassau Inn.

So Scott still loved me best.

Dear Scott,

I want more than anything to come to the prom. I
want to see you in your world, charging around, full of
action and purpose. The Cottage Club. The Triangle
Club. The Tiger. Just saying those names makes my head
spin. A man's world. I am so sick of being around nothing but girls, girls, girls.

I will write to Mother right away and see if she will
agree to come east to chaperone me. But I must warn
you. She can be narrow-minded sometimes and may
think 16 is too young for a prom.

In truth, I couldn't get up my nerve to write my mother about the
prom. All I'd said about Scott Fitzgerald when I'd gotten back from
St. Paul was, "Marie's got some attractive friends." Ever since the
unfortunate business with Aldus, Mother and Daddy didn't approve

of me thinking about any one boy as "special." And I certainly had never mentioned the thick envelopes with the Princeton postmark that arrived in my mail cubby every two or three days. I'd managed to convince my parents that I was getting lousy grades because I was a dumbbell, not because I was spending my study halls answering letters. If I asked to go to a prom with some unknown St. Paul boy, my mother would say, Now who is this boy again?

How could I describe Scott? He lets all emotions spill out, like I do, and doesn't feel obliged to keep himself tucked in and screwed down like other boys. He asks me all sorts of profound questions and seems to really value my opinions. In my mother's unimaginative eyes, my special bond with Scott would seem like nothing more than a childish infatuation.

As luck would have it, fate provided me an excuse to back out of the prom.

Dear Scott,

I am, as our friend Marie would say, in heap big trouble. And for once, I'm not even guilty. Who ever said life was fair!

Let me start at the beginning. Last Saturday was the senior dance, when the seniors are allowed to bring actual males on campus. The other students were restricted to our dorms so we wouldn't bark or drool. It was a balmy night, so we went to bed with our windows open and listened to the tinkly tunes floating over from the gymnasium.

Then Marie and I heard crunching in the gravel under our windows and a couple of male voices calling up. There was laughter from the girls next door, and then some mad whispering going back and forth. "Come on down," one boy said. "We don't mind if you're in your nightgowns." Then Marie stepped up to the window and told them they better pipe down. The boys yelled back "Mind your own beeswax," and pretty soon Marie was whispering along with the rest of the girls.

I had your last letter under my pillow, and was feeling glad that such silly stuff didn't interest me anymore. Next thing we knew, the dorm mother's door slammed. Marie and the other girls jumped back into bed, and the boys ran off into the night.

But it was too late. Miss Meister, the housemother, positively identified four girls hanging out the windows —the two girls next door, Marie, and me. Hillard hauled us into her office. Called us hussies who had tried to spoil the dance for the senior girls. Said that she would have suspended us, but because there was only three weeks of school left, she is being merciful and putting us on bounds.

I am sick about missing the prom. I'd give anything to see you.

Scott's next letter held a single sheet of paper. A skull and bones with a dejected frown was drawn in the middle. The caption read "She can't come!"

Dear Scott,

Golly, sorry I gummed up your plans for the prom. (I'm not supposed to say gum up. Mother says only salesgirls in the Loop chew gum.) But my guess is you found a few baby vamps to fill your dance cards.

Now I have a proposition.

Mother is coming to New York when school lets out
and we are going to spend a couple of days at the Plaza,
as she says, bumming around. I think she is feeling a
little guilty about sending me off to Westover.

One evening she is going to a lecture on Staffordshire
figurines at the China Collectors' Club. She's gotten me
two tickets to *Nobody Home* and has told me to invite one
of my school chums. She didn't say that my school chum
couldn't be male, so I'm inviting you!

Just think. A whole evening together alone in New
York. Anything could happen.

Your Ginevra

Scott wrote right back. "New York. You. I can't wait."

Dear Scott,

The show is at 8:00 at the Princess Theater. I'll meet
you in the lobby by the ticket window at 7:30.

Don't breathe a word of this to anybody! Mother
would have a fit if she knew I was going to the theater
with a strange man unchaperoned. Not that you are a
strange man of course, but Mother thinks that anyone
she hasn't been properly introduced to must be a Bar-
bary pirate.

4

Nobody Home

Scott was late but I didn't mind. I wedged myself into a green marble corner by the ticket window, and studied the couples promenading through the brass doors. The women were wearing tiny hats that perched on their heads like a boy's cap, and their skirts were black and so narrow that they walked in a kind of China doll shuffle. I reached up and fingered the floppy brim of my organdy hat, which had seemed so snappy when I bought it at Carson Pirie's in December, and tried to smooth down my dress, which poked out like the petals of a daisy.

When a handsome couple stepped up to the ticket window, the woman shot me a suspicious glare. She was probably an old girl or someone's big sister on the lookout for wayward Westover girls—Hillard had spies everywhere. I turned sideways and examined a billboard deep in the shadows.

I caught a flash of bright yellow sailing against shiny brass, and whirled around to find Scott. After all the pages of Princeton letterhead, and the hours of mooning in a dorm room at dusk, here we were face-to-face again. We shook hands and stepped back, as if to see if the flesh could hold up against the wild imaginings. I was shocked all over again that Scott was so short, almost my height. But then I took in the elegant profile with the firm chin and the finely arched nose. His collar was an iridescent white, fixed with a casually off-center pin, and the jacket was smartly tailored but unbuttoned, as if he'd tossed it on in the cab ride over.

I grinned and he grinned back, the upper lip making a witty curve. "You look lovely," he whispered, even though everyone was jostling by too fast to eavesdrop.

"So do you."

An usher in a black-braided jacket rang a bell to announce the curtain, and I fished the tickets out of my purse. Scott snugged my hand into the crook of his elbow, and the usher showed us to perfect seats—only six rows from the front but tucked off to one side, so we could watch like spies. The Princess was cozy, with blue-and-white tapestries on the wall like a grandmother's parlor. When the lights faded and two girls in zebra-striped pantaloons did a Castle walk across the stage, I felt as if they were putting on a private performance just for us.

I wasn't paying close attention to *Nobody Home,* but it seemed like all the other musicals I'd ever seen. A boy meets a girl in a charming way in a picturesque spot—he retrieves her blown-off hat in front of the Ferris wheel at the San Francisco Fair. The lyrics were all too clever to make much sense:

> Now bed's always been my pet study
> I've tried every sort on earth,
> Fat beds, and thin beds, and twin beds,
> I took to my bed from birth.

After the opening number, Scott's hand crept over, twined its fingers in mine, and held it fast on top of his knee, which was gently tapping out the beat of each song. After the first act, I let my head rest on his shoulder and felt the soft scratch of his jacket. His neck smelled different than it had in St. Paul—fancy shaving soap mixed with cigarettes and the sugary residue of whiskey.

The play ended with the predictable scene. The boy and the girl are back in front of the cardboard Ferris wheel, and he is once again sprinting after her hat.

As the cast took their curtain calls and the houselights brightened, something about this silly play suddenly struck me as oddly moving, and tears welled. Maybe it was because from the sixth row, I could see the stagehand crank a rope to make the Ferris wheel spin or because the actress who played Pauline, the heroine, wasn't young. Her wig had slipped to show dark roots, and the face powder had caked in the lines around her mouth.

Scott, still clapping, glanced over. "Are you crying?" he whispered, sounding amused.

"Love stories always make me cry, even when they turn out happily. Because the best part has come to an end." Maybe I cried because I was afraid that this might be the best part of my romance with Scott—an illicit pair hiding in a dark theater, our upturned faces bathed in stage light.

He reached over and tenderly wiped each eye with his thumb. "What nonsense. Why can't we live the best parts over and over again?"

We rearranged ourselves and slowly wandered out of the theater. The sky had turned black now, so the street lamps and theater signs shimmered with halos. A spotlight crisscrossed the distant sky, as if it were searching for a stray airship. The other couples formed a restless line for cabs, impatient to get on to the next part of their evening—a late-night supper at the Ritz, Ziegfeld's *Midnight Frolic* at the New Amsterdam.

"I wish we could go someplace, but Mother will be back from her China Collectors' Club and wondering where I am," I said wistfully.

"You have time for a cup of tea, don't you?" Scott pleaded. He pointed at a tiny shop next to the theater—TSARINA TEA ROOM was written in flaking green paint across a steamy window.

It was narrow as a closet inside, with wrought-iron tables along one wall only big enough for two. We wedged into the one empty table next to two girls who had promenaded in the first act and still had their stage makeup on. The menu was typed in Russian, with crude English translations scrawled above in red ink.

A waiter appeared with a long gray beard and the kind of red drum hat worn by circus elephants. I pointed at something called a gooseberry blintz. "I'll have that, I suppose."

"Just a cup of tea for me," said Scott. The waiter padded off in slippers and we were left by ourselves, grinning stupidly.

"I've been dreaming of this moment ever since our bobsled ride." I was babbling.

Scott leaned forward, pressing his knees against mine under the tippy table. "Me too."

"The play was clever, don't you think?"

"To tell you the truth, I wasn't really listening."

"I liked Pauline's costume."

"She made you cry."

"It seemed so sad that she has to pretend to be eighteen when she must be at least thirty. Probably no boy would want to chase her hat anymore. After the show, she walks home to a boarding house on a bad street. She shakes out birdseed for her canary, and sings him a few lines."

"Isn't it peculiar, how sweethearts meet," Scott sang in a pretty decent baritone. "Do you remember the first play you ever saw?"

"My grandfather took me to *Babes in Toyland* when I was about four. The toy soldiers had black fur mustaches and red circles painted on their cheeks. I got so scared I started to whine, and the usher asked us to leave. It was very embarrassing. How about you?"

"I was in ninth grade at Newman School in Hoboken. We got one outing per semester, and I took the train into the city and saw *The Quaker Girl*. I decided Ina Claire in her little gray dress and white bonnet was the love of my life." Scott dropped his chin and looked for a moment like a smooth-cheeked fourteen-year-old in his Sunday best. "Until I met you," he added.

Our waiter delivered a pancake piled high with yellowed cream and greenish berries. I mashed them together with a tiny fork and took a cautious bite. "Why does foreign food always taste like curdled milk?" I asked.

Scott laughed, as if I'd meant to be witty. He pulled a dented flask from his pocket and poured a large dollop into his teacup. "Medicinal spirits. I have weak lungs. Want some?"

"Better not. Mother would give me hell if she smelled liquor on my breath."

He screwed the cap back on and gave his tea a stir. He still had those nice thick lashes, I noticed, which set off the color of his eyes, which in this light looked halfway between green and blue.

"Tell me everything about school," I ventured. "How'd your exams go?"

Scott shrugged. "Maybe not so well. But let's not talk about that. Let's talk about us. Am I still at the top of your list? I need to know." His hand disappeared under the table and dropped on my knee.

"Of course you're the top boy on my list." My hand slid down my lap until it covered his. "Not that I keep a list. And not that I know any other boys. I've been locked up at boarding school for the last year, remember?"

"Maybe so, but Marie says you get letters from a dozen other boys. I think she's just trying to prepare me for the day you throw me over."

"Not a dozen boys. Just John Pullman, and he wears specs."

"And how about that boy who's off in Montana shearing sheep. Just because of you."

"I told you. I'm a reformed woman." I held up my hand as if I were making the Boy Scout pledge.

"But you're probably going to all sorts of parties this summer where there will be new boys."

"Not really," I lied. Mother had already sent me a list of invitations I needed to answer, but they were the usual stuff—tea dances, luncheons after tennis tournaments, a vaudeville put on by the hospital's Ladies' Auxiliary. It would be the same old tiresome group of boys that I'd gone to dances with since I was ten. Only one of the invitations flickered and rumbled like distant fireworks. Old Joe McCormick was giving an engagement party for his daughter in his brand-new mansion on the lake. I was already wondering if there would be mysterious older men from faraway places.

"Maybe we should get engaged, and then I wouldn't have to worry anymore." Scott nudged my shoe with his. "I'm sure there's a jewelry store around here that's still open. I'll ask the waiter."

I noticed the two actresses at the next table exchanging smirks. The banter that had seemed so amusing in our letters now sounded foolish spoken out loud. "Come on, Scott. Be serious. Are you going to be in St. Paul this summer?"

"Yes." He sounded petulant.

"So you see. You'll go to parties, too."

"Not many," he said. He pulled out his flask and dumped the rest of the "spirits" into his now empty teacup. Maybe he was getting a little tight. "Mostly I'm going to be stuck in my parents' depressing house, and thinking of all the ways my mother embarrasses me."

"Come on. You make it sound like your parents live in a tenement. You must be doing something interesting with your time." Scott was starting to look pathetic.

"Well, actually, I'm planning to start a novel."

"There you go. That's the ticket. What's your novel about?"

He straightened up and his eyes took on a roguish gleam. "You."

"That would make a boring book. What could you possibly say about me?" I admit that this scheme made Scott seem more attractive. None of the boys back in Lake Forest even pretended to do artistic things like write books.

"Let me think." He leaned back and sized me up. "Rich girl lives in an Italianate mansion with about a quarter mile of terraced lawns and many unused rooms. Her mother is an ineffectual type who frets that her only daughter is completely out of control. The father is handsome but snobbish, and worries that the daughter will marry the wrong type."

"First of all, I don't live in a mansion. I have a little sister, so I'm not an only daughter. Daddy is handsome but not a bit of a snob. You better come for a visit this summer so you can get your facts straight."

"Really?" Scott sounded pleased. "When?"

"Whenever you want. Stay for as long as you like. Mother and Daddy will be tickled that a real writer is making a study of us."

In the cab ride back to the Plaza, Scott and I sank into comfortable darkness. He leaned me back, snaked his arm around my waist, and kissed me full on the mouth. Now that we weren't in the back of a bobsled being watched by Marie Hart and all the rest of St. Paul, I could let myself go. I matched him kiss for kiss. Yes, everything had been perfect, I decided, gazing past the rim of Scott's ear as streetlights pinwheeled by.

I found myself daydreaming in bland words, as if I were already describing it in a letter to Marie. *Nobody Home* was cheerful and loads of fun, the Tsarina Tea Room was so queer. Scott was just as handsome, just as fascinating as he'd been in St. Paul. Thank goodness we didn't "fall flat." Sometimes these boys are such a letdown the second time around. And he's writing a book about me and coming out to Lake Forest to do "research!"

"In August," Scott murmured, with a last kiss on my neck.

"In August."

5

Houseguest

The racket from Mr. Jensen's tractor woke me up. I flipped over in bed and frowned at the open window. Why couldn't he mow the grass in the afternoon? There were only three weeks left before I went back to school, and I needed to catch up on my sleep. I closed my eyes and considered the day. The semifinals of the men's tennis tournament at the club started at three, but it was pretty pointless to go—most of the men were nearly thirty and married. Then again, I could wear my new lawn dress with navy blue piping. I checked the little leather travel clock on the bed stand—it was half past eleven. Maybe I still had time to go downtown and get a shampoo first. I'd drop by and see how Mother's seamstress, Mrs. Turner, was coming along on my costume for the McCormicks' party. She didn't have much time left. I counted the days on my fingers—five more until what the *Tribune* had called "the party of the season."

I slipped on my robe and padded barefoot along the hallway and down the stairs. I flipped through the stack of morning mail on the hall table. Nothing for me except an-

other letter from Scott. Even though he'd been back in St.
summer, he still wrote on Princeton stationery, which seem
little dishonest now that he'd flunked three final exams and w
back on probation. I tore it open sloppily with my thumb.

> Dearest G.,
>
> I wish you'd write me back. It's been almost two
> weeks. I hope this doesn't mean you've fallen for that
> dark Chicagoan with the gleaming smile after all!
>
> I was waiting to hear from you about the best dates to
> stop in Lake Forest on my way back to Princeton. Since
> you didn't answer my last letter, I've gone ahead and
> made travel plans. I'll arrive in Lake Forest Aug. 15 on
> the noon local. I'll leave on the 22nd. That's only a
> week. Hardly enough time to see my girl again and get
> my facts straight for my book.
>
> I remember how I wanted to kiss your tears away
> when you cried during *Nobody Home*. I just hope I don't
> forget myself and kiss you in front of your parents.
>
> Till the 15th!
>
> Your Scott

I jammed the pages back into the envelope and sank down onto
a spindly hall bench. If only I had bothered to read his last two letters—the fifteenth was tomorrow!

I decided to follow Daddy's advice on how to deal with a sticky
situation—puzzle it through step by step. On June 8, at a table in
the Tsarina Tea Room, with my knees pressed tight to Scott's and
a wisp of steam rising from a brass pot, a visit from Scott had
seemed like a thrilling idea. Now, with Scott twenty-four hours
away, I was filled with dread. What had happened?

't sent me after *Nobody Home* seemed just as
'd sent to Westover. He hoped my mother
hair and chapped lips. He'd seen all sorts
trip back to St. Paul—a man who sold
valise, two Vassar girls who wanted to
y, a Methodist minister with a Persian cat in a
ote him right back, saying that I missed him desper-
y, that I'd played tennis with my friend Millie at the Onwentsia
Club and beat her 6–3, 6–2, and then we'd played a round of golf
and she beat me. Afterward we drove in the Jordans' electric to the
drugstore for root beer floats.

Two days later I got another letter from Scott that sounded less
cheerful. He had set up a "writer's garret" for himself on the third
floor of his parents' house, but it was hot and filled with dead flies.
He was writing a play about me called, tentatively, *The Debutante,*
even though I wasn't a debutante yet. He was also doing some
studying because he would have to take makeup exams in September. It took me a few days to answer him this time. I told him I had
been cast in a vaudeville to benefit the Lake Forest Hospital and
had spent all afternoon rehearsing the maxixe with Deering Ryerson, Weezie's brother.

Scott's next letter arrived a day later. Why hadn't I answered
him, he asked, sounding peeved. He had a few research questions
for me. What were my height and weight? Who was my favorite
matinee idol? I dashed off the answers—five foot four, 107 lbs.,
Douglas Fairbanks.

I didn't hear from Scott for almost a week, and when I did, he
was vaguely accusatory. Was I falling for any of the boys in the
vaudeville? He knew how easily I went head over heels for complete strangers. And he had another question—Was I fickle because
I had a weak character? Life was getting hectic—I had vaudeville

practice every day, and there was usually something going on at the club every night, so I didn't answer him right away. Before I knew it, there was another letter with another nosy question— How did my parents meet? Were they still "in love"? And another with another.

And my goodness, the spelling mistakes—"definate," "illegable." They'd gotten so embarrassing that as soon as I hit one, I'd stuff the letter back in its envelope and fling it in the bottom drawer of my dressing table. In the last few weeks, even though the vaude-ville was over and I had time on my hands, the letters had piled up, unread and unanswered, like autumn leaves in a storm drain.

I'd tried to find the right moment to let my parents know about his visit, but how could I explain Scott? I couldn't tell them about the bobsled ride or the letters or *Nobody Home.* I certainly couldn't tell them that some strange Princeton boy wanted to do research for a book about me. So I'd said nothing, with the vague hope that Scott might decide not to come for a visit after all.

Well, as Hillard put it, now I had to "pay the piper," whatever that meant.

Through the dining room doors, I could see my mother's head bobbing up and down over the flower urns along the terrace. Even though she had two maids and a gardener, there were a few house-hold chores that she insisted could only be done properly with her own two hands—polishing the Perry silver hot chocolate pot that had been rescued from the Chicago Fire, washing each prism of the crystal chandelier with newspaper and vinegar, and deadhead-ing the flowers in the urns.

Brandishing Scott's letter like a spear, I padded through the dining room, across the already-sun-baked flagstones, and leaned a hip against one of the fake Tuscan urns until Mother glanced up. A steamy haze had settled on the back field past the lawn where

Daddy had fashioned a crude three-hole golf course. The crickets roared and the golf flags flapped limply in the heat.

Mother straightened, pushed back the brim of her straw gardener's hat, and squinted toward my robe and now-dirty bare feet. "You're just getting up at . . ." She checked her watch. "Noon? Don't expect Mrs. Coates to make you breakfast."

"I'm not hungry." The last time I'd asked Mrs. Coates, in a perfectly courteous way, for coddled eggs and a piece of toast, she'd muttered, "Coddled girl."

Mother went back to snipping off withered petunia blossoms. She had special outfits for each of her chores—a butcher's apron, a basket for clippings, chamois work gloves, dainty rubbers that fit over her summer shoes—which took her longer to put on and take off than the job itself. "You didn't get home by ten."

"I didn't? What time did you fall asleep?"

"Around eleven."

"I must have come in right after. Sorry." In fact, we'd made a tureen of planter's punch and scrambled eggs at Millie's pool house around eleven.

"Did you pick up your room like I asked?"

"It's almost done."

"Did you write your thank-you note to Aunt Minnie for the pincushion?"

"I just got up, Mother. I'll do it after lunch."

"That's what you said yesterday. Did you organize your stocking drawer? There're at least five pairs with runs." This is the way things went with my mother—she'd keep reeling off chores until I popped a gasket.

I held Scott's letter between my index fingers and spun it like a pinwheel. "Can we change the subject? I just got a letter from Scott Fitzgerald. He's Marie Hart's friend I met in St. Paul last Christmas, remember? The one I said was so attractive who goes to Princeton. He's clever and writes plays and things."

"Dimly," she said with a snip.

"Well, he just wrote, saying he's planning to drop by on his way back to Princeton."

"You didn't say yes, did you?" She dropped the shears into the basket and yanked off her work gloves—she hated the disorder of houseguests.

"I may have, by accident. Anyway, he's getting here tomorrow."

"He's not spending the night, is he?"

"A couple of days. Maybe even as long as a week." I shrugged, as if the matter was out of my hands.

"A week!" She raised the brim of her sun hat, her eyes narrowing with suspicion. "Why would a boy you hardly know think he could come for a week?"

"How should I know?"

At the far edge of the golf course, a lean boy in overalls was bent over the tractor, squirting the axle with a spouted oilcan, like the Tin Man's in *The Wizard of Oz*. So it was Mr. Jensen's helper who'd woken me up—that seemed more forgivable. I adjusted my bathrobe so it drooped over one shoulder and stared till he looked up and waved with a sunburned arm. Maybe later I'd take him a glass of ice water.

"If you have a guest, I guess you can't go to the McCormicks' party," Mother concluded, as if this would surely change my mind.

Oh, rats. I'd forgotten about the party. "No one will mind if I bring him along." I turned and strolled back toward the house.

My stomach had started to rumble, so I detoured through the kitchen to see if I could pinch a snack from Mrs. Coates. She was standing at the pastry table, cutting the crusts off watercress finger sandwiches. I slid three onto a napkin and sat down at the kitchen table next to her six-year-old son, Julian.

"Those are for your mother's bridge party," Mrs. Coates said, setting the carving knife down with an ominous smack.

"Mother won't mind if I have a few. I haven't had any breakfast."

Mrs. Coates was a comely young woman, but the bitter turn of her mouth made her look dowdy and middle-aged. Mr. Coates was a plasterer who always seemed to be out of a job.

"Hi, Julian." Julian had his mother's thick curls and fine features. When he wasn't in school, he sat quietly in the kitchen flipping through my old books, which he'd found in the nursery. "Whatcha got today?"

"Hi, Ginevra." He held up the book cover so I could see the bent ears and shredded trousers of Br'er Rabbit.

"My favorite story is about the Tar Baby. I tried to make a tar baby once by smearing mud on one of Evvie's dolls. Can you read all those big words?"

"Of course he can," said Mrs. Coates. He's not a bonehead student like you, her tone implied. She was ambitious for Julian—she'd told Daddy that she put aside a dollar a week for his college fund.

"I mostly look at the pictures," he said with a modest smile that made me think this kid was going to go far.

"You get back to your book, Julian, so Ginevra can get herself dressed."

The next day, I convinced Daddy to let me drive the electric to the train station to pick up Scott. "Why can't Jensen take you in the Packard?" he asked.

"Can't I do something by myself for once?" I wanted to face my houseguest alone so I could set some ground rules. Don't mention your letters or your "writing." No calling me "my girl." And for God's sake, no kissing.

I arrived half an hour early and paced up and down the blacktop platform, my white shoes turning sticky and black with tar.

Across the street, two burly men balanced on a scaffolding slung across the front of a new row of shops, slapping fake Tudor stucco on with trowels as if they were frosting a cake. One nudged his cap—"Hey, girlie." I gave a halfhearted wave back.

The crossing gate started to clang and flash as a two-car local chugged slowly up the track from Highland Park and squeaked to a halt. A single door unlatched and passengers stepped down one by one—old man Blair, past ninety with a humpback and a cane who still put in a half day in the city, Mrs. Brewster buttoning up her summer gloves, Mrs. Seaman's seamstress shouldering a carpetbag stuffed with mending. Then a pause, long enough for me to think that Scott had missed the train, that I'd been spared.

The conductor jumped down, swung a battered suitcase onto the platform with a scrape, followed by a small, dapper figure fishing in his pocket for a bit of change. The door slammed shut, the train lurched northward, the other passengers drifted off, leaving Scott Fitzgerald blinking blindly in the noonday glare. I stood to one side and watched as his eyes adjusted. Yes, I recognized the bright hair parted in the middle, the graceful nose, the sloped shoulders, all done up like a dandy in a white linen suit and white buck shoes.

"Ginevra," he yelped, the lovely lips turning upward into a grin, and he trotted toward me, his suitcase banging against his shin. I held out my right arm for a handshake, stiff as wood to fend him off. He stopped and dropped his bag, clutched my hand in both of his, brought it tenderly up to his chest, and rocked unsteadily back on his heels.

"You came," he announced simply. Anyone who was watching—as I was sure the plasterers and the seamstress and even old man Blair were—would know without question that this was my sweetheart.

I tugged my hand away and took two giant steps back. "Of course I came." My tone was matter-of-fact. "Did you think I'd leave you stranded?"

His gaze swept over my person, first down, then up. "You look as if you've just bounded off the tennis court."

"Thanks." That morning, I'd taken pains to look poorly in the hopes of cooling Scott off a bit. I was wearing the same white lawn dress I'd had on the day before, now wrinkled and damp. I hadn't bothered to brush my hair, just raked it back with my fingers and twisted it tight with three hairpins. I headed toward the car with Scott jogging behind.

"You're driving?"

"More or less," I said. I wasn't quite sure where reverse was, so I jammed the car into a gear and pressed the pedal, sending the car jackrabbiting backward across the street. Scott smiled, unalarmed, and placed a steadying palm against the glove box.

As we lurched down Green Bay Road, he kept up a patter of polite conversation. "Lake Forest is famous, you know."

"For what?"

He gestured down a freshly cut driveway lined with livery trucks. "The palaces of meatpackers."

I would have shrugged and said what nonsense, except he was pointing at the stone ramparts of Mr. Cudahy's Norman castle that was rising up against a pancake-flat horizon.

I swayed up our drive, and when the house loomed into view, I yanked hard on the brake lever, which caused a wave of gravel to ricochet off the side door like a Gatling gun. Scott exhaled, sank down against the red leather seat, and took in every detail as if he were committing it to memory, to be jotted down later in his diary.

The house was made of Portland cement dyed a sandy pink to match a Tuscan villa Daddy had picked out of a picture book about the Grand Tour. On either side of the front door stood crumbly, lichen-covered statues of Bacchus and Pan, which the architect had paid an impoverished Italian duke to hack down from his own front door, then crate and ship to the New World. The grape arbors, topiaries, and spindly cypress trees hadn't grown high enough to disguise the mowed bluestem prairie grass. A brisk wind flapped the green-and-white-striped awnings over each window. The only landmark was a line of telephone poles across the flat horizon.

"See, I was right. You do live in an Italianate mansion," Scott said, pleased with himself.

I trotted up the front steps and threw open the screen door as if I were late to a dentist appointment and needed to hurry Scott along. The house seemed mercifully deserted—Daddy was still in the city, and Mother had gone to a fancy luncheon for the Infant Welfare Society, which helped the babies of factory workers.

Scott wandered down the hallway, his heels squeaking across the buffed black-and-white tiles. He put a hand on the iron banister and peered up at the ten-foot salon portrait hanging in the stairwell of three little Bavarian princes with big heads and short legs. "Your relatives?" he asked with a wise-guy smile.

"I hope not. Daddy bought it because he liked the fancy gold frame."

He inspected the living room and dining room, then stopped at the doorway of Daddy's office. "Oh, hello," he said.

Evvie, my eleven-year-old sister, was sitting at Daddy's huge partner's desk with her Postage Stamps of the United States album, examining a page with a magnifying glass. Evvie prided herself on being as unlike me as possible. Pale and freckled, she dressed as much like a boy as Mother allowed, in sailor blouses, bloomers, and open-toed sandals like Breton fishermen wear. She kept her string-straight hair whacked off into two stubby pigtails. She'd won the sixth grade Latin prize, played the oboe, and had many self-improving hobbies along with stamp collecting.

"You're Ginevra's houseguest," she said, a statement, not a question.

"I'm Scott Fitzgerald and I'm pleased to make your acquaintance," he said in the tone one uses with cute children. Strangers found Evvie charming until they realized she liked to repeat comments that people made about one another and stir up trouble. For example, the time she asked me with innocent eyes, "Why did Daddy say that sending you to boarding school was the only way to save what was left of your reputation?"

"Are you really in love with her?" Evvie asked, pointing toward me with a pair of tweezers.

Scott's face reddened, as if he had on two spots of rouge. "I'd say I like her a lot. Don't you?"

"No." Evvie picked up a large pair of library shears and started to snip the stamps off a pile of old envelopes. Suddenly I spotted at least ten fat, creamy edges right in the middle of the stack. The envelopes of Scott's letters—she must have snitched them from my drawer. She probably read the letters too and was waiting for the right moment to recite some choice lines.

I linked my hands through his elbow and tugged him free. "Let me show you the guest room. Then we can take a walk and I'll give you the tour."

"That's what I was hoping," he said, his face turning an even brighter shade. Ten minutes later he was on the terrace smelling of lavender soap, his hair wet-brushed, tie straightened, and the corner of a crisp handkerchief peeking out of his breast pocket.

Even though I wanted to be out of earshot from Evvie, I wasn't all that eager to be alone with Scott, so I took my time explaining the garden. "These are Mother's perennial beds. She just put in the coral-bells, so there aren't as many blooms as there will be next year. I got tired of my goldfish when I was ten and dumped him in the fishpond, and if you look long enough you'll see him. He's turned into a monster—a foot long with black rotten spots." We stared at the green slime and leaf rot at the bottom of the pond for a couple of minutes, but not a stir from Maurice.

I led Scott across the lawn toward the first hole of the golf course. He paused at the top of the tee and surveyed down the fairway to an emerald putting green that hovered like a mirage.

"You have your own golf course?" He sounded a little appalled.

"Just three holes. But they're tricky with swamps and tree roots, so if you play them three times, you get a pretty good game. My friend Millie Jordan is coming to play with us tomorrow. She's crazy about golf."

"Sounds like fun," Scott said halfheartedly. He pulled a cigarette case out of his pocket, the brass one I thought was smart back in St. Paul. "Mind if I smoke?" He lit up before I could answer and took a few desperate puffs. "Let's walk down there." He waved his cigarette where the path detoured toward the Skokie Ditch.

I pulled a stalk of Queen Anne's lace and whipped the ground as I walked. The path zigged and zagged through the high grass, then dipped down to a sluggish brown stream.

"This looks like a good place to sit," said Scott, lowering himself onto a flattish bump.

I noticed that the seat of his white pants would get grass-stained, but didn't think it was ladylike to say so. I perched a modest three feet away.

"I used to wade in there," I said blandly.

"I've been dreaming of this for two months!" Scott exploded. "Night after night in my attic. You have no idea." He leapfrogged over, grabbed my waist, tilted me back, and kissed me. A mad, wet kiss, just like the ones that had made me go limp in the cab ride back to the Plaza. Now his lips felt rubbery.

"Mmm," I murmured politely, as if I'd bitten into a peculiar candy. I slipped both hands against his chest and pushed him back firmly, then slid myself another three feet down the bump. "Can I have a cigarette?"

His pale eyebrows made a furrow while he fumbled one from his case and lit it. I inhaled with tiny puffs, holding it awkwardly between my thumb and index finger. Even though I liked the idea of being a daring girl who smoked, it still made me woozy. I pointed the lit end at him, just in case he considered making another lunge. "I don't think we should kiss anymore."

"Why *not?*" he pleaded.

"Someone might see us." This seemed unlikely—we were sitting at the bottom of a sunless ditch.

"You didn't worry about kissing me in a bobsled or a taxi cab." He sounded miffed. "Besides, what difference would it make if someone did see us kiss. Everyone knows you're my girl."

"Well, that's just it, Scott. My parents don't really know that."

"They don't?"

"My parents are kind of stuffy. They think sixteen is too young to be serious about any boy."

"So what did you tell them about me?"

"Lots of things." I waved the cigarette around while I picked my words. "I said you were a friend of Marie's. You belong to all the best clubs at Princeton."

"Did you tell them I'm going to be a writer?"

"I left that part out."

He tossed his cigarette butt into the water, and watched as it floated for an instant and then sank under the murky surface. "You sound like I embarrass you."

"Don't be so melodramatic." I reached over and patted his bony knee, like I did when I teased Evvie and made her cry. "When Mother and Daddy get to know you, they'll love you just as much as I do. Then you can call me 'my girl' all you want." I jumped up and tried to smooth the creases out of my dress.

By the time we straggled back to the house, Daddy was setting out decanters and mixers on a silver tray in the living room. "Who goes there?" he bellowed, and came striding out to the front hall, right arm extended. At forty-four, Daddy still had the broad shoulders and nipped waist of his days as a Yale tackle. The only signs of age were a few white strands that had crept into his thick crop of ebony hair and a dignified looseness in the jowls. Looming a full head above, he made Scott look as dainty as a paper doll.

"Name your poison."

"Gin, neat, sir."

Daddy nodded with approval as he filled a toddy glass to the rim; he liked men who drank plain liquor without any funny stuff thrown in. He settled on the oversize damask couch, threw a comfortable arm over the back, crossed his legs. Scott perched himself nearby on a low, tufted armchair covered in candy-stripe silk, which Mother called her sewing chair—not that she ever sewed.

"So you're a Princeton man."

"Yes, sir. Starting my junior year."

"Went to Yale, myself. Class of Ninety-three."

"I was bothered until the middle of last year that I wasn't going to Yale," Scott mused.

"Then why didn't you?"

"I'm not sure I could have passed the entrance exams." Scott smiled, as if he expected a gold star for his honesty. "I always thought Yale had a neat, hard brightness. Yale is aristocratic and Princeton's just snobbish."

"I'm not sure I get your drift," Daddy said, who did not believe in what he called "hair splitting." "Are you on the athletic teams?" Daddy cast a doubtful look toward Scott's scrawny shoulders.

"I was on the freshman squad, but I busted up my knee the first week and had to give it up." Marie Hart told me that Scott had scraped his knee the first day, which had given him a handy excuse to quit before he got cut. "So I joined the Triangle Club. I was elected secretary this year."

"Triangle is the one where the boys dress like chorus girls?"

"That's it. I'm considered the prettiest one."

Daddy grinned politely. "Can I refill your drink?"

"Please."

"You're from Minneapolis, I gather."

"St. Paul. On the other side of the river."

"The Twin Cities."

"That's right. My father works in wholesale groceries," Scott added, as if he'd been asked.

Daddy glanced over to where I had dropped onto an out-of-the-way stool. "Ginevra, you look as if you've been herding swine."

"I was showing Scott your golf course. I'll change for dinner." As I walked up the stairs, I heard Daddy start to grill Scott about his golf game.

"I sometimes played golf at the White Bear Yacht Club," said Scott, sounding slightly tight.

I took pains getting dressed—Daddy loved to make a fuss about how I was turned out for dinner. I selected a dress with six bold black stripes down the skirt which flattered my hips, brushed my hair a hundred strokes and rolled it high, put on a dangerously liberal application of rouge and lipstick.

According to Mother, Daddy was something called "a man's man," which she implied was a great achievement. This meant that he did all things well in a plain way without boasting or calling attention to himself. Mother said that Daddy had not been a member of Bones or any other secret society because Deke had been good enough for him. He had been so popular in college that he'd had fifteen groomsmen, and she'd had to ask girls she hardly knew to be bridesmaids. He preferred golf to tennis, which he said made a man perspire too much. He was well read, but preferred books by dead Americans such as James Fenimore Cooper; he knew French and German but refused to speak anything but English. His favorite meal was Yankee pot roast, and he wouldn't eat dishes with French sauces or puréed vegetables. He would not sing except in church and was suspicious of men who liked amateur theatricals and motion pictures. Hired help, from Mrs. Coates to Mr. Jensen, adored him because he didn't pretend they were equals but wasn't above rolling up his sleeves to dig a posthole. Even though he gave no thought to his clothes, he looked like a department store mannequin. I was afraid that in the eyes of a man's man, Scott Fitzgerald was not going to measure up very well.

Having exhausted the topics of both summer and winter sports, Scott turned his attention to my mother over dinner. "You have no idea what a stir your daughter caused when she visited over Christmas. No one could talk about anything else for weeks."

"Oh, really?" Mother said, bringing a hand to her throat in alarm. She'd learned over the years that it was usually a danger sign when someone mentioned that I'd caused a "stir." Next she'd hear that I'd been caught smoking a cigarette, or that I'd snuck into a walk-in ice chest with some boy, and that my name had been struck off Miss So-and-So's list for next year's dance. "Has your family always been from St. Paul?" she asked.

"No, actually, my father is a southerner. From Rockville, Maryland," Scott said with enthusiasm, relieved to have been tossed a conversational bone. He'd realized by now that the list of subjects to avoid was lengthy—including one's accomplishments, one's profession, anything to do with money, art, literature, and now, me. Genealogy, since it was a subject pursued by great-aunts and librarians, was probably safe.

"I'm named after my great-great-great-uncle Francis Scott Key, who wrote 'The Star Spangled Banner.'" In one of his letters, he'd told me Key was a "vague relation that my father claims," but maybe Scott was having a hard time keeping his facts straight. He'd switched to wine over dinner, and his face in the candlelight had taken on the moist shine of a drunk. Being able to hold his liquor was another man's-man quality he lacked.

"You know the story about how he was looking out a porthole of a ship in Baltimore Harbor, and that after the smoke from all the cannon shells had cleared, he saw that our flag was still there." Scott made an explosion sound, then crooked a hand over his eyes as if he were staring out to sea. "Family legend has it that he didn't really see it at all. He'd gotten disgracefully drunk on the captain's rum and been locked in the brig all night. One of his fellow sailors described the part about bombs bursting in air, and he stole it. So you see, I'm descended from a long line of frauds."

My parents nodded politely, but Evvie sized him up with newfound respect. "You're a lot more interesting than Ginevra's usual boys," she concluded, her mouth full of strawberry shortcake.

6

Dismal Swamp

I decided the best approach with Scott was to go about my usual business. The first morning after his arrival, I sat at Daddy's desk and caught up on thank-you notes—one to Aunt Minnie in Galena for the "cunning" pincushion made of five little stuffed Chinamen and one to old Mrs. Thorne for a luncheon she'd invited me to back in June. Scott sat in the Morris chair in the corner with an ashtray propped on one of the wide arms and made a half-hearted stab at flipping through a geometry textbook for his makeup exam. Every time I'd glance up I'd catch him studying me, his mouth curled up in a foolish grin.

"You don't seem to be getting much studying done," I said, turning back to the sheet of robin's-egg-blue notepaper with GP printed in raised white letters.

"Conic sections. Not making any more sense than it did last June. Lucky thing I signed up for tutoring at school. Rooney manages to get half the football team to pass their makeup exams. I'll study on the train back to Princeton." His resolve sounded faint. He slammed the book shut, dropped it on the floor, and slid a wistful glance out the window at the back field. "I wish we could be alone. Let's go for a walk down to that drainage ditch."

I waved my note to dry the ink. "We better not. Evvie might tell Mother we'd been sneaking off." I folded the note into an envelope, picked up my pen, and started on another one. Scott sighed, walked over to the bookshelf, and started fiddling with the patent model for the Perry Fireproof Vault.

After lunch Scott tagged along while I did errands at Market Square, the row of Tudor shops that had just been built in the town center to provide amenities for the meatpackers' palaces. First we went to the library to return books, then on to Krafft's Drugstore, where I bought a new toothbrush, and Garnett's for some stockings. While I went upstairs to Mrs. Turner, the seamstress, to have my outfit for the McCormicks' party fitted, Scott perched on a bench outside O'Neill's Hardware. I dawdled for forty-five minutes over the new fabric samples from New York and dress patterns in *McCall's* magazine.

I found Scott eating a powdered doughnut. He was deep in conversation with Mr. Jensen, who was holding two lengths of galvanized tin gutter. Scott wiped a dusting of sugar off his chin. "I've been telling Mr. Jensen all about our bobsled ride and how you hit St. Paul like a blizzard."

Mr. Jensen's gloomy Scandinavian features twitched slightly, the closest he ever came to a smile.

"Sorry I've been such a rotten hostess," I said on the car ride home.

"I'm glad we're close enough so you don't feel you have to make a fuss." He fixed me with a dreamy expression, as if he were watching his bride walk down the aisle. "Besides, I enjoy watching you pick out toothbrushes and stockings."

The next morning, Millie Jordan came over for nine holes on Daddy's golf course. Poor Millie now had to play golf at our house four days a week. After she'd beaten the pants off Angus McNair, the pro at the Onwentsia Club, the board had passed a new rule forbidding women on the course Thursday through Sunday. Not that any male was willing to play with her anymore, including her own father. I told Scott that he could play with Millie, whom I described as "not a half-bad golfer for a girl." I'd stroll along as a spectator.

On the first tee, Scott plucked a driver out of the golf bag he'd borrowed from my father, hefted it, arranged his fingers on the grip one by one, as if he were following a diagram, and took a few showy practice swings. Even I could see that his hips swiveled too far around and that his shoulders ended up at a cockeyed angle.

"Have you played much?" Millie asked in the low, confiding voice she used to lull her competitors into thinking this was a casual round of golf. She was wearing a custom golf outfit she'd had run up by a tailor—a man's linen jacket and pants that were full enough to pass, barely, as a kind of tight skirt. Her hazel eyes were flecked with yellow, like some predatory cat's. She wore her hair twisted under a golf cap, so from a distance she looked like a sunburned, freckled fourteen-year-old boy.

"Quite a lot. At the country club in St. Paul," said Scott, sliding one driver back in the bag and selecting another. "You can move your tee closer," he added with a gallant wave down the hill.

"That's not necessary," Millie said pleasantly. Like a ballerina making a pirouette, she set her ball on the tee, chose a club, and polished its head with a piece of chamois that hung off her belt. When she stepped up to the tee, a veil seemed to drop over her face as she stared hard at the ball for a moment, then raised her focus to the pale circle of green in the distance, with its flag fluttering in the morning mist. With a smart crack of the club, the ball made a lazy arc through the sky and dropped precisely ten yards from the edge of the green, as if it had been following whispered instructions.

"I see you're quite good at this." Scott sounded amused.

"She is," I said. "She won the ladies' title in the state tournament in June. She'd have gone east to compete in the Women's Amateur but her parents wouldn't let her."

"Why not?"

"They're afraid if I win any more championships, I'll never find a husband." Millie kept her gold-leaf eyes fixed on her ball, analyzing which iron would chip it within a foot of the hole. "Which is silly. I'm going to end up a spinster even if I start letting the boys win. Okay, Scottie. Your turn."

Scott chucked the driver back in my father's bag. "You don't have to let me win. In fact, I loathe golf and I'd rather not play. Ginevra and I will just watch and admire."

"All right," said Millie, not even bothering to protest. She hated playing with duffers who took five strokes for every one of hers, chatted, and lost track of their scores. "Now let's see how I do today with the Dismal Swamp." Millie made up fond nicknames for every golf hole, as if it were a lover. She called Daddy's three holes the Dismal Swamp, the Devil's Ditch, and the Isle of Woe.

Millie marched ahead toward her ball, her golf bag slung across her back as if it weighed no more than a handbag. Scott lurked along the edge of the mid-fairway, watching her with a peculiar attention as she lined up and executed a neat chip shot with an eight iron, which sent the ball bouncing within a foot of the cup.

"What's so fascinating?" I whispered, almost miffed that he had turned his fawning toward Millie.

"I guess I've never met a girl before who was a serious athlete. Look at the way she holds her shoulders back and moves her feet without looking down. It's like she first learned to walk on a golf course. Do you think she'll never get married? She's got a pretty face."

I considered Millie's features under the narrow brim of her

golfer's cap—the arched brows, the delicate nose, the tidy row of small bright teeth. They might have been pretty on another girl who knew how to make a sideways glance or a long, slow smile. A girl who used lipstick and cold cream, who didn't let herself get burned into leather like a squaw. "Millie's only interest in boys is beating them on the golf course. She can't be bothered to flatter or flirt, so boys don't think of her as entirely female." The remark came out cattier than I meant it to.

"She seems like an odd friend for you."

"Opposites attract, I guess." In truth, we were friends by default; the other Lake Forest girls seemed to find both of us untrustworthy. "So you're falling in love?"

"No." He sounded distracted. "I'm just interested in unusual types. For my writing," he added.

His eyes stayed fixed on Millie as she knelt down on all fours, laid her cheek on the green to line up her putt, then sank the ball. She shouldered her bag and headed toward the next hole, tossing and catching the ball with one hand as she walked, like a pitcher on his way to the mound.

"You should put her in your book about me," I said.

He lifted his gaze and gave a polite smile. "There's a thought."

7

Pockmarked Moon

On the third day of Scott's visit, the temperature had cracked 100 by noon, so Mother decided on a light supper of cold salmon on the terrace. Meals on the terrace were always a production—Mr. Jensen spent an hour unrolling the green-and-white awning and tethering it with ropes around the sandstone urns, dragging a cast-iron table and six chairs under the skimpy shade, and lighting off four smudge pots to ward off the swarm of mosquitoes that headed off the ditch at sunset. Then Mrs. Coates set the table with the special outdoor china and linens—chair cushions and a tablecloth that matched the striped awning, and emerald glass plates and goblets. All afternoon, the smudge pots smoldered under the awning and the furniture baked under the steady beat of western sun, so that by seven o'clock, we felt as if we had sat down on the racks of an oven. Scott appeared to have on the same suit and shirt he'd arrived in, now with a thin rim of gray at the neck and damp under the arms. Mother shielded her eyes from the fireball sunset blasting under the awning, and watched Daddy flake his salmon apart suspiciously as if he expected maggots. Outdoor suppers were never a success.

She turned her distracted attention to the houseguest. "What do you think of our Lake Forest, Mr. Fitzgerald?"

Scott set down his fork, which held a half-eaten asparagus spear, and took a pensive swig of his third gin. He swept a critical eye at the fake stucco walls and the pilfered marble statuary, at the stunted cypress arbor and the prairie grass creeping into the bluegrass lawn despite Mr. Jensen's daily squirts from a metal drum of weed killer. Large beads of sweat had formed along his fine brow; in a moment they would start to stream, but he was too well mannered to mop them up with his napkin. "You always hear Lake Forest spoken about in hushed tones, even in St. Paul. The Mount Olympus of the Middle West." His voice was slow and gravelly—the gin had made him wax profound. "It just seems like it's trying too hard."

"Trying too hard to do what?" Daddy asked.

"To forget that forty years ago its grandfathers were stuffing sausages. And selling fireproof vaults." He was too stewed to realize he was being rude.

Daddy gave a short, tight grin, pretending to be amused.

"That's what Grandpa says," Evvie chimed in. For the last two days, she'd joined us for dinner instead of eating at the kitchen table with Mrs. Coates and Julian. She'd even brushed the burrs out of her hair and washed the soot off her elbows.

"Does he? Good girl, Evvie," Scott said. Evvie fiddled with her hair bow.

"So, Ginevra. I hope you're showing our guest a good time," Mother said in a bright, let's-move-on voice.

"She's doing an excellent job," Scott offered. "I watched her buy a toothbrush and some stockings. And then we both watched Millie Jordan play golf."

Mother shook her head sadly. "That girl gallivanting around the country with a golf bag. I feel so sorry for her parents."

"Oh, come on, Mother. You make it sound like she's run off with the circus. If Millie were a boy and the captain of the Yale golf team, you'd say how lucky the Jordans are."

Mother's plump shoulders shrugged under starched linen. "But she's not a boy, is she?"

"Scott's been making notes about us," Evvie said importantly. "To use in his writing."

Daddy placed his knife and fork at four o'clock over his uneaten salmon. "You mean one of those plays where the men dress up like women?"

"Oh, no, sir. A real book. I plan to become a writer when I'm done with college."

"I don't think Mrs. Perry would be happy if Ginevra's toiletries appeared in a book," Daddy said in a final way, as if that was that. He blotted the corners of his mouth with his napkin and then set it on the table. "So, Mr. Fitzgerald. You must be heading back to college soon."

"Not until Sunday, so Ginevra and I have got three final days with each other." He reached unsteadily across the table between the salad plates and water goblets and squeezed my elbow. "Maybe you and Ginevra would like to come to the Yale–Princeton game, sir. You could stay as my guest at the Cottage Club," he added grandly.

"I'm sure you'll be very busy with your classes," Daddy said with his jaw set to one side, as if he were testing a cracked filling.

"Oh, not very." Scott leaned back, drained his cocktail, then shook the glass so the one remaining cube clacked like a maraca.

Later that night I lay sprawled across my bed, scribbling a few lines in my pocket diary.

> Scott Fitzgerald, Marie Hart's friend, has been visiting
> for a few days. For some reason, he doesn't seem as at-
> tractive as he did when we went to see *Nobody Home* in

June. Marie would say it is because I am a snob, but now I find him immature.

Played golf with Millie. The McCormicks' party is in two days and I'm wild with excitement.

It has been hot as blazes all week. Mother says it needs to rain soon or the new grape arbor won't last the winter.

There was a soft knock on my bedroom door. "We need to talk," a voice whispered, and Daddy opened the door a crack and slipped inside.

The last time Daddy had stepped into my bedroom was when I'd had my tonsils out at age eleven and he'd been sent up to comfort me with a bowl of orange jelly. But after I'd reached what Mother mysteriously called "the tender age," Daddy usually summoned me to his office when he wanted a tête-à-tête.

He stood at the end of my bed and pivoted slowly, taking it all in—the pink-sprigged bedspread wadded in a ball on the floor, studio portraits of boys in prep ties jammed into the edge of the mirror frame, a jumble of hairpins and cold cream pots on the dressing table, invitations and magazines piled on the desk. Four days' worth of stockings and satin slips were tossed in the lap of a pink wingback chair. He puffed out his cheeks in a disapproving way, as if he were about to launch into a lecture on the virtue of tidiness, then seemed to think better of it. Dragging the dressing table bench over to the head of the bed, he sat down. I propped myself up on the bed, readjusted my bathrobe lapels so they closed more discreetly, and tucked my diary back inside the night table drawer.

"Ginevra," he said, leaning toward me, his hands gripped as if in prayer. "I think it's time for you to consider your conduct."

"What's wrong with my conduct?"

"This friend of yours. Scott. He seems to think you two have some sort of. . . . understanding."

"Why do you say that?"

"Evvie tells me he wrote you almost every day this summer."

"Just because he writes me doesn't mean I write him back."

"Now he seems to think you'll be his guest at football games and proms, and that he has claim to your exclusive attention."

"I was friendly and polite to him, just the way you and Mother have taught me. It's not my fault if he takes things the wrong way and starts to imagine things." I inhaled the fatherly scent of cigarettes and cognac.

His shoulders softened. "Not your fault. But you have to be firm with these boys." "Boys" was meant to include Aldus Hutchinson, who last I heard was still too distressed to return to Harvard and had been ordered by a psychiatrist to spend another year at his uncle's ranch on the outskirts of Glacier Park.

Daddy cleared his throat and pried his collar loose from his damp neck. "Dear, you are seventeen."

"In three and a half months."

"This is a critical time in your life. You must be selective, and judge whether a young man is worthy of you. Does he know how to conduct himself in the world, does he occupy himself with worthy enterprises? These are the questions you must ask yourself. And by the same token, any decent young man will judge whether or not you are worthy of him. And if he sees that you are spending your time with unformed boys who brag about writing books and drink too many gins, he will think less of you. The first time I saw your mother, I knew before we'd even spoken that this was a woman who was fit to be the mother of my children." The memory of his first glimpse of Ida Avery at the Field Museum

Esquimaux Exhibition made him raise his eyes to the open window and gaze out into the steamy darkness.

My mother, Ida Avery, was the only child of a retired lawyer and his sickly wife. She had spent her first nineteen years cloistered inside their cottage on the old end of Prairie Avenue, being tutored by her father on Emerson and fetching beef tea for her mother. Since her parents thought it was unseemly to comment on one's personal appearance, no one had ever told my mother that her masses of auburn hair, cornflower-blue eyes, and twenty-inch waist made her a beauty. She would have died a spinster if her mother hadn't decided, in the single adventurous act of her life, to visit the new Field Museum one Sunday afternoon.

Pushing her mother around in a wheeled wicker chair that they rented at the door, Ida headed toward the North American Indian Hall. She steered her mother through a looming forest of totem poles toward a crowd gathered in front of a life-size model of an Esquimaux camp. A mannequin stood in front of a papier-mâché igloo mounted on a wooden platform painted white to look like an ice floe. He was dressed in a sealskin anorak and bent over an iron kettle while a stuffed Husky dog sat by a gut sled. Suddenly the mannequin started to move, began to chop at something with a stone hatchet. Ida blinked in the dim light and realized that it was no dummy at all, but a real live human.

"The word 'Esquimaux' comes from the Algonquin and means eater of raw meat," said a uniformed guard, who appeared to be acting as tour guide. A chorus of disgusted murmurs rose from the audience. "Chu here is a genuine Esquimaux our scientists brought back from their expedition last summer to Cook Inlet. He is approximately seventeen years of age. Since the Esquimaux keep no birth records, scientists must base an estimate of his age on the condition of his teeth." Chu stepped forward, pushed back his hood to show off the shape of his Mongoloid skull, opened his mouth wide so everyone could appreciate the blackened stumps.

"Chu is making his midday meal, which consists of whale blubber and seal heart." He put a gelatinous yellow chunk in his mouth and chewed with gusto.

"Food like that will give you worms. Poor savage doesn't know better," Ida's mother pronounced to the crowd. As a professional invalid, she took a clinical interest in gore.

Suddenly bile rose up in Ida's throat. She took a dizzy step backward, and then she was falling, falling. The next thing Ida remembered was lying flat on the hard floor, enjoying the cool of the marble against her neck. Where's my hat, she wondered. She heard her mother's dim cry in the background. "Sit up, Ida. Sit up. Don't make a spectacle of yourself."

Then she heard a strange male voice. "Rest now, Miss Avery. You've had a shock." A dark young man with earnest eyes and noble features was bending over her—she had admired this face many times before.

When she felt strong enough to stand, the man insisted that she slip an arm around his muscular middle while he lead her to his carriage. His name was Charles Perry, he explained, and—what a coincidence—he lived right across Prairie Avenue from the Avery house. Ida didn't have to ask which house was his. In the gloomy, still hours when she was not reading Thackeray or massaging her mother's feet, she would perch on the horsehair settee in the front parlor and observe the comings and goings at the Perry mansion across the way. She'd watched it go up seven years ago—a four-story brownstone affair with a slate mansard and fussy filigree balconies over each of the long front windows, filled with newfangled devices like central heating and electric servant buzzers. Ida was especially taken by the Perrys' dashing son, who galloped down the front stoop two steps at a time as if he had a football tucked under his arm. He was usually with a rowdy group of college boys or an ingénue resplendent in watered silk and egret. Ida was so resigned to her snipped-off life she didn't even feel envy—the Perry house was as strange and distant as the Eiffel Tower in a snow globe.

Charles Perry called the next day with a handful of wilted lilies he had snatched from a vase and spearmint lozenges that the Perrys' Bavarian cook had boiled up from a secret recipe.

"I looked into those guiltless doll eyes and found myself confiding things I'd never told another soul. That at Yale, I'd spent too much time with men of weak character and overimbibed. That I'd once allowed myself to become engaged to a silly society girl just because every other boy was in love with her. That it was time I became serious about a profession and that I planned to apprentice myself at the State Street Bank. Your mother was such a lamb that she didn't even realize she was being courted until I pulled a velvet box out of my pocket a month later."

Daddy's voice grew husky as he reached the moral of his lecture. "You see my point, Ginevra?"

The shepherdess bedside lamp bathed his face in a tender glow— the sharp nose, lopsided from an ancient football injury, the firm chin with a slight dent in the middle as if left by the sculptor's thumb, had grown more handsome under the sag and blur of middle age. Twenty years later, he still acted as if Ida Avery was a catch. He didn't seem to notice that her waist had doubled after two babies, the auburn hair had faded to plain brown, that she was just an ordinary middle-aged woman.

I lunged forward and wrapped my arms around his bristly neck. "I want to find a man just like you." But someone like the young

Charles Perry—on the cusp of manhood, suddenly turned serious and full of purpose, assessing every girl he met with newly critical eyes—would not choose me. He would see Scott Fitzgerald orbiting around me like a pockmarked moon and pass me by.

8

Luau

Scott did not take Daddy's hint and decide to head back to Princeton before Constance McCormick's engagement party. Two days later he was sitting across from me at the breakfast table as I read the *Tribune*'s rapturous description: ". . . this evening's event promises to be the brightest star in the glittering constellation of the Lake Forest summer season."

Constance McCormick was the kind of no-nonsense girl with erect posture and a robust stride whom my mother called "handsome." Ever since her debut three summers ago, she'd thrown herself into worthy causes like collecting discarded books from Astor Street mansions for the Hull House library, and seemed on her way to becoming a spinster who chaperoned dances and wore glasses on a chain around her neck. Then last Christmas, Horace Armour swung back into town after spending a year in Hawaii doing something vaguely exotic like building a pineapple-canning factory. Even though he could have had any fluttery girl he wanted, he chose Constance.

According to the *Tribune,* Old Joe McCormick, the steel

tycoon, was pulling out every stop to celebrate foisting off his un-marriageable daughter.

> To honor the South Seas proclivities of his future son-in-law, Mr. McCormick is hosting an authentic "luau," which means feast in Hawaiian. The menu will feature suckling pig roasted over a bonfire and pineapples shipped by steamer directly from the Dole plantation in Maui. Hawaiian musicians will serenade the happy couple with authentic South Seas love songs. The engagement of his oldest daughter provides Mr. McCormick with an opportunity to show off "Xanadu," the fantastic Moorish castle with tiled roofs and minarets he has just completed on a bluff overlooking the lake. The dress theme for the party is "Hawaiian."

I tucked the society section under my napkin, watched as Scott picked up his coffee cup with a shaky hand, steadied his elbow against the table, lowered his mouth, and took a loud slurp. An unforgiving slant of morning light made his face look puffy and gray-tinged, and decades older than nineteen. The pale yellow of his hair seemed unnatural, as if it had been painted on with a brush.

"I have to go to some dreary engagement thing for Millie's cousin." I left the names vague—Scott's ears would prick up at the mention of McCormick and Armour. "I *tried* to get out of it—everyone will be over thirty. Even Millie's made an excuse not to go. Says she has to play in a golf tournament in Lake Geneva. But Mother insists that I at least put in an appearance." I rolled my eyes. "The good news is that you don't have to come. You can have dinner with Evvie while I'm being bored to death."

"I won't desert you. I'm good with grandmothers," Scott said, spreading a layer of marmalade on a piece of toast and taking a cautious bite as if his teeth hurt.

"It's sort of a costume party, I think. You didn't bring anything Hawaiian, did you?"

"I love dressing up." He grinned. "Too bad I didn't know about this a couple of months ago. The costume closet at the Triangle has a whole tribe of Hawaiian costumes. I probably could have gotten someone to send me a couple," he said vaguely.

"Oh, well. We'll just have to find something in Evvie's dress-up box," I said.

By which I meant he would have to rummage around in Evvie's dress-up box. I'd already had my costume made up by Mrs. Turner. Neither of us had any idea what a Hawaiian dress looked like exactly, so I picked out the most tropical-looking sample in Mrs. Turner's swatch book—an upholstery fabric covered with big red day lilies. Then I sketched up a dress that I thought looked "native" —a swoop of fabric draped over one shoulder, tied tight around the middle with a wide red sash. The design didn't allow for many undergarments, so Mrs. Turner had sewn on a few carefully concealed hooks to close any peekaboo gaps. Midafternoon, I headed back to my bedroom. "I've got to wash my hair," I told Scott.

I rinsed my hair with two egg yolks to bring out the shine and brushed it dry so it would hang straight. With my back to the mirror, I slipped the dress on. I adjusted the folds over one shoulder and pulled my hair around to one side so it cascaded over the bare shoulder. I tied an extra piece of flowered cloth around my forehead like an Indian, slipped on a pair of Chinese silk slippers Aunt Minnie had brought me from her trip around the world, and fastened on Grammy Perry's old coral necklace and earrings. I spun around, my heart sputtering at the sight of an exotic stranger staring back in the mirror. My face had a feverish glow, as if I had been basking in a tropical sun; the day lilies bloomed across breast and hip. I looked as much like a Hawaiian princess as a girl from Lake Forest could.

I ran a finger along my bare shoulder and down my arm. This is what it would be like to be touched by a lover—rough, urgent hands running across my white body, my naked skin against his. A "lover"—I'd never used that word before, even in my private thoughts. My most daring words were "kissing" and "petting." Then there were other words I knew somehow but hadn't ever heard anyone say—intercourse, copulation . . . Marie and I had giggled over an ad in a cheap ladies' magazine for tooth powder—"She's Got Sex Appeal!"

I thought of the book of postcards I'd found hidden in the back of Daddy's desk drawer under a stack of check stubs. "Scene Erotiche dell'antica Pompeii" stamped across the front in broken gold letters. Frescoes of men doing unspeakable things to women, exactly what was hard to say, since the plaster was flaky in all the crucial places. Forcing the women to sit on top of them, or bend down on all fours with their rear end poked up in the air. The first time I'd found the postcards I jammed them back, slammed the drawer shut, ran to the powder room, and washed my hands twice with sandalwood soap. Two days later I snuck the postcards into my skirt pocket, locked my bedroom door, and took a good long look. These weren't husbands and wives, I decided. They must be gladiators and slave girls, captured from Bible places like Gilead or Nob.

I didn't want to think how Daddy had ended up with such vile things. Mother and Daddy had visited Naples three springs ago, and the hotel had arranged a tour of an ancient city being dug out from under fifteen feet of ash. "It sounded quite interesting," Mother said, with an if-I'd-only-known shrug. Under a broiling

Mediterranean sun, they climbed down rickety ladders into dusty pits just to see some bit of mosaic or a decapitated statue. Maybe the guide handed the postcards to Daddy when Mother was climbing up from one of those pits, and he was too polite to refuse. He stuck them in his vest pocket and then into the back of a drawer when he got home, too embarrassed to throw them in the trash for the maid to find.

I leaned my bare shoulder against the sunwashed wall and thought about my talk with Daddy. Friends of Horace's would be at the party tonight. Older men who were finished with school and were making their way in the world. Maybe one of them would find me worthy and I would make Daddy proud.

I heard Evvie's screechy laugh from somewhere down the hall. Then Scott's voice, not the exact words, just the rise and fall of it, followed by more giggles. I imagined them kneeling in front of Grandpa Perry's steamer trunk, which Evvie used as a dress-up box, covered with yellowed canvas and peeling stickers from the *Oceanic* and the *Athens*. Scott would slip on a pair of withered spats, and a rust-stained hoop skirt, leap up on a chair, and launch into a falsetto chorus from *Fie! Fie! Fi-Fi!*

Tired to death in Paris, London makes us glum . . .
Now to Monte Carlo we have come.

At six, I heard Daddy crunch up the driveway, the clink and clatter as he set up the cocktail tray on the terrace. I padded down the stairs in the Chinese slippers, crept outside where Daddy lounged on a chaise, his face buried in the evening paper. When he finally glanced up, I started to dance my own version of a hula—my bare arms undulating like waves, my hips swaying. He stared, mute, his neck and cheeks reddening as if he'd suddenly gotten a sunburn.

For some reason, seeing Daddy lying on his back with a startled expression made me think of the Pompeii frescoes all over again.

"Where do you think you're going in that getup?" My mother's voice behind me, the clip-clop of her heels against the flagstones as she trotted toward us with an ice bucket on a tray. I halted my dance midwave and my father jumped to his feet, as if we'd been caught doing something naughty.

"To Constance McCormick's costume party. Remember I told you that Mrs. Turner was making me a dress?" In truth, I hadn't told her it was a costume party, much less that I'd ordered a custom outfit, because she might have tossed cold water on the plan.

"You're hanging out everywhere," she observed. With brusque hands, she recrossed the dress folds so they cinched tightly over my chest, then tied the sash with a double knot.

"Yoo-hoo. I'm ready too," Scott announced, parading out the French doors with a fringed shawl tied around his waist and a geranium tucked behind one ear. He held a croquet mallet aloft as if it were a scepter, and Evvie trailed behind like a royal attendant, wearing a turban fashioned out of a salmon-pink guest towel. Scott made a slow pirouette in front of my parents.

Mother's scowl faded, and she looked at Scott almost fondly. "Oh, I see now. It's just a silly costume party. You had me worried for a minute, Ginevra. I thought you were trying to look like some kind of . . . what's the nice word for it? Temptress."

The McCormicks' house, with its limestone columns and carved stone lions, had somehow been transformed into something shadowed and pungent. The long driveway was lit by flickering torches sunk into the ground. Two colored men in grass skirts beat sticks against a hollowed-out log. A pit had been dug in the front lawn and filled with smoldering pigs. Before Scott and I hit the front door, I yanked him into the hollow of a privet. "You can leave your costume here," I whispered. "You don't want people to think you're an ass."

"Oh, I don't care," he started, but then caught my warning tone— that I would never forgive him if he made *me* look like an ass. He tossed the flower and the croquet mallet under the thicket. "But I'm keeping this," he said, patting the scarf around his middle. "The fringe will quiver when I tango."

I sprinted a few steps ahead so I could make my entrance solo, the sarong clinging to my ankles, my hair billowing. Constance Mc-Cormick was the first in the receiving line, in her usual pale blue lace and pearls; the only concession to the tropical theme was a red carnation perched uneasily behind one ear. Her mouth jerked to one side, just like when she'd been the chaperone at the Winter Club Snowflake Dance three years ago and had caught me with Deering under a pile of overcoats in the boys' cloakroom. She turned to Horace Armour by her side, an overly blond fellow with a sunburned scalp and blunt, cheerful features. "This is the Perry girl," she said, as if I were out of earshot. "One of Millie Jordan's little friends."

I grabbed his hand with both of mine and held it tight. "Constance was sweet to invite me, even if I'll be a wallflower."

"Why would you be a wallflower?" he asked, his distracted gaze aimed over my shoulder at the new guests piling up in the receiving line, including Scott, who already had a tall drink in his hand.

"Look at me," I said, coaxing his pale, incurious eyes to lower. "I'm the only one in costume." I waved my bare arm toward a gaggle of girls streaming out of the powder room in the usual glove-length sleeves and ruffled necklines. "I've made a spectacle of myself."

"A lovely spectacle," Horace murmured. He wasn't the type of boy who made racy remarks to girls, and he looked a little sheepish at his daring. "Your hair all loose like that reminds me of the native girls who used to clean fish along the beach in Maui. Don't you agree, Constance?"

"I wouldn't know, dear," she said, her eyebrows pinching together as if she was remembering the reasons why she'd always disliked me.

"Billy Granger's here someplace. He just got back from learning to fly biplanes with the French army. Let me introduce you." He grasped my bare elbow and started to steer me toward a somber man with military posture lurking in a back corner of the hallway next to Mr. McCormick's hunting trophies. Before Horace could take a step, Constance's tiny, freckled hand landed on his shoulder, clenched like a talon.

"You remember Mrs. Schweppe?" she asked, reeling him back to her side and shouldering me out in the process.

Well, I could introduce myself to the aviator, I decided. Scott, thankfully, seemed too busy to tag along—he stood at the end of the receiving line with his ear tilted toward a humped dowager, who poked a gnarled finger at his sash. Billy Granger was the son of Daddy's golf partner. He was famous for building gadgets with junked automobile parts and was one of the few society boys smart enough not to flunk out of Sheff. But the title "aviator" now gave him a shimmer of romantic doom.

Photographs of pilots appeared almost daily on the front page of the *Tribune*—in belted leather trench coats and woolen puttees; the only part of the face visible underneath goggles and helmet was a reckless smile. "Captain James Lawrence, age 19, was killed five minutes after takeoff from Granger Field in Gurnee when his Curtiss airplane stalled and crashed into a nearby cornfield," the gruesome caption read. "Wings and tail were snapped off on impact."

I snuck up behind the soaring form of Billy Granger. His bulky shoulders strained the seams of his dinner jacket, which he must have borrowed from Horace. On his feet, scuffed brown oxfords—

Horace's patent leather pumps were probably three sizes too small. He was standing with his face to the wall, making a thorough inspection of Mr. McCormick's stuffed heads, which hung one on top of the other for twenty feet to the top of the vaulted ceiling. He stared up at the snarling mouth of a stuffed boar's head and then snarled back. I burst out laughing.

He whirled around so fast a cowlick of straight black hair flopped down over his eyes. "Oh, sorry," he stammered, slashes of red rising up along his cheeks. "I didn't know anyone was watching."

"Do you speak boar?"

"Not usually, I mean, no," he remarked toward his oxfords. "I don't know anyone here, so I'm trying to keep myself busy. I'm not very good at parties, I guess," he observed sadly.

"I'll talk to you. I don't know anyone either," I said. Billy Granger was desperately handsome, the way an aviator should be. His eyes were a pale gray, like the horizon at dawn. The bones of his face were sharp and angular, as if they'd been dashed off in lines of India ink.

He frowned at my sarong. "Are you passing out hors d'oeuvres or something?"

"I'm a guest." I flipped my hair over one shoulder and smoothed the lily over my hipbone, feeling oddly pleased that I could pass for a servant. "It's supposed to be a costume party."

"I hadn't noticed."

"I've seen you before. I was about seven and you were thirteen. Your father was playing golf with my father at the Onwentsia, and you were their caddy." I remembered a grumpy boy with a pimply chin and crooked argyle socks.

"Dad didn't want to pay fifty cents for a caddy so he made me do it for free." He still sounded bitter. "Finally I made the excuse that the fresh-cut grass kicked up my hay fever and quit."

"Horace said you've been training to be an aviator in France." My voice grew hushed at "aviator" and "France"—could there be any two more glamorous words in the English language? I backed toward a pair of uncomfortable-looking gilt chairs, plopped down on one, and patted the seat of the other. "Sit down. I want to hear everything."

"You do?" Billy Granger cracked a smile for the first time, showing off a lot of big square teeth like Teddy Roosevelt's. "I was more of a mechanic than a pilot, really. So many frog pilots have been shot down they're short-handed on the airstrips. So I got a chance to work on planes, even though my French is rotten and half the time I didn't understand what they were telling me to do. *Merde* this, *merde* that, *vite, vite, vite*." He gave a Gallic shrug and turned his palms upward; they were rimmed with yellow calluses. "But I got pretty good at adjusting the timing so the engines wouldn't stall. After a while, even an ace like Nungesser wanted me to tune up his Nieuport before he took off, because none of mine ever crashed. I became sort of a good luck charm, like a rabbit's foot." As he talked, he stared toward the middle distance, as if he were still searching the sky for the silvery wink of wing struts to come lurching through a puff of cloud. His features were a fetching mixture of boy and man, I decided. His eyebrows peaked with wonder, as if he'd just wired together an electric doorbell; his delicate upper lip sprouted a respectably bristly mustache.

He pulled a brown Turkish cigarette from his jacket pocket. "Mind if I smoke one of these? One of the filthy habits I picked up from Nungesser."

"Go ahead. I wish I could smoke too," I said, taking a loud sniff. It smelled nasty, like singed rubber.

"Frenchwomen smoke. I found it shocking at first, but I got used to it." I had a racy image of Billy huddling with a woman in the dim corner of a café over tiny glasses of some poisonous green liqueur. Her skinny calf dangling below a short hemline, her hair hennaed bright orange, her bottom teeth stained with tobacco and lipstick.

"Do you fly planes too?" I asked hopefully. A mechanic, even if it was for French fighters, didn't have nearly as much appeal.

"A little." His tone was sheepish, as if I'd discovered a shameful secret. "Nungesser gave me a few flying lessons. I can take off, do a halfway decent landing. I'm going to get some official pilot training this fall in Dayton. So if Wilson ever quits being a sissy and sends our troops to France, I can be one of the first pilots in the American air service." His fingers clenched, as if he were tugging on a control stick.

The patter of the party—the men's laughs, the clanking of silver platters, the strum of a lone mandolin somewhere out on the terrace—faded. Here was the hero I'd been searching for—unfazed by the distant rumble of war, the sputter and swoon of airplanes.

"But wouldn't you be scared?" I reached over and squeezed his upper arm, which bulged like a weightlifter's. "My father says that being an aviator is very dangerous." That was one of the few facts I remembered from Daddy's recitation of the war news over breakfast every morning. Usually "mustard gas" and "Triple Alliance" and "Big Bertha" got garbled together into a background hum. But now that a real live person like Billy Granger could go to war, I would pay more attention. I hoped the American pilot's uniform wouldn't be that army brown—the color of dog droppings. A midnight blue with a wide belt would be smart, with a leather trench coat tossed across the shoulders like a cape.

"It's risky, I guess. But then I tell myself to remember what we're fighting for. The Huns are streaming over Europe, and U-boats will be in New York harbor if we don't stop them. I'm fighting to protect my mother and my sisters and maybe, someday . . ." he paused, took a thoughtful puff of his stumpy cigarette ". . . a wife."

Suddenly a shadow fell across us. "There you are, Ginevra. I've been searching everywhere." I glanced up at Scott, bobbing and swaying over us like a giant Pinocchio puppet, his arm outstretched, his nose pointed and red. The shawl around his waist had sagged, the fresh drink in his hand sloshed from side to side.

Billy started to rise to his feet. "I'm Bill Granger."

"Don't get up. I need to take a load off my feet." Scott sank into the gilt chair next to Billy, his legs splayed out as if he were about to take a siesta. "I'm Scott Fitzgerald, an old friend of Ginevra's. I met her last Christmas in St. Paul on a bobsled ride. It was twenty below, and we were under a buffalo robe." Scott gave Billy a lascivious wink. "You look like an old friend, too."

"We've just met," I said coolly. "Bill is a friend of Horace Armour's. He's been flying airplanes with the French army, and he's going to be a pilot in the American army as soon as we join the war." Not just a silly college boy, my tone implied, who "writes," plays dress-up, and is flunking geometry.

"Girls love to talk about the war, don't they," Scott said, giving Billy's upper arm a nudge. "I read an article in the *New York Herald* last week that said a pilot on the front lasts an average of three days before . . ." He whistled like a howling wind and nose-dived his hand toward the floor.

Billy slowly stood, glancing in the direction of the receiving line, which seemed to have broken up. Couples were drifting arm in arm toward the dance floor on the terrace. "I can't stay," he added vaguely. "I've got to be at the airstrip at the crack of dawn."

"Sorry you have to rush off," said Scott, sinking back farther, so his highball glass rested on his stomach.

"Well, goodbye, Miss, ah . . . Ginerva. Nice talking to you." Billy gave me a brisk bow, then swung around to Scott. "You too." He beelined toward the front door as if there were a Sopwith Pup on his tail, his pants riding up like knickers.

"Snappy shoes," Scott snickered.

"Shhh. He'll hear you," I hissed, but Billy didn't give us a backward look.

"Why would you care? He was a bore. I was afraid you'd be stuck with him all night."

I glowered toward the floor.

"Oh come on, Gin-er-va! Please tell me you're not taken in by all that we-must-save-the-women-and-children-from-the-bloody-Hun stuff. The biggest dullards at Princeton are the ones who are suddenly all keen on signing up, just because it gives them something to talk about besides bond prices and football passes. They know that anyone looks fascinating in a uniform."

"Daddy says pilots are brave."

"Just because someone can get himself killed in three days doesn't mean he's brave. It means he's too stupid or unimaginative to know better."

I searched the crowd for Billy Granger's black coxcomb hair and earnest brow, but they were gone without a trace. "I enjoyed talking to him. He cares about things," I pronounced simply.

"A dance will cheer you up," Scott said, rising to his feet, still with no clue that I was seriously annoyed.

The mandolin out on the terrace had been joined by a piano and the thumping of a tom-tom in some Polynesian version of the turkey trot. Well, it wouldn't hurt to take a spin around the dance floor. Maybe Billy Granger was lurking at the end of the stag line and I could apologize. Sorry about that boy, I'd say. He thinks he's being funny.

With my hand held aloft, Scott paraded me to the middle of the dance floor, dropped his arm around my waist, and sidestepped gracefully into a turkey trot. Well, at least he was a decent dancer. In the wax-smooth Chinese slippers, I could only stand on tiptoe and be spun around like a doll. After three swoops and whirls, a broad hand thumped down on Scott's shoulder and my heart skittered for an instant—maybe Billy Granger had come back. But then I found myself pirouetted into the lumbering, bearlike embrace of John Pullman.

Tender eyes, round like acorns, stared down at me through rimless glasses. "I was hoping you'd be here," he said with a happy sigh, his breath smelling like a cherry cough drop. John Pullman was a brainy boy who'd had a crush on me in third grade and let me copy his answers on a long-division test. Since then, he'd sprouted up like Ichabod Crane, his straight blond hair already receding off his forehead.

"Oh, hello there." I gave a distracted smile toward his chin. "How's your summer been?"

"Pretty bad, actually. I'd hoped to go on a walking tour of Greece, but Father had me tightening bolts on the assembly line."

"I'm sorry," I said. Mr. Pullman had poor John's career all figured out—he'd work his way up from the factory and be a vice president of Pullman Car by thirty. John wasn't allowed to do anything impractical—such as majoring in classics.

"That's some dress," he whispered, tightening his grip and snagging my hair on his cuff link in the process. "Pretty daring for old Lake Forest."

"You're sweet," I said, pushing him back a couple of inches—I remembered Daddy's warning not to be too nice to romantic boys. I peeked past John's shoulder for a glimpse of Billy Granger, but no luck. "Could you dance me over to Horace Armour? I need to ask him a question."

"Oh, sure," said John, resigned that his time was up. He shuffled me backward to the center of the dance floor, where the happy couple were doing a workmanlike tango.

"Hello again," I said to Horace as John stumbled off with Constance. Horace studied a scuff on the parquet floor and jangled the change in his pocket—Constance must have scolded him for flirting with me. "I enjoyed talking to your friend Billy Granger. Did he leave already?"

"I think he had to be somewhere in the morning."

"Maybe I'll drop him a note," I said humbly. "Would you know his address?"

"Gosh, sorry. I don't. I better get back to Constance." With that, he strode over to John Pullman and cut in with a proprietary tap.

Before I could feel deserted, an arm slipped around my waist and bent me over in a tango dip. "Care for a dance?" Scott said, sounding drunker than ever.

"I'm tired. Let's go home." I turned and trudged toward the door, my hair by now hanging in a tangled clump, my sarong bunched over to one side. I kept my eyes fixed ahead, but heard the waves churning in my wake.

"There's the little Perry girl. She has such a pretty face," an old woman said.

A younger female voice answered back. "She was the one . . ."

"Oh, yes. I remember now." The old woman's voice was less kind now.

Scott trotted unsteadily behind me. "Wait up. Not so fast," he called. "They're just bringing out the pigs."

9

Poor Boys

We stepped under the porte-cochère, and Scott propped himself up against an ivy-covered trellis. All that was left of the Hawaiian paradise were smoldering torches, wilted orchids, and the smell of charred pork. When the valet pulled up with the electric, I sprinted past Scott and climbed into the driver's seat. "You're not in any shape to drive," I said loud enough for the colored men to hear. As I inched the car homeward, staring out into the feeble two-foot beam cast by the tiny headlamps, I had an image of Billy Granger's ramrod-straight back striding out of my life forever.

I heard Daddy's voice scolding me: You have only yourself to blame. You let Aldus Hutchinson, that poor boy, buy you a ring and ruin his life. Vanity, vanity. Then you did the same thing to Scott. Allowed him to think love letters and kisses in bobsleds meant something. Yes, you told yourself you loved him back, but be honest. You were in love with his attentions, not with the boy himself.

I snuck a sideways glance at Scott, who was dozing against the passenger door, mouth open, with a string of spittle dribbling from one corner. I nosed the car up the dark driveway and ratcheted the hand brake up. "Scott." I reached over and jiggled his limp arm. "Wake up."

He jerked upright with a snort, stretched, smiled sleepily. "Back already? Looks like everyone's gone off to sleep. Let's have a nightcap on the terrace."

"You need to leave tomorrow."

His expression slowly grew alert as he took in that I was serious. "I can't leave until Sunday. I thought I'd told you. My room at Little Hall won't be ready until then."

"You need to leave tomorrow," I repeated.

"You're not still sore about Billy Granger, for crying out loud. Trust me, I did you a favor by chasing him off."

"It's not just tonight."

"Oh, really? What else have I done?" Suddenly his voice was as hushed and sober as a Sunday school teacher's.

I exhaled so hard I fogged the windshield. "You haven't done anything. This is all my fault. I meet boys and get carried away. I liked you a lot when I met you in St. Paul, and I loved all your letters, because you really are clever with words. And our evening together at *Nobody Home* was like a fairy tale. But now Daddy says I've misled you into thinking we have an understanding."

Scott's long upper lip flinched as if someone had raised a fist to him. "I should have known that your father would disapprove of me. He probably said that poor boys shouldn't think of marrying rich girls."

"Who said anything about getting married? And besides, Daddy's not a snob. Mrs. Coates and Mr. Jensen adore him." I tried not to think about Marie's long-ago warning: Scott's different than you, Ginevra. "Daddy thinks I need to be more serious. And you need to be more serious too. You need to pass your courses and think about your future. You shouldn't waste your time mooning over me."

Scott stared straight ahead. Backlit in the porch light, his pro-file looked distinguished and stirring, as it had in the back seat of the bobsled. "No one will ever love you as much as I do. You know that, don't you?" His voice was calm—it was a statement of fact, not a plea.

"You should get some sleep," I said, resisting an impulse to reach out and pat the top of his head. "You need to catch the nine o'clock local if you're going to make the noon express to New York." With that I stepped out of the car and trotted across the driveway, peb-bles slipping into the sides of my Chinese slippers.

I woke up to the clang of Mr. Jensen's drum of weed killer being wheeled across the lawn. A bar of hot morning light seeped in under the curtains. The stop and start of Mother's voice talking on the telephone echoed up the stairway.

I settled back under the covers, clamped my eyes shut, and tried to recall Billy Granger's features. The way his eyes became clear as seawater when he gazed into the distance. The manly way he held his cigarette between thumb and index finger. The plain, grave way he spoke, as if every word mattered. In truth, the fact that he had no interest in me made him more enticing. If he'd jotted down his address on a slip of paper and begged me to write, I probably would have been bored with him already.

Scott's shoulders had drooped like an old man's as he'd plodded up the stairs, his fancy leather pumps scuffing along the carpet. I should have been kinder, let him twirl me around the dance floor a few times and bring me a plate of roast pig. I pictured him in the guest room now, packing up his soiled shirts and geometry text-book, swiping his hair with two hairbrushes, straightening his tie in the oval mirror over the bureau, snapping his suitcase shut.

I heard the guest room door slam, footsteps out in the hall,

Scott's voice saying something unintelligible to Evvie, probably that his train was leaving in less than an hour. I should make sure he had a proper breakfast before he left and drive him to the station in the electric, I told myself. It was the least I could do. Instead I rolled onto my side, pulled the covers up to my chin. The pillowcase had a comforting smell of bleach and laundry soap, the sheets were worn soft as flannel—I burrowed under and fell back to sleep.

I heard an imperious rap on the door and then footsteps marching over to the bed. I opened one eye and found Evvie scowling down, her arms crossed over her bony chest. "Get up, will you? Scott's leaving in ten minutes."

I swung my legs to the floor, raked my fingers through my hair. "Tell him I'm coming." I found my kimono under a heap of clothes, shoved my feet in the Chinese slippers, and padded down the stairs. He was standing on the front stoop with Mr. Jensen, who had pulled up his truck, ready to give him a lift to the station. Mr. Jensen scowled at the half-tied belt of my bathrobe and my messy hair—no daughter of his would parade around in such a state in front of male houseguests.

Scott was dressed in the same white suit and white bucks he'd worn the day he arrived, rumpled and worse for wear. He glanced over at me, squinting as if the morning light was hurting his eyes. I stuck out my hand. "Have a good trip back. I know you'll pass your exams with flying colors, and you'll be back on top at the Triangle Club."

He grasped my hand in both of his. They felt unusually large and capable for such a slight man. I wondered if I'd noticed his hands before. "I'll do my best," he said, trying to sound jolly. "Thank you for being such a perfect hostess." He sounded sincere.

"I don't know about perfect. I'm afraid you didn't have much fun last night."

"I'm sorry you didn't have much fun either." He moistened his lips as if he was about to say more, but then noticed Mr. Jensen checking his watch and Evvie lurking in the doorway. "I'll write when I get to Princeton."

"You better run or you'll be late." I waved like a beauty queen in a parade as Scott swung his battered suitcase into the back, climbed into the passenger seat, and Mr. Jensen stepped on the gas. Just as the truck was about to pull onto Green Bay Road, Evvie charged up the drive, flailing both arms like she was drowning. "Bye, Scott," she yelled. "I'll miss you."

I trotted back upstairs to my bedroom, Evvie trailing along behind. She plopped down on the bed, swinging her legs, and watched as I divided my hair into three sections and started to brush it out.

"You should have come down when Scott was having breakfast. I think it hurt his feelings. I sat with him so he wouldn't feel too lonely."

"I overslept. Thanks for taking care of him."

"I don't know why you had to be so mean. He's not as dumb as your other boyfriends. At least he can make up funny songs."

"It's hard to explain," I said in a patronizing, big sister tone. "At my age, I have to spend my time with suitable boys. Being suitable is a lot more complicated than making up funny songs. Daddy will explain when you're older."

"Things like 'poor boys shouldn't think of marrying rich girls,' right?"

I spun around. "I didn't say that. Scott said that. He thinks Daddy disapproves of him because he isn't rich, but that's not true."

"Baloney," said Evvie, an expression our mother said was vulgar.

I didn't have the strength for a squabble with Evvie. "Okay, you're right and I'm wrong. Satisfied?"

She shifted her attention to my sarong, which twisted along the floor where I'd dropped it last night like a shed snakeskin.

"I'm not going to wear that again. You can have it if you want."

"Honest?" The scowl melted.

"Sure. Let me show you how to tie it."

Evvie jumped off the bed, positioned herself in front of the mirror, her arms held out like a scarecrow. I draped the sarong over her sharp shoulder blades and then wrapped the sash double around her skinny waist.

"Do I look as good as you?" she asked, spinning around so she could inspect herself from every angle. She jutted her chin out to disguise her overbite.

"Better than me," I said, and Evvie grinned at the possibility. "Let me do your hair." I twisted her lank, not-very-clean hair into a knot on top of her head, with loose strands springing out like devil's horns. "Just one final touch," I said. I rooted around in the back of my stocking drawer for my contraband lipstick and rouge. I held my finger up to my lips. "Promise you won't tell Mother."

"Cross my heart," Evvie said solemnly, placing her hand over the tiny bump of a breast. She closed her eyes and hung her mouth wide like a goldfish.

After I'd finished, I held the rouge compact up to her face so she could inspect herself in the smudgy mirror. "Don't keep licking your lips or it will come off."

"But it tastes like candy," she said with a dreamy smile, my mistreatment of Scott forgotten. All I had to do to win Evvie over was be a nice big sister. It was so easy—I should try it more often, I decided.

"What happened to the Princeton boy?" Daddy asked in the middle of dinner, looking out at the terrace as if we'd accidentally left him there with his cocktail.

"He had to get back. He's in charge of the Triangle Club this year, and has lots to do," I said. It seemed disloyal to mention tutoring school, or that I'd ordered him to leave early.

Daddy nodded, his gaze still fixed on the flagstones. "He seemed like a feckless fellow. But you never know. Those are the kind of boys who can surprise everyone and make something of themselves." Daddy could be merciful now that Scott was gone and his daughter was safe.

A week later, a thin envelope with a Princeton seal arrived.

> Dear Ginevra,
>   I am sorry we parted on such unfriendly terms. Please know that my affection for you is unwavering. You are the only girl I will ever really love. But if you are still determined to cast me off, I would be grateful if you would destroy my letters. I pored out my heart and soul on those pages, and I don't want you to hold them up as incriminating evidence.

I gathered up as many of Scott's letters as I could find, some of them still unopened, and deposited them in the trashcan outside the kitchen door on top of a mound of coffee grounds. I decided Scott the aspiring writer would prefer a more romantic version of how I disposed of his letters.

> Dear Scott,
>   I carried all your letters out to the back field and burned them, as instructed. There were so many that they almost started a brush fire!
>   You don't need to worry that I'd hold your letters against you. I never took them seriously.

You sound like you have a guilty conscience. Did you write me things that you did not mean?

You might as well destroy my letters too.

And by the way, it's poured (as in flowing liquid), not pored (to examine closely).

Your Faithful Friend,

Ginevra

Part Two

10

Red Cross Cadet

Two weeks before I was due back at Westover, I finally wrote a letter to Marie Hart. Neither one of us had been very good about keeping in touch over the summer.

> Yesterday, Mother had the gardener haul my school trunk up from the basement. I just about cried! Last night I had a nightmare about creamed chipped beef and Hillard's sermon about the prodigal son.
>
> Now about decorating our room. I am bringing a Yale banner and six satin pillows which we can pile on the beds and turn into comfy chaises. Does that suit m'Lady's fancy?
>
> I met a dark handsome aviator this summer. Unfortunately, he has no interest in poor little me. I'll tell you all about him after lights out.
>
> Guess what? My friend Millie Jordan isn't going back to Miss Porter's for her senior year! She wants to play in a golf tournament in Hot

Springs in October, and another one in Santa Barbara
after New Year. So her parents caved in and have hired
her a tutor for the year. What a lucky dog.

I saved my version of Scott's visit until the end.

> P.S. You've probably heard that I was a complete louse
> to poor Scott. It wasn't really my fault. Daddy is so wor-
> ried about the war and everything, and he just put his
> foot down about having a houseguest stay longer than 4
> days. I can't say I blame him. You know how Scott can
> carry on about the Triangle Club and the Cottage Club,
> and I think he wore out his welcome. Please don't be
> cross at me.

Marie's response came by return mail.

> Oh, dear! I should have written you back in July. I'm
> afraid I have some bad news about rooming together.
>   It turns out that dear old Dad was upset about our
> misadventure during the Senior Dance, and has been
> lecturing me all summer about "turning over a new
> leaf." For some reason, he decided that you led me
> astray. I'm afraid I might have given him the wrong im-
> pression about you. I told him that you spend your study
> halls writing letters to boys, and I think I might have let
> on about you secretly meeting Scott in New York in
> June. I'm such a complete idiot! He wrote Hillard and
> asked her to assign me a roommate who was, in his
> words, "as sober as Martha Washington." So who do you
> think my new roommate is? Lizzie Harkness, that prig!

Poor Daddy has enough on his mind these days. He
says a war will ruin his business and we'll end up in the
poorhouse. He says I need to get top grades at Westover
this year, so I can go to college and earn a living if I have
to. Golly!

Please don't be peeved with me, G. You're still my very
best friend, and I want to hear all about your aviator.

P.S. Scott wrote me a gloomy letter about his visit to
Lake Forest. Says you threw him over with "supreme
boredom and indifference." That's a direct quote. He
flunked geometry again, so can't be secretary of the Triangle. He says that now he's lost both you and Princeton, he hopes there's a war so he can enlist. I was very
stern with him. I told him it was high time he face facts
about you, and that if he enlisted, he'd probably shoot
himself in the foot on the first day!

I jammed the letter back into the envelope, crumpled it into a
ball, and tossed it toward the wastebasket under the dressing table.
It missed and skittered across the floor. I sank down on the school
trunk that Mr. Jensen had dropped in the middle of the floor and
bitterly surveyed the things I'd spread out on my bed to pack. Five
white uniform dresses freshly laundered and starched. A French dictionary, two new composition notebooks, and a box of Ticonderoga
pencils. The Yale banner and the six satin pillows with fringe.

I slowly bent my mind around Marie's poisonous words. She had
chosen Lizzie Harkness to be her roommate instead of me. She
called Lizzie a "prig" just to soften the blow. Lizzie was from a filthy
rich New York family who had just erected a showoff tower in the
middle of the Yale campus. She was the star wing on the field
hockey team and head chapel girl who wore a long red robe and lit

the altar candles before Hillard's sermons. As much as I hated to admit it, she was even genuinely pretty—with thick red hair and no freckles. I didn't believe for a minute that this had been Mr. Hart's idea. Marie had thrown me over with supreme boredom and indifference. And now I would have to room with some other sad-sack girl who couldn't find a roommate either.

Marie was stupid. Westover was stupid. "Stupid, stupid, stupid," I whispered fiercely. I couldn't help thinking this was somehow Scott Fitzgerald's fault. He'd probably told Marie I was a big snob after all, and she decided to give me a taste of my own medicine.

The next day I set my alarm clock for six o'clock so I could have breakfast with Daddy before he left for the train. I scooped the fleshy white out of a soft-boiled egg while Daddy read from the front page of the *Tribune*.

"'Tanks will aid victory at Somme. A small sector of British tanks has made important gains on one sector of the Somme. According to Winston Churchill, a strong British tank force is the key to destroying the trench barrier on the Western Front and ending bloody and fruitless trench warfare.'" His voice trailed off.

"Go on."

"Let's find something more cheerful for your breakfast." He unfolded the society section. "'Mrs. Swift named president of local Red Cross brigade.' That's better, I suppose."

I walked over to the windowsill and started to pluck withered leaves off the pots of pink geraniums—one of Mother's jobs. "Do you think we'll go to war?"

Daddy set down the paper. "I think we'll end up getting sucked in, even if Wilson is reelected. But there's no need for you to worry." He reached over as if to pull me onto his lap, then, realizing I was too big for that, gave my elbow a brisk pat. "It's not as if U-boats are going to be popping out of Lake Michigan, or anyone you know will ever have to fight in a trench. I'm too old, and all the boys in your grade will be deferred until they finish college, by which time the war will be long over."

"We *do* know men who will fight," I corrected. "I was talking to Billy Granger at the McCormicks' party. He volunteered with the French air patrol. Now he's getting trained as a pilot so he can be in the first squadron of American planes in France."

I sank down in the empty chair next to Daddy. "You remember the discussion we had a few weeks ago? I've decided you're right."

"Right about what?" he asked absently. He'd gone back to the front page with the photograph of a zeppelin shot down in flames over London.

"That I should be more serious about my life. That's why I think I shouldn't go back to Westover."

He lowered the newspaper.

"It seems so frivolous to be memorizing Latin declensions and *Annabelle Lee* when the whole world is about to blow up into war. I want to make myself useful and help people."

"How could little Ginevra Perry make herself useful?"

"Help Mrs. Swift with the Red Cross. Lots of ways."

"I did tell you to be more thoughtful." He gave me an indulgent smile. "I didn't tell you to quit school."

"I'm not saying I would quit school. I just don't want to go back to Westover."

He rubbed his forehead, as if all my whining was giving him a headache. "But I thought you liked the girls at Westover."

"No, I don't! They're catty and backstabbing. Marie told her father all sorts of lies about me. And now he's written Miss Hillard and said I'm not good enough to room with her."

"I'm sure you're exaggerating," he said, folding up the paper and checking his watch.

"I am not. Ask Miss Hillard yourself if you don't believe me."

"All right, then. I will."

Daddy sent Miss Hillard a special delivery the next day, and her response brought Daddy around to my side.

> Dear Mr. Perry,
>
> Mr. Hart did write me with concerns about Ginevra's behavior and her undesirable influence upon his daughter. At his request, we have assigned Marie a more suitable roommate.
>
> Westover holds its students to the highest standard of conduct. We believe that the lapse of any individual student undermines the morale of all students. Therefore we have decided that Ginevra would benefit from additional supervision. The housemother, Miss Meister, has agreed to house Ginevra in her apartment.
>
> We trust that you will find this arrangement satisfactory. Please let me know if I can provide any additional assistance. I am
>
> Yours Most Sincerely,
>
> Marguerite Hillard.

He pounded the table so hard that the salt and pepper shakers toppled over. "Marguerite Hillard can go straight to hell. 'Undesirable.' 'Additional supervision.' She makes you sound like a criminal. I wouldn't send you back there if it was the last school on earth." I hung my head in what I hoped seemed like a grateful and obedient way, and forced back a triumphant grin.

And so it was decided that I would spend my senior year being tutored along with Millie Jordan. Daddy's study was converted into a proper schoolroom, with two desks and a small chalkboard. Our tutor was a retired history teacher from Highland Park High School named Miss Adelaide Lombard. She wore the same green serge dress each day, with removable collars and cuffs. She brought a sack of dreary textbooks she'd used at the Southern Illinois Normal College forty years ago, and for the first month made an honest effort to teach us something. She trudged us through an hour each day of Latin and French grammar, British literature, algebra, and ancient history. In the afternoon, she assigned a theme for us to write in a marble-papered composition notebook, which she graded for penmanship and grammar.

I meant to be a diligent student, but every time I tried to simplify an improper fraction or translate sentences into French, my mind drifted away. I wondered if I would run into any soldiers the next time I went shopping with Mother in Chicago. There were so many enlisted boys who hadn't gotten their orders yet and just loitered around street corners so they could show off their uniforms. Maybe I'd even run into Billy Granger. I flipped to the back of my composition notebook and scribbled a picture of his wide shoulders in an army tunic, his rugged head with a khaki cap.

Millie was even more restless than I was. She came to our lessons already dressed in golf knickers, with her hair pulled back in a tight knot so it wouldn't fall in her eyes when she putted. She sat by the window, gazed longingly down toward the Dismal Swamp, and let out pitiful sighs, like a dog waiting for his walk.

By the end of October, Miss Lombard had given up on the notion of teaching us anything. "Why don't we read some of these nice books on your father's bookshelf?" she suggested, bumping her index finger down a row of leather-bound spines. She pulled down *Middlemarch* for me and *The Hound of the Baskervilles* for Millie. "When you're done, you can write me a little book report, and then I'll assign you another." After that, our days were spent curled up in the two Morris chairs by the fireplace, flipping pages and slurping cups of cocoa that had turned cold.

I decided that George Eliot had much more to teach me than Miss Lombard. I may have occasionally shown poor judgment, but I'd never made such a hash of things as that silly Dorothea Brooke. I'd never marry some horrible old man with white hairy moles growing on his face.

Even if I wasn't attending to my studies, I still wanted to prove to Daddy that I was serious about helping people. Three afternoons a week, when Millie had a golf lesson at the club, I reported to Mrs. Swift's house on Mayflower Road, where the Lake Forest brigade of the Red Cross met. I was issued a cadet uniform—a gray flannel pinafore with a red cross appliquéd across the front, and a white kerchief to bind back my hair like a nun's. I had Mrs. Turner make a few tucks so the pinafore showed off my waist, and managed to coax ringlets to spring loose from the corners of my kerchief, and the effect was the Gibson girl goes to war.

Maisie Swift was an enormous woman with mountains of pink, damp flesh folding helplessly into extra stomachs, chins, and elbows. Her heap of premature silver hair was coiled into a top-knot, and her perfect doll's face was nestled down between two dumpling cheeks. Maisie Swift was dim, but was put in charge of charity events anyway because she was the richest woman in town, and if things got in too much of a muddle, she could enlist the help of her husband's secretary and bookkeeper. Our brigade included three ancient widows, a dozen of the young married set, and me. Mrs. Swift set us to work knitting mittens and mufflers in army-green wool, probably because she had once read a novel about noble Confederate women huddled together to sew overcoats and blankets for their poor husbands so they wouldn't freeze in a Yankee cornfield.

I got a Christmas card from Marie Hart with a sheepish note scrawled on the back. "Westover's an awful bore without you. Lizzie

Harkness has turned out to be a complete pill. She's so stuck-up
about being a senior proctor that she even gave me two demerits for
being 'disrespectful.' Hope you aren't sore about the roommate
mix-up! Scott still sounds pitiful."

I included a gracious note on my Christmas card. "Am having
loads of fun being a Red Cross cadet. I'm doing my part to keep our
soldiers happy!"

In early February a huge headline announced "Wilson Breaks
with Germans." Daddy showed me a map on page 2, with every
ship sunk by U-boats marked with a black German cross. It looked
like Europe was being smothered by a swarm of locusts. "You know
what this means, my girl?" he asked. I nodded, even though I had no
idea, not really.

When Congress declared war in April, the mood in our brigade
grew somber. Our conversations turned from gossip to war news.
College boys had been spared from the draft, but not the husbands
of the young marrieds. I would see them at Sunday lunch at the
club in their drab wool uniforms tailored by Brooks Brothers, their
upper lips shadowed with the tender shoots of new mustaches.

"George has been called up. He has to report to Camp Devens
in three months," said Sally Farnum, glancing fretfully at her stomach, which was just starting to poke out. George would be gone
before the baby arrived, she said, and he would face all sorts of
dangers even if he didn't get sent to France. The camps were filled
with enlisted men who were crawling with TB germs and lice, and
might "accidentally" miss a target on the rifle range and hit an officer instead.

I steered the conversation to the boys I knew. How about John
Pullman? I asked. Safe and sound at Yale for another year, and
then who knows? The army doesn't really like to take sissy boys,
you know, said Elsie Sturgis, who ought to know, since her hus-

band, Jack, was considered a bit of a sissy boy himself, and a drunk to boot.

"Any word about Horace?" I asked Mrs. Armour, who was his aunt.

"He applied for a commission two days after he got back from his honeymoon. Says it's his patriotic duty to serve, but poor Constance."

"And what about that friend of his, the pilot?"

"The Granger boy? I heard something about him. Oh, yes. He's off in Ohio somewhere learning how to fly planes."

"I saw him at the McCormicks'," Elsie said. "He certainly has turned into a dashing figure. Any girl would be lucky to land him." She shot me a tiny sideways wink.

"Doesn't he have an understanding with Peg Denton?" Sally asked.

"I think Eliza Denton and Franny Granger are the ones with the understanding. Their cabins are side by side on Indian Point, and they've been plotting since little Peggy and Billy were both in diapers."

"It's good that Billy's known Peg a long time," said Elsie. "Maybe he hasn't noticed she weighs two hundred pounds."

The nattering of the women faded to a low hum as I digested these new tidbits. Yes, Billy Granger was divine—everyone thought so. When he came home on leave, exhausted and demoralized, maybe he would appreciate the attention of a Red Cross cadet. He'd forget all about Peg Denton, although it was hard to believe he thought about her much anyway. She was a butterball, to say the least.

The problem was how to get our brigade to do something more useful than knitting lumpy, deformed socks that no soldier would ever be desperate enough to wear. I showed Mrs. Swift a clipping from the *Tribune*.

The War Department spends $156.30 to outfit each
doughboy. Each soldier is issued 107 pieces of fighting
equipment including a gas mask, 50 articles of clothing,
and 11 cooking implements. The War Department does
not provide any luxury items. The most thoughtful gift
for your doughboy is a simple care package containing
cigarettes, tinned meats and hard candies.

What a clever idea, said Elsie Sturgis, dropping her knitting nee-
dles with a clatter onto the parquet and snapping open her pocket-
book.

Now that our offerings could be purchased rather than handmade, our fingers flew as we stuffed cardboard boxes with Win-
stons and tins of fruit drops. In May, a photograph of me appeared
on the *Tribune* society page dressed in my uniform and surrounded
by hundreds and hundreds of care packages. The caption read, "Mrs.
Gustavus Swift pronounces Miss Ginevra Perry 'invaluable' to Red
Cross war effort."

By the time Pershing's men had landed on French soil, I was
spending every afternoon at Mrs. Swift's side, packing, sealing, and
stacking boxes, all the while asking idle questions about our various young men. "What's the latest news about Horace?"

"He's training somewhere down in Alabama, and thinks he'll
ship over by October. Constance is expecting, of course."

"Of course," said Elsie Sturgis, rolling her eyes heavenward.
Along with being a sissy and a drunk, Jack Sturgis seemed deficient
in the baby-producing department as well.

"Any more news about the Granger boy?" I asked.

"I did ask Frances Granger at the Casino Club because I knew
you were particularly interested, and she said . . . what was it, now?
Oh, yes. Billy's coming home for a month in September."

The next day I brought a clipping about the squalid living conditions at Camp Sheridan down the road from Lake Forest. Men were crowded into drafty, unhygienic tents, and were so idle during their off-duty hours that they got into fights in taverns along the railroad. Wasn't it our patriotic duty to open up our homes and offer wholesome entertainment to the officers at least? A splendid idea, Mrs. Swift and all the young marrieds agreed.

We planned a ball for mid-September. It shouldn't be just another boring tea dance with a piano player and a punch bowl, I insisted. For one evening, the men should be able to step into a magical world and leave all their worries behind.

But we can't pretend the war isn't happening, said Sally Farnum. That would be disrespectful to our men.

Finally we decided on the theme "Over There!" The nice parts of "Over There," we explained to Mrs. Swift. Not the trenches and hip-high mud part.

I was put in charge of the decorations, and filled a sketchpad with watercolors to show the ladies. We would transform the top floor of the Winter Club into Montmartre. There would be a replica Moulin Rouge that spun, and round tables with checked cloths along the sides of the room like a street café. We'd serve French-type food like red wine and moldy cheeses, and get the band to play the latest songs from Paris, like "Après la Guerre." I designed a whole set of "gay Paree" costumes for the hostesses to wear—cancan girls, waiters, street vendors, nuns.

"What are you going to go as, Ginevra?" asked Elsie Sturgis.

"I'm not going to wear a costume."

"Lady Godiva, eh? I should have guessed," she said, lighting another Lucky Strike. She was the only one in the brigade who dared to smoke around Mrs. Swift.

"I thought I'd just help out behind the scenes."

"What a good girl."

I made sure that Mrs. Swift enclosed a note in Billy Granger's invitation. "Your mother reports that you will be on leave in time for our little fete, and I do hope you will be able to attend. I promise that there will be plenty of très charmantes filles!"

"We should probably invite Peg Denton, too," I said halfheartedly.

"I'm not sure she'd be very comfortable dressing up in a costume. She's a little . . ." Elsie searched for a tactful word. "Broad in the beam?"

I obsessed over every detail—the design of the dance cards, the fabric for the costumes, the red paper lanterns that hung from the ceiling. I appeared once again on the front page of the *Tribune* society section, standing on a stepladder in a painter's smock, dabbing the finishing brush stroke on the spire of Sainte-Chapelle.

> Miss Ginevra Perry has researched photos to make sure that every detail is accurate in her backdrop of the Paris skyline for tomorrow night's "Over There!" Officer's Dance hosted by the Lake Forest Brigade of Red Cross volunteers. "I want everything to be perfect for our soldiers," says Miss Perry.

I couldn't resist the opportunity to gloat. I sent a copy of the clipping to Marie Hart, who was now a freshman at Macalester. "Isn't the outfit killing! But it sure beats our old Westover uniforms! How's college? It must be very boring with all the eligible boys off at war. I'm busy day and night with the Red Cross."

On the night of the dance, I stationed myself behind a wooden desk in the drafty front hall of the Winter Club, dressed in my pinafore and kerchief, where I handed out dance cards and boutonnieres and hung hats in the cloakroom. I'd read up on where each one of the men was stationed and the latest movement of the American troops in Europe so I could make sympathetic chitchat.

"How's Camp Dix?" I asked John Pullman, who seemed if anything younger and more tentative in his brass buttons, jodhpurs, and cavalry hat.

"All right, I guess," he said, absently plucking the petals off his carnation and stuffing it in his pocket.

"So when is the First Division shipping out?"

"First of next month. How about a dance?"

"I'm stuck here for the duration. But there are lots of other girls," I said, pointing toward Millie, who was dressed as a waiter with an apron and a penciled-on mustache. I'd forced her to come, and she slumped against a fake lamppost. John gave a hollow smile and trudged toward her.

For three hours I greeted boys, with no sign of Billy Granger. Even though he hadn't answered our invitation, I still had a mysterious faith that he would come, that he'd be tugged here by the sheer force of my will.

In truth, despite the Moulin Rouge whirling away, the flickering glow from the paper lanterns, the husky yearnings of an actual Parisian chanteuse, the coos from a bunch of pretty girls in skimpy costumes, "Over There!" was turning out to be a somber affair. When I walked through at ten o'clock with a tray of foie gras hors d'oeuvres, the boys were clustered around the café tables, heads hung together, puffing at Cuban cigars. I caught snippets of their grim mutterings, the slang of war—"latest figures," "booby-trapped," "rainbow division," "billet," "Hindenberg Line." The only two who seemed to be having any fun were, surprisingly, Millie Jordan and John Pullman. She was marching him across the dance floor in a brisk tango, and he actually seemed to be laughing.

At five past eleven, I started to pack away the unused dance cards and carnations. A door slammed somewhere and heavy boots strode across the waxed floor. I glanced up to see Billy Granger before me. He wore a tight brown tunic unadorned except for a plain leather belt, a soft cloth cap, boots splattered with mud. His face was now angles and shadows, the gray eyes eerily pale, the chin tinged with a day-old beard.

"Hello, Ensign," I said, straightening my kerchief.

He gave me a vague, impersonal smile, showing off the Teddy Roosevelt teeth. "I'm William Granger. Sorry I'm so late."

Did he really not recognize me? "Ginevra Perry," I offered, which didn't stir a flicker of recognition. "The dance is thataway. There's plenty of food left. Go on."

"All right. Thanks." He headed toward the doorway, then stopped and turned back. "Nice to meet you."

"Nice to meet you too," I said, keeping my eyes fixed on the box of cast-off dance cards and carnations.

After a few minutes, I wandered over to the doorway and peeked in. Billy Granger had joined the group of men around the café table, and was puffing away on one of their Cuban cigars. He was holding forth on something, waving the cigar in the air to make a point, while all the other men leaned toward him as if they didn't dare miss a word. The chanteuse announced that this would be her final song, and I turned back to my post; the men would soon be needing their hats back.

"Ginevra, wait," a woman called. Elsie Sturgis was tripping toward me in baggy fisherman trousers and espadrilles laced up her ankles. Her hand was clenched onto Billy Granger's sleeve, tugging him along like a two-year-old. "I told Ensign Granger that you've been working all night and you deserve at least one dance." She stopped, huffing and puffing, and gave him a shove in my direction.

"I'm not much of a dancer," he said, gazing wistfully at his cigar.

"It's your duty, I'm afraid. Ginevra's our most devoted volunteer." Elsie gave me a sly wink as if to say, see, I'm not such a witch.

He sighed, ground out his cigar with his muddy boot, took my arm, and led me past the café tables, past the line of neglected society girls whose cancan ruffles had drooped. We stepped onto the almost deserted dance floor just as the chanteuse was breaking into "After the War Is Over." Billy wedged me in a stiff-armed embrace and started in on a robotic waltz, as if he were following footsteps painted on the floor.

"Told you I was no good at this," he said, glancing over my shoulder at the two soldiers left at the café table, who were lighting fresh cigars.

"I'm glad Elsie forced you to dance with me. I've got a confession to make."

"What?" Puzzled eyes squinted down at me.

"We've met before, at the McCormicks'. I probably shouldn't even remind you, because I was so horrible. I was the girl in the sarong with the drunk."

His mouth flattened into a line. "I remember now. The one who said pilots last an average of three days on the front."

"He was nobody. Just some boyfriend of my old roommate. Can we start all over again?" I tilted my face under his rigid jaw and gave a pleading smile. His arms softened a bit. "What do you think of our decorations?" My backdrop had started to buckle in the middle, so the Eiffel Tower looked like it was swooning. "Does it look like Paris when you were there with Nungesser?"

"Pretty close."

"Where are you going next?" I whispered.

"The naval station in Key West. I'm in charge of training pilots."

"Just like you hoped. Your dream came true."

"Right." There was a tremor in his voice.

There was nothing left to say. I nestled my cheek into the brown wool, which smelled like leather, machine oil, and Turkish cigarettes. The singer directed her last chorus toward the aviator with the Red Cross girl enfolded in his arms, not so much dancing as swaying side to side.

> After the war is over,
> And the world's at peace,
> Many a heart will be aching,
> After the war has ceased.

When the music stopped he stepped away, straightened the leather strap across his chest, glanced toward the door—his duty done.

"Do you think I could send you one of our care packages?"

"I guess so." And then, realizing he might seem ungrateful, he said, "I mean, I'd like that. Thank you, Ginevra."

A few days later, I called his mother to find out his preferences. "Well, let's see," she said, another enormous, vague woman from the Mrs. Swift school. "He used to collect Civil War lead soldiers. And when he was a Boy Scout, he never could have enough pocketknives."

"I'm wondering what he might like now, as a grown man, Mrs. Granger."

She seemed taken aback, as if I'd asked something slightly improper. "Fishing, I suppose. And any kind of game, especially chess, because he is so clever with numbers. He's very enthusiastic about the Chicago White Sox. He likes plenty of starched handkerchiefs. And even though I disapprove of smoking, he seems to prefer Dunhills."

The next week, I sent a care package unlike any other received at the Key West Naval Aviation Training Station. Smoked salmon and foie gras from Marshall Field's fancy food section, the *Tribune* sports section about the White Sox victory in the World Series, a carton of Dunhills, a traveling chess set that folded into a wooden box, and, even though the Prohibitionists had ruled liquor for servicemen strictly contraband, a silver flask filled with Daddy's best single malt. And at the bottom of the box, a photograph of me in my Red Cross pinafore in a Mark Cross leather frame. Over the next few weeks, I sent two more care packages with a collapsible fishing pole and tackle, a deck of monogrammed playing cards, a box of La Coronas and a silver cigar clipper, a box of Brooks Brothers handkerchiefs, a baseball signed by Buck Weaver, and (a whimsical touch, I thought) a Boy Scout pocketknife.

Four weeks later, I got a perfunctory thank you on a penny postcard.

> Dear Genevra (spelling?),
>   Thanks for all tasty victuals and smokes. I had no idea Red Cross Care packages were so luxe! How'd you guess I like Dunhills and chess? You're a real pal.
>   Yrs. Sinc.
>   Ensgn. Wm. Granger

I sent a penny postcard back.

> Dear Ensign Granger,
>   No more care packages until you send me a proper letter.
>   Yrs. Sinc.
>   Ginevra (with an i) Perry

Then I used the strategy that had worked with the few indifferent boys I'd met in my four years as a flirt. I waited; and the longer

I waited, the more deeply I fell in love with Billy Granger. I cut a smudgy picture of him out of the *Tribune* rotogravure section, pasted it onto a shirt cardboard, and tucked it away inside my untouched Book of Common Prayer. Every night I would go to bed whispering a letter to him. "Tonight there was another tea dance at the Winter Club. All the soldiers were so conceited, and yet not one will face as much danger in two years as you face in a single day."

Two weeks later, a pulpy military-issue envelope arrived, my name spelled properly in a bold, masculine hand.

Dear Ginevra,

I apologize for my shabby postcard. I can't tell you how much your care packages have meant to me.

I am writing this from the infirmary. One of my trainees crash-landed on the airstrip. We tried to pull him out, but it was too late, poor fellow. Anyway, I got a pretty bad burn on my arm (the left one fortunately— that's why I can write you!) and they are confining me to bed rest so it will heal up properly.

I have your picture on my bedside table, and all the other men asked if you are my sweetheart, and I said I wish you were.

I must have seemed very rude and dull when we met at your lovely little dance. I'm afraid I was feeling pretty distracted about shipping out to Key West. Little did I know how much I would miss the aid and comfort of a certain Red Cross cadet. I hope you don't mind if I write you on a regular basis. A letter back would please me more than you can imagine.

Yours Truly,

Billy G.

Over the next four months, Billy's letters arrived every few days, each one longer and more confessional than the last.

> I never guessed that training other men would be so dif-
> ficult. When I try to explain how a plane works, I get all
> muddled up. I'm not clever with words like you are. I
> guess I'm much more comfortable in the machine shop
> with engines and tools that don't say anything.

> The rudders on the last batch of Jennys are stiff and tend
> to jam. We complained to Curtiss, but they don't give a
> Goddamn (pardon my French). They have no idea what
> it's like not to be able to steer a plane that's 400 feet up
> in the air. . . .

> We lost two men in a training flight today. One just fin-
> ished his freshman year at Vanderbilt, and I had to write
> a letter to his parents. We are all pretty cut up.

Mother found me getting weepy over one of the sadder ones. I was propped on the stone wall by the fishpond so I could see the clouds reflected in the water, which reminded me of Billy in his airplane.

"What's the matter, dear?" she said, dropping her pruning shears. But when I told her about Billy's grief over the tragic death of the college boy, she scoffed. "Frances Granger's son? I thought he was just interested in ham radios." She bent and plucked a fallen willow branch from the murky water.

"I wouldn't expect you to understand," I said stiffly. How could she, when she hadn't seen the true Billy in his letters—silent but tenderhearted, filled with manly complexities.

In late June, I got an unusually thin letter.

I will be home for a short (too short!) furlough over Fourth of July. Will you have dinner with me? I have an important question to ask you.

Your Billy

11

The Triumph of Youth

had a special black dress made for the occasion, daringly low cut for an eighteen-year-old girl, with
chiffon butterfly sleeves. When he stepped into our front
hall on a stormy night in July, I thought yes, this is the man
I have been waiting for. He loomed tall, his hair and leather
trench coat were dripping, his face was haggard after six
months of aerial disasters. "Ensign," Daddy said with odd
humility, extending his hand.

Billy took me to the dining room of the Palmer House—
not the most romantic or fashionable restaurant in Chicago,
but considered fancy.

He stared disapprovingly at the leather-bound menu,
shaking his head.

"Anything wrong?" I asked.

"Look at these prices. I hate to see gouging just because
there's a war."

"My menu doesn't have prices," I said.

"Of course. What would you like?"

There was tournedos with béarnaise, and quail in
orange sauce, and oysters fresh from the Chesapeake. Even
though I should have been much too nervous to eat, I

suddenly felt famished. "What do you think I should order?" I asked
meekly.

"Well, my mother likes the roast turkey with stuffing."

"Then that's what I'll have," I said, closing my menu. It was
thrilling to have a man make decisions for me.

I sipped my champagne cocktail slowly, waiting for the "important question," but Billy wanted to continue in the confiding tone
of his letters. Through cocktails, the main course, and dessert (he
ordered rice pudding for both of us—another one of his mother's
favorites), he talked on. Back when he was at Yale, he'd thought
he'd try out for the White Sox as a pitcher after graduation—the
Yale coach thought he had a decent shot. But the war had made
him see things differently, had made him realize that becoming a
professional baseball player was just a schoolboy's dream. Now he
had to think of what he would make of himself after the war was
over. "If I survive," he added.

"Of course you'll survive," I said, my voice hushed and fervent.

Well then, if he did survive, he planned to start an airplane
manufactory. "Those Curtiss men are a bunch of boobs and need
someone to give them a run for their money," he said. His capable
hands—pitcher's hands—rearranged the spare silverware so it
looked like the skeleton of a cockpit.

"But who will need airplanes when the war is over?" I asked.

"Mark my word, Ginevra. In five years the postal service will be
sending their mail by air. In twenty years, you'll take an airplane to
New York just like you would a train." He set the silverware down
and fixed his attention on me. "You're not wearing your Red Cross
uniform," he said.

"No." I shrugged my shoulders so the butterfly sleeves fluttered
prettily.

"I probably should have noticed that before." His pale eyes trav-
eled over my body—from my face to my shoulders and finally to the

V-shaped edge of my neckline. He stared long enough that the top of my scalp started to burn. "You're so lovely. I still can't believe someone like you would ever bother with someone like me."

"Why do you say that? All the ladies at the Red Cross say you're dashing."

He shrugged. "I've always been a dud with girls. At dances, I could never think of anything clever to say, so I spent a lot of time outside inspecting the cars. The only girl who put up with me is good old Peg Denton, and that's just because our mothers are friends."

I burst out laughing. "You're not fourteen anymore, Billy. In case you hadn't noticed."

He looked back at my neckline. "I've noticed." He slid his closed fist across the table. The angry end of his scar peeked over his cuff. His hand opened; an old-fashioned purple velvet box nestled in his broad palm.

"I've grown to care for you so much these last few months. I was hoping you would be willing . . ." His voice trailed off and a flush crept up his neck, as if he had admitted something embarrassing in front of a stranger. But he should know that I wasn't a stranger anymore.

I stroked his scar with a fingertip. "Yes, Billy?"

"I was wondering if you would consider becoming engaged to me," he said, lifting his bashful eyes to mine. He couldn't quite bring himself to say the word "marry." He licked his lips. "I love you," he added in a raspy whisper, as if his throat hurt.

I gazed over his shoulder at the high, arched windows. A crack in the stormy sky had opened, and a wisp of moonlight peeped through—a good omen. I spoke slowly, stating each word like a vow at the altar. "I would be honored to be your wife."

His face broke out into a relieved grin, then he took a long swig of ice water, as if he'd just hiked up a mountain.

I took the box in my hands but didn't open it. I'd been waiting my whole life for this moment, and I wanted to savor every second. The lilies of the valley in the bud vase gave off a sad, sweet scent. I noticed a little patch of whiskers to the left of his chin, which his razor had missed, and one of his knuckles had a scrape as if he'd fallen on the playground. The room had turned oddly quiet, and I glanced up to see the waiters and other diners watching us like doting parents.

Billy finally reached over and snapped open the box. "It was my grandmother's," he explained, as I slid a clump of dim diamonds and fussy Victorian filigree onto my wedding-ring finger. "Not her engagement ring. They were too poor when they got married to have one. My grandfather bought it when Granger & Sons made its first hundred thousand."

My father had told me a less romantic story about how the Grangers had made their money—by selling lumber for ten times what it was worth in the two months after the Chicago Fire.

Billy's eyes narrowed with disappointment at the ring, which hung down over my knuckle, as ridiculous as a giant's ring. "My mother said you might want something more à la mode." So Billy had told his mother of his plan to pop the question, and she had approved enough to turn over the family ring.

"I love it," I murmured. "I love you."

Billy stopped his parents' Plymouth at the top of our driveway, pulled up the hand brake, and reached for me. The rain had started again, and streamed down the windshield like a waterfall. His kiss was so tentative and off-center that I wondered if he had ever kissed a girl before. I kissed him back, my mouth supple, open, guiding his hands so they circled my waist, inhaling the delicious scent of his leather coat. He let out a small groan, and tried again, hard and fervent this time. A quick learner, I thought.

After what seemed like hours, Billy disentangled himself with another groan, a regretful one this time. "I wish we could get married right away. I don't think I can wait."

"I can't either." If I waited, all the thrill might fizzle away, like it had with Scott. If we were married, the first kiss would be preserved forever, like rose petals in the pages of a book.

"But I'm going back to Key West."

I wrapped my arms around his neck. "I'll come too."

At breakfast the next day, I announced that I was going to marry Billy Granger when he had his next furlough in two months. Mother and Daddy set down their forks and exchanged sober glances. "Ginevra, I'd like to speak privately with you in my study," Daddy said.

We settled face-to-face on the Morris chairs. Daddy bent down and rubbed his eyes, as if he had a blinding headache or was wiping away a tear. He reached over and grasped my right hand (not the one with the hideous ring) tightly in both of his. "Ginevra, please try to listen." His voice was resigned, as if he already knew he'd lost this battle.

"What?" My tone was truculent.

"Your mother and I have discussed this. We hope you understand that this is a very important step—the *most* important step a girl can make. Why do you have to get married in such a rush? You are only eighteen."

"In case you hadn't noticed, there's a war on."

"Which, according to the papers, will be over in less than six months. And there you'll be, married to Bill Granger for the next fifty years."

"He's the kind of man you told me I should pick. He's wise. He has character. He's brave and willing to sacrifice his life for his country. Other men respect him." And all the girls admire him, I wanted to add.

"I did say you should pick a man with character. And Bill is a good fellow, I admit. Responsible, hardworking, clever with radios and airplanes and such. But that doesn't mean he'd be a good husband. At least not for you."

"Why not for me?" He made it sound as if I had some kind of infirmity that required extra care.

"Because you need a husband who has some pep and imagination. Bill is a Granger, and the Grangers are a dull lot. The only place they vacation is some shack on Lake Michigan because they're all so crazy about fly-fishing. That pile of bricks on Michigan Avenue doesn't even have central heating because Gerald is so Scotch. The only thing Frances Granger ever talks about is her dreary charity for unwed mothers. Bill probably gave you that old ring because he was too cheap to buy you a new one."

I jerked my hand back and cupped it protectively over Billy's ring. "That's unfair. You don't know Billy the way I do. He says such sweet, funny things in his letters. And he's full of pep, for your information," I added. Like last night, in the car.

"All right, then. I see there's no changing your mind." He bent down and gave my forehead a dry, sad kiss.

After a hint or two, Billy took me shopping for a diamond solitaire the very next day—at a nice local jewelry shop, not something ostentatious like Peacock's. I tactfully picked the third largest one in the tray.

Fortunately, everyone else was much more enthusiastic about my engagement. When I dramatically pulled off my glove and displayed my ring at the next Red Cross meeting, the ladies burst into applause, and Mrs. Swift had the maid bring out the sherry even though it was before noon.

"A wartime bride. Could there be anything more romantic?" Elsie Sturgis murmured. It sounded like one of her usual jabs, but her eyes were wet with tears.

Evvie was happy mostly because she got to be a bridesmaid. "Can I wear a grown-up dress with no sash," she begged. "And shoes with a heel?"

Even Millie, who normally had no use for mushy stuff, warmed to the idea of marriage, especially the part about moving out of my parents' house and Billy and me having an apartment of our own. "Maybe I should get married too," she mused, adjusting an argyle sock. "Then I could come and go as I please and play in as many tournaments as I want."

"But who would you marry?"

"I don't know. John Pullman, maybe. He writes me all the time from Camp Dix."

"Oh, don't do that," I said with such force that Millie reared up her head, offended. "You can do better," I offered. What I wanted to say was poor, sweet John Pullman can do better—he deserves someone who loves him.

Billy sent me darling little packages nearly every day from Key West, wrapped in brown paper and twine—a bottle of pinkish sand, a pair of silly earrings made of dried seahorses, a stuffed baby alligator dressed as a bathing beauty. "These are the finest gifts I can find," he wrote. "It's very primitive here, not at all what a Lake Forest girl is used to. I can hardly wait. I'm counting the days." How could Daddy have ever thought that Billy was dull and unimaginative?

"Key West will be like going to Girl Scout camp," I wrote back. "Not that I've ever been to Girl Scout camp! I can hardly wait. I'm counting the days."

Billy and I were married two months later when he had a three-day furlough. The ceremony was just the way I had envisioned it—solemn and simple. Elsie Sturgis, my unlikely cupid, was maid of honor; Millie and Evvie were bridesmaids.

The entire *Tribune* rotogravure section was devoted to my wedding, and the write-up seemed to appreciate the drama and historical significance of the occasion even if my parents had missed it.

THE TRIUMPH OF YOUTH

What a realization of the supreme power of youth is forced on us by these so-called "war weddings." The old and wise will look on with awe at the valorous determination of the young to snatch happiness from the tremendous conflagration which is burning up our outworn failure of a civilization. The flames light up the radiant faces of our boys and girls as, two by two, they join hands and smilingly undertake to cope with the great catastrophe.

In the shadows of the outer circle, their elders look on, stretching out detaining but ineffectual hands, in helpless anguish. They are part of a closing chapter. To their sons and daughters belong both the present and the future. Each of these war marriages is a further manifestation of the triumph of youth.

The groom is stationed at the naval aviation camp at Key West. Due to Ensign Granger's brief furlough, the couple must forego a traditional honeymoon and hurried from the reception to catch the 6:05 at Union Station.

The 18-year-old bride seemed unperturbed at foregoing a wedding trip. "My place is with my husband," she said. "My duty is to provide him with companionship and support."

The bride of an aviator must be of heroic stuff to keep smiling these days. But that's what our American girls and women are. The whimperer is rare.

12

Honeymoon in Key West

Because the train was crammed with soldiers and there was not a sleeping compartment to be had, we spent our honeymoon night sitting side by side in a passenger seat, holding hands and watching the Indiana wheat fields whisk by in the lemony dusk. I pointed out a crooked gingerbread cottage by a crossing. We could see a man and a woman through the parlor window. "Look. They're dancing," I said. "It's their anniversary. 'Come to Me Tonight' is playing on the gramophone. It has a skip, but they don't even notice. Two old basset hounds are snoring away by the fire."

"You see love stories everywhere," Billy whispered tenderly. He bent over to give me a passionate, open-mouth French kiss.

We arrived almost forty-eight hours later at the naval station's married officers' quarters, a dozen attached ramshackle bungalows under a stunted row of palm trees, with our marriage unconsummated. The red disk of a sunset balanced on the rim of the stagnant ocean, blasting the curled shingles, the parched lawn, the jagged, meaty plants, with an ungodly heat. More like a missionary outpost in darkest Africa than a summer camp, I thought.

It was early evening, just past suppertime, and Billy's fellow officers and their wives were sprawled on the paintless front porches. Two toddlers in low-slung diapers squirted each other with a hose on the patchy front yard. When our jitney pulled up, the men stepped down off the porch and sauntered up to Billy, slapped him on the back, slid me sidelong looks. They were all very blond, with sunburned scalps and necks, dressed in their uniform pants and undershirts. No man I knew would ever go out his front door in just an undershirt, no matter how blistering hot it was.

"Well, look who's back with his child bride," one said. "Bet you didn't catch much of the scenery," said another. They had thick Southern accents, with names like Prescott and Baird. After greeting Bill properly, they turned their attention to me, inspected me in a remote, respectful way. This was the way it would be as a married woman—men filtering their attention through my husband, directing their innuendoes and racy remarks toward him, not me.

Then their wives ambled down off the porches—birdlike girls who looked about Evvie's age, in frilly, handmade clothes. About half of them had terrifying, pregnant bellies. They gave me handshakes with limp fingers, one after the other, and introduced themselves with lazy, deferential voices. "How d'you do, Miz Granger." They had what Daddy would call "cornpone" names—Fay, Hettie, Suellen. Then they stepped back and swept brazen stares over my engagement ring, the gold GPG initials on my new suitcases, my unscuffed white kid shoes. Their smirks told me that they knew I was about to step into the shabbiest, most paint-peeled bungalow and sleep with my husband for the first time four feet from where they sat.

Billy tucked two suitcases under his arms, grabbed the other two, sauntered onto the front porch, and kicked the warped door open with his heel. "We've had a long trip. I think we're going to turn in. You coming," he paused, "um, dear?"

The wives dropped their eyes to the ground, started to pat their sweaty tendrils back under hairpins as if they were suppressing a laugh. Well, I wasn't about to be the butt of anyone's joke, especially not these Hetties and Suellens and Fays. I put on my most rapturous smile, the one I'd used on boys since I was fourteen, and directed it straight at their husbands, and kept it there until they turned away, blushing. "I *am* tired," I said, stretching my elbows out like a kitten and stifling a yawn. "Night, y'all," I sang out, trotting to the front door with eager steps and slamming the door behind me.

The bungalow consisted of one large room with brown-stained tongue-and-groove walls and ceiling, a two-burner hotplate, ice chest, two broken-down chairs, a card table, and in one corner, a bathtub. A back hallway had a cubicle with a swaybacked double bed and a water closet. Not particularly clean, but there were fresh broom marks across the floor. I walked around and shut every window, trapping in the stifling, moldy air, then pulled down the stained shades and tested them to make sure they wouldn't spring back up. I picked up the package of navy-issued linens that had been left on the threshold, went to the back hall, and made up the bed. I stepped out of my skirt and blouse, folded them over a suitcase, unpinned my hair, and stretched out on the bed. Mustard light and the shrieks of the children filtered in through the stained parchment shades.

All my daydreams about Billy Granger hadn't included marital relations, as my mother called it. But kissing Billy was exciting, I told myself, staring up at the sagging ceiling. And looking at Daddy's Pompeii postcards was exciting. So touching Billy, and having Billy touch me, would be exciting too.

I heard the kitchen sink running, and then there was Billy standing above me in his uniform pants and his undershirt. There were tufts of dark hair sprouting across his chest and under his arms. He gave off a sharp smell that soap couldn't quite cover. I reached up for him with one arm and clamped my other hand over his mouth. "Quiet," I whispered, my lips on his ear. "Quiet as you can."

Over the next few days, I figured out how to "keep house." Mother had told me I should hire a colored girl or maybe the wife of one of the enlisted men to cook and tidy up. "You have no idea how to cook or clean," she had warned with a shudder, "especially in an army barracks. You might poison Billy by accident with tainted food." But none of the Hettie-and-Fays had help, so I decided to make do.

In the early mornings, before the sun pulsed through the palm fronds like hot breath, I would walk down the crushed seashell path to the canteen and buy groceries for dinner. It was always the same—tinned peas and salmon, crackers, two bottles of root beer—the kind of picnic Evvie and I used to serve up to our dolls in the potting shed by the fishpond.

In the evening after our playhouse supper, we dragged the two chairs onto the busted front porch. Bill uncapped the root beers and we drank them straight out of the bottle because we didn't have proper glasses. The other officers and their wives were standoffish, so we made do with our own company. Our conversations sometimes sounded stilted, like the ones I'd staged between my bride-and-groom dolls.

"How was your day, dear?" asked Billy on a typical evening, leaning back and inspecting me with husbandly pride. He was dressed in his undershirt and uniform pants like all the other aviators, and his tan neck and pale arms were covered with a fine sheen of sweat, which was attractive, I decided. It was the way a real man was supposed to look.

"I swept out the house and I changed the bed sheets. Then I did some washing in the sink." I pointed with pride to three of Bill's undershirts and my nightgown flapping on the clothesline. They didn't look as white as the clothing on the other officers' lines—their wives probably knew of some soap flakes that worked better than the bar of yellow soap I'd found in the sink. But my laundry looked good enough to me.

"Did you fly an airplane today?" I asked.

"No, I was giving the trainees a lecture on safe landings and take-offs. I drew diagrams on a blackboard. I think I'm better at that than I am in the cockpit."

"Any news from France?"

"No orders for more pilots. Still no planes to fly." He gave a help-less shrug. By the time American factories started producing enough planes, the Germans would have surrendered. All these trainees would never go anywhere but back home, which was fine by him.

After we finished our root beers we played checkers, the only game we were an even match for, because my Uncle Silas had taught me some sneaky moves one summer at Mineral Springs. Billy kept a running tally on a piece of cardboard he'd tacked to the front door. I was ahead by two games, but I suspected he was letting me win.

After checkers we went to bed, where we made love. I was still trying to decide what I thought about sex. At first it had been thrilling, as if I were being initiated into a secret club with myste-rious rituals. I loved to watch how transported Billy became, clos-ing his eyes, an animal sound rising up in the back of his throat.

Making love with Billy seemed pleasant enough but not nearly as pleasant as kissing in the back seat of a car under a starry sky. Kiss-ing was a great wave of anticipation that built on and on, where making love was over and done with in no time flat. I started to wonder if sex was overrated. I could not understand why people in

Pompeii had gone to all the bother to paint erotic frescoes. Or why women in novels, like Hester Prynne, had risked getting pregnant and being banished to a shack in the woods just so they could make love to someone like Arthur Dimmesdale. It didn't seem worth it, unless I was missing something.

In the afternoon I wrote letters home. I did not want Daddy or Mother to think for a single minute that they had been right about my marriage—that Billy Granger was a dull fellow, or that I wasn't tough enough to handle a honeymoon in a barracks. I did my best to paint our marriage as a madcap, romantic adventure.

> You should be very proud of me. I am learning how to sweep! At first I moved the broom frantically back and forth, but all that did was stir up a huge cloud of dust, which then settled back down and made everything dirty again. The trick is to sweep very *slowly,* gather all the dirt up into one large pile and push it out the door.
>
> When I was hanging my wash out, my next-door neighbor, a girl named Suellen Fogg, noticed that my hands were chapped and suggested I put some lard on them. What's lard, I asked, which she seemed to think was hilarious. Turns out that she grew up on a farm in the Ozarks, and lard is a kind of fat you cook out of a dead pig. She gave me a can of lard, and it looks sort of like white butter. I smeared a thick layer all over my hands, and now they are as milky and smooth as a baby's bottom. (Even though I'm not sure if a baby's bottom is milky or smooth.) When I get home, I think I will put lard in small blue jars and try to sell them at Marshall Field's for a dollar apiece as "Mrs. Granger's French Hand Pomade."
>
> Billy had a day off last week and we took a picnic to

the beach. I made sandwiches out of potted deviled ham
that Billy said were delicious. He taught me how to surf
cast, which means that you stand in the water to your
knees and cast a line into the waves. I didn't catch anything, but Billy caught a sand shark. It was an ugly beast
with jagged teeth, and I made Billy throw him back.
Billy bought me a kite at the canteen. He told me not to
let it out too far, but I let it fly higher and higher until
the string ran out and it floated across the ocean. Billy
says that it's probably drifting over the Western Front by
now, and will get mistaken for a SPAD.

Billy and I are having so much fun together. We tease
and laugh all day long.

Your loving daughter,

Mrs. William Granger

One morning as I was strolling over to the canteen, my string
bag swinging, grinding the pink dust into the milky flesh of my kid
shoes, I heard the choke of an airplane engine and the squeal of
metal on metal. Then there was the heartbeat of silence, the whis-
tle of wind, and finally the crash. I stood mesmerized at the inky
plume of smoke that rose up in the field past the landing strip, the
stink of burning rubber mixed with gasoline, the wail of distant
sirens and women shouting. Some poor woman has lost her husband, I thought. Then everything turned golden and distant, I felt
giddy with a hallucination of Billy dead. Not his body in flames, in
pieces, but me dressed all in black in the front pew of St. Stephen's
Episcopal Church, where two months before I had stood in white.
I blinked hard and knew that Billy was too sensible, too much of a
Granger, to get himself killed. And with that realization, I felt disloyal and ashamed.

Just when the novelty had started to wear off canned peas and gray laundry and sweeping, the commander issued a warning about an influenza epidemic spreading through the military camps, and urged all dependents to return home. I told Billy a little old flu didn't scare me, but he insisted I leave. "What would I do if something happened to my wife?" he said, his eyes turning moist.

Daddy wangled me a reservation in a first-class Pullman. The seats had been covered in sterile sheets, and the few passengers were required to wear surgical masks and gauze gloves. I had ridden to Florida in twilight and dawn, but now I returned at midday. The train stopped by the gingerbread cottage on the crossing. Children's clothes and a woman's petticoat flapped on a clothesline; a five-year-old Model T with rusted fenders was parked in front. The house was not squalid or sad, just ordinary. There was no reason to think that the man and woman I'd seen through the front window had been dancing to faraway music. I could see that clearly now.

13

Who's Who and Why

The first time I realized that Scott Fitzgerald had become a famous writer was in September of 1920. I remember the date because Dr. Robey's nurse had just telephoned to inform me that the results of my blood test had "confirmed the doctor's suspicions." In the slang that I used with my married women friends, the rabbit had died.

Will-Bill had not even turned one. I had told Billy I didn't want to get pregnant again soon, and he had said, "Don't worry. I'll take care of it." After that, our love-making proceeded exactly as it ever had, but I assumed, because he was six years older and had gone carousing around Paris with French aviators before the war, he was using some nonobvious but effective trick for preventing the conception of babies. Silly me.

I wanted to dash out of our apartment, hail a taxi on Lake Shore Drive, and head straight to Millie Pullman's or Elsie Sturgis's, not that either one would have offered me much sympathy. Millie had married John Pullman six months after I'd married Billy, but babies didn't seem to be in the picture. Millie wasn't interested in anything that would get in the way of her golf swing, and John had had mumps at Yale, which she said "puts a kink in the hose." Elsie had never had children and didn't much like them. "Will-Bill's cute, I guess, but I think I agree with my father. He said children were only interesting when they could read the *Tribune* and discuss it intelligently."

Besides, I couldn't run anywhere, because it was Thursday and Eileen, the nurse and cook, had the afternoon off. She'd put Will-Bill down for his nap before she left, so at least I had a few moments of peace and quiet, but I was stuck. I sank down into the puffy middle of the down sofa in the living room, crossed my arms, and gloomily surveyed every object—the peach-striped, box-pleated curtains, the silver cocktail set on the built-in bookcase, the bleak Corot landscape over the fireplace, the Meissen plates propped on the mantel. The apartment building was finished the month after we were married, and I'd persuaded Daddy to put a down payment on a three-bedroom with a maid's room. I wanted something brand spanking new, the last word. No dark moldings, heavy drapes, or dusty chandeliers for me.

When we moved in, there was a front-page article in the *Tribune* society section—"Trend-setter Mrs. William Granger Says Young Marrieds Want All Modern Conveniences." The article included photos of me turning a chrome bathtub faucet, reclining in the built-in window seat with the latest volume by a poet named Carl Sandburg (a prop provided by the photographer), putting packages in the electric dumbwaiter, even placing a teakettle on the four-burner Roper stove, not that I'd ever cooked anything more complicated than scrambled eggs and toast. I think that being photographed for that story had been the happiest moment of my married life so far.

I poured myself a glass of sherry—I was not usually an afternoon drinker, but why not?—lit a cigarette, and started to shuffle through the tidy stacks of magazines on the glass coffee table. I had subscriptions to the most popular ones—Mr. Mencken's *Smart Set, Vanity Fair, Cosmopolitan, Metropolitan Magazine*—but never had much time to do more than thumb through the fashion photographs and the soap ads. Today I was going to sit down and read something. Elsie was always talking about the latest novel, which I'd never even heard of. I told myself that just because I was married to a man who never read anything but aviation reports and I now was going to be the mother of two—*two!*—of his children, didn't mean I had to let my brain shrivel up.

Suddenly, Will-Bill started to thrash around, kicking the sides of his crib—already he was turning into a muscular giant like Billy—and making guttural noises that verged on a full-fledged cry. He could fuss for a little bit longer. I picked up the *Saturday Evening Post* and flipped back to my favorite column: "Who's Who and Why—Frivolous Facts about the Great and Near Great."

I skimmed over a few of the frivolous facts—that the famous writer had been sent off to a Catholic boarding school because he scribbled stories in the margins of his schoolbooks, that he'd written his first novel while on watch at Fort Leavenworth, that he'd papered his room with 123 rejection slips. I studied the photograph of a fair young man sitting on a stone stoop, his hands clasped around his knees, his angular face squinting into the sun. The caption read, "In three months, he wrote eight stories and sold nine: F. Scott Fitzgerald." It took me a full second to realize that this was Scott. The boy who had pestered me with dozens of letters and had embarrassed me with his talk about writing a famous novel was now a Who's Who.

I started the article at the beginning and read slowly, whispering the words, searching for any mention of myself. But no, he skipped from writing the play for the Triangle Show as a freshman to dropping out three years later to join the army. He ended the article with a flippant summary: "My first novel, *This Side of Paradise*, came out. I got married. Now I spend my time wondering how it all happened."

I remembered dimly that Elsie Sturgis had told me about *This Side of Paradise*. She didn't say who wrote it, only that it was shocking for some reason. Elsie liked to keep abreast of everything that was shocking.

Will-Bill launched into a full-force wail. As I walked down the hall to the nursery, I considered the other piece of information. Scott had gotten married. Was it a girl from St. Paul or some exotic from New York or California? Whoever she was, I was sure she was boldly beautiful and had some artistic talent like painting or writing songs. Scott would marry a heroine so he could write a book about her. And to think, he might have written a book about me, if I hadn't sent him packing.

Will-Bill was standing up, rattling the sides of his crib with his round red fists, his cries getting louder, more indignant. He was a handsome boy with a thick thatch of blond hair and noble Viking features. I felt my usual mix of maternal pride and shame that I was such a witless, incompetent mother. When he saw that it was me and not Eileen, his face fell grave, the blue eyes opening round. "It's me, Will-Bill. It's your mommy," I said, trying to sound hearty and in charge, like Eileen.

I grabbed him around his solid middle and heaved him up and over. "There you go. Oopsie daisy." I tried to swing him onto my hip but I missed—he hung on my shirt to stop the slide, his sturdy legs kicking for purchase, and started to cry again. "Please don't worry," I pleaded. "Mommy is going to take you for a walk." Then I caught a strong odor—he'd soiled his diaper. If he was just wet I might have waited, but something would have to be done about this.

I hauled him onto the changing table and undid his pants. A wave of nausea hit me, just as it had during my first pregnancy. "We're going to make you all clean," I said in a soothing voice. He fell into a nervous silence and gnawed at his knuckle. I opened a bureau drawer and tried to guess which outfit Eileen would choose. I wrestled him into corduroy pants and a sweater appliquéd with a duck, which I hoped wouldn't be too warm for the weather, and called the doorman to carry down the baby buggy, a contraption with rubber bumpers ordered from Harrods.

"Taking the baby for a bit of a stroll, Mrs. Granger?" the doorman asked, sounding more surprised than I thought was polite. He wrestled the buggy through the double glass doors onto the sidewalk, and I carefully lowered Will-Bill in. He slid sideways with a thump, his clothes skewed, his face watchful.

"Here we go, baby. This will be fun." Moving the carriage was like rolling a boulder. When I had gone on walks with the baby before, I'd always strolled gaily next to Eileen while she pushed, teasing her about being such a slowpoke. I trudged eight blocks to Kroch's bookstore on Michigan Avenue, the late afternoon sun burning my back, the sides of my bobbed hair sticking to my cheeks with sweat. I arrived at Kroch's just at closing, considered pulling the carriage up the three front steps, but decided I'd better save my strength for the haul home. I wedged the buggy against a curbstone so it wouldn't roll. "You stay here," I said to Will-Bill, peering down with a reassuring smile. I straightened out his sweater and handed him a stuffed elephant.

The salesclerk was old Miss Grant, the only person I knew who still wore a pince-nez and an oilcloth butcher's apron. Was Scott's book really scandalous, or just modern? This was my mother's bookshop, after all. "I'm looking for a new book. Just came out. The title is . . . let me think. This side of something. Hmmm." I rummaged through a tin of colored pencils on the counter.

"Paradise. By a Mr. Fitzgerald. We just got some more of them in. Can't say that I've read it, of course. Will that be all, Mrs. Granger?" When she handed me the package, I realized I'd left my purse at home.

"Could you put it on my mother's account, please?"

When I got home, I put Will-Bill in his crib with a bottle. He sucked it languorously, tugging at one sock, until his eyelids blinked heavily and closed. Eileen strictly forbade me to let Will have an afternoon bottle and nap—she said it threw off his schedule and spoiled his appetite for dinner. Well, he seemed happy, and I needed a moment to myself. I'd just have to stand up to Eileen for once.

I made myself a proper cocktail, a whiskey and soda, because it was almost five o'clock. Then I dug to the bottom of a stack of phonograph records and put on "The Wang Wang Blues." In the evening, when Billy came home from his airplane factory, he usually needed soothing music, like Caruso or Strauss waltzes. All the pounding of metal, fumes, and solvents gave him headaches. I propped myself on the window seat so I could see the sun set over the lake, the book balanced on my knees.

The story was about a boy named Amory Blaine with green eyes and handsome features, who moves to Minneapolis, goes to Princeton, and writes a musical for the Triangle Club called *Ha, Ha, Hortense.* In other words, Scott, but with a few romantic embellishments thrown in. Amory had spent his childhood in fancy hotels with tutors and butlers, was a looming six feet, was the star quarterback on the football team.

Then on page 60 came the event I'd been waiting for. Amory, now a sophomore, was back in St. Paul for Christmas. At a dance at the Minnehaha Club, he was introduced to a beautiful out-of-town guest named Isabelle Borgé.

"She paused at the top of the staircase. The sensations attributed to divers on spring-boards, leading ladies on opening nights, and lumpy, husky young men on the day of the Big Game, crowded through her." Isabelle gazed down the curved stairway, saw "two pairs of masculine feet," and wondered whether "one pair were attached to Amory Blaine," the handsome college boy who'd been coached to fall in love with her, just as she had been coached to fall in love with him. In the past month, "he had assumed the proportions of a worthy adversary." When he said something clever, she felt like a minor character had stolen the star's line, and that she must grab the lead back.

Their mating dance finally reached "a very definite stage" where they needed to slip off to a remote corner of the Minnehaha Club, away from the "lesser lights" who fluttered and chattered downstairs. She told him he had "keen" eyes and "awfully nice" hands that looked as if they played the piano. He confessed that he was "mad about" her. "Their hands touched for an instant, but neither spoke. Silences were becoming more frequent and more delicious . . . the music seemed quivering just outside."

Just as Amory was about to kiss her, Isabelle had a moment of insight. "The future vista of her life seemed an unending succession of scenes like this: under moonlight and pale starlight, and in the backs of warm limousines and in low, cosey roadsters stopped under sheltering trees—only the boy might change." Amory's "whisper blended in the music . . . they seemed to float nearer together. Her breath came faster . . . Lips half parted, she turned her head to him in the dark." At the end of the evening, they parted with a solemn handshake. Later that night, as she crept into bed, Isabelle wondered what he would say in the letter he would write that night.

Back at Princeton, Amory sat by an open window every night at eight, stared at a snapshot of Isabelle, and wrote her thirty-page letters about how much he thought about her and would never fall in love with another girl, "and so on in an eternal monotone that seemed . . . infinitely charming, infinitely new."

But Amory's romantic illusion of Isabelle didn't survive their next meeting. When he tried to hug her, she cried "Ouch!" and accused him of making a pea-size bruise on her neck with his shirt stud. After that, she showed her true colors—she curled her lip and sulked. At first I thought you were self-confident, she said; now I see that you're just conceited. And you talk about Princeton too much.

The next day, Amory sneaked away on a morning train without saying goodbye, wondering why he had wasted his affection on such a cold, shallow girl. Then he decided that she was "nothing except what he had read into her," and that knowing him will turn out to be the high point of Isabelle's life, that no one else will ever "make her think."

So, Scott had put me in a book after all.

I placed my palm over the page and stared out at the window as if I was seeing the landscape clearly for the first time. The sky was streaked with mother-of-pearl clouds, a seagull poked at a sandwich wrapper on the beach. The water was flecked with the white patches of day sailors, a dozen of them headed in every direction. On the sidewalk below, two women waited at a crossing with their dogs, an Airedale and a cocker spaniel, tugging against their leashes. At the far edge of the horizon, a barge steamed northward toward Ludington, leaving a frothy plume of wake. I felt dizzy, breathless with rapture. Rapture in its most primitive sense—as if I'd had a vision, seen my soul lift up and fly away.

I flipped back to Isabelle poised at the top of the staircase and reread the entire section again, substituting "I" for "she." I had "the social and the artistic temperaments found often in two classes, society women and actresses." "Flirt smiled" from my large brown eyes. I spoke with an "enthusiastic contralto." I could do "remarkable" things "socially with one idea": it was as if I "held it off at a distance and smiled at it" and then "played a sort of mental catch with it."

I seemed to be the model for what Scott called a P.D., "the Popular Daughter." The P.D. "becomes engaged every six months between sixteen and twenty-two, when she arranges a match" with a serious young man who considers himself her first love. A P.D.'s day is filled with "furtive excitement"—a cocktail in a hotel lobby, followed by theater, "a table at the Midnight Frolic," a three-o'clock after-dance supper in an "impossible" café. In Scott's book, my sixteen-year-old self had been fixed in amber, poised at the top of the stairs.

I pulled a sheet of writing paper and started to write a fan letter.

> Dear Scott,
>   Forgive me for being a "Romantic Egoist," but I thought I recognized myself in your wonderful new book. The meeting between Isabelle and Amory at the Minnehaha Club and the endless love letters from Amory reminded me of one Ginevra Perry and one Scott Fitzgerald when they were very young. Could it have been only five years ago!

Just the idea of writing a flirtatious letter to a man, a married man at that, made me jump to my feet and pour out another drink. My letters, ever since I'd gotten married, were so tiresome—bread-and-butter notes, accounts of the baby to Aunt Minnie in Galena. I considered the next paragraph.

> A few of your predictions for this "Popular Daughter" did not come true, I'm afraid. I did not become engaged every six months between sixteen and twenty-two. Nor

was my life an unending succession of moonlit nights in
the backs of warm limousines.

Do you remember the aviator we met at the McCormicks' party?

The image hit me with such force that I set down my pen. A girl
with a tangle of dark hair and a garish red sarong, with Billy
Granger sitting ramrod straight on one side, and Scott Fitzgerald
slumping drunkenly on the other. One man I thought was mesmer-
izing, the other I thought was merely irritating.

I married Billy Granger a year and a half later, a day
before he was due back at the naval aviation station in
Key West. We live in a cunning new apartment on Lake
Shore Drive, and have a baby boy.

If you're ever in Chicago, please come for dinner. I
would love for you to get to know Billy. He's still crazy
about airplanes, and now he's started his very own airplane factory.

I stopped, wondering if a cozy dinner with Scott and Billy was
such a good idea. Being married to an aviation pioneer sounded a
lot more thrilling than it really was. Granger Aviation was really
only a Quonset hut near Ashburn Field with some salvaged airplanes where Billy and a metallurgist from the University of
Chicago were trying to invent an aluminum alloy skin for long-distance airplanes. Every couple of months, we would gather on the
airstrip at dawn and watch a "test flight." Billy would take off in a
stripped-down Jenny covered in patches of corrugated Duralumin
and loop around the field for a couple of minutes while Dr. Furst
measured its speed and lift with various gadgets. On weekends,

Billy was usually too tuckered out to do much more than play a few holes of golf with John and Millie, followed by a steak sandwich at the club grill.

I imagined him trying to make Scott understand the potential significance of Granger Patent Duralumin Panels. "Metal-sheathed airplanes are the future, and Duralumin is both strong and light. But you see, Scott, it has two problems. It bends with compression, and it can melt from the heat of the engine. Our patented process adds both corrugation for rigidity and extra magnesium for heat resistance. That's the ticket." At this point, Scott would check his watch and say that he better make it an early evening because he was catching the morning express.

Maybe I could suggest a quiet hotel luncheon instead. But by then I'd have a huge belly—I imagined Scott's elegant face falling as I waddled up to his table in a balloon dress. Better not include anything about my life now; leave that part to his imagination. Maybe it would be safer, less disappointing not to write a letter at all.

When Eileen came home an hour later, the sunset had faded to a single rosy thread. She pulled off a green felt hat and untwined the challis scarf from Liberty's I'd passed along because it had moth holes. "Where's the baby?" There was suppressed alarm in her voice.

"He's having a nap," I said, trying not to sound intimidated. "He was so tired after our walk that I put him down with a bottle."

"But what about his supper?"

That's right. Eileen had left a dish of minced beef, mashed potato, and puréed carrots to warm up. Forgot about that. "He was waiting for you."

14

Stork Scissors

The next day, after Bill had left in his grease-stained tweed jacket for the airplane shed and Eileen had taken Will-Bill for her morning get-together with the other Irish nurses in Grant Park, I slipped *This Side of Paradise* out from underneath the window-seat cushion and nestled down to savor the rest. But Isabelle did not reappear, not even to say she'd changed her mind and was really in love with the sensitive boy who "wrote stuff" after all.

Amory had loved several girls after Isabelle. There was Rosalind, the messy debutante who made swan dives into the shallow end of swimming pools. There was Eleanor Savage, who railed against being a female and not being able to play around with any boy she wanted without "sentiment." She wrote Amory poems with brazen lines like "That was the day . . . . and the night for another story." In the last four years, while I had done nothing but pursue and marry Billy Granger, decorate an apartment, play golf, and get pregnant twice, Scott had had a whole novel's worth of gropings with fearless women.

I shut the book and set it carefully on the bookshelf next

to the silver cocktail shaker, then rummaged around in Eileen's bureau until I found her mending basket. With a pair of tiny scissors shaped like a stork, I cut "Who Was Who—And Why" from the *Saturday Evening Post*. Then I slit pages 57 through 94 out of *This Side of Paradise,* and stitched the loose sheets together with the unbleached thread Eileen used for mending. I carried my little bundle around the apartment searching for a safe place to hide it—a sanctuary. Finally, I slipped it in a chintz-covered accordion folder Mrs. Turner had made me for—God help me—recipes.

A few days later, I was at Madame Jacqueline's Beauty Shop for my weekly attempt to get my hair tamed. I had had my hair bobbed a month after the Armistice along with every other American woman under the age of thirty. While the fine, limp hair of the average female sprang into fluffy curls that showed off a well-shaped head, my thick hair whacked hung like two horsetails. "Ginevra's started a new fashion," said Elsie Sturgis, "the barnyard bob."

Once a week, Jackie (who was "French" via Fond du Lac, Wisconsin) slathered my hair with lanolin so it would bend, wrapped it around tin curlers, and stuck me in a rear alcove next to an electric coil heater. Usually I occupied myself with the *Tribune*'s daily crossword, but today I focused in on a yellowed, waterlogged stack of *Saturday Evening Post*s wedged in under the shampoo sink. I started flipping through them, one after the other, past articles on the League of Nations, stories by Booth Tarkington and Zane Grey, flower garden poems by ladies with three names, and a recipe for a new Volstead Act concoction made with ice cream called a sundae.

When I got back to the May issues, I hit pay dirt—two stories by Scott, and I skimmed them for a glimmer of me. The first one, "The Ice Palace," was about a lazy Georgia belle who visits her fiancé's family in St. Paul, nearly freezes to death in an Ice Palace during a winter carnival, and flees back to the languid South. Sally

Carrol was clearly based on some other girl, maybe the girl whom Scott had ended up marrying. The only thing we had in common was a horrified reaction to the doilies and gewgaws of a St. Paul sitting room.

But in the second story, "Bernice Bobs Her Hair," I once again got a head-spinning jolt of recognition. Not in the boring Bernice visiting from Eau Claire, who gets her hair bobbed at a barber. The character I identified with was Marjorie Harvey, the mean cousin, who manipulates Bernice into getting her hair bobbed. Marjorie treats Bernice, the unwanted houseguest, the way I treated Scott in Lake Forest. She criticizes Bernice's hick clothes, deserts her at parties, and tells her, "I suppose if you're not having a good time you'd better go. No use being miserable."

Jackie came in to check my wave and surveyed the dunes of magazines strewn around my feet. "Can I help you find something, Mrs. Granger?"

"I was looking for an article. Do you think I could take this home?"

"Take 'em all, for all I care." She dropped to her knees, which gave a reproachful crack, and started scooping them up.

I cut out "Bernice Bobs Her Hair" with a pair of Jackie's shears, folded it into my purse, and that night slipped it in the recipe folder with Isabelle Borgé and "Who's Who."

And so began my secret hobby of following the comings and goings of myself in the writings of F. Scott Fitzgerald. When the mail was pushed through the slot at 10:15 every morning, I set upon it, yanked out the latest issue of *Saturday Evening Post* or *The Smart Set,* then shut myself in the bedroom and sat at my desk with the stork scissors poised. I licked my index finger so it would stick to the glossy page.

Every month or two, after dozens of magazines and hundreds of pages, I'd unearth a nugget about Scott. A book ad, for example, with a brooding author photograph and a caption that read like the inscription on a bust—"The Novelist of the Rising Genera- tion." Snip, snip, and into the recipe folder. As with any bad habit, I didn't want to think too much about why I did it. I only knew that finding myself in a clipping gave me a forbidden thrill, as if I were leading a secret life. I was sixteen again, poised at the top of the staircase, looking down at a dozen male feet. All I had to do was choose the pair I wanted.

A month later I was in Elsie Sturgis's apartment. She had sum- moned me on the telephone. "I need a confidante," she said, her voice on the verge of tears. We sat side by side in a love seat in a bay window in her bedroom. Her tall figure was bent over, her face in her hands, and I noticed the gray strands peppering the bottom layer of her shingled hair. The couch was covered in chintz pat- terned with green parrots in bamboo birdcages, faded on the tops of the tufted arms where the sun hit. The coffee table had three overflowing ashtrays and two white rings where glasses had been left. The single bed had newel posts that were carved to look like swans' heads; a mauve satin comforter puddled on the floor.

"Jack is suing me for divorce," she said, straightening. She was wearing her usual "at home" outfit—men's silk pajamas and men's leather slippers.

"Oh, dear," I said. "I'm so sorry." I patted her hand, which had brown spots on the back and chipped nail varnish. I hadn't seen Jack Sturgis in months, come to think of it—Elsie was always out and about by herself. This was the first couple I knew who were actually divorcing, and I felt shocked.

They were a curious couple, to be sure—she older, taller, more masculine than he was—and they didn't have children. But most of the couples I knew were oddly matched in some way. Millie and John Pullman, for example—she was athletic and outgoing, he was shy and bookish. Or Horace and Constance—he was debonair and she was dowdy. Or Billy and me. That didn't mean any of us would consider getting a divorce.

I searched for what to say next—the "why" of it didn't seem like any of my business. "Has he moved out?"

"He's been living at the Saddle and Cycle Club for six months, in one of the back bedrooms where the grooms used to sleep. I thought everyone knew," she said with some of her old spunk.

"So your life won't change so much?" I asked hopefully.

"Oh, my, yes. Jack's horrible lawyer says I'll have to move into some little three-bedroom by the stockyards. And I can't keep Lois on my alimony, not that she ever does anything but take nips from the Seagram's. I'll have to settle for a colored girl one morning a week, and give up the Casino Club. I might even have to get a job."

"A job? Doing what?" A friend of my mother's had been forced to get a job after her divorce, fitting brassieres at Field's. Whenever we ran into her in the fitting room with a measuring tape draped over her shoulder and a pincushion hooked on her belt, Mother's eyes would fill.

"I was thinking of trying to be a teacher at Miss Pratt's. I graduated from college, you know. Bryn Mawr. Even won a Latin prize."

I had an image of Elsie turned out in snappy suits bought on sale from Carson Pirie's which she rotated every third day, and good shoes resoled once a year, and an apartment furnished with castoffs that she'd had cleverly slipcovered in an outré fabric with black squiggles and squares. For a while, we'd get together for matinees every two weeks and dinners when Billy was out of town. Then the visits would dwindle to lunch at the Women's Exchange at Christmastime so we could exchange gifts.

"I'm so sorry," I said again, feeling useless.

"Don't you go getting a divorce, even if you think Billy's a stick-in-the-mud. Not unless you have husband number two all lined up with a license and a ring." Elsie jumped to her feet. "Let's not be so glum." She came back with two sherries in smudged glasses, dropped the Victrola needle on "Chin-Chin," started flipping through the latest *Collier's*. "Maybe this is my problem," she said, pointing to an ad for Ban-or.

This was better—discussing the promises made in ads. I picked up a *Hearst's* that was jammed between the couch cushions. "'Do you have halitosis? Even your best friend won't tell you.'"

"How about piano lessons?" She held up a drawing of a shy young man pulling up a piano stool in front of a sea of jeering faces with the caption "They laughed when I sat down—Until I started to play!"

I stopped at a fuzzy-focus photograph of a dazzling couple posed as movie stars. The woman's perfect, careless face was framed by marcelled waves, her unsmiling eyes were fixed hard on a spot in the distance, a strand of pearls hung askew across a deep neckline. The man leaned toward the camera with a lordly air, his chin tipped down so the light hit the fine planes of his cheek and brow. His fingers rested on the velvet and ermine of his wife's lap. I tossed the picture to Elsie. "She's beautiful, don't you think?"

Elsie held the photograph up to the window so she could read the caption. "'Mrs. F. Scott Fitzgerald started the flapper movement in this country. So says her husband, the best-loved author of the younger generation.'" She studied it for a few seconds more. I considered confessing that he was my old boyfriend, someone I could have married instead of Billy. "She's got a strange squint, like she's planning to put a hatchet through his skull," Elsie observed. "And he's a fairy."

"But he's married."

She answered with a sphinxlike smile.

"How can you tell?"

"You just can, doll face."

Five months later, I landed on the maternity ward of Rush Hospital after I started to hemorrhage. The baby, a boy, was born five weeks early. "You needed emergency surgery to stop the bleeding," Dr. Robey told me, refusing to meet my eyes. "I'm afraid it's unlikely you'll be able to have more children. But this one will pull through if we can fatten him up."

The nurse brought the baby into me—a scrawny bundle wailing so hard his skin had turned an angry red. A tuft of pitch-black hair poked up on top of his head like an exclamation point. "He won't have anything to do with a bottle. Could you give him the breast, Mrs. Granger?"

"I'll try," I said, sounding dubious. I'd attempted to nurse Will-Bill, who'd clamped on and sucked away for a few minutes, then shrieked for a bottle. The nurse set the baby in my arms, unbuttoned my nightgown, pulled out a swollen breast that seemed to belong to someone else, and plugged the baby's mouth with a hard purple nipple. A moment of silence while he inhaled, then he broke free and spluttered with rage.

"I don't know why he's so cross," the nurse said.

I did. He knew what his mommy had been thinking when she was pregnant—all those bad, dark thoughts. That's why he'd made his escape early, a suicide's leap. She was such a bad mother that now she couldn't have any more children.

"Let me try again," I said. He gave a few feeble pulls, then nestled his head against my breast like it was a big pillow and slept. Don't worry, Mommy will be much nicer, I promise. I tried to smooth the spiky hair, but it sprang up—runaway black hair, just like mine.

"It worked," the nurse said, sounding surprised. "If he wakes up, try to feed him again. We need to get some meat on his bones." She cranked the bed up, propped some pillows behind me, and deposited a stack of magazines on the bedside table.

While the baby slept, I flipped through them on my old search, and there, in *Metropolitan Magazine,* was a snippet from Scott's brand-new novel, called the *Beautiful and the Damned.* The story was about another one of Scott's disagreeable society girls, this one named Gloria Gilbert, who was married to an equally spoiled man named Anthony. In the middle of a weepy fight, Anthony and Gloria start to discuss what kind of baby they will have.

"There are . . . two distinct and logical babies, utterly differentiated," Anthony says. "There's the baby that's the combination of the best of both of us . . . and then there is the baby which is our worst —my body, your disposition, and my irresolution."

"I like that second baby," Gloria says.

Maybe it was my postpartum wooze, but I felt as if Scott had planted a secret message in the story for me to find. The baby slept on, my nightgown button imprinted on his cheek; his fist had wrapped around my pinkie. Will-Bill was all Billy—sturdy, cheerful. But this one seemed to have my small bones and moody nature, and I knew I liked the second baby best.

Billy wanted to name him Gerald after his father, but I wanted something more modern. How about Avery, I suggested, Mother's maiden name. Sort of like Amory Blaine.

"Who's Amory Blaine?" asked Billy.

15

House Party

It was the annual house party at the Armours' twenty-room cottage perched on a bluff over Lake Charlevoix. Three couples had been coming for six straight years now—the Horace Armours, the William Grangers, and the John Pullmans.

Billy and Horace had organized the first house party back in 1919 when they were fresh back from the war. We'd always been an uneasy group, but now we seemed to rub against each other like wool on sunburned skin. Horace, who'd made a fortune speculating in steel stocks, was nervous that Billy would ask him to invest in Granger Panels, an idea that was clearly going nowhere. Constance thought Millie spent too much time gallivanting off to Santa Barbara and Hot Springs while John stayed in their dusty apartment making bachelor suppers of scrambled eggs and toast. I thought the Armour boys, Nicky and Bert, bullied five-year-old Avery, and Constance thought Avery was a crybaby.

Every day we followed the same routine. In the mornings, the children practiced their swimming strokes off the dock under the barely watchful eye of the Armours' nanny. Horace took the adults for a spin around the lake in his new high-speed runabout while we sipped watered-down old-fashioneds from a thermos and tried to recover from our hangovers. Then the couples were divided into three teams for competitive games—Millie and Horace, Constance and Billy, and John and me. After lunch we played eighteen holes of golf, which Horace and Millie always won. After dinner we'd play bridge, which Billy and Constance always won. John and I weren't bothered that we never won at anything, which is probably why we were paired off in the first place.

Now it was after dinner, and the adults had gathered in the vaulted great room for bridge. The children had been banished with the nanny to the boathouse, which had a Ping-Pong table and a dartboard. The day had been stifling for northern Michigan, but now a frigid drizzle drummed on the cedar roof. John Pullman, always a considerate houseguest, pounded at the warped windows until they finally shut. He jammed balls of yellowed newspaper and birch twigs under a pile of ancient spruce logs in the two-story stone fireplace, then lit off the pile so it sparked and sizzled like a Roman candle on the Fourth of July.

Constance had unfolded the bridge table in the far corner, snapped on a green felt cover, and set out monogrammed bridge pads, pencils, and coasters. I curled up on a sagging leather couch by the fire and shivered. Even though everyone else was still in the knickers and vests they'd worn golfing, I'd dressed for dinner in a silk dress I'd just bought in the latest color, called seafoam, with scarabs embroidered on the kimono sleeves. I opened a bag from Kroch's bookstore and pulled out Scott's latest novel, *The Great Gatsby.* I'd raced through it the day before, but now I wanted to parse it out slowly, word by word. *Her face was sad and lovely with bright things in it, bright eyes and a passionate mouth, but there was an ex-*

citement in her voice that men who had cared for her found difficult to forget: a singing compulsion, a whispered "Listen," a promise that she had done gay, exciting things just a while since and that there were gay, exciting things hovering in the next hour.

"That's four spades for us," said Constance, jotting figures on her pad. "One hundred sixty points for us. We're one game from rubber."

"Club," said Billy, sounding cocky. Billy still had the lean build of the young aviator I'd married, but the military mustache was long gone and the dark hair was starting to thin.

"Pass."

"Three clubs," Constance answered in a blasé tone, which meant she was sitting on a powerhouse.

"Three no trump, I guess," said Millie, who had a hard time paying attention when she wasn't playing golf. One muscular calf was slung over the other, and her foot jiggled . . . . *there was a jauntiness about her movement as if she'd learned to walk upon golf courses on clean, crisp mornings.*

"That's ridiculous. You can't have a thing," Constance scoffed. "All right. Your funeral. Pass."

"Here you go, partner," said Horace, laying down his hand. "Four points." He tilted back in his chair, lit a cigarette, then gave me an appraising glance. "That's a smart dress, Ginevra. You should take Constance shopping sometime. She could use some sprucing up." Making a pile of money had changed him. *Now he was a sturdy straw-haired man of thirty with a rather hard mouth and supercilious manner.*

Constance adjusted her cardigan over her matronly chest. "Why would I want to spruce up? The boys would just put their sticky fingers on me, and you'd never notice anyway." Her voice was brittle—everyone knew that Horace kept a girl in town.

"Well, I think you look just fine," said Billy gallantly. "Of course,

I never dress up myself. At work, I'm always up to my elbows in monkey grease and solder." Billy never missed a chance to mention his airplane factory.

"How's it all going with that metal stuff? What's it called?" Constance asked, shuffling the cards.

"Granger Patent Duralumin Panels. We're putting the finishing touches on our first prototype. You and Horace should drop by some afternoon."

"We'll do that. Horace is always looking for the next Firestone and Pittsburgh Steel. Aren't you, dear?" She set the deck in front of Horace and rapped it once with her knuckles, hard. "Your deal."

Horace flipped the cards around as if he were tossing daggers.

"You shouldn't be reading in such poor light, Ginevra," said Constance. "That's how Charlotte Brontë ruined her eyesight, you know."

"I'm fine."

"What is that book you find so fascinating?"

"It's a novel by F. Scott Fitzgerald," I said. I'd never told Billy that the drunken boy who had insulted him at Constance and Horace's engagement party had turned into a famous writer. Not that he or anyone else would have been interested.

"Are we supposed to have heard of him?" Horace asked, who was suspicious of anything popular with the masses.

"Maybe," I said vaguely. "He's quite à la mode."

"I think that cover is very disturbing, with those big eyes staring at you. You would be better off sticking to the classics. There's a compete set of Trollope in my bedroom. Have you read *Barchester Towers?*"

"I'll read it next."

John dropped down at the end of the sofa, perched an amber glass ashtray on his knee, and opened a volume in tattered red cloth.

"I stick with the classics myself," he said, holding it up so I could read the spine—Cicero's *Letters.*

There was a scratching like a mouse scrabbling across the floor, and I glanced up to see Avery standing in front of me. His dark hair and wool shirt were soaked through, giving him a drowning muskrat look, and he was panting, as if he'd just sprinted up a hill.

I lowered my book. "How'd you get so wet?" I wrapped my blanket around his shoulders and steered him toward the fire.

"Nicky and Bert locked me out of the boathouse." He grasped a box of pick-up sticks in his dead-white hands. "Will you play a game with me?"

"I'm sure Nicky and Bert didn't really lock you out," Constance said. "You go back and tell them that Mother says they should be nice to you."

"Come on, Avery. I'll play a game with you," John said, shutting his book, and sitting cross-legged on the stone hearth. "What have you got there?"

"Pick-up sticks."

"Ah, yes. You lever the sticks off so they don't make the others move. Is that the gist?" he asked gravely.

"Right," said Avery, letting the sticks fall with a clatter. "I'll start."

"I hope you'll try to go swimming tomorrow, Avery," Constance said. "A little cold water never hurt anyone. I think your father needs to throw you in from the end of the dock."

"Oh, that won't be necessary. You'll jump in, won't you, Avery?" Billy said, trying hard to sound jolly. He didn't like to admit that Avery wasn't like all the other children.

"No," Avery said in a small but mulish voice. His knee jerked, which made the pile of sticks topple sideways.

"Don't worry, Avery," John said in a soothing tone. "No one's going to throw you off the dock."

"What's that book about, anyway?" Constance said, trying to recover her dignity.

I closed it around my thumb and dropped it into my lap. "It's about a girl named Daisy Buchanan, who is lovely and beguiling. During the war a poor boy named Gatsby falls in love with her, but gets shipped off to England before he can propose. When he gets back, it's too late. She's married a rich man named Tom Buchanan, who's from Lake Forest and has polo ponies."

"Never heard of him," Horace said.

"It's a novel," John said. "It's not about real people."

"Well, there is one character who's a little like someone we know—a famous lady golfer who's Daisy's best friend."

Millie perked up. "Actually sounds like a book I might want to read."

"Well, not really. The woman cheats in a tournament by kicking her ball out of a bad lie."

Millie shook her head so her bobbed hair fanned out into a halo. "I'd never do that. I wouldn't need to."

"Anyway," I continued, "Daisy and Tom live in a mansion on Long Island, and Gatsby moves into a house on the other side of the bay so he can stare at the green light on the end of Daisy's dock. It turns out that Gatsby has been plotting all along on how he can win Daisy back. He's made a fortune and throws big parties so Daisy will drop by. And Daisy is all ready to fall in love with Gatsby again, because her husband is unpleasant and has a mistress."

At the word "mistress," Constance frowned at her bridge pad.

"But then Daisy accidentally runs over the mistress with Gatsby's car and kills her. Gatsby takes the blame, but then the mistress's husband shoots Gatsby, and nobody comes to his funeral. That's the end of the book." *She vanished into her rich house, into her rich, full life, leaving Gatsby—nothing.*

As usually happens, summarizing the plot only made the book sound ridiculous. And if I'd described the beautiful parts—Gatsby's pile of fancy shirts and his resolves written in the back of *Hopalong Cassidy*—they'd come off as trivial. *Bathe every other day. Read one improving book or magazine a week . . . . Be better to parents.*

"I only like books about nice people," Constance said.

"I can understand thinking about a girl you once loved for years and years," said John.

"Stop being pathetic, John," said Millie. "John's had a mad crush on Ginevra ever since they were at the Bell School," she explained to the bridge table.

"I'm not being pathetic. I'm being polite about Ginevra's book." *There must have been moments even that afternoon when Daisy tumbled short of his dreams—not through her own fault, but through the colossal vitality of his illusion.*

"I think it sounds very depressing," Constance concluded. "You really should read *Barchester Towers*."

16

The Professor

In the summer of 1926 we decided to skip the Armours' annual house party. Billy said he was too busy to get away. The prototype plane covered in a shiny pelt of Granger Patent Duralumin would make its maiden flight at Le Bourget on September 1 in front of whirring newsreel cameras. Billy bought Will-Bill a set of miniature tools so he could spend a day at the factory "helping." The factory ran double shifts. When I called, Billy answered by bellowing, "Who is this? Could you speak up?" over the buzz of electric drills and metallic thunks of hammers.

Mother insisted that I spend July out in Lake Forest. "Mary Paula will watch the children. You can sleep late in your old bedroom, just like before you were married. Billy can come on the weekends. Besides, I need your help."

"With what?"

"It's your sister," she said grimly. "I'll explain when you get here."

The boys and I took an afternoon train out to Lake Forest, and by the cocktail hour I was sitting on the terrace with a nice tumbler of Daddy's bootleg bourbon while

Mary Paula, the cook who had replaced Mrs. Coates, tried to coax Avery to take a bite of a lamb chop and climb into the bath. Mother sat opposite me with a pile of Evvie's weekly letters. "So, what about Evvie?" I said, taking a long sip.

"Starting last November, every letter contains a reference to this Eliot Schumacher." She slipped on her glasses, unfolded the gray deckled sheets one after another, and read excerpts in a troubled tone. "'A graduate student at Harvard named Eliot Schumacher took me to tea at the Gardner Museum on Sunday which was very pleasant.' And this. 'Saw Ben Hur with my friend Eliot at the Park Square Theater.' And then this. 'Eliot's mother has been visiting from Grand Island, Nebraska. We took her to the Boston Symphony to hear Brahms 2nd and I think she enjoyed herself.' Well, after that I wrote Evvie and asked her about the background of this Eliot."

"And . . . ?"

"His parents are German emigrants who don't speak any English. His father was a lineman for the Union Pacific until he died of TB, which Evvie seems to think is romantic. Now his mother runs a boarding house for railroad workers. He's a scholarship boy at Harvard and what do you suppose he's studying?"

I shrugged.

"German literature, so he can be a professor, probably at some Lutheran college back on the prairie."

"Really, Mother. What's wrong with being a professor? You make him sound like a con man."

"I'm sure he's coming out to announce they're engaged. He's figured out she's got money. I want you have a heart-to-heart sisterly chat, help set her straight."

"I'm not sure I'm the person to set anyone straight," I said mildly, refilling my glass. Mother seemed to have forgotten that Billy had sunk most of my money into Granger Aviation. "And besides, I don't think Evvie needs advice on how to live her life from me or anyone else. She seems to be doing just fine without our help."

Evvie was still the directed, purposeful girl she'd been at eleven. Unlike her dumbbell sister, who hadn't bothered to finish high school, she'd graduated from Wellesley and was now going to library school at Simmons. Who did Mother think would make a better match than Eliot Schumacher—some witless society boy like Bobby Poole, who was still setting up Civil War battles with his lead soldiers at the age of thirty-one?

Eliot and Evvie arrived the next day on the eleven o'clock train. Even though she'd developed an attractive figure, Evvie dressed in the style of a Boston bluestocking—a gabardine suit in a sensible navy blue, a tiny string of cultured pearls she'd gotten when she was confirmed at thirteen, and a shapeless cloche hat that looked as if she'd knitted it herself. Eliot was dressed in a similarly careless fashion—a wrinkled seersucker jacket, crooked bow tie, and slightly flattened straw boater. He blinked up at the statues and topiaries through thick glasses and patted a piece of flyaway sandy hair down on top of his already balding pate. "My, my," he said in a voice as flat as a Dakota wheat field. "The Villa d'Este."

"Oh, no, Mr. Schumacher," Mother explained. "This is not a real Tuscan villa. You will only find those in Tuscany, which is in Italy. This is a reproduction."

"You don't say, Mrs. Perry. Right here in Illinois. Will wonders never cease."

Over lunch, Eliot presented my mother with a thick volume bound in brown cloth. "*The Magic Mountain,* by Thomas Mann," my mother read nervously. Her tastes tended toward Westerns, such as Zane Grey's and *The Virginian.*

"It's by a German writer whom I admire a good deal."

"That's what you are studying, of course. I hope it's not in German, because I don't know German, although I probably should. It's very long, I see. What's it about?"

"It's set in a tuberculosis sanitarium."

My mother sucked in a breath through her small doll's lips. She had been frightened of TB ever since her cousin had developed a spot on her lung; it was said she'd been infected by an Irish chauffeur, and she'd had to spend two entire years in bed. "Oh, dear. I suppose it reminds you of your father," she said to Eliot.

Evvie's scrunched mouth told me it was time to step in. "I'm looking for a book," I said, prying it out of my mother's grip. "May I have a turn with it first?"

"Be my guest."

After lunch, I followed Evvie upstairs and sat on her bed while she unpacked. She slung her suitcase onto the rack and hung her clothes up with a petulant banging of hangers and closet doors. A drab, gray evening dress with a high neck could have belonged to a Hull House worker.

"Eliot seems very nice. Brainy too." I hadn't been in Evvie's room in years, and I glanced around at the framed academic awards and diplomas hanging over a tilt-top desk, the felt Wellesley banner over the bed, the neat row of French grammars and Dickens on the bookshelf. None of the frivolous clutter of my girlhood room.

"He is!" she exploded. "Mother's gotten it into her skull that's he's interested in my money. Eliot despises capitalism. He's the secretary of the John Reed Club at Harvard."

I wasn't sure who John Reed was, but guessed that being a member of his club probably wouldn't help Eliot's cause. "Remember they didn't approve of my engagement either."

"There was nothing wrong with the Grangers' pedigree. They just thought you were too young. This is different. They're such snobs."

True enough. Mother disapproved of Eliot for the same reasons that Daddy had disapproved of Scott Fitzgerald. "I'll try to bring Mother and Daddy around."

"Thanks, Gin." She hadn't called me that since I was about thirteen. "I didn't expect you to be so understanding." We stood side by side for a moment, then she reached over and gave me an awkward, bony hug, and I could smell her lily-of-the-valley toilet water. "Would you mind paying a little attention to Eliot? I don't want him to think my whole family is stuck-up."

"Don't worry. I'll make him feel at home."

The next day I invited Eliot to take a walk on the prairie. I led him down a stubbly path that cut through the bluestem grass, past the milkweed pods, the black-eyed Susans and Queen Anne's lace, the darting flutter of monarchs and fritillaries. We climbed down the embankment to the Skokie and settled side by side on a spongy log a few inches from the water.

"Evvie and I used to go wading here up to our waists. When we went back to the house, we'd leave muddy drips from the back door all the way to our bedrooms."

Eliot took off his jacket and rolled up his sleeves, showing off surprisingly muscular and tan arms. "It's hard for me to imagine you and Evvie doing anything that normal kids did, like mucking around in a creek."

"We weren't supposed to. Mother said there were poisonous snakes and hobo camps down here, not that I ever saw either one. She probably just didn't want us to get our clothes dirty. I had to force Evvie to come with me. She was always the good girl, and I was the bad girl who got her in trouble."

"You don't seem like a bad girl anymore," he said, glancing at my starched lawn dress that stopped a modest three inches below the knee, white stockings not rolled but fixed with garters, and linen shoes.

"I suppose not." I let out a discontented sigh. The reasons my parents thought I was bad—flirting with boys, leading Aldus Hutchinson on—all seemed so harmless now. "Evvie tells me you're secretly engaged."

"Yes. I'm a lucky man," Eliot said, with unexpected passion. "I'm crazy about her. I'm . . ." As he paused to find the right word, he slipped off his glasses and dropped them into his front-shirt pocket. Without glasses, Eliot looked more like the son of a Union Pacific lineman than I would have thought possible. "I'm besotted," he admitted with a helpless shrug.

How had Evvie, with her barber-chopped hair and drab clothes, managed to make a man besotted? I wondered if any man had ever been besotted over me. Billy probably had been in the beginning, but over the years seemed to have found the airplane factory a more enticing place than home with me. And of course Scott had been besotted back when he was nineteen, but after I'd cast him out, he'd come to his senses and moved on as well, with the dazzling flapper whose photograph turned up everywhere.

"Have you picked a wedding date?"

"The sooner the better," Eliot declared, pulling a handkerchief from his back pocket and mopping off his ardent brow.

"Since I'm going to be your future sister-in-law, I want to learn more about you," I said, kicking off my shoes. I reached under my dress, unhooked my stockings and rolled them off, dipped my toes in the murky water of the Skokie.

Maybe he was a good storyteller, or maybe I was in an attentive frame of mind, but I found the story of Eliot Schumacher intriguing. His father, Adolph, had been an educated man, a philosophy student at the University of Heidelberg, where he had met Eliot's mother, who had the romantic name Isolde. "They were radicals," Eliot said. "They believed in free love and overthrowing the kaiser."

When they heard the secret police running up the stairwell, they escaped out a window and eventually made their way to Nebraska, where Isolde had an uncle. Isolde found a job as a cook in a boarding house for railway workers, and Adolph worked as a lineman. "Papa had to trudge along the tracks in winter and chip ice off the switches. He'd always been sickly, and the winter I was born he developed a cough. I still remember the red spots on his handkerchief. Five winters later, he hemorrhaged and died. Mama slaved away until she'd saved enough to buy the boarding house and send me to the best university in America."

"My life seems so boring compared to yours," I said.

"If having an exciting life means having your father die at age twenty-nine and your mother having to do other people's laundry, then I guess I'd settle for boring."

"Oh, Lordy. That came out all wrong. I just mean my life has been so easy. I've never suffered, never had to work for anything."

"Consider yourself lucky."

"I do," I said, even though at that moment Evvie seemed like the lucky one, not me.

We straggled back to the house, damp and disheveled, and found my parents and Evvie assembled on the terrace for the cocktail hour. Evvie squinted, as if the western sun was hurting her eyes, or as if she was having second thoughts about having asked her sister to be hospitable.

"What can I get you, Mr. Schumacher?" Daddy asked, his hands poised over a tray of the finest Canadian liquor that could be found south of the border.

"I'm not much of a drinker, sir. A beer, I suppose." Eliot rolled down his sleeves, put his glasses back on, and resumed the professor role.

My father tilted his head back and roared, an imperious rich man's laugh. "Sorry, Mr. Schumacher, we don't have beer here. I'm afraid you'd have to go to Milwaukee for that. How about a whiskey and soda."

Eliot took a cautious sip. "Very refreshing, sir," he said affably.

Billy rolled in with a shower of gravel and a slam of the front door just as we were sitting down to supper. His shirt was clean and his hands scrubbed, but he still reeked of gas fumes and glue. "Sorry I'm late. They were bolting the wings. I personally inspect every single bolt as it goes in. If it's not sunk flat, it causes wind re-sistance," he explained. He looked haggard — the Paris Air Show would be the last chance for Granger panels to hit it big.

During dinner, Billy tried in his flat-footed way to be interested in Eliot. "I don't suppose German professors earn very much, do they," he observed. He pushed a piece of prime rib through a puddle of gravy and chewed it on his back molars. Billy always had a hearty appetite after a day at the factory.

"It depends what you're comparing a professor's salary to," Eliot said, with another affable smile. "Compared to a factory worker in, say, one of the Chicago meat-packing plants, or a mail clerk at Sears and Roebuck, a professor earns a good deal. Compared to a businessman, I suppose it would depend on what economic sector. May I ask what your line of business is, Mr. Granger?"

"Please, call me Bill. I am the president of a small aviation company."

"Does the president of an aviation company earn a great deal?" Eliot asked in a mild way.

"I don't earn a salary in the conventional sense."

"So you earn an unconventional salary?" Eliot assumed a con-fused expression. Evvie had told me he'd been the Nebraska debate champ.

"I don't earn any salary at the moment. We're developing a

patented Duralumin airplane skin that has the advantages of being both strong and lightweight." His hands moved as if they were stretching a piece of putty. "We are planning to demonstrate the prototype before the Paris Air Show in December. So with luck, we'll get some orders from Boeing and Junkers for their long-distance airplanes. Mark my word—when the first plane flies across the Atlantic, it will be covered with Granger patented panels."

"There must be other companies trying to develop competing products."

"That's not likely to happen. We have our test flight in two months." I thought Billy's bravura rang a little false. He probably didn't want to admit that there was any possibility for failure in front of my father, his major investor.

Daddy continued Eliot's interrogation. "So when you become a German teacher, I suppose you'll teach Goethe. I read Goethe in fifth form."

"I am planning to concentrate on modern literature."

"Modern literature. That sounds like an oxymoron." The definition of "oxymoron" was something else Daddy had learned in fifth form.

"Many critics feel that the way we will best understand the advances of the new century is through the arts. Novels about social change by writers such as Theodore Dreiser, Sinclair Lewis, Willa Cather . . ." Eliot floundered, glancing around at a sea of blank faces.

"F. Scott Fitzgerald," I offered.

"Good example—*The Great Gatsby.*" Eliot gave me a grateful nod.

"He's an old friend of mine," I explained. "He actually sat at this very table. Mother, you remember Scottie from St. Paul. Very blond, almost pretty?"

Mother shook her head firmly. "I'm certain there's never been a writer in this house."

"I remember him," Evvie said, shooting me the same reproachful glare she'd used ten years ago. "He wrote Ginevra stacks of adoring letters, followed her around like a puppy, and she tossed him out without a thought. I'm glad he's succeeded. It was obvious he was going to make something of himself, at least it was obvious to me. I'm surprised you read his books, Ginevra. I wouldn't think you'd be interested."

"Even I can change, Evvie. And admit I misjudged someone."

During my next walk with Eliot down by the creek, I couldn't resist bringing up the subject again. "You probably were surprised that I used to know F. Scott Fitzgerald."

"A little," he said, not sounding impressed. He plucked the petals off a black-eyed Susan and flicked them in the water, where they floated like tiny yellow canoes. "I read an article a couple of years ago that said he'd moved to Paris. All the great writers are moving to Paris. He has a very exotic-sounding wife named Zelda."

The woman with the face of an Indian princess and the latest style of bobbed hair. "During my junior year at Westover, he wrote me almost every day."

"Really," Eliot said, giving me a reappraising glance, which compared me no doubt to the beautiful Zelda. "Do you have any of his letters here? I'd love to have a look, if you don't mind."

I was afraid I would lose my newfound status with Eliot if I admitted I'd tossed Scott's letters out by the dozens. "They got packed away when I got married. Evvie's right. I treated him shabbily. This may sound conceited, but I think he considered me his first love. Have you read *This Side of Paradise?*"

"It's required reading for all college freshmen."

"Do you remember the scene where Amory meets Isabelle at the Minnehaha?" He nodded, although he still looked unconvinced.

"Well, Scott's describing the first time he saw me at a country club party in St. Paul's."

"Right. A 'speed' who's been kissed."

I dropped my head down in mock shame, and in doing so managed to brush my shoulders against his. "I told you I was bad."

He gave an uncomfortable smile, then stood to pitch the bare stalk of the black-eyed Susan into the stream before resettling on the ground a good two feet away from me.

"So you're F. Scott Fitzgerald's muse. Did he model any other characters after you?"

"A few, I think. I even keep a file of his stories back in Chicago. They flatter my ego." Why was I admitting this to him? "Please don't tell Evvie. It makes me sound so silly."

"Are you Daisy Buchanan?" His voice was intrigued, the way it had been when he talked about the modern novel, even though he still kept his distance.

"I'm not sure I want to be the model for such an awful woman. But yes, the way Daisy is so careless and takes Gatsby's affection for granted, maybe that's the way I used to be. And the way that Gatsby idealizes Daisy into something she's not, that's Scott."

The sun was slanting low in the bluestem, and Eliot cast an impatient glance up the embankment toward the house. "We should head back. Your father's probably setting out the hooch."

I didn't want our conversation to end, didn't want to give Eliot back to my sister. I am ashamed to say that I lunged over and wrapped both hands tightly around his thick upper arm. "You should write a novel," I whispered, bringing my face closer. "You tell such wonderful stories."

In one graceful, catlike movement, Eliot stood and detached himself, leaving my arms hanging in midair as if I were praying to the Virgin Mary. He busied himself polishing his glasses, rolling down his shirtsleeves, brushing off his pants. "I don't think I'd be much of a novelist. I'd better stick to teaching."

I jumped to my feet, straightened my hair and my stockings—

trying to act as if nothing had happened, as if I had not just made a grab for my sister's fiancé.

Suddenly Eliot stopped and crossed his arms in front of him with feet planted—like a teacher standing at the blackboard. "You know, Ginevra, this is probably none of my business, but since you're going to be my sister-in-law, here goes. You don't seem very . . . fulfilled. There's more to life than rereading stories an old boyfriend wrote about you. You're still a very attractive woman who has a great deal to offer."

I met his eyes, and hoped he didn't notice the mortified flush across my cheeks.

"How do you think I should go about becoming fulfilled?" I wasn't sure if he was suggesting I volunteer for the Salvation Army or find a lover.

"I don't want to sound like a Laura Jean Libbey, but why don't you try to find pleasure in the life you've got rather than the life you haven't?"

"And how do I do that, Professor?"

Eliot shrugged. "I'm sorry. That's something you're going to have to figure out for yourself. One more thing I should mention." His voice was carefully nonchalant. "Evvie and I have been lovers for about six months. I hope that doesn't shock you."

That night, as Billy and I were getting ready for bed, I reached over and put a hand on his shoulder, felt the knot of muscles under his bathrobe. "Worried about the air show?"

"A little," he said, casting me a wary glance. I didn't usually show much sympathy for his troubles with Granger Aviation.

"Elsie Sturgis says the franc is worth practically nothing." Elsie had spent the winter living in style on her tiny alimony in a Left Bank apartment. "And I spoke with Mother, and she said the boys could stay here for a couple of weeks and Mary Paula's sister could come in to help. So I was wondering if you might like me to come along. Lend a little moral support."

"You'd do that?" He gave me a pathetically grateful smile. "I'll be busy getting the prototype ready. I won't be much company."

"That's all right. I can go sightseeing on my own. I'm a resourceful girl." A plan was taking shape in my head. I would wander about Paris, visit the bookshops, talk to some expatriate Americans in those Left Bank cafés they flocked to. I'd find out where Scott lived. Then one day he'd be hurrying down his street, elegantly dressed in a custom-made English suit, his handsome face lost in thought, and there I'd be. "Scott?" "Ginevra?" "What an amazing coincidence." This is what Eliot had meant about finding pleasure in my own life. No more daydreaming about Scott—I would make him real.

17

Shakespeare and Company

Six weeks later, Billy and I disembarked from the *Aquitania* with twelve crates containing the disassembled pieces of the Granger prototype airplane. Billy and the two mechanics he'd brought along headed off in a truck for Le Bourget, and I boarded a late-night train for Paris. I had booked us into the Lutetia, a Left Bank hotel Elsie Sturgis had recommended.

"Why can't we stay at the Ritz, like everyone else?" Billy had asked.

"And sip champagne cocktails at Harry's New York Bar with a bunch of bankers' wives from Peoria?" I clucked my tongue.

The next morning I pushed through the plate glass door onto the Boulevard Raspail with the vague plan that I would somehow track down Scott Fitzgerald. All I had to help me was my hardly opened Larousse from Westover and the map Elsie Sturgis had drawn on a piece of moiré stationery of "the real Paris." I unfolded the map. An ink line marked "Raspail" crossed another marked "St. Germain." The Seine was drawn with wavy lines at the top, landmarks designated with squares: Notre Dame, Palais Lux, Pantheon. Elsie had been too tipsy to remember any other names, so she had marked spots along the boulevards with X's like a pirate map. The largest X on the St. Germain was identified—"Favorite café, the 'Deux' something." I folded the map back in quarters and tucked it in my pocket, determined to find my own way.

I'd never been to Paris before. Daddy had promised he'd take me on a grand tour when I turned sixteen, but by that time the war had broken out. When the war was over, I was a married lady with a baby on the way. I hoped that I would blend into the crowd of snappy Frenchwomen. Before I'd left, I'd gone to Field's for the snazziest dress I could find—a linen sheath in a color the saleslady called "lapis lazuli." But in the hard light of the Left Bank, the color looked as garish and hopelessly American as the cornflowers in Aunt Minnie's garden. My reactions to the sights and sounds of the real Paris felt depressingly provincial. The horns of French cars went *beep beep* rather than *honk,* blood dripped from the *lapins* dangling by their hindquarters in the butcher shop window, and pooled on the sidewalk. A lean Frenchwoman slinked by in a dress the color of ashes, all asymmetry—the right side of her shingled hair three inches longer than the left, the left hem of her skirt a foot longer than the right. A three-foot strand of pottery beads swung dangerously to and fro like a mace. A veteran stood propped in a doorway with an empty pant leg and shirtsleeve pinned up, expertly rolling a cigarette with his remaining hand, a tobacco pouch dangling from his teeth.

I rounded the corner onto the Boulevard St. Germain and started searching among the cafés for one with "Deux" in its name. I found the Café Les Deux Magots a couple of blocks up—a vast establishment with three tiers of outdoor tables, all jammed. I wedged into an empty wicker chair in the middle tier and scanned the crowd for what I imagined an expatriate writer would look like—

an unshaven man in a fisherman sweater who was sharpening a pencil with a pocketknife, or a woman with a tortured expression, hunched over a tiny volume of poetry. I spotted four Northwestern boys who'd been on the ship with us, and one raised a glass of bright orange liqueur in my direction. Two men dressed identically in black suits, like off-duty waiters, sat at the table to my left, cigarettes smoldering in saucers, silently studying newspapers in Cyrillic type. A Dutchwoman with four children sat to my right, their cheeks puffed out as they blew over cups of hot chocolate.

A waiter in a stained white apron appeared at my elbow. "Un café au lait, s'il vous plaît," I said, wincing at the hideous clang in my accent. I should have paid better attention during my French classes at Westover.

"Yes, madame," he answered.

While I waited for my drink, I searched the crowd in vain for a glint of Scott's fair head, although who was to say that his hair was still blond, or that he even had hair anymore.

I pulled out Elsie Sturgis's map to figure out where to walk next. In the void between the Boulevard St. Germain and the Palais du Luxembourg, she'd scrawled a large X labeled "American Bookstore." I dropped a handful of coins on my saucer and set off, wandering in concentric circles around Elsie's floating mark. I searched the storefronts for rows of books, but all I found was a dusty toy store, where I bought two lead soldiers dressed as crusaders for Avery and a pocket telescope set for Will. I ended up on a gravel pathway in the Jardin du Luxembourg and watched a boy with stick legs like Avery's chasing a sickly squirrel. In the blast of August sun, the roses had withered and the leaves on the linden trees were edged with brown.

In the frigid stone crypt of St. Sulpice, I dropped a few centimes in a dented tin box for four offertory candles, and thought hard about my prayers before I lit them. For the safety of Billy's plane I asked, imagining a sleek silver plane as it banked a smooth turn over the Paris skyline. And for Will, picturing him on a canvas cot at his scout camp: please let him win the best-scout award, the one desire of his seven-year-old heart. And for Avery, kneeling on his bedroom floor, cutting pictures out of train magazines for his scrapbook: please make him less odd, less alone. I lit the last wick on the remains of a dying candle, sputtering in a pool of wax. And for myself: help me find Scott. I amended my prayer: help me find what I'm looking for.

On a side street north of the Odeon, I finally came upon a storefront with a display of English books, their pages curling in the sun. SHAKESPEARE AND COMPANY, LENDING LIBRARY AND BOOK-SHOP was painted in peeling gold letters over the door. I dimly remembered having read that this store was scandalous for some reason.

I opened a glass door covered with English advertisements and timidly stepped into a large room with untidy bookshelves running up to a twenty-foot ceiling. Framed photographs of brooding authors hung in a jumbled rogues' gallery over a marble mantel. I paused at a front table stacked with new books and journals, waiting for a salesclerk to appear. From a back room, a woman was speaking rapid-fire French into the telephone. "Can I help you?" she called out to me in an American accent.

"Just browsing," I said. "No hurry." The woman resumed her chatter and I wandered over to the authors' wall for a closer look. A distinguished man with a tidy mustache wore glasses with one lens darkened, as if he were blind in one eye. A stout woman with a man's haircut and a shawl wrapped around her shoulders like a peasant. The only faces I recognized were long dead—George Eliot, Shakespeare. I didn't spot a portrait of Scott.

A yellowing broadside was tacked to a back wall—*The Outrage of Ulysses*. Now I remembered where I had heard of Shakespeare and Company—it had published a shocking novel that had been judged obscene in America and banned. Elsie had bragged about how she had smuggled a copy past customs in a trunk with a false bottom.

"Is it a good book?" I had asked her.

"It's very complicated. And long," she had said vaguely. "No one actually reads it. That's not the point."

I thumbed through the new novels stacked on the front table. Sherwood Anderson, Sinclair Lewis, nothing by Scott.

The phone clacked down, and a birdlike woman strolled from the back room dressed like Little Lord Fauntleroy in a velveteen jacket with a drooping bow at the neck. "Looking for something in particular?" she asked. She probably thought I wanted a copy of *Ulysses* to shock the folks back home.

"We're here for a test flight at Le Bourget, or at least my husband is." For some reason, it was important that this woman not think of me as a mere tourist. "He's unveiling his new plane. So I have time on my hands."

I picked up a journal crudely printed on pulp paper, called *This Quarter*. "It looks like every writer in Paris drops by here."

"Quite a few."

"An old friend of mine is a writer. I think he and his wife are living in Paris now." I ran my finger down the table of contents. Ezra Pound, Carl Sandburg, James Joyce.

"And who's your friend?"

"Scott Fitzgerald."

"Oh, my, yes. Scott and Zelda. I think they've found life in Paris very diverting. Maybe too diverting."

"I was hoping to look them up. Would you have their address?"

"Last I'd heard, they'd decamped to the south of France." She saw my shoulders slump. "I think there was something about them in the *Tribune* a couple of weeks ago. Let me see if I can find it." She stooped down and started to root through a stack of newspapers under a desk. "Here it is." She folded the paper open to the second page, cleared a spot on the desk blotter, and gestured me toward a rolling chair. "It's in 'Left Quarter Notes.'"

> News of celebrities comes from Juan-les-Pins, from a person who calls himself Alison Keyes. It is apparently becoming the thing for American and other artists to stay there during summer. First, it seems that the F. Scott Fitzgeralds are there. That is as far as they got on that rumored trip around the world. He is said to be doing a new novel, which is no great news, for he usually is, when he isn't doing something else. Still, if he can make it as good as *The Great Gatsby,* it will be worth the wait. I wonder what fantastic activities are now making up his real life?

The woman climbed on a footstool to return some battered books onto a high shelf. She had no more time for gossip, but I wasn't ready to leave. I'd come all the way to Paris to find Scott, and this was as close as I was going to get, so I might as well make my confession to her.

"I haven't seen Scott since he was nineteen. I expect he's changed a good deal."

"I'm not sure about that. His friends would say he still acts like a drunken college boy. Breaking glasses, running around the Place de la Concorde in a vendor's cart. Showing up at people's apartments at five in the morning. Waking the baby, irritating the concierge. Hemingway made me promise not to give Scott his new address."

"But his wife must have settled him down a bit."

"Zelda?" She spun around on her footstool so I could see her eyes give a merry roll and her head cock to one side. "She's even wilder than Scott. He spent a whole paycheck on a pearl necklace that she gave to a Negress she was dancing with at a nightclub. She leaves a bowl full of money on the front hall table for deliverymen to help themselves. Now they complain that all Scott's thousands are gone." She trotted down the footstool for another stack of books to reshelve. "Of course, she's lovely and he has the face of a movie actor, so everyone forgives them."

I didn't have the courage to ask any more questions. I stood up and folded the *Tribune* to the front page.

"You can leave him a note if you like. People treat me like the Left Bank branch of American Express." She gestured toward a pigeonhole box on top of the mantel filled with odd-shaped envelopes and paper scraps. "I'll pass it along next time he drops in, which should be in a few months."

I imagined my note pulled out and inspected by every expatriate writer spending an idle afternoon at Shakespeare and Company. Maybe there were a few other notes for Scott already waiting. "That's all right. It's getting late." I realized I should buy something, of course, after plying her with so many questions. "I don't suppose you have anything new by Scott. I've run out of things to read."

"I think we've got something newish, somewhere." She climbed down from the footstool and searched under a stack of *An American Tragedy* and *Arrowsmith*. "Here it is. I only ordered one copy. It's stories, I'm afraid." It was a slim book called *All the Sad Young Men,* which seemed about right for my forlorn mood. She nimbly wrapped it in brown paper, snipping the twine with oversize library shears.

"Now tell me your name so I can report back to Scott."

"Ginevra Granger. Formerly Perry. From Chicago."

"Ginevra from Chicago. All right—I'll try to remember," she said, thrusting her hands deep inside the pockets of her velvet jacket. The phone rang in the back room, and she trotted off to answer with brisk steps, as if she'd forgotten already.

Billy said he would be working till the wee hours at Le Bourget, overseeing the installation of every panel of Granger Duralumin, so I dined alone back at the Deux Magots. Now that I was no longer looking for Scott, I sat myself at a remote table along a darkly paneled wall under the watchful eyes of two wooden Chinamen perched on a column. The deux magots, I guessed, whatever they were. I asked for an extra candle so I could read *All the Sad Young Men,* and ordered the *plat du jour*—a beef cutlet and scalloped potatoes. The Dutch tourists and boisterous college boys had drifted off in the early evening, replaced by sturdy older couples silently soldiering through their *saucisson.*

At the second story, called "Winter Dreams," I felt the old tingle of recognition. A golf caddy, Dexter Green, from Black Bear, Minnesota, falls in love with a lovely rich girl, Judy Jones, on the golf course. I sawed off a piece of gristly beef with a dull knife, and washed down the beef with a hardy swig of red wine, savoring the moment. Here I was, once again, reading about myself in one of Scott's stories. But this time I wasn't in my chaise or in a hairdressing salon in Chicago, I was in the Deux Magots. Even if Scott wasn't here, I was inhabiting his world, his cafés, his bookstore.

In Gatsby fashion, Dexter becomes a man of means—by building a chain of laundries—to capture Judy Jones's attention. She acts interested just long enough to make him break off an engagement with another girl. Judy Jones was like Isabelle and Daisy and Scott's other bloodless girls who stomp over a poor boy's heart without a second thought.

But in the final two pages, "Winter Dreams" takes a dark turn.

Dexter Green, who has fled the Midwest to escape the memory of the unfaithful Judy Jones, is now a middle-aged banker turned cynical about women and love. One day he runs into a man who knows Judy Jones.

"Awfully nice girl," the man reports. "I'm sort of sorry for her." Her husband, Lud Simms, drinks and runs around while she stays home with their kids. No shred of her beauty remains, even though she is only twenty-seven. "Lots of women fade just like *that*," the man says with a snap of his fingers.

In the end, Dexter Green stares out at the sun sinking behind the New York skyline "in dull lovely shades of pink and gold." Losing the dream of Judy Jones's beauty is worse than having lost her love, he thinks, as painful as if he had married her and watched her "fade away before his eyes." Dexter tries to remember her gingham golf outfit and the soft down on her neck but realizes these things "existed no more."

I stabbed the tiny silver fork into the untouched heart of a pear tart, closed the book, set a pile of franc notes on top of it, and threaded my way through the now bustling tables toward the street.

A waiter came running after me, catching me by the elbow. "Votre livre, Madame," he said, holding it aloft. He squinted at my face as if he was trying to figure out if this odd American tourist was suicidal or just drunk.

I couldn't think how to say "I'm done with it." "C'est rien," I said, severing my connection with a chop of the hand.

I wandered down the Boulevard St. Germain toward the Boulevard Raspail as if in a trance, oblivious to the neon café lights, the jostling throngs of tourists back in evening finery, the smells of grilled fat and strong coffee, and "Bye Bye Blackbird" playing on a gramophone.

Scott's golden words had conjured his own romantic version of

Ginevra Perry, made me more beautiful than I really was, more enticing, crueler, more capable of reckless love. And now, in "Winter Dreams," Scott had realized the truth about me. The moonlit verandas and the soft deep summer rooms had been knocked over like a stage set, and there I stood, the same person I had always been. A conventional society girl who had settled into a conventional society marriage and simply faded away.

I imagined his face sagging with disappointment at the sight of me, just like Dexter Green's. Scott was lucky that I'd thrown him over so he could find his soul mate, Zelda—a woman who was truly beautiful and bold, leaving a litter of francs and pearl necklaces in her wake.

I remembered Eliot Schumacher's words, spoken by the still brown water of the Skokie—"Why don't you find pleasure in the life you've got?" At the time, I'd thought he'd meant, chuck your humdrum life and have a romantic fling. Now I realized Eliot was saying just the reverse. Stop dreaming of an impossible romance and find joy in the husband, the children, the life you have—in Billy, Will, and Avery.

I turned onto the Boulevard Raspail, tucked my purse firmly under the arm of my cornflower-blue dress. The bursar on the ship had warned me about the dangers of women walking unaccompanied in a questionable neighborhood at night. Nasty Frenchmen could snatch my bag or, even worse, think I was in Paris for a divorce and therefore open to lewd suggestions. But I seemed to have turned invisible, like poor Judy Jones, and I glided back to the Lutetia unmolested.

That night, I lay in bed waiting for Billy with the shutters open, the street lamp outside the window giving the room an underwater glow. It was after two when I heard the heavy brass bolt thrown back. Billy tiptoed in, wearing the leather trench coat from his aviator days and a tweed cap like a garage mechanic's. I sat up and switched on an ebony night lamp shaped like an obelisk.

"You didn't have to wait up for me," he said, sounding weary to the bone but pleased.

"I had the concierge send up some food," I said, pointing at a slab of ham slathered with mustard on a peasant loaf and a bottle of German beer.

"I guess I did forget to eat today," he said. He slipped off his jacket and cap. The lapels of his gray Brooks Brothers suit were streaked with axle grease. I caught a gleam of white scalp through his matted hair.

"How's it going?"

"We got the tail section assembled, but the engineers say it's eighty pounds too heavy. We need to make it lighter somehow." He let out a defeated sigh—for five years he had been pounding and pressing Duralumin until it was no thicker than tissue paper, but still it was not thin enough. "It's a lunatic asylum out there. Cameramen are lined up, waiting for us to crash. How was your day?"

"I saw the Jardin du Luxembourg and St. Sulpice. It was a little lonely, really. I think you were right. We should move to the Ritz."

"But I thought the Ritz had too many American tourists." He smiled—I didn't frequently admit I was wrong when it came to matters of taste.

"Well, I'm an American tourist. I don't know why I ever pretended to be anything different. Besides, Millie's coming in a couple of days from Scotland, so I can have a pal while you're out at Le Bourget."

Over the next week, Millie Pullman and I made every stop suggested in a volume I'd picked up at Brentano's called *The Paris That's Not in the Guidebooks*. We had our toenails painted maroon at Elizabeth Arden's at the Rue de La Paix. We had lunch at Ciro's and

had *cinq à sept* at Harry's New York Bar, where I had to monitor the
number of champagne cocktails Millie consumed so she wouldn't
fall asleep in the taxi. One night we went to Bricktop's nightclub,
where Millie danced with a Negro named Jimmy and I danced with
a man with dyed black hair who said he was a Romanov prince and
needed a loan for cab fare. We spent an entire afternoon at the
House of Chanel having drop-back gowns modeled for us, then
sneaked back to a shop behind the Comédie Française where they
made knockoffs for a quarter of the price. I bought a tunic and sandals made by Isadora Duncan's brother, and Millie bought an ugly
abstract painting of a bicycle by an Italian who might someday be
famous. We even spent a morning at the Louvre searching for the
Mona Lisa. Millie wanted to find that bookshop over on the Left
Bank where we could get copies of the shocking book Elsie was
always carrying on about, but I managed to talk her out of it.

On our last day, we went out to Le Bourget to witness the test
flight of Billy's plane. On a clear morning at approximately 5:30
A.M., a custom-built Fokker F.VII Southern Cross monoplane took
off from Le Bourget Airfield, Paris. Its length was 28 feet, and it
had an extended wingspan of 46 feet. It was outfitted with a 223 hp
Wright Whirlwind 9-cylinder air-cooled engine, Hamilton con-
trollable pitch propeller, Pioneer altimeter and turn and bank in-
dicator, and Granger Duralumin panels. A crowd of over two
hundred had assembled to witness the historic flight. Loaded with
an extra fuel tank and with no headwind, the plane barely obtained
enough lift to clear telegraph wires at the end of the runway. The
plane bobbled and swayed for a few moments, then righted itself
and headed northeast across a potato field. Then, without warning, the plane plunged to earth a mere 500 feet from the runway.
The pilot, American ace "Tiger" Lyons, was pulled from the fiery
wreck. Although Lyons suffered significant burns on his arms and

a crushed femur, he survived. Experts attributed the crash to the excessive weight of the Duralumin panels.

After the crash, Granger Aviation vaporized like a smudgy trail of exhaust. The scrap metal and machine tools were auctioned off. The mechanics and pilots drifted westward to California, where airplane factories were sprouting up in orange groves. All that was left were a few sample panels of Granger Patented Duralumin, stored in Daddy's garage.

Billy surrendered his dream of becoming an aviation hero with remarkable speed and grace. On the voyage back from France, he spent most of his time in the men's lounge studying the stock reports in the pile of week-old newspapers. The day we got back to Chicago, he made an appointment with Horace Armour, and within a month he'd joined the firm of Armour Cudahy as a stock analyst. "Beats freezing my rear end off in a Quonset hut. If every chauffeur in town can make a killing in the market, why shouldn't I? At least I know how to add a column of numbers," he said. Soon he was poring over ticker tape and annual reports with the same zest he'd had studying the test results of the National Aviation Commission wind tunnel. He didn't even seem bothered when the Spirit of St. Louis, clad in some other type of corrugated metal, landed at Le Bourget eight months later.

Part Three

18

Century of Progress

Three weeks after Black Friday, Daddy toppled over on the platform of the Lake Forest station, just as the doors of the 6:50 businessman's express snapped open. A mild heart attack, Dr. Proxmire diagnosed, but the chambers were dangerously enlarged. He warned Daddy that he might not survive another Chicago winter—a mere chest cold could finish him off. Daddy decided to retire early so he and Mother could spend their winters in Florida, which was a respectable place to live now that land developers had drained the swamps and built nice golf courses. Mother found them a Spanish-style hacienda with antique tiles that had been built in a brand-new resort on Boca Grande.

But Daddy balked at the idea of selling his precious house to strangers. "Why don't you and Billy move in," he pleaded. He was seated in a wicker settee on the terrace with his feet in slippers and a plaid blanket over his lap. The mane of black hair had started to turn gray and wispy, his football player's neck had become stringy. "You were so happy here. I can still see you dressed in a Hawaiian getup for some party at the McCormicks', doing a hula dance on the terrace. Remember when you had so many tricks up your sleeve?"

"Come on, Daddy," I said, giving his knee an impatient pat. "I'm a middle-aged lady. No one wants to see me dancing the hula, not even you. And I'm too old to have any tricks up my sleeve."

Daddy wouldn't let the idea go. "Think how much fun Avery would have mucking around in the Skokie. It would do him good. He's turning into an apartment boy who doesn't want to get his feet wet."

I let Daddy talk me into it, and by the next fall, I was back where I started from—on Green Bay Road. Billy had proved to be clever about stocks, clever enough to see that things were getting out of hand in 1929 and to sell most of his holdings before the crash. But even if we weren't as broke as most of our friends, we couldn't keep the house in Daddy's grand style. Billy had the golf course plowed under and turned the garden beds into a baseball diamond for the boys. He let Mr. Swensen go and cut the lawn with the Ford tractor himself, dressed in the coveralls and tweed cap Mr. Swensen had left hanging on a nail in the shed.

The boys started at the Bell School—Will in sixth grade and Avery in fourth. Right from the start, it seemed as if Daddy's prediction was right: all Avery needed to turn into a normal boy was to be pushed out the back door onto the prairie. With Will trailing behind as self-appointed watchdog, Avery went skating on Saturday afternoons with the other ten-year-old boys at the Winter Club and afterward scalded his mouth on watery hot chocolate. He rode his bike along the train tracks and left pennies to be flattened by the Skokie Line milk run. He whittled a canoe out of a birch log, burned his name and address on the bow, launched it in the Skokie, where it floated two hundred feet and got snagged in a drainage pipe. He did less well at the Bell School, but his older brother, with his straight blond hair and his earnest brow, hovered nearby, watching, and was usually able to set things right. When Avery stole a silver dollar from Michael Clow's coat pocket, Will gave him two silver dollars back not to tell anyone. At night, they sat side by side over Avery's arithmetic book, Will dictating the answers to the long-division problems, which Avery copied on lined paper in a minute script.

As for me, I tried to follow Eliot's advice and find pleasure in the life I had. I started to look at Billy fondly, finding things to admire. He was a goodhearted and patient father, throwing pitches to Will for hours in the back field to improve his batting, helping Avery arrange his battalions of lead soldiers across the bedroom floor in the exact formation of the Battle of Agincourt. Billy had lost his aviator figure, but he was still handsome in a bulky, middle-aged way. I'd stopped being annoyed when he called me "old girl."

I led the life of a typical Lake Forest matron, and discovered that I was quite good at it. I played golf with Millie once a week at Onwenstia and developed a decent short game. I was elected vice president of Constance Armour's charity to collect winter clothing for needy children in the Chicago slums, and spent two mornings a week boxing up galoshes and flannel trousers. Billy and I joined the Green Bay Play Readers Club, where I had a knack for roles as jaded divorced women and Billy had a secret talent for playing buffoons. I don't know if all this was what Eliot had in mind when he said I should be more "fulfilled," but I felt fulfilled enough.

After my trip to Paris, I didn't keep a clip file on Scott anymore, not that I'd come across any clips to add. After the crash, Scott's stories disappeared from the pages of *Hearst's* and the *Saturday Evening Post*. The problems of debutantes and Ivy League boys seemed passé—now writers were supposed to be interested in coal miners and sharecroppers whose land had dried up and blown away.

Even if he wasn't publishing anymore, I liked to think that Scott was surviving the Depression unscathed, was still cavorting around the Place de La Concorde with Zelda in a vendor's cart.

I happened to be standing in the hallway slipping on Mother's old gardening rubbers in May of 1933 when I got a long-distance phone call, person to person, from Scott Fitzgerald. In the few seconds it took for the operator to connect us, I tried to absorb the shock that I was actually going to speak to Scott. Not the way I'd thought of Scott for the last ten years—as words on a page, as a touched-up photograph in a stylish magazine—but the man himself. Then I felt the usual flood of dread about person-to-person phone calls, because they were only used to deliver terrible news.

"Ginevra?" The voice was tinny and slow, like a warped phonograph record played at the wrong speed.

"Scott? I can't believe it. Are you calling from Paris?"

"No, no. That was years ago. I'm in Baltimore."

"Baltimore?" Not St. Paul, not New York, not any of the places I'd imagined Scott all these years.

He sighed, as if the story was much too complicated to explain over a scratchy telephone wire. "We needed a quiet place for me to finish my novel and for our eleven-year-old daughter, Scottie, to go to school. And for Zelda to get better. We even found a house to rent called La Paix." He let out a laugh that didn't have a drop of mirth in it.

I didn't think I should ask what Zelda was getting better from. "How'd you find me?" I sat down on a bench and started to twist the phone cord around my finger.

"From Marie. She told me you'd moved back to your parents' house."

"I'm sitting in the hallway right now," I said stupidly. This was the last place I'd seen Scott, how many years ago? Sixteen, no, seventeen. "I was crazy about all your books. I always knew you'd be famous."

"No, you didn't," Scott said. There was a peevish edge to his voice that made me wonder if he might be tight. "Say, Ginevra. I have a big favor to ask."

Oh, Lord, I thought. He's going to ask to borrow money. "Of course, Scott. Anything."

"Zelda's coming to Chicago next week. She wants to see that new World's Fair. And I was wondering if you could have lunch with her. She's always wanted to meet you," he added lamely.

"I'd love to take her to lunch. I can meet her at the fair if she'd like. I haven't seen it myself," I said, giddy with relief. He only wanted a small, easy favor—to take his wife out to lunch. "I'm dying to meet Zelda, too. I met a woman in a bookstore in Paris who says she's lovely. Very original."

"She was. I mean, she is."

"All right, then. You let me know what day and where she wants to meet."

"One more thing." His voice dropped so I could barely make it out.

"Yes. Can you speak up?"

"Zelda's been sick. With a nervous condition. She's been at the Phipps Clinic at Hopkins, but she's better now. Her doctors say this trip is a rest cure."

"All right. I'll keep lunch quiet, I promise."

There was another pause. "Zelda's just published a novel."

"Oh, really! Good for her. I'll get a copy. What's it called?"

"*Save Me the Waltz*. It's good, I think. But please don't read it as a portrait of Zelda and me."

"Don't worry. I won't do that," I soothed. "When's your new novel coming out?'

"Next year. It'll be my best," he said, as if he was trying to convince himself.

"I can hardly wait." The operator broke in with the five-minute warning. "We better hang up."

"We didn't talk about you."

"My life's very ordinary. It's just what you'd expect." After all, I'm Judy Jones, I thought. "Zelda can give you a report."

"You two are going to hit it off," he said in a dreamy way.

After I hung up, I slumped back on the bench, brooding. What had made Scott's voice sound so different, so old? It had lost its boyish bounce, I decided; the words didn't come firing out at you, *rat-a-tat-tat.*

I tried to piece together the odd bits of information he'd tossed in. They had left Paris for Baltimore because they needed "a quiet place." So Scott was still writing, something brilliant by the sound of it, free from the distractions of the Left Bank. He had a little girl the same age as Avery, with the winsome name Scottie. I imagined a face with Scott's graceful mouth and fine nose under a cap of buttery hair.

I wondered what exactly had Scott meant when he said Zelda had been in a clinic with a "nervous condition." Most of the people we knew in Chicago who had had "nervous conditions" were drunks who had been sent off to sanitariums to dry out. Sometimes the term was used for women who had done unacceptable things like run off with the gardener or hand out leaflets about birth control. So was Zelda a drunk or a hellion? Based on the description I'd heard from the lady at Shakespeare and Company, she could be either.

Then there was the favor itself. Why would Scott ask his old girlfriend, whom he hadn't seen or spoken to in years, to take his wife to lunch at the Century of Progress? I imagined all sorts of cruel motives. He wanted to get back at me for throwing him over—see the beautiful, talented woman I married instead of you. Maybe Zelda wanted to meet the model for Judy Jones. Even worse, maybe Scott had dreamed up this bizarre encounter to put in one of his books. In any case, I admit I was curious to have a look at Scott's wife and hear the details of their glamorous life.

I had to call four bookshops to track down a copy of *Save Me the Waltz*. As Scott promised, Zelda's novel followed the facts of their life together—at least the ones I knew. A coddled Southern belle named Alabama marries a handsome Yankee artist she meets during the war. He is lionized as the voice of the modern generation. They have a daughter named Bonnie, they undertake a life of drunken parties from New York to Europe and back again. If all these events were true, then what of the others? The husband becomes an abusive alcoholic. The wife first has an affair with an aviator and then trains to become a professional ballerina so obsessively she goes mad.

I found Zelda's author photograph more intriguing than the novel. A laughing, tan beauty with a tousled bob, dressed in a tutu and satin toe shoes perched on top of two wooden trunks. Their address was dashed off in black paint across the slatted front—
FITZGERALD, FELDER ST. MONTGOMERY ALABAMA.

Zelda and I agreed to meet at the north entrance to the fair, next to the Field Museum. "I will carry a yellow rose so you will recognize me," she wrote, which seemed unnecessary—how could I not spot the ballerina?

I stood for several minutes by the bustling north gate and scanned the crowd for a woman in pink tulle, waving a yellow rose. The temperature on the giant Havoline thermometer pushed toward ninety, and I fanned myself with the fair guidebook. I spotted a small middle-aged woman with a red rose by her side, sitting on the bench by the ticket booth. She was dressed in a dowdy navy-blue suit with lace-up oxfords and heavy, flesh-toned stockings, like a librarian on holiday. I tried to get a glimpse of her face, but she was wearing a tightly knit hat that covered her hair, and her face was downturned, poring over the guidebook and checking off items with a pencil.

I stepped closer. "Excuse me?" I couldn't bring myself to say "Zelda." What if the real Zelda was just walking up and saw me mistake this odd, mousy creature for her?

The woman squinted up at me. There was a vague resemblance, but the face was years older, with chapped, red skin—what Zelda's mother would have looked like if she had worked as a field hand. Just before I was about to say "My mistake," the woman grabbed the rose and jumped to her feet. "Ginevra? I'm glad you recognized me. The flower seller only had red roses." She was short and skinny as an old hen, but she still had a belle's voice, with a heavy Southern lilt. When she offered me her hand, I noticed it had the same flaky, raw look as her face. A skin ailment, like the eczema Avery got in the fall when school started.

"You're just as beautiful as Scott said," she observed in a matter-of-fact way. When she smiled, the skin around her mouth cracked like dried clay.

"I already knew what you looked like," I said. "Your photograph is in every magazine."

"Was," she corrected.

I unfolded the fair map. "Scott said you shouldn't get too tired, so I was thinking we could start at the Art Institute and see *Whistler's Mother,* which they borrowed from the Louvre, and then over to Horticulture Hall, and then maybe a nice quiet lunch at the Heidelberg Inn. How does that sound?" I spoke in a hushed, sickbed tone, now that I realized that "nervous condition" was a polite way of saying "mental illness."

Her face fell. "I was hoping we could just wander about and take it all in. I want to see what the world of tomorrow is going to look like," she said in a meek tone, as if she was always bossed around by killjoy adults.

Well, why not? I thought. I wasn't her nurse. "Lead the way," I said. She took off like an overexcited seven-year-old, with me trotting to keep up. She sped right by the educational exhibits—"The Story of Physics," "Advances in Dentistry"—and stood transfixed by anything bright-colored and shiny. She watched a revolving display of sixteen Nash sedans in an eighty-foot glass tower for a full ten minutes. Every few feet, she bought a souvenir teaspoon or beaded Indian bracelet for Scottie and a snack for herself.

All the while, she carried on a nonstop monologue that didn't seem to require any response from me.

"Of course, Scott drinks too much. My sisters and mother always thought he was a dipsomaniac and didn't want me to marry him. Now half our friends say I had a nervous breakdown because of Scott's drinking, and the other half say Scott drinks because I'm crazy. Look—the Goodyear blimp. I was in love with an aviator once, on the French Riviera, but then Scott got very jealous and made me send him away."

We'd made our way to the Midway, where the educational exhibitions gave way to blinking signs and squawking loudspeakers. "This is more like it," Zelda said, leading us toward a replica of Lincoln's childhood cabin hewed from rough logs. A pimply thatch-haired boy with bare feet and linsey-woolsey trousers was pretending to chop logs and read at the same time.

Zelda stopped by the split-rail fence and called over to him. "Whatcha readin', Abe?" she asked in a flirtatious, honeysuckle voice.

He looked up, embarrassed. Tourists weren't supposed to talk to the living exhibitions. "I dunnow," he said in a southside accent.

"You better study harder if you're gonna be president and free the oppressed Negra," she drawled.

"Screw you," he whispered, and Zelda tipped her head back and let out a bleak laugh, her eyes turning flinty as if from some inner fire.

"Let's get some lunch—my treat," I offered, although it was hard to imagine she was very hungry after an eggroll, a corn fritter, and a dish of spumoni. We wandered up the Midway past the Negro Plantation Show and the Battle of Gettysburg cyclorama. I turned into the Streets of Paris and steered her toward a reproduction café that had the same wicker chairs and umbrellas as the Deux Magots. Maybe Zelda would find this familiar, soothing.

Suddenly she reared up like a skittish horse and planted her feet on the cobbled pavement. "Why would I want to go to Paris?" Her voice was aggrieved. "Paris is where everything started to go wrong for Scott and me. He made me stop dancing and sent me to the hospital. This isn't even the real Paris." She scowled at my face as if she'd never seen it before.

"Sorry—stupid idea. You pick the restaurant. You're the out-of-town guest," I said, steering her back to the blare of the Midway.

"Let's go there," she said, pointing toward a red-and-white big top with a banner flapping from the tent pole—"Fisher's Circus Cook House." A strong man decked out in fake tiger fur and pasted-on handlebar mustache escorted us over dank-smelling sawdust, seated us at a trestle table propped on a rain barrel, and handed each of us an oversize fork.

"Can we have menus?" I asked.

"This is the circus, lady. Don't get no menus."

A midget dressed like Tom Thumb brought us tin plates with strings of sausages, baked beans, and a bunch of cooked carrots. Zelda shrugged happily and poked her fork into one of the sausages—the dark demon seemed to have crawled back into its cave. "This is fun," she announced.

"I'm surprised you wanted to meet me."

"It was Scott's idea," she said with a shrug. "He always talks about you. He says you were his first love. I think he was hoping that if we met, I'd act more like you. He's always trying to reform me."

"I'm sorry. That sounds tiresome."

"A long time ago I felt jealous, but I'm past that. Besides, you seem nice. You're taking me out to lunch." She tossed a chunk of sausage to a miniature poodle dyed blue who was snuffling around our feet.

"I read your novel. I found it very affecting," I said.

She shifted her scrawny frame on the bench and looked away; the storm clouds were gathering again. "None of the reviewers thought so. Scott didn't want me to publish it in the first place. He said it would make us a laughingstock, and I proved him right. Ha!" There was a painful pause. She bounced her fork against the rim of the plate, as if it were a cymbal. "Do you write?" she asked.

"I'm afraid I'm just one of those society women who play golf and dither around with charities."

Zelda let out a sigh that seemed to reach to the bottom of her soul. "You're lucky. Scott and the doctors think my artistic impulses are dangerous. They have forbidden me to write another novel."

She stopped and gave a deliberate smile, as if she were remembering her doctor's pleas to avoid agitated thoughts, to follow the rules of polite conversation. "I'm so rude. I haven't asked you a single question about your life, and Scott will want to know everything. You married an aviator instead of Scott. He must be handsome."

"Back then he was, I guess. Even average boys look handsome in a uniform. I think Scott was the first person to tell me that. And

Billy's not an aviator anymore, I'm afraid. His prize plane crashed, his company went bust, and now he's a stockbroker. Turns out he's much better at stocks than he ever was at planes."

"But you were madly in love with him, weren't you?" she leaned forward and asked in a cozy whisper.

My shoulders hunched over, embarrassed by the spectacle we made—two middle-aged women confessing crushes like school-girls. "I was only eighteen. I hardly knew Billy. I was in love with the idea of being in love."

Her gaze turned far away and she shook her head slowly back and forth. "I was madly in love with Scott. Even when he was stewed all the time and we had terrible fights. We were so happy to-gether. Not just once, but happy a thousand times."

Sadness washed over me, for this worn-out soul who could still speak so passionately about love. "I don't think I've ever felt that deeply about anyone," I said, my voice catching. We fell silent for a few moments. She chewed on a forkful of baked beans; I wiped my damp face with a dingy napkin.

I moved on to a blander subject. "Tell me about Scottie."

"Scottie's a very self-reliant little girl. I don't know who she takes after—I guess she takes after herself," Zelda mused. "Scott thinks I'm not a very attentive mother. It's not my fault if I've hardly been home in the last three years, and Scottie feels she doesn't have to listen to me anymore." A pause, as she remembered that when asked about one's children, one should ask back. "What are your boys like? I'm sure you're a perfect mother."

"Will's pure Granger through and through, so I don't think I have much to do with how he's turning out. Good at things like ice hockey and baseball, and a poor sport when he loses. Very quick with numbers. Can be pretty literal-minded about art. When I took him to see the Seurat at the Art Institute, he said, 'Didn't he know how to do regular painting?' He's off at camp in Minnesota right now winning archery and swimming ribbons. And then there's Avery, who's a mama's boy. He's very sensitive, gets his feelings hurt, and refused to go to camp with his big brother."

I tried to keep the airy tone that other mothers used when chatting about the quirks of their children. As if it were the most normal thing in the world for a boy to jam himself into a crawlspace in the attic when it was time to leave for camp, and yelp like a wounded rabbit when Billy grabbed a skinny shin and tried to pull him out of the shadows.

Zelda cocked her head, as if she were listening to instructions whispered into her ear. "Do you think you'll have any more children? You're not too old," she said, squinting toward my middle.

I shook my head. "I had a hard time when Avery was born. I can't have any more children, which makes me sad. I was so young when I had the boys. I think I'd do a better job now."

Zelda's mouth twitched to one side, which made me regret I'd said anything about second chances. "Think you can handle a few more exhibits?" I added.

She jumped up and grabbed her bulging purse. "I need to exercise. The doctor said I should walk five miles every day."

Zelda came to a halt outside a tent with a huge sign: DULFOUR'S FREAK SHOW—HUMAN MISTAKES—25 CENTS. Underneath hung stylized portraits of the attractions—*The Gibbs Sisters, Siamese Twins Alive, India Rubber Man,* and *The Armless Wonder.* I was afraid she would make us go inside, but she only shuddered. "I saw a movie about circus freaks last year that gave me the horrors. Beauty and normalcy seem so arbitrary, don't you think?" Then she hooked her arm through mine and marched me full speed out of the Midway and south down the promenade toward what looked like a flying saucer hovering over the water.

As we walked closer, we saw it was the hexagonal House of To-morrow, made of glass panels and steel tubes perched on a sand dune. We paid the dime admission and climbed the steel steps, past the garage with its car and biplane, to the diamond-faceted turret. Zelda ran an appraising finger over the metal venetian blinds, the tubular chairs covered with fake polar bear fur, the rubber floor springy as a trampoline.

We stepped out onto the observation deck, and Zelda hung precariously over the metal railing. She turned her ravaged face toward the velvety lake breeze, looking for a moment so radiant that I could imagine her young again, when her cheeks and hair were smooth and honey brown.

"You should have a house just like this. See, your husband would even have his own airplane hanger," she said. "Scott would be so disappointed if you did not have a perfect life."

Two months later I got a crudely wrapped package from the Phipps Clinic. It was a watercolor of a hexagonal house perched on a coral-pink beach overlooking a turquoise sea. A dark-haired girl who resembled me at eighteen leaned on the deck railing with her gaze fixed on the horizon, as if she were searching the skies for her aviator to return home.

19

Myrna

Zelda would have been disappointed—there were no aviators in my life. The only young man I stared at and obsessed over was Avery.

In 1934, when it was time for Will to start high school, he decided on a day school in Evanston rather than going east to boarding school like all his other friends. Although he wouldn't admit it, Billy and I knew he didn't want to leave Avery.

Living out in the country had not turned Avery into a normal boy after all. In the eight months after his thirteenth birthday, Avery had grown six inches. His nervous, sharp features had elongated into a handsome, angular face. His black hair, which he tossed back with a jerk of the chin, hung in a rakish wave over his forehead, and the film on his upper lip was so thick that he needed to shave every two days. Teachers complained that he drew cartoons of movie stars in his notebook and never seemed to be listening. He refused Will's offers to ride bikes and toss baseballs. Every day after school he dropped his book bag in the hall, pounded up the stairs, and retreated behind a locked bedroom door.

Avery spent his afternoons and his nights, as far as I could tell, reading movie magazines—*Photoplay, Silver Screen, Modern Cinema*. With a pair of manicure scissors, he cut out pictures of starlets very precisely, each curl and finger separated, and pasted them to the wall above his bed. The women had one feature in common—they were all dark brunettes. Photos of Norma Shearer, Maureen O'Sullivan, Claudette Colbert dressed in everything from pantaloons to peignoirs, soon covered the entire wall.

At first he was satisfied with going to the Saturday matinees at the little Deerpath Theater near the railroad station. Will dutifully followed along, even if he'd seen the movie the week before, to make sure Avery didn't get into any scrapes. Then Avery insisted that they go into Chicago every Saturday to one of the cathedral-size movie palaces that showed the latest Hollywood releases.

One wintry afternoon, as they stepped out of *Naughty Marietta* at the State Lake, Avery stopped in his tracks, transfixed by the red marquee of the Chicago Theater on the other side of State Street which blinked GARY COOPER IN THE LIVES OF A BENGAL LANCER. He checked his watch, grabbed Will's sleeve. "We can catch one more show," he said, zigzagging across four lanes of traffic.

Will clapped a calming paw on Avery's shoulder and tried to steer him toward Northwestern Station. "Avery, no," he said, in the patient voice he used with his brother. "We don't have enough money for another show. Besides, I'm supposed to go somewhere tonight." He'd already missed a morning hockey game, and he didn't want to miss Barbie Boreland's birthday party.

Avery didn't seem to hear. "Don't worry. I've got money," he chirped, standing in the ticket line, bouncing on the balls of his feet. Will knew that if he tried to drag Avery away, he might have a tantrum—a throw-himself-down-on the-pavement, kicking, whining fit that was shameful for such a large boy. Will told himself that he didn't mind seeing *The Lives of a Bengal Lancer,* and that Barbie Boreland's party would probably be boring.

Avery flashed two red tickets in front of the usher and tried to hustle past. But the usher's hand lashed out like a snake, caught Avery by the wrist, pried his fingers open. Two used, torn ticket stubs fluttered to the floor. "Trying to sneak in?" He smiled, showing four front teeth capped in silver. He summoned the manager, who marched Will and Avery into the office behind the projection booth.

"I can pay," Will said, opening up his wallet and pulling out all his cash—three one-dollar bills. Avery sat dazed by the flickering lights of the projector.

"I don't want your money now," sneered the manager. "Don't they teach you not to steal in Lake Forest?" All Will had to do was say that his brother was not right in the head and tap his temple, and the man would have set them loose. But Will stayed loyally mute, his head hung in shame, while the manager called Billy. Avery watched the first forty minutes of *The Lives of a Bengal Lancer* from the projection booth until Billy arrived and made him leave before the end.

"I'm sorry," Will blurted when they reached the car, and burst into tears.

"Shhh," said Billy, reaching out to pat his knee in the darkness. "It's not your fault."

Later that night, Billy and I sat in Daddy's old office with the door closed, face-to-face in the old, battered Morris chairs, our knees touching. Billy, who was not normally a drinking man, poured himself a tumbler of straight Scotch. "We have to face facts. The boy is off." The mustache Billy had grown back was sprinkled with gray the color of iron filings. His pale eyes, which used to snap when describing the advantages of Duralumin panels, looked dried out, as if they weren't producing enough tears.

"Lots of boys steal things at his age. It's a phase." I sounded unconvinced.

"Will didn't. And it's not healthy for him to be around Avery all the time. Will would be better off in boarding school, so he doesn't feel he has to be Avery's keeper."

I winced at the word, but in truth Avery did need a keeper. "I can go with him to the movies on Saturdays. I don't mind." Avery's problems were my fault, after all. It was because I had had evil thoughts when I was pregnant with him, wishing that he would shrivel up and disappear like an apple core left in the sun.

The next September, Will enrolled at Hotchkiss, and I became Avery's movie companion. Avery insisted that our Saturdays together follow a precise ritual. In the morning he studied the movie listings in the *Tribune,* and after great deliberation selected two. We took the ten o'clock local into Chicago, and ate bologna sandwiches with mayonnaise, mustard, and one leaf of lettuce, washed down with a thermos of black coffee. We walked from the station and were in our seats by noon for the cartoons and newsreel. We sat in the twelfth row on the left-hand aisle. Avery would not allow us to buy popcorn or candy, which he found distracting. After the first show, we walked over to the Old Heidelberg Restaurant for bratwurst with side dishes of mashed potatoes and beets and apple strudel for desert. Then we caught a late afternoon show and were able to catch a six o'clock back to Lake Forest in time for a late dinner.

All the while, Avery kept up a steady stream of Hollywood gossip that he'd gleaned from his movie magazines. "The Selznicks had the bathtubs for their new house in Santa Monica carved from single blocks of Carrara marble." "Clark Gable says that if he has to shave his mustache off for *Mutiny on the Bounty,* he's not doing it."

I liked to think I was helping Avery keep his obsessive interest in movies within socially acceptable limits. "You know it's all right to talk to me about movie stars," I said. "But with the boys at school, you should pick topics that they're interested in, like the Chicago Cubs. You're so good at memorizing facts. You should read the sports page every day, and then you can talk to them about what player made a home run or what pitcher is getting traded to the Cardinals."

In truth, seeing two movies every Saturday and discussing movie stars by their first names was much more interesting than a round of golf with Millie or packing boxes of mufflers and flannel pants with Constance. On those Saturdays, all of Avery's strengths shone through—his humor, his capacity to retain and analyze thousands of facts. He's not an oddball, I thought, he's a boy wonder, just like Irving Thalberg, who transformed orange groves into Sherwood Forest and Tahiti.

By the time Avery turned fifteen in 1936, his taste in movies had started to evolve. He said Norma Shearer had as much talent as a store mannequin who'd had elocution lessons. Jeanette MacDonald looked like she was inflicting her songs on Nelson Eddy like a punishment. The perfect woman was Myrna Loy in *The Thin Man*. Avery admired her in the opening scene, when she finds that William Powell has already had six martinis and she tells the waiter, "Bring me five more martinis, Leo, and line them right up here." That's the way a woman should act, he said—matching her man drink for drink, wisecrack for wisecrack.

Avery joined something called the Men-Must-Marry-Myrna Club, which sent him a monthly newsletter of adoring Myrna facts. Her father came up with her name when his train went by a station called "Myrna." John Dillinger was so in love with Myrna that he sneaked out of hiding to see *Manhattan Melodrama* at the Biograph, where the G-men were waiting. Asta's real name is Skippy, and once he bit Myrna's hand so hard she had to get two stitches.

Myrna thinks that her legs are fat, so that's why she's always shot from the knees up. We would see every Myrna Loy movie again and again until another one came along.

Avery showed me a picture of Myrna on the cover of *Photoplay*, impish chin tilted up, soft brown curls tossed back, one finely penciled brow arched coyly. "I think your hair might look nice like that," he said. "And you should make your eyebrows really thin too." I took the photo to the head stylist at Elizabeth Arden and got a soft permanent and my eyebrows tweezed and penciled into comets. I bought Woodberry Cold Cream, which Myrna promised had given her complexion its dewy gleam. On one of our Saturdays, Avery pointed out a dress in a Marshall Field's window with a mandarin collar and a wide leather belt. "That's what Myrna was wearing in the train scene in *Libeled Lady*." Even though Billy would think it was too pricey, I splurged. For Christmas, Avery gave me costume-jewelry clips with enamel jaguars. "Sort of looks like what Myrna wore with her leopard evening gown in *After the Thin Man*, don't you think?"

No one seemed to notice my sudden resemblance to Myrna Loy, but they did say I'd smartened up. "It's about time, too. You were getting so dowdy. You've still got a knockout figure," Millie Pullman observed. "You don't have a boyfriend, do you?" She winked—Millie told me that she'd had a few "rolls in the hay" with the new golf pro at the club.

"Only Avery," I said, with a coquettish lift of my Myrna eyebrow.

One day in late September, Avery did not come home after school. Around dinnertime we called the school secretary, who reported that Avery had not been in school that day. That he had called to say he had a broken filling and an emergency appointment with the dentist. We checked the Deerpath Theater, walking up and down the aisles as a scratched print of *It Happened One Night* flickered across the screen. Then I waited at the train station in case Avery showed up on a late train, while Billy drove to Chicago to check out Avery's favorite theaters. He started at the grandest—the Uptown, the Oriental, the Chicago—and worked on down the list, through the night, till he searched the Music Box at eleven. Then Billy called the police. Billy and I sat through the night at the kitchen table with cold cups of coffee, watched silently as a bleak sun rose up over the crusted snow.

The Cleveland police called the next afternoon. Avery had been arrested for loitering in a hotel corridor and had confessed his story to the police. He'd read in *Modern Screen* that Myrna Loy was to fill in for Ilka Chase for a week "as a lark" in an out-of-town production of *The Women*. Instead of going to school, he caught a morning train to Chicago, boarded the Twentieth Century at Union Station and was in Cleveland forty-five minutes before the curtain rose. He chatted up the girl in the ticket booth, who told him Miss Loy had booked a suite at the Hotel Cleveland. He was discovered hiding behind a fire door down the hall from Miss Loy's room by a hotel detective, who called the police, who threw Avery in the tank for the night.

Under normal circumstances, the police captain said, they would see this as nothing more than a schoolboy stunt, and release Avery to his father's custody with a stern lecture.

"But isn't this a normal circumstance?" Billy asked.

"I'm afraid not, sir." Upon questioning, they learned that the name Avery Granger was familiar to Miss Loy. Her office had received fan letters for over a year, sometimes as frequently as once a day. Normally Miss Loy's letters were opened and answered by a secretary, but the contents of these letters were found to be so disturbing that they were brought to Miss Loy's attention. The writer claimed not only that he loved Miss Loy, but that he knew she returned his love. He alluded to her secret plan to leave her husband and run away with him. The letters had been turned over to the Los Angeles police, where Avery's name was kept on file as a potentially dangerous person.

Because of his young age and his obvious mental instability, Miss Loy did not want to press charges. All she required was that the parents provide proof that the boy was under treatment from a licensed psychiatrist and that they sign a statement that the boy would not attempt any further contact with her.

When Avery returned with Billy the next day, his clothes were rumpled and stained, his cheeks were gaunt from three days of nothing but black coffee and pastries, but his manner seemed undaunted, carefree. His eyes were lit up as if an endless movie was now playing inside his head. He pulled a playbill out of his pocket, and reverently unfolded and smoothed it. "Myrna was so wonderful, Mother. You should have been there."

Dr. Proxmire gave us the name of Dr. Henry Lucas, chief psychiatrist at Michael Reese Hospital. "He's the top. Trained in Vienna with the man himself." Billy and I met with Dr. Lucas to discuss Avery in his stale office with overfilled ashtrays and a desk stacked high with yellowed files. I had never met a psychiatrist before, and he was exactly what I'd expected—a portly man with a funereal black suit, rimless glasses, and a vaguely British accent.

"The boy may be a little odd, but he's not having a nervous breakdown," Billy announced. "There is no history of insanity in either of our families. There is certainly no need for him to be sent to some kind of asylum."

The doctor shrugged, his eyes fixed on a dictionary stand against the back wall. "I can't say. I haven't met the patient."

"But when will you know what's the matter with Avery?" Billy insisted.

"I can't say that I will ever 'know' your son. Or, as you say, what is 'the matter' with him."

"Maybe he's just anemic," Billy added.

And so it went for another hour, each one of Dr. Lucas's cryptic remarks making Billy more and more agitated, and reducing me to silent tears, which probably reinforced the doctor's suspicion that bad parents were at the root of Avery's problems. Finally, we agreed that Avery would be admitted to the general pediatric ward, rather than the psychiatric ward, of Michael Reese.

"If anyone asks, we'll say he's rundown and needs iron shots," said Billy.

Two weeks later Avery was home again, well rested and fifteen pounds heavier. The visit had been fun, he said, because the nurses brought him movie magazines and had seen every one of Myrna's movies too.

"How did you like Dr. Lucas?" I asked.

"Not much. He smelled funny and never said anything."

"So what did you talk about?"

"A little bit about Myrna, but he didn't seem that interested. He'd never seen any of her movies, not even *The Thin Man*. He asked a lot of questions about you."

Dr. Lucas sent his report to Billy at his office at Armour Cudahy.

Patient: white male, 15 years, 5'9", 118 pounds

The patient is suffering from mania with obsessive ideation.

Patient appears to have an extreme Oedipal fixation, which he has projected onto imaginary relationships with movie actresses. Mother is exacerbating Oedipal phase by encouraging patient's obsessive behavior. Mother escorts patient to multiple movies per week,

and has allowed him to dress her up like a particular
actress named Myrna Loy.

It is recommended that the patient have three hourly
appointments per week. In order to reduce Oedipal fixation and obsessive ideation, patient should only be allowed supervised contact with mother.

Although a boarding school situation might be opti-
mal, the patient is not deemed stable enough to function
within a structured and rigorous school setting. It is
therefore recommended that he work with a tutor at
home until his delusional behavior is curtailed, at which
time he may resume his education.

Billy and I met back in Daddy's office with the doors closed,
face-to-face in the Morris chairs, but our knees were not touching this time. We both had large tumblers of Scotch. Dr. Lucas's
report lay face-down on the carpet, where it had slipped from my
fingers.

"You know, Mother never wanted me to marry you. She thought
you were too self-centered to make a good mother," Billy said. "Of
course, the last thing I was thinking of was whether or not you'd be
a good mother. You were so lovely, and I was flattered that you
seemed to be in love with me."

His tone was mild, bewildered, as if he were muttering to himself. He went on as if he didn't expect me to answer. "Then after we
were married you didn't seem to like anything about me. You didn't
like it when I touched you, you didn't like being pregnant with our
children. You actually seemed relieved when the doctor said you
couldn't have any more babies after Avery. You treated me like I
was a mistake you had to live with. Boring old Billy and his airplanes, boring old Billy and his stocks. And yet I'm the same person

I always was." The light was fading fast outside, but neither of us bothered to turn on the desk lamp.

His words shamed me. I'd always thought Billy was too oblivious to realize that our marriage was a dried-out husk. "You deserved a better wife," I said at last. Someone like Peg Denton, who'd never married and still grinned and patted her hair into place when she spotted Billy at the club.

He nodded his head. "Yes, I did."

"For what it's worth, I tried to be a good mother to the boys. Especially to Avery, since he seemed to need me more."

"By dressing up like Myrna Loy?" Billy said, meeting my eyes for the first time, his mouth twisted in a wintry smile. "Yesterday, I went to Lucas and asked him point blank if he thought I should divorce you. He said no, 'the patient needs the home situation to remain intact.' So we're stuck with each other, old girl."

That evening, after Avery had been sent to bed with a sleeping powder dissolved in hot chocolate, Billy moved his clothes and toilet bag to the maid's bedroom in the rear of the house, where Mrs. Coates had once taken her afternoon naps. He would handle advertising and interviewing candidates for Avery's tutor, he said. My input was not needed or welcome, thank you.

20

The Tutor

A week later, Billy informed me he'd found a tutor for Avery—a law student from the University of Chicago. "Says he used to spend time in this house when he was a little boy. His mother was your parents' cook, I think. Thought it might be good if he knew the lay of the land, what kind of people Avery is from. His name is Julian Coates."

I remembered an earnest little boy sitting at the kitchen table, plowing through my old copies of *Br'er Rabbit* and *The Wizard of Oz* while his mother cooked. Mrs. Coates had quit working for Mother and Daddy during the war to work at the Evanston hospital. Last I'd heard, her ne'r-do-well husband had disappeared, and she'd taken night classes to become a registered nurse. "Always thought she was too good to be a servant in Lake Forest," my mother had said, still sounding indignant.

Julian pedaled up from the train station on a three-speed Raleigh and arrived at our doorstep, damp and flushed. He had his mother's sharp blue eyes and springy brown curls, in bad need of a haircut. He was dressed more like a delivery boy than a law student, with worn corduroy pants lashed around the ankle and a frayed tweed cap. He slowly wandered down the front hall, giving every room a once-over.

"Doesn't look as grand as it used to, does it?" I said. I'd simplified things when we'd moved in, replaced the wallpaper and silk curtains with beige paint and linen, removed the salon portrait, let the marble tiles get scuffed.

"Still looks pretty grand to me. I used to tell people my mother worked in a palace."

Billy sat us both down at the dining room table to review the schedule for Avery's tutoring, "so that there will be no misunderstandings." He patted a stack of textbooks at his elbow. "These are the books he was using in school this year. I had his teachers send their lessons for the rest of the semester so he can keep up with his classmates and get credit for the year." Julian started to flip through the books.

"In addition to his studies, you'll take him into Chicago for his appointment with his psychiatrist three times a week." Billy watched Julian's face for a reaction. This was the first time I'd heard him say that word—he'd told the school and our families that Avery was taking a six-month leave from school because of anemia from infected mastoids.

"All right," said Julian, without lifting his eyes from a map of the Peloponnesian War he'd found in Avery's Latin textbook.

"Besides the daily lessons and the doctor's appointments, it will be up to you to keep Avery occupied in constructive ways appropriate for a fifteen-year-old boy. Do you have any suggestions?"

"Probably the same kinds of things when I was his age. We can ride bikes and hit a tennis ball around. We can go into the city and go to the Field Museum and the Art Institute and catch a matinee . . ."

"He can't do that. There are some peculiarities about Avery's case that you should know about." Billy opened a folder, pulled out Dr. Lucas's report, and handed it to him. Now Julian Coates would know right from the get-go what kind of mother I was, what he was up against.

As Julian read it his face reddened, and one of his legs jiggled under the table. "Okay," he said, handing it to Billy and turning his attention back to the Peloponnesian War. "No movies then."

Next, Avery was dragged out of bed to meet his new tutor. "Oh, good," he said pleasantly, offering his hand, his pajama sleeve sliding back up his skinny arm. He didn't quite understand why he wasn't in school anymore, and seemed lonesome now that he wasn't allowed to talk to me or read movie magazines. As they stood shaking hands, they both bounced nervously on the balls of their feet. With their lean frames, untidy clothes, dark hair standing on end, they looked more like brothers than Will and Avery ever had.

Satisfied that he'd left matters in capable hands, Billy went off to work.

"We need to find someplace where you can work," I said to Julian, leading him through the living room, down the hall, into Daddy's study. I could set up a schoolroom just like the one I'd had with Millie.

We hadn't had guests at the house since Avery ran away, and I suddenly looked at the place through the eyes of a stranger. The framed photographs of the boys had such a thick coat of dust that they seemed to be peering out through a veil. Empty tumblers of Scotch were lined along the windowsills; the desk was piled high with unopened mail and unread newspapers.

"Let me tidy this up," I said, making a tray of the old newspapers, stacking the glasses on top and heading off to the kitchen.

When I came back, Avery was sitting at the desk examining two books that Julian had pulled from his canvas sack—*Mein Kampf* and *The Young Manhood of Studs Lonigan.* Julian slouched in one of the Morris chairs, smoking a cigarette and reading the *Chicago Sun,* which no one I knew read because it was the pro-Roosevelt paper.

"I've cooked up kind of an offbeat educational plan for Avery," Julian said. "I never liked reading Caesar and Wordsworth when I was fifteen, so why should he? I thought he might like to try some newer stuff. For his history lesson, he can read the newspaper every day to see what the Fascists are up to next, and write me weekly reports. I'm not sure Mr. Granger would approve, though."

I picked up *Studs Lonigan* and traced a finger over the drawing on the cover—a young man with a battered felt hat pushed back on his sweaty brow, his burly hands wrapped around a broom handle, his eyes lifted heavenward as if he was dreaming of finer places and finer women. "I don't think Mr. Granger has to know."

Since we only had a part-time cook who came in the evenings, I made them lunch of creamed chipped beef on toast and served it up at the kitchen table.

Julian ate as if he hadn't had a good meal in a while, mopping the plate clean with a piece of toast. "This is where I used to have most of my meals when I was a little boy. My mother was your grandparents' cook," he explained to Avery. "I used to sit at this very table and watch her make finger sandwiches and fried chicken."

"That's neat," Avery said in a vague way. He had a myopic world-view—it was hard for him to imagine that adults were ever children, or that people used to live in this house before he was born.

"I remember your mother used to put money in an account every week for your college," I said. "She must be proud of how you've turned out."

Julian turned up his frayed cuffs. "I'm not so sure about that.

She wishes I'd get a job as a clerk at a Catholic law firm and stop reading books by socialists."

"So what does she think of you working here?"

He set down his coffee cup and laughed—a cocky, youthful laugh that showed off a lot of bright teeth. "I haven't told her, but I don't think she'd like the idea."

I picked up their plates and carried them over to the sink. "She let us know she disapproved of us. Especially me. She thought I was a lazy, spoiled girl, which of course I was."

Julian folded his napkin in a noncommittal way, as if he had no opinion on the subject.

"So why did you come back?" I asked.

"Mr. Granger's advertisement was posted at the law school. When I saw the address, I decided it was too big a coincidence to ignore. I think I was just curious to come back and see if this place was real. Sometimes I wondered if I made it all up."

That afternoon they resurrected Avery's old bicycle from the garage, pumped up the tire, oiled the chain, raised the seat, and pedaled off to the library. Other volumes of "newer stuff" piled up on the desk—*Call It Sleep* and *Tortilla Flat*. Julian tacked a map of Spain and had Avery plot the victories of the Loyalists in Old Castile, Navarre, West Aragon, Catalonia. Julian came up with interesting side trips after Avery's appointments to Dr. Lucas—a lecture on the night sky at the Planetarium, a play called *Waiting for Lefty* by someone named Clifford Odets.

Julian, Avery, and I settled into a routine. After they had spent the morning on lessons, I would make them lunch. It was the only time of day when I got to talk to Avery without Billy's scrutiny, and I'd pepper him with questions just to keep him with me a little longer. I read the *Sun* and dipped into the stacks of books left on the desk late at night, after Billy and Avery had gone to bed.

"Scary what Lindbergh says about the German air corps. Looks like no one can stop Hitler," I ventured.

"Goering's promised Lindbergh a commission in the German Air Corps, so Lindberg will say anything," Avery said.

"Lindbergh's always been a Fascist, ever since they kidnapped his kid," Julian added.

One day Julian announced that they were going into the city early. "We're going to see the murals before Avery's appointment." A WPA mural at the North Branch Post Office was causing a fuss —some outraged postal patron complained that it was filled with Communist propaganda.

"Sounds like fun. I wish I could come along," I said.

"Well then, come. Who says you can't, Ginevra?" Julian said, using my given name for the first time.

"No one, I guess." As long as Julian was along, I wasn't breaking any of Lucas's orders.

The mural, which was a tribute to Illinois farm products, covered a twenty-foot wall above the stamps and parcel post windows.

"See that bearded farmer driving the tractor? They say he looks like Lenin," Avery announced in a high voice that ricocheted down the canyon-shaped lobby. A woman pulling magazines out of her mailbox straightened and glared. "And see those women wearing overalls and babushkas? People say that no farm wife from Illinois would dress like that." The woman marched over to the clerk at the parcel post window as if to complain.

Julian and I both started to giggle. "Maybe you should pipe down a little, buddy," said Julian.

Avery didn't even bother to lower his rapturous gaze. "Why should I?"

Julian and I dropped Avery at Dr. Lucas's office on Clark Street and went around the corner to the Ajax Coffee Shop, where we sat in a booth by the window so we could see Avery when he came out. I ordered black coffee, and Julian ordered cherry pie with a scoop of vanilla ice cream.

"How do you think Avery is doing?" I asked.

"I think he's doing fine. Really, Ginevra. He doesn't want to talk about Myrna Loy all the time. Reading the paper and discussing Alf Landon and the Rome-Berlin Axis seems to keep him grounded in the actual world."

"Do you think he can go to a regular school next year? Billy wants him to go to Hotchkiss with Will."

Julian dumped another dollop of cream in his coffee and gave it a thoughtful stir. "You've got to face facts that Avery is always going to be an eccentric kid. He's not going to bend himself to fit into someone else's mold. He likes to make his own rules."

I stared at the gouged tabletop and let the words "eccentric kid" sink in for a few moments. "Eccentric" sounded a lot better than "strange" or "off," the words that were usually used to describe Avery. Musical prodigies and nutty inventors were called eccentric. I glanced up and found Julian studying me in a somber way that reminded me of his mother.

"Sorry," I said. "I just get so distracted when I think about Avery. Let's change the subject. Do you still live with your mother?" It felt slightly improper to be asking Julian personal questions, as if I were violating one of Dr. Lucas's rules.

"I used to, but we get on one another's nerves, because she still treats me like I'm ten and wants to tidy up my dresser drawers. So thanks to the munificent salary from the Grangers, I can now afford a lovely efficiency in Hyde Park. It looks out on an airshaft and it smells like curry from the Indian medical student next door. But it feels like a palace. So what about you, Ginevra? How'd you end up back at your parents' house?"

"For the usual boring reasons. Daddy had to move to Florida because of his heart, and the boys needed more room to run around, so it all made sense."

He shook his head, chewed his lower lip in a disappointed way. "It doesn't make sense to me. I remember how you used to dress up in all these glamorous costumes, with boys swarming around like flies."

"You make me sound like a rotten banana," I said airily, but I was flattered.

"I always thought you'd do something dramatic, like become a movie actress or marry a Romanian prince."

I made an apologetic shrug. "Evvie's the only one of us who did something interesting. She married a professor who's now the dean at Williams, which is hardly a Romanian prince. I'm afraid we've let you down."

"That's all right," Julian said with a melodramatic sigh. "Illusions die hard."

"Yes, they do," I said, smiling. For the first time in a long time, I remembered what it felt like to be an eighteen-year-old girl who had silly conversations and laughed about nothing.

After that, I joined Julian and Avery on their expeditions into the city. We went to Marshall Field's to see the Christmas decorations, to a record store to listen to the latest Benny Goodman in a soundproof booth, to an exhibit of modernistic furniture by a German architect who'd fled the Nazis.

While Avery had his appointment with Dr. Lucas, Julian and I chatted over coffee and pie in the window booth at the Ajax, and I found myself admitting a few of my shameful secrets. I talked about Will, now a huge, grim boy who played catcher on the Hotchkiss baseball team. "He writes me dutiful letters. 'Dear Mother, I am doing well in mathematics. Dr. Blair read from Paul's First Epistle to the Corinthians. Thanks for asking if you can send me anything, but I'm all squared away. Yours Sincerely, William Granger.' He blames me for the fact that our family is such a mess. At least he writes to his father about normal things like baseball and mixers."

I told him about Evvie, now pregnant with her fourth child. "She's always charging around with a hundred useful projects. Hosting a tea for incoming freshmen at the dean's house. Leading a discussion for faculty wives on the situation in Europe. She and Eliot are in a bell-ringing group. I was jealous when she got engaged and I made a pass at Eliot, but he never told Evvie, bless his heart."

Julian told me about his father, who drank a dozen bottles of beer every night and fell asleep in a chair, listening to Jack Benny on the radio. "But he wasn't allowed to laugh, because Mother was so furious, sweeping under his feet or banging pots in the kitchen." Then one day he didn't come home. "After a couple of weeks, Mother told me that he'd moved into his sister's house in Cicero, and that we were better off without him. And after that he'd turn up every now and then. He showed up one Easter Sunday, and came to a couple of my track meets. He didn't seem to want food or money. Just rubbed my shoulder and got teary. He gave off this sick sweet smell, as if his pores were sweating syrup. Then when I was fourteen we heard from his sister that he'd 'passed.' She didn't say from what. But even a drunk father is better than no father, and sometimes I wished Mother hadn't been so judgmental and driven him off."

When he asked me why I'd married "Mr. Granger," I ducked the question. "I was way too young when I married Billy, and I acted like a little brat when I figured out he was just a regular man, not the aviator I'd made up. But we've come to appreciate each other over the years, even if the business with Avery has been a strain."

Julian crossed his arms and started jiggling a knee to let me know he wasn't buying any of it. Avery had probably told him that Billy had moved into the maid's room.

"So what about you?" I said. "You must have a girlfriend."

"Why do you say that?"

"I would think girls your age would find you attractive."

"I had a girlfriend. Helen Pomeroy, who went to Chicago with me. We talked about getting married for a while, but she had to support her mother. Now they've moved to Houston because her mother developed asthma. I hear from her every now and again. She's a secretary for some oil speculators, so I'm sure she'll land herself a millionaire."

He studied my face. "I would think boys would find you attractive."

I laughed. "That was a long time ago."

"You'd be surprised. I bet some of them still do."

It had started to snow, the flakes coming down in large wet clumps. We slipped down the snowy sidewalk to the vestibule of Dr. Lucas's office building. We were ten minutes early, and the light had burned out in the brass fixture.

"I guess we'll have to wait in the dark."

I turned to Julian, took his elbow in my gloved hand. I opened my mouth to say, That's to thank you for being so kind. Julian placed his hands on my hips and brought me close so I could feel his belt buckle pressing into my middle. He hunched down and kissed me, a long, passionate kiss. Then he straightened and pushed me back a few paces, and we stood staring at each other in the afternoon gloom, breathing hard, until we heard Avery galloping down the marble stairs.

Two days later, for Avery's next appointment, without any discussion, we drove the car into the city, with Julian behind the wheel.

"Why aren't we taking the train?" Avery asked.

"Because your mother and I want to see the exhibit on Mexican crafts at the Armory," Julian answered, without missing a beat.

"Sounds boring."

"That's what we figured you'd say. So this way we'll be back before your appointment's over."

"Okay." As soon as Avery had disappeared behind the brass grill of Dr. Lucas's building, Julian was backing out, heading toward Michigan Avenue, cutting down a maze of side streets that only a native could know. He pulled up in front of a limestone building with crenelations along the top that made it look like a small fortress. ROBIN HOOD EFFICIENCY APARTMENTS was written in neon letters over the door. Julian yanked up the parking brake, hopped out, ran around to my side, and opened the door. His face was serious, determined. He offered me his arm, as if I were his maiden aunt coming for a visit.

"I'm afraid it's five flights up," he said.

"Good exercise." We walked up the stairs at a leisurely pace so we wouldn't arouse the super's suspicion—me in front, Julian in the rear, jangling the keys in his hand.

He unlocked the door, stepped back, and gestured me in. He turned the dead bolt so slowly that it did not make a single click. The room was as spare and immaculate as a monk's cell—a narrow bed covered with a Navajo blanket, abstract art reproductions thumbtacked to the wall, a stack of orange crates jammed with books, a complicated-looking phonograph with records arranged neatly in a stand. In the corner, a writing desk with a Mason jar of pencils but no papers. The curtain was already drawn, a piece of red embroidered silk that gave the room a rosy glow.

He's prepared his room for us, I thought, turning around to face him. He kissed me once, a mere brush of the lips, as if to say, we don't have time for that. He slipped off my coat, folded it, and hung it over the chair, then did the same with his own. He unzipped my dress and slid it off slowly, as if he were luxuriating in every new inch of flesh. Next my slip, then my stockings, until I stood before him naked.

"You are so beautiful," he said, astonished. Then he removed his own clothes, and we lay side by side on his narrow bed and at first simply touched each other, as if we had never done such a thing before and never would again. And then Julian made love to me, not with me, but to me, with his young, insistent, greedy body, and I was the one astonished.

Julian held his bare arm above our faces, turned it so we could read his watch in the pink dusk—4:12. Avery's appointment had ended at four. We got up and with our backs to each other got dressed, then raced down the stairs. We drove in silence, Julian concentrating on every stop sign and light, as if he was willing the traffic to move faster. A block away from Lucas's office I spoke. "Avery can't find out about this."

He reached over for my hand, his expression so intent it almost looked angry. "Trust me. Avery will never know." The waiting room of Lucas's office, with its single chair and *National Geographic*s was empty, as was the vestibule where I had dared to kiss Julian. I stumbled around the corner to the pay phone in the Ajax diner, dread rising in the back of my mouth, wondering which theater to search first. And there in the booth by the window sat Avery with a cup of coffee, an empty plate smeared with cherry pie goo, and a fork poised over a half-eaten wedge of blueberry.

He gave us a sweet, sleepy smile, like a three-year-old who has just been woken up from a nap. "Hi, there. If you didn't come in five minutes, I was going to try the lemon meringue." The corners of his lips were stained blue.

We slid into the other side of the booth, a good three feet between us.

"How was the exhibit?" he asked politely. I studied his eyes for some hint of rage, but they were flat as a stagnant pool.

"Very interesting. Weavings made by peasant women . . ." Julian trailed off, at a loss for words.

"And pottery and some religious figures. All very colorful," I continued, pleased at how convincing I sounded.

For the next two days, Julian and I circled around each other, in an elaborate mating dance. We did not touch, we did not glance at each other even when we were certain that Avery was not watching. Yet every time I could hear Julian's raspy laugh or quick step in another room, I felt like an iron nail tugged by a magnetic force field. Images raged as if I had a fever—our bodies together on his narrow bed, the red silk fluttering from the seep of cold air under the sash. I counted off the time until Avery's next appointment with Lucas—two days away, one day, six hours. I scanned the newspaper for possible alibis and found an exhibit of illuminated manuscripts at the Newbury.

We followed the same routine as the last time—dropped Avery off, then wove through the maze of side streets, only this time I slid across the seat and pressed myself into Julian, kissed his neck, touched him through his pants. "Not too much of that," he laughed, "or I'll crash."

No leisurely pace this time—we bolted up the stairs, slammed the door behind us. I was the one who undressed him, not bothering to fold his clothes but simply tossing everything into a heap. Afterward, Julian put on a record of Bix Beiderbecke, and I fell into a lazy drowse, lulled by footsteps scuffing up the stairwell, the thunks of the heating pipe, the *rat-a-tat-tat* of chilly car engines trying to turn over.

Suddenly Julian was shaking my shoulder. "Christ. It's ten of five." The sky had turned dark, a streetlight shone outside the red silk—covered window. Julian sped through the streets headlong, slamming on the brakes once for a boy who scuttled out from between two parked cars. When we pulled in front of the Ajax, there was Avery's face in the front booth pressed against the glass, his mouth twisted into an anxious frown.

I rapped on the window and hurried in. "Sorry, sorry."

His table was littered with three empty pie plates and strewn newspaper pages. "Why are you so late? I ran out of money, and she said if I didn't order something else I'd have to leave," Avery whined, poking his thumb toward a surly waitress who was wiping up the counter with a gray dishrag.

"There was an accident. The traffic was stopped for blocks." The waitress stopped the dishrag and shot me a skeptical look.

"I don't believe you," said Avery, his voice rising.

I patted his shoulder. "Shh. Let's talk about this in the car."

"I think you were just having fun at your stupid exhibit and you didn't care if you made me wait."

"Let's go." We let Julian off at the elevated, and on the drive back to Lake Forest I tried to jolly Avery along. "I'm sorry. Really. It will never happen again."

"It better not, or I won't go to Lucas's anymore." His arms were folded over his chest, his dark hair hung in a petulant wave over his eyes. "Anyway, he says I'm getting better."

"He does?" First I felt relief, and then, shamefully, panic. If Avery stopped going to Lucas's, there would be no more afternoons with Julian. I can't give him up, I thought. I was a half-dead person until Julian jolted me back to life—I won't turn back.

"Yeah. He says I don't have such a one-track mind anymore. I'm reading newspapers and books instead of movie magazines. I'm talking about Alf Landon and John Steinbeck instead of Myrna Loy."

"I agree. Dr. Lucas has helped you a lot."

"Lucas had nothing to do with it. Julian is the one who's helped me."

My pulse spluttered just to hear his name said out loud. Julian, Julian. "Well, that's right. Julian too." His lovely, lean body arching over mine in the gauzy light.

We turned on Sheridan Road and drove in silence for half an hour. We are not really hurting Avery, I told myself. Avery loves me, Avery loves Julian. He wants us to be happy.

"Oh, and guess what?" Avery said, turning to me with a tentative smile, pushing his hair back. "Lucas said I could try going to movies again. It would be sort of a test, to see if I could handle it. I'd have to go to ones that don't have Myrna in them, of course." He watched my face. "What do you think?"

I took a few moments to digest this suggestion. It was hard to believe that Lucas had given Avery permission to see movies again. But Avery was getting better, obviously, and maybe overcoming his obsession was part of the final cure. It must be the truth, I decided. Avery was incapable of telling a lie, and besides, I wanted to believe him, I needed to believe him.

"All right," I said carefully. "We'll give it a try. But there will be restrictions. And if you start writing letters to movie stars or gluing their pictures all over your wall, the privilege will be revoked."

"Don't worry. You can trust me," Avery said, excitement creeping into his voice. He stared at the headlights bouncing off the blackened windshield as if it were a flickering screen.

The next day, when Avery was holed up in Daddy's office writing an essay on the roots of the Stalin-Trotsky schism, I confessed my scheme to Julian in the pantry. "I probably shouldn't have agreed. I just couldn't think of any other way for us to still see each other."

Julian turned and faced me, his eyes narrowed as if he was notic-ing flaws for the first time. "I guess a movie now and then won't do him any harm," he said, pulling me close. I buried my face in his neck, inhaled the Borax that he used to wash his shirt every night in the apartment sink.

21

Matinee

On the day of Avery's next appointment, I searched the movie listings in the newspaper. *Swing Time* was playing at the State Lake. Too romantic, and Avery might develop a fixation on Ginger Rogers. *Romeo and Juliet*, at the Chicago, was a possibility—hard to find fault with Shakespeare, after all. But it starred Norma Shearer, one of Avery's dark-haired loves before Myrna. Finally I picked *The Story of Louis Pasteur* at the Oriental, which sounded educational and didn't even list a female star. Julian and I reviewed the plan with Avery in the car ride into the city.

"You can only see this show at the Oriental. No slipping off to another theater. I'll be waiting in front at six o'clock," I said.

"So how are you going to kill time while I'm at the movies?" Avery asked. Julian and I exchanged a frantic glance—was this a pointed question? I didn't think so—his voice sounded guileless as always.

"I'm going home. I've got a class at seven," Julian offered.

"And I've got errands in the Loop."

"Why do women always have so many errands?" Avery asked.

"That's a profound question, my boy," said Julian.

Three hours to ourselves—what luxury. Julian meandered through the side streets to Dorchester Avenue, we sauntered up the stairs, and took our time in every other way. He boiled water on the hot plate and made us oolong tea in paper-thin porcelain cups. I wrapped myself in his red plaid bathrobe and wandered around inspecting his things. His undergraduate diploma from the University of Chicago, all in Latin; the only words I recognized were *magna cum laude*. A faded snapshot of Julian in a track uniform, poised mid-stride on the starting line, ready to sprint off at the burst of an unseen gun, "New Trier" written in script across the flimsy undershirt. I knelt down and read the titles of the books jammed on the shelf. Rows of sober tomes by John Dewey, Charles Beard, George Santayana. Then novels and slim volumes of poems piled on top. *The 42nd Parallel* by John Dos Passos, *The Harp-Weaver* by Edna St. Vincent Millay. I memorized the titles so I could check them out of the library—I wanted to read everything that Julian had read. I pulled a cheap, warped book from the bottom of a pile—*This Side of Paradise*.

I held it up for Julian to see from the bed. "Did you like this?"

He squinted at the garish cover portrait of a petulant boy lounging in the front seat of a roadster. "The famous novel of flaming youth" was stamped across the top in red letters, like a brand. "Oh, right. A friend from New Trier gave me that as a joke when we graduated. It used to be the hot book for college boys. I never actually read it. Have you?"

I climbed back onto the bed. "Fitzgerald was an old boyfriend, believe it or not."

He gave me an uncertain smile, not sure if I was pulling his leg. "Really?"

"He came to visit me in Lake Forest. Maybe you remember him. He was a sophomore at Princeton. Very blond, very slight."

He flipped through the yellowed pages as if he was having a hard time putting his lover and this ancient author together. "I do remember one boy, but I thought he was a friend of Evvie's. He once had breakfast at the kitchen table, and Evvie talked to him like he was an invalid. Eat up, she said. The bacon is good. Just take one bite."

Oh, Lord. Scott's final morning after the McCormicks' party. "I'd thrown him over, ordered him to leave, and good old Evvie was trying to make sure he had a decent breakfast before he got on the train."

The book dropped from Julian's fingers. He slipped the robe off my shoulder and kissed my collarbone. "Did you and Fitzgerald do stuff like this?"

I shook my head. "Hardly." I've never done stuff like this with anyone else but you, I wanted to say. When I left, Julian was asleep in a tangle of bed sheets and empty teacups.

I pulled up in front of the Oriental just as the show was getting out, watched the crowd drift out under a mandarin roof made of yellow blinking lights—a harried mother tugging two freckled-faced boys done up in their Sunday best, two young women dressed in practical suits like secretaries, a lone man examining the movie posters in the brass case by the ticket booth. I made up stories about what had brought them to a Wednesday matinee of *The Story of Louis Pasteur*. The kids on a spree from some hamlet downstate. The two women's boss was away on vacation, so they decided to live dangerously and leave work early. The man had lost his job but hadn't told his wife yet. Most of the scenarios I imagined seemed to involve lying or sneaking off.

Just when the crowd had thinned and I was feeling the first prickle of alarm, Avery came bouncing out, his hands thrust deep in his pockets, with a blissful, faraway look that I hadn't seen in a long while. When he spotted me, the smile faded to the normal range and he jumped in the car.

"How was it?" I asked. There was a pause—he didn't seem to be listening. "Avery?"

"Oh, sorry. It was wonderful. Louis Pasteur was a great man. All these children were dying of undulant fever and he saved them."

"And you didn't feel too overwhelmed going to the movies again?" I studied his face in the flickering glow of the marquee.

He examined the tops of his hands as if there might be some telltale sign—shaking, a rash. "No, I seem fine."

On the way home, he chatted away about non-movie star topics—like the stadium that Hitler was constructing in Berlin. "It'll hold over two hundred thousand people. Julian says Hitler's just using the Olympics as a stage for Nazi propaganda and America should withdraw its team. But I think we should go, because what better way is there to show up Hitler than to have a Jew or a colored man win?" Lucas was right, I decided; Avery could handle a movie now and then. Maybe someday soon, he could handle other things too—school, a girlfriend, a job.

Once a week I picked out a movie on a dull subject and with few female stars. Julian and I would drive Avery to the city, drop him at Lucas's office, and then dash across town to Julian's apartment. During our three hours together, I pretended that we had a real relationship that was deepening, that Julian and I had a future. I cooked him scrambled eggs and fried bread on the hot plate while he played me his favorite records—Gene Krupa at Carnegie Hall, songs from a new show called *Porgy and Bess*. We looked at his senior portrait in the New Trier yearbook—with slicked-down hair and a bow tie—taken a mere eight years ago.

Julian told me more about Helen—that she had a slight limp

from having had polio when she was three, that they had been lovers but she was too nervous about getting pregnant to enjoy it. "The best part for her was getting her period once a month."

I told him the truth about my marriage. "He wanted to divorce me after Avery ran away. But Lucas said we should stay together for Avery's sake. You've probably guessed that he sleeps in the maid's room."

"I guessed."

When Will came home for Christmas, I was afraid he would notice the electric charge between Julian and me, or think it curious that Avery was allowed to see a movie once a week. But he seemed mostly grateful that Avery had recovered, and was in the care of someone as capable as Julian. His only complaint was that I seemed to be avoiding Julian. "You're such a snob, Mother," Will scolded. "You shouldn't look down on someone just because his mother used to be a cook here and he reads the Democratic paper. You know, lots of boys at school support FDR."

"I suppose I should be more open-minded."

In the last week of March, Julian and I dropped Avery at Lucas's office. A wintry wind whipped up Clark Street, flapping the tattered FDR posters pasted on every streetlight. As usual, I reviewed the plans as Avery climbed out. "So I'll pick you up at the State Lake at six o'clock. *Tale of Two Cities,* remember. Don't go anywhere else."

"Okay. So where are you going?" He always asked.

"The Rembrandt exhibit at the Art Institute."

"But I thought you'd already seen that."

Had I already used that as an excuse? "I'm going again."

I remembered every detail of my afternoon with Julian, because it turned out to be our last. We made love in a way that had evolved in four months from a hundred-yard dash to a minuet—

every sensation prolonged, savored. Afterward, I touched a small scar on his shoulder blade that looked like a rust-colored blister. "What's that from?" I asked. I was always discovering something new about his body.

"I was playing with sparklers one Fourth of July when I was five, and a cinder landed on my shirt and smoldered through. I always thought it would go away, but I guess it's there to stay."

I bent down and kissed it.

"What about you? Any scars on your Woodberry complexion?"

"Just one." I raised my leg so he could see a silvery streak across the back of my knee. "My sister Evvie threw a croquet wicket at me. I had to get a tetanus shot."

Julian ran his finger over the ridge. "Was she the type that threw things?"

"More like I was the type who got things thrown at me. I was a mean older sister."

"That's hard to believe."

"I wish you could meet Evvie and Eliot. You'd like them." I couldn't keep the wistful tone out of my voice. Julian and I would never be a normal couple who had friends or went places—we only existed in three-hour stretches in a Hyde Park efficiency. When I left, Julian was in his plaid bathrobe, sitting at the built-in kitchen table reading the newspaper and sipping tea, looking like a young husband on a Sunday morning.

When I pushed out the heavy glass door of Julian's building, I noticed the sky had turned dark and ominous, the last flakes of winter were spiraling downward. Just like the first time I kissed Julian, I thought. We'd survived an entire season. My next thought was, I have to pick up Avery before the snow gets heavier. I trotted across Dorchester Avenue to where I'd parked the car, its windows now covered with a dusting of white, and yanked open the door.

"Hello, Mother," said Avery. He sat slumped down in the passenger seat, the collar of his coat pulled up over his ears, his hands jammed down in his pockets. "Sorry. I didn't mean to startle you." His breath made a dense cloud.

I stumbled into the driver's seat, eased the door shut, turned the key in the starter, my mind trying to grasp how Avery came to be in the car, outside Julian's apartment. "How'd you get here?" I finally asked.

"I took a taxi." His teeth were chattering.

The starter clicked a few times, then the motor sputtered to life. I pushed the gas pedal, flicked on the windshield wipers to clear the snow, wiped the inside of the glass with a handkerchief. Don't ask questions, I told myself, let him do the talking. A few puffs of warm air seeped out of the heater.

"I went to the State Lake like we planned, but the projector was broken and the show was canceled. So then I walked over to the Art Institute to find you, but it turns out that the Rembrandt show closed back in January. I wandered all around the Art Institute looking for you. The gallery that has the big painting made all of dots, and the one that has the marble statues of Greek gods. There's a taxi stand outside, so I decided to come over to Julian's and he could tell me what to do next. But then I saw the car, and thought I better just wait here. I'm sorry I didn't stay at the State Lake. I know you told me not to go anywhere else."

"You did the right thing." I put the car in gear and eased it out of the space. "I'm just sorry you got so cold." I kept my face pointed straight ahead at the hypnotic swish of the wipers so he wouldn't see the fear in my eyes.

I drove in silence for mile after mile, down Green Bay Road through Evanston, Winnetka, Highland Park. The snow stopped and melted into harmless puddles on the pavement, the car turned steamy hot, and Avery took off his coat. At a stoplight, I forced myself to glance over at him.

He was staring at me with his chin dropped like a child who was about to get scolded. "You're not mad at me?"

Why did Avery think I was mad at him? Because he'd left the State Lake, or because he'd found out that Julian was my lover? Don't ask, I told myself. He has a child's mind, he doesn't grasp the adult world. Badgering him about what he heard, what he suspects, will just do more damage. "I'm not mad at you. I have no reason to be mad at you," I said softly, reaching over and lifting his chin up with my gloved hand.

I said nothing to Julian when he came the next day to tutor Avery. The wisest course was to go ahead with our daily routine, I decided, and then maybe Avery would decide that our car parked at Julian's was of no significance. All day, I watched Avery and Julian from afar. In the morning, they worked on a wall chart they were keeping on the Nazi military buildup. Avery filled columns with tiny drawings of goose-stepping soldiers, fighter planes, tanks, and submarines. Then I overheard Avery recite the first few stanzas of a Vachel Lindsay poem, with Julian hammering out the beat on a tabletop. *Walking lepers followed, rank on rank, / Lurching bravos from the ditches dank . . .*

Avery stopped. "You're going too fast," he complained, laughing.

"You're going too slow," Julian answered. The same cheerful banter as always.

The next week, as we were planning for his afternoon appointment with Lucas, I decided to play it safe. Avery was running his finger down the movie listings. "How about *Modern Times* at the Paradise?" he suggested.

"Let's skip the movie today, all right? I'll just wait for you at the Ajax, and we can head home after your appointment."

Avery sucked in his cheeks and folded the paper shut, looking like a child who had been falsely accused. "All right," he said in a meek voice.

I dropped Julian at the elevated and Avery at Lucas's, then went around the corner to the Ajax. I sat in the front booth by the window, ordered coffee and blueberry pie. I tried to read an article in *Collier's* by Eleanor Roosevelt about her work to improve infant health care, but my mind kept side-slipping onto the image of Avery's scrawny body stretched out on the frayed velvet chaise in Lucas's office. I imagined the damning things Avery might tell Lucas. "Mother told me that she'd pick me up at the State Lake, but the show was canceled because the projector was broken. So I went to Julian's apartment, and there was her car parked right in front . . ."

When I glanced up from my hallucination, it was ten past four —Avery would be along any minute. I had a second cup of coffee and a bite of pie, which had turned cold and gelatinous. At four-thirty, I walked over to Lucas's office—maybe he was waiting for me in the lobby. No Avery. I glanced up at the light fixture that had started it all—two fresh bulbs twinkled innocently. I walked up the two flights to Lucas's office. The door was ajar. I knocked, peeked around the corner, and found Lucas sitting at his desk, scribbling furiously in a small notebook.

He squinted at me. "Can I help you?"

He didn't recognize me, which shouldn't have surprised me, since he'd only seen me once, with my face bloated from tears. "Do you know where Avery is?"

"I could ask you the same question. In the future, if he is going to miss an appointment, I wish you would do me the courtesy of canceling." Then, seeing the alarm in my face, he pointed at his desk. "Use the phone if you want."

Rotating my back to Lucas and cupping my hand around the receiver, I called Julian. "Is Avery there?"

"Why would Avery be here?" he said, sounding sleepy.

"Because he was there Tuesday. I didn't tell you. He was waiting for me in the car outside your building."

"What?" he said, so loud that I had to jerk the receiver away. I glanced over at Lucas, who was still jotting away, his eyes fixed conspicuously downward.

"We'll talk about this later. Run down and see if you see him on the street. I'll wait." The phone thunked against a tabletop, followed by footsteps and the slamming of a door. I watched the wall clock long enough to see the minute hand jerk forward three times, Lucas's pen scratching away the whole time.

Then footsteps back, Julian's gasps. "No sign of him. Now what?"

"I'm going to call Billy, and we'll search the theaters. We've done it before, you know." I hung up the receiver very tenderly, as if I were placing a baby down in its crib. Then I picked it up again and called Billy's office.

Lucas was leaning back in his chair, his fingers set tip to tip. His expression was weary, as if once again humans had reverted to their old incorrigible ways despite his best efforts. "I will wait here in case the boy shows up."

Billy and I searched every downtown movie theater. Have you seen a boy like any other sixteen-year-old—five-foot-nine, thin face, uncombed brown hair, tweed jacket? we asked. The next day, two Chicago detectives came out to Lake Forest to interview us. Billy and I sat side by side in the Morris chairs in Daddy's office, the policemen standing in front of us, one to ask the questions, the other with a pad to write down everything we said. "Is there any reason why your son might want to hurt himself? Has anything happened recently that could have upset him?"

And so I told them about Avery finding my car parked outside
Julian's apartment. As I spoke, I studied Avery's chart still thumbtacked to the wall behind them, counting the fifty-six Nazi foot
soldiers, each one representing ten thousand men, as they goose-
stepped right off the edge, like sheep stampeding over a cliff. When
I was finished, I caught the two detectives exchanging a glance that
said, this big fancy house and all this stinking money, and she has to
screw the kid's tutor. Figures, doesn't it?

They asked for Julian's name and address. "He doesn't know
anything about this. Really," I said, my voice quavering, as if I was
telling a lie.

The next day, the story appeared at the bottom of the front page.
"Prominent Businessman's Son Reported Missing." They ran Avery's
picture from eighth grade at the Bell School. "Detective Faulkner
of the Fifth Precinct issued a statement that they are investigating
the case as a runaway, although they have not ruled out foul play.
The boy's tutor, Julian Coates of Hyde Park, was the last person to
see the boy on the afternoon of March 30. Coates was questioned
by police and released."

We told my parents and Evvie and Eliot that there was nothing
they could do but wait and hope. Julian did the discreet thing—he
disappeared from view. Will insisted on coming home from boarding school to help his father search the movie palaces and elevated
stations again and again, catching catnaps in the back seat of the car.

On the fifth day of Avery's disappearance, Billy and Will rode
on the deck of a police launch that cruised up the Chicago River and
directed a searchlight on the bridge pylons where bodies washed
up. I stayed in a chair at my kitchen table, drinking coffee and trying
to read a new novel that Millie Pullman had brought over to distract
me called, appropriately enough, *Gone With the Wind*. I needed to
wait by the phone, Billy told me, in case they had news.

The phone rang, and as I picked it up, I had an image of Avery's wet face resting against a stone block as if it were a pillow. "Ginevra, he's here," said a joyful male voice. "This is Eliot," he added.

"Where is 'here'?"

"Williamstown. Evvie heard a scratch at the door like a dog. And there was Avery!"

"Is he all right?"

"Hard to tell." Eliot's voice was suddenly subdued. "He'd lost his coat somehow and was chilled to the bone. And I don't think he's had anything to eat for days. Evvie's got him wrapped in blankets and is feeding him some soup."

"Put him on."

"I can't, I'm afraid. He doesn't seem to be able to talk. We've called a doctor."

The doctor described it as a catatonic state. His temperature was 96, his pulse rate was 52, his eye dilation had a delayed response to light. Avery was taken by ambulance to Massachusetts General Hospital. Billy and Will took an airplane to Boston the next morning, and I was not asked to come along. After a week of intravenous feeding and hydration, Avery's condition stabilized, but he was still mute. In consultation with Dr. Lucas, the doctors recommended that the patient be transferred to McLean Hospital in Belmont for evaluation. Five weeks after Avery's disappearance, Billy's lawyer sent me the McLean report.

> During four-week hospitalization, the patient's catatonic state has gradually abated. Patient is now willing to converse with doctors and family members and demonstrates normal affect. Patient participates in scheduled activities and occupational therapy . . .
> Patient still suffers from selective amnesia of events

prior to March 30 when he ran away . . . Patient
becomes agitated when asked by doctors to discuss
mother . . .

Patient has requested to live with aunt and uncle,
Evelyn and Eliot Schumacher. Professor Schumacher
is Dean of Williams College in Williamstown Mass.
Schumachers have a stable home environment and are
willing to act as patient's guardian. It is therefore recommended that patient live with the Schumachers and
continue psychiatric treatments on an outpatient basis.

Enclosed in the envelope was a legal document for a "divorce of
the marriage bond," filed by William Granger against Ginevra Perry
Granger. In the line next to "proper grounds," someone had typed
in "adultery."

22

The Crack-Up

On May 30, 1937, I took down the chart of the Nazi military buildup and the map of the Loyalist front in Spain, folded them in two, and stuffed them in the trash can outside the kitchen door. I cleared the desk of Julian's books—*Mein Kampf, Studs Lonigan, Appointment in Samara, The Cantos*—packed them in a liquor carton, and wrote "Julian Coates, 4817 Dorchester Avenue, Apt. 5C" on the outside. An address I had visited over a dozen times but never written down before. I stuck in a note scribbled on a slip of Avery's lined paper. "I am so sorry. None of this is your fault. Be well. G."

I covered the furniture with sheets, pulled the curtains, dead-bolted the doors, and walked away from my old life with two suitcases.

I found a furnished one-bedroom in a respectable but slightly down-at-the-heels residential hotel called the Seneca. Most of the other tenants were retired school-teachers. The only personal possession I'd brought besides clothes was a framed photo of Avery and Will, taken six years ago when we moved to Lake Forest, skating at the

Winter Club. They were bundled up in plaid scarves, woolen hats with earflaps, mittens. Avery stood on his skates, ankles buckled inward, grinning triumphantly at the camera. Will had an arm wrapped around Avery's middle, keeping him upright, his chin resting on top of his little brother's head.

Billy communicated with me through lawyers. Papers had been filed and the divorce would be finalized in six months. Since I was the guilty party, I was not entitled to any alimony but would retain title to the Lake Forest house. Due to the "mitigating circumstances," he was applying for full custody of the children. I would be granted visitation rights "as deemed appropriate by medical authorities."

My parents sent me cheerful postcards from Florida of beach cabanas and palm-lined boulevards. Evvie and I had decided to spare them the sordid details of my divorce, and they were careful not to probe too deeply. "Can't understand why you picked the Seneca, of all places," my mother wrote. "Maybe it's improved." "It was 82 degrees yesterday," Daddy wrote. "You and the boys should come down for some sunshine. If they can't get excused from school, why don't you come by yourself?"

Evvie wrote me weekly reports about Avery's progress.

—Avery is doing a wonderful job settling into our household routine. He is very diligent about making his bed every morning and clearing his dishes after a meal. He seems to enjoy my cooking and is fattening up nicely. According to the scale in the bathroom, he has gained almost ten pounds and now weighs 133.

—Avery is becoming very popular with his little cousins. Charlie demands that he give him piggyback rides all around the block, and Jane will not go to bed

before he has read her the *Three Little Pigs* in his scary big
bad wolf voice.

—Eliot has been driving Avery to his weekly appointment at the Austen Riggs clinic in Stockbridge. His new
doctor is George Libby. He is barely thirty, and just finished his training at Hopkins last year. Eliot and I feel
that he may connect better with Avery than an old-
world doctor like Lucas.

—Eliot and I have been trying our best to keep Avery up
with his lessons. We have gotten textbooks from
Williamstown High School. I have been working with
him on irregular French verbs, and am trying to get him
through *Othello*. Eliot has been working with him every
night on geometry, but says he was never much good at
the subject himself, so it's the blind leading the blind.

—Will is planning to come for a long weekend before
he heads back to school. Avery has missed his brother a
good deal and speaks of him often. I think it is lonely for
Avery not to be around boys his own age.

—I realize this is a dark time in your life. I know you are
not ready to face a visit with Mother and Daddy in Boca
Grande, but at least try to keep yourself busy. Don't let
yourself fall into a morbid state.

Even though I was grateful for Evvie's kind words, I was not doing
very well keeping myself out of "a morbid state." I made no effort to
keep in contact with our old friends in Lake Forest, and the only

people who got in touch with me were Elsie Sturgis and Millie Pullman, who had finally decided it was time to "face facts" that she had
more fun on a golf course than she did in the company of her husband and that she should get a divorce. Every Thursday they took me
out to dinner and a show. "The gay divorcees' night on the town,"
Elsie called it, but in truth it felt like a visit to an invalid's sickbed.

"Ginevra, please eat some of your lamb chop. You are wasting
away to nothing," Elsie said.

"Try to smile," said Millie as we walked into the theater. "This is
supposed to be a comedy."

When I didn't have plans with Millie and Elsie, I wandered
around like a ghost. Once I took a bus over to my mother's old
house on Prairie Avenue. It was now a derelict boarding house with
a cardboard sign taped to the window—ROOMS BY THE WEEK OR
BY THE MONTH. I stood in front of the parlor window and looked
across to the spot where the grand Perry mansion had once stood,
and which was now a weedy, vacant lot. I took the elevated to the
Loop and had coffee and blueberry pie in the front booth of the
Ajax, went to the latest exhibit at the Art Institute, took in a matinee at the State Lake. Every time I glanced up or turned around, I
expected to see Julian, with his unkempt hair and clothes, walking
toward me with a jaunty step.

One time a magazine clipping fell from one of Evvie's letters.

> I came across this in a back issue of *Esquire* and thought
> you might find it interesting. Sad, isn't it? He was so
> famous, and he seems to have fallen so far.

I hadn't seen Fitzgerald's name in print in a few years; I couldn't
even remember in what closet shelf or box I'd stashed my old clip
file.

I sank down in the threadbare loveseat in my "parlor," flicked on the lamp with the yellowed shade, and smoothed out an article called "The Crack-Up," by F. Scott Fitzgerald, dated February 1936. There was no author photograph.

> There is another blow that comes from within—that
> you don't feel until it's too late to do anything about it,
> until you realize with finality that in some regard you
> will never be as good a man again.

It was Scott's dark night of the soul. For seventeen years, he'd believed that "life was something you dominated if you were any good," but "ten years this side of forty-nine, I suddenly realized that I had prematurely cracked." Now he lived in a dollar-a-day room in a little town where no one knew him, lived off potted meat and crackers, and didn't change out of his pajamas for days on end. He spent his days moving around "great secret trunks" in his head. "My self-immolation," he concluded, "was something sodden-dark."

I jumped up, whirled around in horror, taking in the faded wallpaper, the windows painted shut, my larder filled with a tin of deviled ham and a box of Uneeda biscuits. I was like Scott—trapped in a rented-by-the-month flat "where no one knew me." I stuffed the article back into the envelope and stuck it in the unread pages of Gone With the Wind. For the first time in years, I felt the urge to track down Scott and write him a letter. It may be small comfort, but I too feel like an old cracked plate.

One day there was a knock on my door, which startled me—I didn't have any visitors dropping by. I swung open the door to find Julian in the hallway with crooked brass sconces. He was oddly aged in six months—the Adam's apple poking out like a doorknob, the trousers hanging down to his hips. His eyes slid over me, up and down, taking in my gaunt neck and the loose folds of my dress. Then he gave me his old grin with the crooked eyetooth—as handsome as ever.

"Come in," I said, wishing I'd remembered to brush my hair and put on lipstick that morning. "It's pretty bleak, I'm afraid." I waved him toward the loveseat, the only seat in the room, and settled on the other end at a discreet distance. "How'd you find me?"

"It wasn't easy. I had to go out to Lake Forest and take a mail clerk out to coffee on her break. Finally she handed over your forwarding address. Told me the gossip she'd heard. That you're getting a divorce. That Avery is living out east with your sister." He turned so his foot crossed the divide, almost touching mine.

"No secrets in a small town."

"'Fraid not. So how is he?" His eyelids winced, as if steeling himself for the answer.

I shrugged. "Better than he was. That's about all we can hope for." We lapsed into a miserable silence, both studying our own lap. "How are you doing?"

"I got my degree. I've got a job, too. As an associate partner for a law firm in Houston."

"Houston?"

He nodded. "Helen and I have been writing." He let out a sigh, raised his woe-filled eyes. "I think we're probably going to get married. That's why I came. I wanted to tell you."

"Don't be sorry. I'm glad. You deserve to be happy."

He looked at the little pile of unread novels on the nicked coffee table and the photograph of Will and Avery skating. "What's going to happen to you?"

"I'm just waiting. For Avery to recover. For Will to finish up at boarding school. For my divorce to be final. Then maybe we can all move back to our old house, and life will be just the way it used to be." I wasn't lying exactly. Avery, Will, and I back together again was the only future I could imagine.

I leaned over and touched Julian's face, ran a finger down the lovely hollow of his cheek. "Please don't worry about me. I'll survive."

His hand reached out and touched my back. Smoothed down my hair, caressed the edge of my ear, the back of my neck. It was the first time anyone had touched me in months, and I went limp against him. Suddenly we were touching everywhere, in our old familiar way, as if we'd last been together yesterday. Every detail of Julian came back to me in a rush—the soapy smell of his neck, the springy curl of his hair, the sharp edge of his shoulder blade through his worn cotton shirt.

Julian pulled back a half inch. "We shouldn't be doing this. I'm going to Houston in three days. I can't change that."

"I know. We're just saying goodbye."

23

The Wilshire Grill

A couple of months later, I came down with a stubborn case of stomach flu. At first I thought I'd gotten food poisoning from a tin of deviled ham, but then it dawned on me that the thing Dr. Robey had told me could never happen again had happened. I went to his office for an examination and was informed that once again the rabbit had died.

I sat perched on a chilly metal examining table, wrapped in a starched sheet, bare feet dangling in midair. "You told me I couldn't get pregnant again," I insisted, shaking my head.

"I said *probably* not. Probably is not a reliable method of family planning." His pen made a reproving scribble across his clipboard—he knew I was a half-divorced woman with no husband, past or future, in sight. Then he let out a re- signed sigh. "I suppose I could give you another D and C to remove excess uterine tissue. Let's schedule it in, say, three weeks. By that time maybe nature will have taken its proper course."

It took me a moment or two to realize what he was offering—an abortion. That is, unless nature took its "proper course." Dr. Robey had probably heard all the gossip about Julian, and had decided that the only proper course for an egg growing inside of me was to shrivel up and wash away.

I still had two more weeks before my "procedure," as Dr. Robey's nurse called it, when Millie Pullman telephoned from the bungalow she'd rented at the Riviera Country Club in Pacific Palisades. It was a little reward, she said, after "sitting on my fanny" for six weeks at a divorce ranch outside Reno to get rid of that stick-in-the-mud John Pullman once and for all.

"I'm taking lessons every day from the assistant golf pro. He just graduated from Stanford, and is very talented, if you know what I mean." There was a pause, as if she was suddenly wondering if that sounded like a snide remark about Julian. "Sorry. Don't take that the wrong way. But please come for a visit. We can play golf every day, and then at night, we'll go dancing at the Trocadero and have our pictures taken outside Grauman's Chinese."

"Maybe I will."

"That's more like it, Gin." There was a scratch as Millie lit a Lucky with one of the kitchen matches she always carried in her pocket. "I know you've been worried sick about Avery, but you deserve a little fun. Time to get back into the swim," she growled.

I bought myself a new suitcase and two drip-dry dresses. I even booked my ticket on an airplane—a DC-3 that had two engines and was guaranteed to be crash-proof. But dark thoughts lurked around every corner. Almost twenty years ago to the day, Billy had said someday soon we'd take a plane like we would the Twentieth Century. I could still see the way he imitated an airplane landing with his butter knife the night he proposed at the Palmer House. Poor Billy had been so full of dreams.

The night before I was to fly to California, I lay motionless on the bed, my fingers laced over my fragile belly like a birdcage. Don't worry, baby, I thought crazily, I'll take care of you.

The spotlight in the alley leaked in around the curtains. I spotted an envelope on the bookshelf with the pages of "The Crack-Up" hanging out like a dog's tongue. I remembered a line—"My self-immolation was sodden-dark."

I sat up, turned on the bedside lamp, found the letter Marie Hart had sent me when I'd written her asking for Scott's address.

> Things seem to be going better for Scott, thank goodness. In his darkest hour, he got a job as a scriptwriter for Metro Goldwyn Mayer, and is now living in Hollywood! At least now he has a regular salary to pay for Zelda's hospital and for Scottie's boarding school tuition. I think he has even managed to dry out, for the time being at least. He always asks about you, after all these years.

I will visit Scott, I thought. He, of all people, knows what it feels like to hit bottom. He will help me, tell me where to go from here.

I will drive over to Hollywood from Santa Monica, I decided. We will have lunch at some famous Hollywood restaurant like the Brown Derby, without the cocktails, of course. He will be more handsome than he had been at nineteen, the way pretty men sometimes are. A few gray hairs and wrinkles will have given his face character, gravity. His eyes will shine with sobriety, his skin will have turned ruddy tan from the California sun.

We will reminisce all afternoon. Remember the clang of heat pipes at the Harts' house. Remember the bobsled ride—the smell of that buffalo robe, the white cloud of our breath. And the letters, all those letters—good heavens, how ridiculous—when we both should have been doing our schoolwork. And then gradually, as the lunchtime crowd thins and the busboys start to set up the tables for dinner, the mood will shift toward the "sodden-dark."

I've made mistakes—so many, I will say, taking his broad, tan hand in mine.

There's still time for both of us to turn our lives around, he will say.

At the airport the next morning, I sent a wire to F. Scott Fitzgerald, Garden of Allah Hotel, Hollywood, California. When I arrived at Millie's twenty hours later, a Western Union was waiting on the hall table.

> Ginevra—To see you again after 21 years. How strange, how wonderful. Tuesday, Beverly Wilshire Grill, at noon.
>   Ever Yours, Scott

I spent the whole morning picking out the right outfit for our lunch. The year 1916, the last time I had seen Scott, was a century ago in terms of fashion. I'd had long hair that I'd worn up, corsets, and fussy hats with ostrich plumes. Since then, my hair had been hacked off, the underwear thrown away, the skirts shortened up to my knees. And now the hair and hemlines were long again, the brassieres and garter belts back, now fortified with elastic.

Since October in southern California was still midsummer hot, I tried a polka-dot navy dress with a white belt and stadium pumps, then tossed it aside as being hopelessly Midwestern-matron-goes-to-the-bridge-club. Finally I settled on a dark green Mainbocher "silhouette" dress with tight sleeves and padded shoulders, which I wore with the jaguar clips Avery had given me because they were like Myrna Loy's. I inspected myself back and front in a full-length mirror, ran an appraising hand over my concave stomach. I'd been so nauseated lately, I was thinner than I'd been in years. I put some rouge and lipstick on to brighten up my pale face. I definitely had more style and substance at thirty-seven, I decided, than I'd ever had at sixteen.

The Beverly Wilshire loomed up like a Hollywood stage set for a luxury hotel—potted palms that flanked the doors were as tall as elms, the brass of the revolving door as bright as gold, the bellboys' uniforms covered with more braid and epaulets than a Fascist general. I crossed a mile-long expanse of velvet carpet that swallowed every sound, down two steps into a plush cavern with bulbous booths in tufted leather and electric lights shrouded behind frosted-glass palm fronds. "Ah, yes, the Fitzgerald party," the maitre d' said, leading me back to a two-person booth tucked deep in a shadowy corner, a hidden place where a studio mogul could seduce his latest starlet.

A slight, elderly man glanced up, slid across the slippery leather, rose to his feet. "Ginevra." A voice with the harsh r's of a Midwestern city perched on a bluff high above the Mississippi.

As my eyes adjusted to the dim light, the features shifted and rearranged themselves until they became Scott, the same and yet grotesquely changed. He still had the full hair and slim build of a Princeton sophomore, but the face looked as if it had been made up for a role in a Hollywood horror movie—the man who has seen his own ghost. The blond hair had turned translucent rather than gray, as if the pigment had been drained out. His eyes were sunken, as if they had been crayoned with ash. The deathly pale was made worse by a snappy houndstooth-check jacket with a silk handkerchief swooning out of the breast pocket and a stiff collar bleached blue-white. He clasped my hand in both of his. They trembled; the skin felt as fragile as tissue paper.

I scooted onto the banquette, and the maitre d' hovered for a drink order. Scott raised a half-emptied tumbler of iced tea—he'd been waiting a while. "I'm on the water wagon—doctor's orders. Want a cocktail?"

"Iced tea is fine."

Scott settled back and studied me in a grave way that made me squirm, as if he was checking each feature against my old self, and then he smiled. Even though his bottom teeth were stained yellow, it was the same sweet, boyish smile he'd given me from the bottom of the staircase at the Town and Country Club. "I wrote my daughter Scottie a letter this morning saying that I've faithfully avoided seeing you all these years."

"Faithfully? That's a funny word choice."

"I told her how I'd flopped in Lake Forest and how you ended up throwing me over with the most supreme boredom and indifference." Talking of his youthful self who had been spurned seemed to resuscitate Scott; he sat up straighter and his voice took on its old zest. "I wanted to keep my illusion of you perfect."

"I was such a stupid, shallow girl. Why would that be anyone's illusion?"

Scott rearranged the stacks of his club sandwich and took a bite, pondering. He seemed surprised that the conversation had taken a turn toward the truth, as if he didn't think I was capable of it. "I guess the perfect illusion was of myself. I want to remember myself back when I cared deeply and took everything hard. Have you read any of my books?"

I nodded. "Every one." Then realized this wasn't the truth. The last book of Scott's I'd bought was *All the Sad Young Men* at Shakespeare and Company.

"So what did you think?" He leaned back, his hands folded like an expectant child. He wanted a fan letter—*You are the most eloquent voice of our generation. Jay Gatsby is the greatest tragic figure in the modern novel—he brought tears to my eyes.* Scott probably didn't get many fan letters anymore.

I pictured myself propped on the window seat in the Lake Shore Drive apartment, holding a book in a pool of fading light. "When I read *This Side of Paradise,* and came upon myself walking down the staircase at the Minnehaha Club, I felt . . ." I stopped, shook my head, tried to come up with the right word. "Flattered. That you'd remembered me at all and thought I was worth putting in your novel. For a while, I read every word I could find, looking for other girls that seemed like me. But then some of your other characters, like Daisy Buchanan and Judy Jones, reminded me of all my flaws."

He leaned over and took a long sip of iced tea through a straw, his eyebrows raised like a question mark. "How so?"

"I'm not like you, Scott. If you cared too much, my problem is that I didn't care enough. I didn't think hard enough about my decisions—who I married, how I treated my husband and my children. I regret that."

The waiter cleared the remains of our sandwiches, which we'd both pulled apart, dissected, and forgotten to eat.

He stared at me with an almost ghastly empathy. "Believe me, regret is another emotion I know intimately. Zelda and I write letters back and forth that are nothing but lists of our regrets. I regret that I got stewed so often, first in New York and then in Paris. All the time I wasted going to parties or recovering from parties when I should have been writing. I regret the cruel things I've said to Zelda, especially when I try so hard not to. Zelda regrets her breakdowns that cost me so much, not only money but my health. We regret that we spent so much money, every last penny, when I was earning so much."

"How is Zelda?" I asked in a hushed voice, probably the way everyone asked about her. "We had such a pleasant lunch at the Chicago World's Fair."

"I'm glad you enjoyed her. She broke down again after she was in Chicago, and her doctors say she'll probably never be able to leave the hospital. Zelda doesn't know that, of course. We all pretend that she's getting better so she doesn't lose hope."

His face blurred as if it were a lens going out of focus, and his eyes welled. I realized, suddenly, that this was the sorrow of a drunken man. The three tumblers of iced tea that he'd downed with such sober purpose must have been spiked.

I reached over and squeezed his hand, which was blotched with brown spots. "Marie tells me things are much better now that you have such a good position at MGM."

"I write screenplays and then they send in some old hack to monkey with the lines and call him my collaborator. Right now, I'm working on something that's not half bad. *Three Comrades,* based on quite a fine German novel by a man named Rilke. I think it will star Margaret Sullavan, Robert Taylor, and Robert Young." At the mention of movie stars, Scott puffed up, which gladdened my heart. He was still proud of his work. "I think we start shooting around Christmas."

"I hope you're getting a chance to write something besides scripts."

"Not right now. By the time I'd left Baltimore, I felt all used up, with nothing left to say. But lately I've been taking notes on all this." Scott nodded toward a jowly man in the next booth who was jabbing his finger at the menu and demanding that the chef make him a special order. "Who knows. Maybe my last novel will be about Hollywood." Last novel, not latest—the word slipped out uncorrected, unexplained.

"And," Scott continued, dropping his eyes in a bashful sweep, "I am seeing a young woman who I think is doing me some good. She makes sure I eat and don't get too gloomy. She even made me switch to Sano cigarettes." He waved one at me, his fourth so far.

So Scott wasn't lonely like me. I tried to look pleased for him. "Tell me about her," I said.

"She's not like anyone else I've known before, which I think is a blessing. She grew up in an English orphanage, believe it or not. She's never had any kind of education and she had to work hard for everything she's ever gotten. First she tried her hand as an actress, and now she's writing a gossip column, which she's quite good at." He spoke with a kind of adamancy I'd seen in other drunks. Yes, I've made mistakes, but now everything is different. This new woman, new job, new whatever will turn my life around. I am a changed man. "Scottie seemed to like her when she was out this summer. It's good for her to be around a woman who knows the value of hard work. Zelda was brilliant, but had no discipline. In the end, that's what did her in."

Scott's new life was like a flimsy parcel held together with brown paper and twine. Maybe he was getting a thousand dollars a week from MGM, was writing a brilliant novel, was being pampered by a plucky English lass. But those shaky hands could drop the parcel at any moment, busting the string and spilling the messy contents all over the sidewalk.

He slumped back in his seat, then glanced over at me as if he could barely remember who I was. "So how is your aviator doing?"

"Last I heard, he was squiring his old sweetheart around town. Everyone says they'll get married the minute our divorce is final." Millie said she'd spotted Billy and the still rotund Peg Denton behind the Onwentsia caddy shack, necking like teenagers.

This news seemed to perk Scott up—he cracked a little sideways grin. "I'm sure you have a new husband lined up too."

Here was my chance to tell him about my own crack-up, but Scott was in no shape to give me advice or comfort. Besides, he didn't want to hear any of my unpleasant truths.

"I do, in fact, but I don't think I better tell you his name, at least not yet." I leaned over the table and dropped my voice to a confiding whisper. "He's a lawyer. But he's got the soul of an artist, and has me reading everything from James T. Farrell to *Poetry* magazine. Quite a departure from Billy Granger. He's much younger than I am—I won't even tell you how much. I've turned into a cradle robber. We're planning to move to Houston so he can keep the wildcatters out of jail."

The fairy tale of a life with Julian spun from my lips like a Hollywood script. The unhappy wife meets a soulful young man, and voilà—they live happily ever after.

With each detail, Scott nodded his head with approval. This was the intriguing second chapter he expected of his Ginevra—I hadn't let him down.

I tossed in one crazy final detail. "We are planning to have a child together, if possible."

"Another child," he repeated, his voice turning almost weepy with wonder. "How I envy you. We gave Scottie the most haphazard upbringing. A different rented flat every eight months, under the care of one incompetent nurse after another. If I had another crack at being a father, I'd oversee lessons and make sure the proper books got read. I'd mold her character so she didn't have any of my and Zelda's failings. Make sure that she's tough where she needs to be tough, and giving when she needs to be."

I nodded gravely, even though Scott was in no condition to be a better father than he'd been the first time around. Then it dawned on me that the only truth in the fairy-tale marriage that I'd described to Scott was the part about the baby.

I thought with an unbearable pang of a beautiful child with Julian's keen face and passions. If only I could have another chance as a mother, but that was out of the question. I would keep my appointment with Dr. Robey after I got back.

When we stood to leave, Scott lurched a few steps, then linked his arm through mine to steady himself. He tried to make it seem like a chivalrous gesture. "Let me escort you back to your car." With his slack, unmuscled arm pinned tightly under my elbow, we zigzagged across the lobby, past the brass and glass awning, toward the parking lot.

"Let's go to your car first," I said, trying to pick out which among the Bentleys and Cadillacs could be his. I should at least make sure he found his car and got the key into the lock.

"Ladies first," he insisted. I realized that he didn't want me to see his car, or maybe—unthinkable in California—he didn't even own one.

He opened the door of Millie's sedan, held my hand while I climbed in, swept the folds of my skirt inside with a flourish, and closed me in with a quiet metallic click. I rolled the window down.

Scott leaned in. "I admit I was nervous at first about seeing you again. But you are still everything I knew you would be." His ancient eyes fixed on my face, as if he was trying to memorize my features. "Send me a wedding announcement with your new name." He spoke with a kind of grave finality, as if he knew we would never see each other again.

"I will." I tried not to take on his doleful tone, but it was contagious. "Who knows. Maybe we'll come to California for our honeymoon. I'll give you a call."

He gave me a courtly bow, and walked away with precise steps, the skin on the back of his neck the color of an ice cube in the unforgiving sunshine. An overcoat was tucked underneath his arm, as if he was dressed for another climate in another place.

The next afternoon I lounged on a chaise in the tiny patio behind Millie's bungalow. Three lemons dangled from a straggly tree, a wave of bougainvillea flapped off a windblown fence like laundry. The soothing chatter of men and the smack of balls floated over from the seventh fairway. My hair was rolled in rags, and I painted a second coat of Love That Red on my toenails. Millie had lined up the assistant golf pro and his brother to take us dancing at the Trocadero. The phone rang, and I hobbled through the low archway and across the tile floor with my toes fanned up, so as not to smudge.

"Pullmans' residence," I said, trying to sound like the maid.

"Ginevra?" a man said.

Scott, I thought, but realized the voice was too deep. Then my heart took a crazy extra beat—it was Julian. Not that there was anything that Julian could do or say to set things right.

"It's John." Millie's now ex-husband. Even though Millie was my best friend, I thought she'd treated John shabbily. He was like Billy Granger—they both deserved more loving wives.

"Millie's out. I'll tell her you called."

"Yes, I know. She's at her golf lesson. Actually, I was hoping to talk to you." He sounded a bit high, but then again it was six o'clock in Chicago—the cocktail hour. "I haven't seen you in ages. How's Avery doing? And how are you holding up?"

"Aren't you sweet to ask. Avery's better. He's still living with Evvie's family in Williamstown. I'm all right, considering that my life has fallen apart."

"I think you're a brave woman," he said, his voice gravelly with conviction. John had always been so kind to me. I remembered his eager face when he cut in on Scott at the McCormicks' party, never guessing that my eyes were fixed over his shoulder the entire time, searching the dance floor for Billy Granger. Fetching me a blanket when I looked cold at the Armours' ghastly house party and playing pick-up sticks with Avery.

I laughed. "Not sure if 'brave' is the word I'd use, but thank you. How are *you* holding up?" Last I'd heard, he was teaching himself Greek in his spare time so he could read Aeschylus in the original. John might have done something interesting with his life if his father hadn't made him a vice president at Pullman Car the day he graduated from Yale.

"Guess I'm lonely," he sighed. "I just moved into my new bachelor pad on Ontario. It's pretty grim. My only furniture is four bridge chairs and a cot."

"It couldn't be worse than my place."

"I'd love to see it sometime. We can commiserate and swap decorating tips," he said.

"I'll invite you for dinner when I get back. I've got a hot plate and a toaster. I'll make you my one and only dish. Creamed chipped beef on toast."

"Bless your heart for taking pity on an old bachelor."

24

Chronicler of
the Lost Generation

Three days after I got back from California, I had John Pullman over for creamed chipped beef on toast, as promised. He arrived at my apartment door with a bouquet of daisies wrapped in a newspaper cone, the first time I'd had fresh flowers since I'd moved in. He had to hunch over to avoid hitting his bald head on the jamb.

I'd tried to set a proper table in my kitchen nook with the two-burner hot plate. I'd bought a yellow tablecloth to cover the scorch-marked table, salt and pepper shakers shaped like roosters, and a bottle of Chianti in a straw basket, even though I still had no appetite for alcohol.

"This is delicious," he said. His Ichabod Crane legs sprawled sideways, since they couldn't fit under the table. "Millie never cooked me so much as an egg in twenty years."

"Compared to Millie, even I'm a gourmet chef."

"I have exciting news," John announced, sounding sheepish, as if nothing he did could ever be considered exciting. "Two days ago I submitted my resignation. After Christmas, I'll be teaching Latin at the Bell School to eighth graders. Now that I'm getting divorced and am an official disappointment to my father, I decided I might as well be doing what I want."

I raised my glass of Chianti. "Bravo, John. It's about time."

"So how about you? Any big announcements?"

My cheerful smile wilted. I set down my wineglass.

John leaned over, his mild eyes squinting behind his pink-rimmed glasses. "What is it?"

"I've made such a mess." I shook my head. All my efforts to brighten things up seemed grotesque, like putting a coat of fresh paint inside a crypt.

"This will pass, Ginevra. Everyone will forget the gossip about your divorce. Avery will get better and move home before you know it."

"It's so much worse than that." I stared at the rooster shakers, and I inhaled slowly to steady myself, and then I told him. About Julian, about the baby, about my appointment with Dr. Robey at the end of the week. I told him about my lunch with Scott Fitzgerald, and my wild, irrational desire to have the baby. "But that's impossible, of course."

John set down his fork and folded his napkin. His long, freckled fingers drummed on the table, and one of his legs started to bounce. "Nothing is ever impossible," he concluded at last.

John Pullman and I were married at the Waukegan Town Hall two months later. Our only guests were the city clerk and her assistant, who served as witnesses. I wore a baggy green suit with a long jacket that did not remotely cover my round middle. John was, to use Eliot's word, besotted. So much so that everyone decided that we must have been having an affair long before our divorces were final, and that John's being sterile because of the mumps was just one of Millie's nasty stories. The baby girl was bald except for a fringe of black eyelashes—just like me, not a trace of Julian anywhere, not that John would have cared.

We moved back to the Perry house, painted the walls apple green and marigold, had the plumbing updated, and replanted the flowerbeds. I didn't send wedding announcements to Scott or anyone else.

When Phoebe was two months old, John and I took the train out to Williamstown to present his new stepfather and half-sister to Avery. The moment he laid eyes on Phoebe, Avery got the same moony expression that he'd had when he talked about Myrna. He begged his doctors to let him move back with me so he could fulfill his new role in life—Phoebe's big brother. "As long as the patient remains under treatment and under close supervision to make certain that his behavior stays within appropriate boundaries," Dr. Libby wrote, "we believe that a nurturing relationship with a younger sibling will be therapeutic."

Avery let her ride on his back, tugging at his hair like reins, built a fort for her with a blanket over a card table, wrote plays that starred her stuffed animals. We gave up on the idea that he would ever finish high school, much less go to college. John got him a job selling tickets downtown at the Deerpath Theater. After the picture started, Avery put a closed sign over the ticket booth grill, and stood at the rear of the theater with an usher's flashlight. Since Avery kept his opinions about the movies to himself, I didn't know what he thought of the new stars who now outshone Myrna— Vivien Leigh in *Gone With the Wind,* Judy Garland in *The Wizard of Oz.*

Billy married Peg Denton a month after I married John, and they settled on her family's farm west of Barrington. Peg raised champion red setters, and Billy became something of an amateur agronomist, researching ways to replant native prairie grass. Billy grew as stout and jolly as Peg, and always seemed to be covered with a dusting of rusty dog hairs and hay.

But not everyone was willing to forgive and forget. Will visited me in the hospital two days after Phoebe was born. He had transformed from a sturdy, clean-cut baseball player into a gaunt, cynical young man in a thrift-store tweed overcoat and dirty tennis shoes. He took two steps into my room, then halted, too appalled by my puffy body in a peach satin bed jacket and the cocooned bundle in the basinet to move any closer. He fumbled in his pocket for a pack of cigarettes.

"It's probably going to need my room," he finally said. "I can move my stuff over to Dad and Peg's house."

"That's hardly necessary. We've got plenty of bedrooms," I said, trying to keep the hurt out of my voice. Of course he was hostile— did I really expect him to make a fuss over my new baby, even if he believed the story that John Pullman was the father? "And she's got a name."

"Oh, right. Phoebe." The word came out like a sneer. "The moon goddess, right?"

When I got home from the hospital, Will's room was stripped bare. All the childhood mementos—the baseball trophies, college pennants, balsa-wood airplanes—had vanished.

On December 22, 1940, I sat in Daddy's old Morris chair, in that study which had witnessed so many of the dramas of my life. Phoebe knelt on the carpet, playing with a battered crèche that had once belonged to Grammy Perry. She'd arranged the sheep and cows like a cancan line across the carpet. The strap of her red corduroy overalls had toppled over a skinny shoulder.

"Naptime sheep," she said, and poked them over one by one with a chubby finger.

"Why don't you sing them a lullaby?" I said.

Avery had instructed me to keep her busy while he finished her present in the basement, a puppet theater. He had cut three square panels out of Masonite, painted them in circus-colored enamel— red, blue, yellow. He had screwed them together with brass hinges, bought some polka-dotted cloth at Garnett's which he'd sewn with sloppy stitches into a ruffled curtain. Now he was painting tragedy and comedy masks on the front panel.

"Do you think she'll like it?" he asked me like an anxious suitor, the intent expression making his face look almost handsome, almost normal.

Phoebe rested her cheek on the carpet, one black braid snaked across her neck. She drew her knees up, stacked one tiny saddle shoe on top of the other. "Rock-a-bye baby," she sang in her oddly husky voice. She reached over and patted each lamb on its chipped head.

Now that she seemed safely distracted, I opened the *Chicago Tribune* and flipped past the ominous headlines on the front page. "FDR Creates Office of Production Management to Organize U.S. Defense." "Berlin: Secret Plans Issued for Invasion of Russia." I couldn't bear to think how every day America was edging closer to war.

On his way back to New Haven in September for his junior year, Will had gotten off at Penn Station and enlisted in the Air Corps. At that very moment, Will was in the Arizona desert learning how to operate a gun from a rotating glass turret on the rear end of a B-17. Will said his squadron was all set to go, the moment FDR decided to stop being such a sissy and do the right thing. The exact thing that Billy had said to me almost twenty-five years ago at the McCormicks' party.

I read *Brenda Starr* on the comics page and a breathless description of the sixteen debs who'd made their bow at the Passavant

Cotillion. And then there it was, on the second page of the society section, in the lower left-hand corner.

> F. Scott Fitzgerald Dies at 44: Chronicler of Lost
> Generation

Scott was dead. How was that possible?

I furiously skimmed the obituary to see what had happened to him in the last three years that could have caused his death, but the facts of his life seemed unchanged. He was working as a motion picture scenarist in Hollywood. He had a wife, Zelda, and a daughter, Frances Scott, who were living in Montgomery, Alabama. He had suffered a first heart attack three weeks before his fatal coronary in his Hollywood apartment.

The rest of the three-inch obituary was an elegy to Scott's failed promise.

> Scott Fitzgerald compared himself to a "cracked plate,"
> not good enough to be brought out for company but
> which "would do to hold crackers late at night or to go
> into the ice-box with the left-overs" . . . Fitzgerald con-
> tinued to show "promise" all through his tortured career.
> His admirers kept hoping for the elusive something
> which would be called great.

As if to prove the point, the blurry photo was at least a decade old. The author bent over his desk, pencil poised, marking a man-uscript—the face turned sideways to show off his famous profile. But even then, the flesh hung loose at the jaw, weighed down by gin and a mad wife and despair.

I rubbed my hand over Scott's picture, as if I could smooth away every wrinkle and blemish. Scott had sat in the chair where I now sat pretending to study geometry while I wrote thank-you notes at Daddy's desk. Every time I glanced up, I'd find those clear green eyes zeroing in on me, dissecting every nuance of speech and dress, cataloging them away for later use.

I stared out the window at the back field, now blanketed with a foot of snow. The path that led down to the Skokie was only a vague dip in the smooth crust. I imagined nineteen-year-old Scott Fitzgerald stumbling up the path toward the house, his fine blond hair damp with sweat, his white linen pants stained with grass. I could hear his voice go high with indignation when I told him we couldn't kiss anymore. "Why not?"

I had meant to write Scott after our lunch at the Beverly Wilshire, but kept putting it off. I couldn't think of a way to explain that I'd married a railroad-car heir, not a boy fresh out of law school, that I was still living in my parents' house in Lake Forest, not on the edge of some Texas oil field. Above all, what would I say about the baby girl that was born six months after I'd seen Scott?

Maybe I hadn't written Scott, but at least I'd thought of him in kind ways over the last three years. When I went to the movies, I always loyally looked for his name in the final credits. Even though I never saw it, I still liked to think that Scott was a success at MGM, that he was back on the wagon despite the slip at the Wilshire, that the plucky English girl was taking care of his health, that his big Hollywood novel would be published any day. When I fed Phoebe spoonfuls of oatmeal, and brushed the snarls out of her wild hair, and read her *Br'er Rabbit* in a quavering voice that made her laugh, I would sometimes remember Scott's pronouncement that if he'd had another shot at parenthood, he'd do it all much better. I was doing it better this time, I told myself.

I let out such a forlorn sigh that Phoebe propped herself up on an elbow and gave me a nervous half-smile, as if she'd been caught doing something naughty.

"Don't worry, sweetie. It's just a sad story in the newspaper," I said in a soothing tone. I stood up and found a pair of library shears in the top drawer of the desk. I cut Scott's obituary out with four neat snips, the last clipping for my accordion file.

25

Property of
F. Scott Fitzgerald

I arrived at the Walnut Room ten minutes early
and asked for a two-person table for two by the entrance
so I could spot Scottie when she came in. Judging from
her sunny manner on the phone, I'd decided that she probably took after her father more than her mother. I remembered the photograph of Scott dressed as a showgirl—slim
legs, natural blond hair, high cheekbones, the sensuous,
curved lips. No doubt about it—Scott's daughter would
be a knockout.

Thank goodness the restaurant had no deep shadows or
plush-carpet silence like the Wilshire Grill. The chatter of
ecstatic shoppers and the babble from the marble fountain
echoed off the walnut panels, like the din of a train station. Three women at the next booth opened their parcels
and pulled identical pairs of kid gloves over waggling fingers, exclaiming, "So soft." A wisp of an old woman with a
humpback blew on a spoonful of clam chowder while her
daughter dragged a shrimp through a pile of red sauce.

If Scott had described me to his daughter, he might have thrown in a few of Daisy Buchanan's glamorous traits—the low, thrilling voice, the fluffy hair that cupped a perfect skull. I had taken pains to dress stylishly, in a black crepe dress with an alligator belt and matching shoes. But even if I fancied that I was still slim and well preserved, I had the usual accoutrements of a fifty-year-old woman—the auburn tint in my hair to cover the gray, the bulging blue veins that snaked across the tops of my hands, the glasses folded by my napkin so I could read the menu. I hoped Scottie wouldn't be disappointed, wouldn't wonder what her father had seen in me.

"Mrs. Pullman?" someone asked. A short young woman with a moon face and mussed blond hair stood by my table.

"Scottie?" I said. Oh, too bad, I thought. She has none of Scott's looks.

Then she smiled, a big, straight-toothed merry grin that seemed to say she was delighted, that I was everything she had expected. Scottie had probably won friends and allies her whole life with that smile. "Sorry I'm late. I got off at the wrong floor, in hosiery, and had to run up two flights of stairs." She set down a tattered Best & Co. shopping bag and slid off her navy suit jacket. As she sat down, I noticed that the waistband of her skirt rode high over a little potbelly—the telltale sign that she'd recently had a baby.

A dour waitress appeared and pulled out a pad from the pocket of her organdy apron. I ordered Welsh rarebit and coffee.

"Me too," said Scottie without looking at her menu. "I'm trying to diet but it's useless. I'm starving." She plunked her elbows down and started chatting, as if she'd known me for years and the only purpose of this lunch was to catch up.

She asked about my children. "Will was in the Flying Tigers and survived without a scratch, thank God. After the war, he decided not to go back to Yale. He works for Boeing, out in Seattle. He just got married, so maybe I'll be a grandmother one of these days." I rattled off the string of half-truths brightly, as if Will and I talked once a week. After the war, Will let me know that he had no desire to return to Lake Forest, or see the new life Avery and I had made with John Pullman and Phoebe. The only news I ever got about Will was through Billy. "Works for Boeing" made him sound like an engineer, not a worker who screwed in bolts on an assembly line. The woman he married was a war widow with two grown children—grandchildren seemed unlikely.

"And then there's Avery. He's a confirmed bachelor, and still lives with us, which suits me fine." Avery was about Scottie's age, I thought with a pang.

"And we have our afterthought, Phoebe. Who is almost thirteen and is already acting like a full-fledged teenager. She has hushed phone calls with her girlfriends and twirls in front of the mirror, and wheedles all sorts of privileges out of her father. I don't think she even really wants the Revlon lipstick or the nylon stockings, she just wants to prove who's in charge. Needless to say, she's just like her dear old mama." At least the part about Phoebe was true.

Scottie told me about her three children, a girl and two boys, and the rambling farmhouse they'd just bought in Chevy Chase. "I'm a hopeless housekeeper, and more like a big sister than a mother. I like the birthday parties, and sledding downhill on the first big snow and making paper dolls. But I hate it when they won't take naps and hang onto my skirt. Of course, I never had any role models on how to be a parent, so no wonder I'm in the dark."

Now that she had broached the subject of Scott and Zelda, I reached over and patted her hand with the platinum rings and chipped nails. "I was so sorry about your father. And your mother, too." I'd read Scott's obituary in the paper, of course, and Marie had written me about Zelda, who had suffered a horrible death in a fire at her hospital.

She nodded stiffly. "Their lives were tragic, and tragically brief. But now they're buried side by side, at peace together at last. I've simply put all their troubles and sorrows out of mind. I like to think of them when they were young, two high-flying generous spirits." It came out as a practiced speech that she'd given a dozen times.

"I had lunch with your father once, years ago, when he was living in Hollywood. He thought you'd turned out beautifully, despite all his troubles," I said, even though I didn't think children ever escape their parents' troubles unharmed. Certainly, my children hadn't. "He said he'd raised you to be tough as nails."

"I had to be, or I wouldn't have survived. I may not have their talents, but at least I have some common sense." The placid mask had slipped a little. She took a sip of ice water, unhappy that she'd been even mildly critical of her parents.

"Your father would be thrilled that his papers are going to Princeton. I never knew a person who loved his college more than Scott."

That seemed to cheer her up—the magic smile came back. "They didn't want them at first. The librarian called Daddy a second-rate Midwestern hack. Now they've changed their tune. I'm hoping someday people will start to appreciate Daddy's books again. There's even a man writing a biography about him, named Arthur Mizener."

I wasn't sure who would be interested in the details of Scott's sad, nomadic life, but I didn't want to hurt Scottie's feelings. "Well, good. Scott deserves to be resurrected."

"So when I was looking for papers for Arthur, I found an old trunk of Daddy's. It had been at his agent's house all these years. And this turned up." She reached under the table for the beat-up shopping bag and handed it to me. "Here," she said, as if she were presenting a child with a large present wrapped in shiny paper and ribbon.

I opened the bag and peered inside at a black loose-leaf note-book like the one Phoebe used at school. I pulled it out and set it on the table. It was heavy and thick as a ream of paper, the cloth cover was faded and dented along the edges. "What's this?" I asked.

She cocked her head mischievously to one side. "Go ahead. Take a look."

I opened the cover. On the first page was typed:

Strictly Private and Personal Letters

Property of

F. Scott Fitzgerald

I turned to the next page, also typed, neatly numbered "*–2–*" on the top left like a book.

[January 11, 1916]
    Westover
    Middlebury, Connecticut
    Monday
    Dear Scott,
    Your letter was marvelous! Marie is right—you do
have a flair for words!
    I'm not used to writing long letters, so please try to
be patient. I thought about you all the way back to Westover. I even wrote silly stuff in my diary like "I'm over
the moon about Scott." I was afraid you might have forgotten your promise to write me, and was beside myself
when I saw that thick envelope with extra stamps . . .

I skipped down to the bottom of the page.

Yours in haste
Ginevra

I turned the next page.
—3—

[January 20, 1916]
Dear Scott,
I admit that the exact features of your face have
gotten a little blurry, so please send me a photograph if
you have one . . .
As for dreams, I dream about spending one perfect
hour with you.

I could feel Scottie's eyes on my face, scrutinizing every reaction. A self-conscious flush seeped over my cheeks. I started to flip
the pages faster.
—7—

[January 25, 1916]
I would prefer a photograph of yourself dressed as a
male . . .

—21— . . .

[February 12, 1916]
Well, I'm not beautiful at all. I think you are trying to
trick me into saying something conceited and making an
ass of myself.

[February 27, 1916]

It makes me feel queer that you see right through me. Am I that obvious? . . .

Really Scott, you are a punk speller! The word is beaux, not beaus . . .

[April 16, 1916]

I want more than anything to come to the prom. I want to see you in your world, charging around . . .

—158—

[May 11, 1916]

She's gotten me two tickets to *Nobody Home* and has told me to invite one of my school chums . . .

—186—

[July 3, 1916]

I don't think you have any right to be cross with me for not writing more often. I've been practicing day and night for the vaudeville. Deering has two left feet and I'm sure our maxixe will make me a laughing stock.

—210—

[August 5, 1916]

I wish you'd stop pestering me with all your nosy questions. For your information, I am not fickle, nor do I have what you call a weak character. I think you

are the fickle one. Your opinion of me seems to have
sunk rapidly.

All my self-important opinions seemed so much worse in print.
I turned to the very last page.

—221—

Dear Scott,
    I have carried all your letters out to the back field and
burned them, as instructed . . .
    . . . I never did take them seriously . . .
    . . . you might as well destroy my letters too . . .

I shut the notebook and finally looked up. "I don't understand,"
I said at last.

"They're your old letters," she said.

"I can see that. But he was supposed to destroy them."

"Well, I guess he didn't." She shrugged. "Or maybe he destroyed
them after he had them typed. Daddy always had a part-time secretary to do his typing."

I cringed at the notion of a prim lady in a cardigan sweater peering at each of my fatuous words through her reading glasses and
then clacking away on a black Remington. "But why would he *want*
to have my letters typed?" I sounded like some thick-headed child
who couldn't understand a long division problem.

"Because they meant so much to him. I think he wanted to pre-
serve them so he could pull them down and read them any time
he wanted, like a novel." Scottie's voice was calm, as if this strange
artifact had a perfectly reasonable explanation.

"I was so self-centered and so mean to him. Why would he want
to remember *that?*"

She leaned back and crossed her arms over her round stomach.

"I think Daddy was trying to remember himself. When things got bad in his life, when Mummy was sick and he couldn't finish *Tender Is the Night* and he was drinking too much, he just wanted to remember what it felt like to be nineteen, in love with a girl." She turned her palms upwards. See? It all makes sense now, doesn't it?

In a way, it did. I could see Scott padding around some drafty rented house late at night, Scottie asleep, Zelda away in yet another sanatorium. He would pour himself a fresh cocktail, pull the notebook of letters off a shelf, and settle down in an armchair with horsehair sprouting out of the seat. And for a moment he would recall the thrill of finding a blue envelope in his Princeton mailbox, the sound as his finger slipped under the flap and tore it free, the sheets of paper fanning out in the soft spring sunshine. I had felt the same rush of pleasure each time I opened my secret file on Scott, found the pages I'd sliced from *This Side of Paradise,* and read *She paused at the top of the stairs.*

The waitress had been watching us, waiting for a lull in the conversation. She briskly stepped between us, and deposited oval plates with four toast points covered by a smooth blanket of cheese and crowned with a sprig of parsley.

Scottie tucked a stray piece of blond hair behind an ear and spread her napkin across her lap, relieved to be done with my letters. She sawed off a square piece and took a hearty bite. "Delicious. What do you suppose 'rarebit' means?"

"I have no idea," I said, slipping the notebook back in the Best's bag and setting it safely on the floor by my feet. When I got home, I'd carry it upstairs and hide it away with the clip file on the back shelf of the cedar closet.

"So tell me about your romance with Daddy."

"Well, it all started at the Westover School. My roommate was a girl from St. Paul."

I told her the story the way Scott would have wanted me to. His hair was bright yellow, like a jonquil, and he wore a soft corduroy vest, which seemed very New York sophisticated. He made me sit in a corner with him, and he sized up everyone in the room with a few choice words, like an artist with a piece of charcoal. At midnight we rode on a horse-pulled bobsled and snuggled under a buffalo robe. The next week, I found a fat letter in my mailbox, and then another and another. Such clever letters—I knew then that one day he'd be a famous writer. In June, we sneaked off to a Broadway play unchaperoned—a shocking thing to do in those days. Later we had funny-tasting gooseberry blintzes at a Russian teahouse. Then he came to visit in Lake Forest, which didn't go very well. Scott was charming but my father could be a snob and didn't approve of a poor boy from St. Paul. We went to a fancy engagement party at the McCormick mansion.

I stopped the story there. No need to describe Scott's wrinkled linen suit and pitiful face when I evicted him the next day, his letters dumped in the trash can on top of the coffee grounds and egg shells. Scottie wouldn't want to hear about how her mother charged through the Chicago World's Fair like a madwoman, how her father had staggered out of the Wilshire Grill into the California sunshine, his face bloated and leached of color, like a corpse.

"So there the three of us were on a bench under Mr. McCormick's stuffed trophy heads—Scott and me and a boy named Billy Granger. Your father was dressed in some silly Hawaiian getup with a fringed scarf around his waist. The Granger boy was very stiff and talked about flying airplanes with the French army. What would have happened if I'd turned right instead of left, if I'd picked the writer instead of the aviator? I've always wondered."

Scottie nodded dreamily, her round cheeks flushed, like a little girl being read a bedtime story. "That would make Daddy happy. He thought you had forgotten him."

Epilogue

February 7, 1981

Mr. George Hobart
Manuscript Librarian
Department of Special Collections
Princeton University Library
Princeton, New Jersey

Dear Mr. Hobart,

My mother, Ginevra Perry Granger Pullman, died in
November. As you probably know, she had a short-lived
romance with F. Scott Fitzgerald in 1916. In sorting
through her papers, I came across letters from several
librarians over the years asking if she had kept any of
Fitzgerald's letters and if she would consider donating
them to Princeton's Fitzgerald Collection. As far as I can
tell, she gave them all the same response—that she had
destroyed Fitzgerald's letters years ago.

My mother was curiously mute on the subject of
F. Scott Fitzgerald. Over the last thirty years, dozens

of biographers and graduate students have requested information. She spoke with two of his earliest biographers, Arthur Mizener and Andrew Turnbull, but after that refused to be interviewed. She was even evasive with me. I became curious about her relationship with Fitzgerald when I read *The Great Gatsby* in a college English class. I asked her what Fitzgerald had been like, and if she was the model for any of the women in his books. She said very firmly that she had "nothing left to say about Scott."

There were no copies of Fitzgerald's books in our house, and I'd assumed that she probably hadn't even read his stories or novels. I also wondered if all the questions about Fitzgerald began to irritate her. Maybe she resented the implication that her romance with Scott Fitzgerald when she was sixteen was the only interesting event in her life.

I confess I had hoped that a few long-lost letters from Fitzgerald might turn up when I cleaned out her house. No letters, I'm afraid, but I did find two curious items, hidden away on a closet shelf behind a pile of old pocketbooks.

The first is a thick file of Fitzgerald's short stories and articles about him, clipped from magazines. There are even some pages from his novels which she tore out. My mother obviously had more interest in Fitzgerald's career than she ever let on.

The second item is a typescript with "Property of F. Scott Fitzgerald" on the first page. It seems to be a typed copy of the letters my mother wrote to him in 1916. There are quite a few of them—the notebook is

227 pages long! I have no clue when or why Fitzgerald had this transcript made, or how it ended up in my mother's possession.

One fact seems clear—their short romance had a powerful significance for both of them. I don't think anyone will ever fully understand why.

Please accept both the notebook and the clipping file as donations from the estate of Ginevra Perry Granger Pullman.

Sincerely Yours,

Phoebe Pullman Warren

Historical Note

Gatsby's Girl is a work of fiction. The romance between F. Scott Fitzgerald and Ginevra Perry is partially inspired by the real life romance between Fitzgerald and Ginevra King, from 1915 to 1917. However, I have purposely altered and reinterpreted both the characters and the events. This novel should in no way be considered a factual account of their relationship or of Ginevra King's life. Because F. Scott Fitzgerald is perhaps the most thoroughly documented and analyzed of all American writers, I feel compelled to specify which aspects of *Gatsby's Girl* are based on fact and which are inventions.

Ginevra King was the daughter of a wealthy Chicago stockbroker, Charles King, who had a summer residence in Lake Forest. She attended the Westover School in Middlebury, Connecticut, and in January 1915 visited a Westover classmate, Marie Hersey, in St. Paul. On January 4, Ginevra met Scott Fitzgerald at a "bob party" that began at the house of Elizabeth McDavitt and ended at the St. Paul Town and Country Club. Fitzgerald was a sophomore at Princeton, a slight but handsome young man who wrote stories for the *Nassau Literary Magazine* and plays for the Triangle Club. Fitzgerald was deeply smitten with the pretty and popular society girl, and wrote her a long "special delivery" letter on the train back to Princeton. She wrote him back on

January 11 on the train back to Westover. For the next six months, Scott and Ginevra conducted an intense epistolary romance, sometimes writing every day, with some letters so long that they needed to be sent in two envelopes. The letters were typical of love-struck teenagers—filled with declarations of devotion and soulful ponderings. In March, Scott got bids from four Princeton clubs, including the Cottage Club. He invited Ginevra to the Sophomore Prom, but her mother refused to come east to chaperone. In June, Scott met Ginevra and her mother in New York and attended the play *Nobody Home*. At the end of spring semester, Scott flunked three of his five exams. He later wrote in his ledger of his sophomore year, "A year of tremendous rewards that toward the end overreached itself and ruined me. Ginevra/Triangle year." In late June, on his way to spend the summer at his friend Sap Donohoe's Montana ranch, Scott stopped in Lake Forest for a short visit with the Kings. During this visit, he met Ginevra's friend Edith Cummings, who later became an amateur ladies' golf champion.

Scott and Ginevra's correspondence limped along for another year and a half, but Ginevra had clearly started to lose interest. Her letters were less frequent and contained lengthy descriptions of other parties and other boys. Scott's junior year was an academic disaster. He was flunking so many classes by Thanksgiving that he withdrew from Princeton, claiming bad health, and returned to his parents' house in St. Paul. In May 1916, Ginevra was "fired" from Westover for talking to some boys visiting for the senior dance from her dormitory window. In August 1916, Scott made a visit to Lake Forest which went poorly. He later cryptically wrote in his ledger: "The bad day at the McCormicks . . . 'Poor boys shouldn't think of marrying rich girls.'" In January 1917, he wrote in his ledger: "Final break with Ginevra." His academic problems continued, and in the spring of 1917, he used the impending war as an excuse to withdraw from Princeton and enlist.

In July 1917, he wrote Ginevra and asked her to destroy his letters. She replied that she'd disposed of them as asked, adding callously that she'd never thought they meant anything anyway. While he was at it, she wrote, he might as well throw her letters away too. Ginevra did destroy Scott's letters, but he preserved hers—a fact she would discover more than thirty years later.

Scott achieved literary fame a mere four years after his devastating breakup with Ginevra. Many of his most famous characters were based on the Ginevra he knew and on the grown woman he imagined she would become: Isabelle Borgé in *This Side of Paradise* (1920), Daisy Buchanan in *The Great Gatsby* (1925), Judy Jones in "Winter Dreams" (collected in *All the Sad Young Men,* 1926) and Josephine Perry in the five Josephine stories (collected posthumously in *The Basil and Josephine Stories*).

In September 1918, Ginevra King married William Mitchell, a wealthy Chicagoan who was serving as an aviator in Key West. After the war, Mitchell became a successful stockbroker. The Mitchells lived in Lake Forest and had three children. Ginevra had only two further contacts with Scott.

In 1933, Scott phoned Ginevra out of the blue and asked her to entertain Zelda at the Chicago World's Fair. At this point, the Fitzgeralds were living outside Baltimore and in desperate financial and emotional straits. Scott was drinking heavily and struggling to finish *Tender Is the Night.* Zelda had been in and out of mental institutions for four years, and it had become increasingly apparent that her illness was incurable. Whether Ginevra and Zelda attended the fair together or merely had lunch is unclear, but Ginevra later told a reporter that Zelda had been uncommunicative and that the visit had been awkward.

In 1937, when Ginevra was getting a divorce from William Mitchell, she looked up Scott during a visit to California. Having hit rock bottom in the mid-1930s (which he described in "The Crack-Up"), Scott had landed a job writing scripts for MGM in 1936. Ginevra and Scott planned to have lunch at the Beverly Wilshire. He wrote his daughter, Scottie, that Ginevra King had been the first girl he ever loved and that he had carefully avoided ever seeing her again "to keep the illusion perfect." Scott had been on the wagon for months but was so undone when he came face-to-face with Ginevra that he got disgracefully drunk. He never saw her again. In December 1940, he died of a heart attack at the apartment of his girlfriend, Sheilah Graham. He was forty-four.

At the time of Fitzgerald's death, his literary reputation was in eclipse. When Scottie attempted to sell his papers to Princeton to raise funds for Zelda, the librarian refused to offer more than $1,000 for the papers of a "second-rate Midwestern hack." During the 1940s, interest in Fitzgerald's work slowly revived. His unfinished novel, *The Last Tycoon,* was published, and his novels and short story collections were reissued.

Princeton Library changed its mind about Fitzgerald, and Scottie donated her father's papers in 1951. In sorting through them, she came across an interesting artifact—a typed transcription of Ginevra King's letters. Why or when Scott had the transcript made is unknown. My guess is that he had it made in the late 1920s when he began the first of his Josephine Perry stories about a spoiled Lake Forest pre-debutante, who was clearly based on Ginevra King. In 1950, Scottie gave the notebook to Ginevra Pirie (she had married John Pirie in 1939). Ginevra was understandably unnerved by this odd memento. Ginevra later wrote Arthur Mizener, Fitzgerald's first biographer, that she found her old letters insufferably boring and self-centered. She told Mizener that she had read very few of Fitzgerald's books, and seemed embarrassed that their short romance had assumed such significance in his work. She hid the notebook at the back of a closet and refused to let anyone look at it, including her daughter and granddaughter. She died in 1980; the notebook of her letters to Fitzgerald and her diary were donated by her family to Special Collections at the Princeton University Library in 2003. Only one of Fitzgerald's letters to her survived—a 1918 note of congratulations on her engagement to William Mitchell.

The personality of Ginevra Perry is based mostly on Josephine Perry, the spoiled sixteen-year-old Lake Forest girl in Fitzgerald's Josephine stories. Fitzgerald wrote the stories between January 1930 and June 1931, when he was badly stalled on *Tender Is the Night* and needed to raise funds for Zelda's continued hospitalizations. The young Ginevra Perry has many of Josephine's flaws. She is narcissistic, entitled, boy crazy, impulsive, and willing to manipulate anyone to get her own way. In the final Josephine story, "Emotional Bankruptcy," Josephine has squandered so much of her emotional energy on silly romances that she is unable to respond to the declarations of an exotic aviator, Edward Dicer, who Fitzgerald implies is her true love. In *Gatsby's Girl,* I couldn't help speculating about what would have happened if she married the handsome but stodgy aviator after all.

Finally, Ginevra Perry differs from Ginevra King in one significant way. Although Ginevra King professed to have no interest in the writings of her old boyfriend, Ginevra Perry feels otherwise.

I have significantly altered the chronology of events of the King-Fitzgerald romance in *Gatsby's Girl.* Their relationship began with the January 1915 meeting in St. Paul and all but ended with his August 1916 visit to Lake Forest. The first six months of their correspondence was the height of their infatuation, but after that, Ginevra's enthusiasm faded. For pacing purposes, I have compressed the Perry-Fitzgerald romance to eight months—from January 1916 until August 1916. I have included events from Scott's sophomore and first junior year.

The letters between Ginevra Perry and Scott Fitzgerald are my inventions. The tone and subject matter of Ginevra's correspondence were suggested partially by the typed transcriptions of Ginevra King's correspondence at the Princeton University Special Collections. Because none of Scott's letters to Ginevra King during their courtship have survived, I have had to deduce their contents (and spelling errors) from three different sources: Amory Blaine's letters to Isabelle Borgé in *This Side of Paradise,* Ginevra King's letters, which frequently commented on Scott's previous letters, and Scott's letters between 1915 and 1916 to other correspondents (for example, his infamous letter to his sister, Annabel, on how to behave like Ginevra King and make herself attractive to men).

Because *Gatsby's Girl* is a novel of literary influences, many phrases from Fitzgerald's writings appear in the dialogue, correspondence, and descriptions.

The Perfect Hour, by James L. W. West, provides a superb account of Ginevra King's romance with Fitzgerald and her later life, with extensive excerpts from her letters and diary. *The Romantic Egoists: A Pictorial Autobiography from the Albums and Scrapbooks of Scott and Zelda Fitzgerald,* edited by Matthew Bruccoli, Scottie Fitzgerald Smith, and Joan P. Kerr, was an invaluable source of early magazine articles by and about Fitzgerald. Other books that were particularly useful in my research included: *Some Sort of Epic Grandeur: The Life of F. Scott Fitzgerald,* by Matthew Bruccoli; *The Far Side of Paradise: A Biography of F. Scott Fitzgerald,* by Arthur Mizener; *Scott Fitzgerald,* by Andrew Turnbull; *Scottie, The Daughter of . . .: The Life of Frances Scott Fitzgerald Lanahan Smith,* by Eleanor Lanahan; *A Guide to F. Scott Fitzgerald's St. Paul,* by John J. Koblas; *Classic Country Estates of Lake Forest: Architecture and Landscape Design, 1856–1940,* by Kim Coventry, Daniel Meyer, and Arthur H. Miller; *Shakespeare & Company,* by Sylvia Beach; and *Century of Progress International Exposition: Official Guidebook of the Fair, 1933.*

Acknowledgments

I am grateful to my mother, Sylvia Peter Preston, who shared her memories of growing up in Lake Forest in the 1920s and '30s. I subjected her to dozens of questions about home decoration, clothing styles, automobiles, trains, stores, hotels, movie palaces, restaurants, and bookstores. When she didn't know the answer, she phoned her friends who are in their eighties and nineties and unearthed some interesting nuggets of information. She also provided original photographs of her godmother, Sylvia Beach, and 1920s interior shots of Shakespeare & Company on the Rue de l'Odeon.

My deepest thanks to Arthur Miller, archivist at Lake Forest College, who provided me with invaluable research materials when I started this project. My deepest thanks to Don Skemer and AnnaLee Pauls for permission to read material in the Ginevra King Collection Related to F. Scott Fitzgerald and the Arthur Mizener Papers on F. Scott Fitzgerald. The Ragdale Foundation in Lake Forest, for providing residencies to write and research this project. The many friends who patiently read and commented on this book in manuscript: Elinor Lipman, Mariflo Stevens, Jane Barnes, Kathleen Ford, Suzanne Freeman, John Sedgwick, Margo Preston Beck, Madelyn Wessel, Ron Falzone, and Megan Marshall. And finally, Chris Tilghman, my first and best editor.

I am profoundly grateful to my agent, Henry Dunow, and my editor, Jane Rosenman, for their continued enthusiasm and support, and to the many people at Houghton Mifflin who helped guide this book into print.